1st Amendment.

$\frac{50}{2}$

The Dangerous Years

MAX HENNESSY

The Dangerous Years

NEW YORK
ATHENEUM
1979

Library of Congress Cataloging in Publication Data

Harris, John, 1916-
 The dangerous years.

 I. Title.
PZ3.H24218Dan   1979   [PR6058.A6886]   823'.9'14   78-72964
ISBN 0-689-10945-8

Characters from *The Lion at Sea* first book who reappear in *The Dangerous Years*

George Kelly Maguire James Caspar Verschoyle Albert Edward Kimister }	Term mates at Dartmouth Naval College, now in the Royal Navy
Admiral Sir Edward Maguire, Bt. Lady Maguire }	Kelly's parents
Charlotte Upfold Mabel Upfold	Kelly's girl friend Charlotte's sister
Albert Rumbelo	Leading seaman, married to Bridget, housekeeper to Kelly's parents
Admiral Sir Reginald Tyrwhitt	Commander-in-Chief, Harwich Force, during World War I
Lieutenant Wellbeloved	Engineer officer, Destroyer *Mordant.*
Lieutenant Seamus Boyle	Watchkeeper in *Mordant.*
Lieut-Commander Fanshawe	Served alongside Kelly during World War I

Part One

1

The rumours had been gathering strength for days. Even in late October stories of a mutiny in the German High Seas Fleet had begun to trickle through and now, finally, news had arrived that the German Kaiser had gone into exile. After four years of discomfort, hardship and sudden death, after four years of grief, misery and deprivation, it was almost over.

Ever since August, 1914, Europe had been engulfed in the greatest war the world had ever seen, but, at last – suddenly, unexpectedly after the setbacks of the spring – the end was now surely at hand. The past month had seen the collapse of Bulgaria, Turkey and Austro-Hungary, and a signal had been received only that morning to say that the war was finally dying.

Sitting in the motor boat of the destroyer, *Mordant*, as it chugged its way back from Stromness, Lieutenant George Kelly Maguire stared round at the wide expanse of Scapa Flow. Scapa was an amazing place, big enough to house all the navies of the world, yet, in its silences, its incredible colours and the extraordinary quality of its northern light, bewitching – a place you either loved or hated. Most people managed to do both.

Somehow, in his strength and stillness, Kelly Maguire resembled Scapa – as if he'd acquired some of its qualities. His gaze reflected the sea, grey, steady, and faraway with years of looking over great distances. His square face was older than his twenty-six years, with narrow crow's-feet of concentration round his eyes and small tight lines at the corners of his mouth. Unruly red hair curled beneath his cap, only partially obscuring the fading pink line of the wound he'd received at Jutland two years before.

He looked again at the land, silent, lonely, and lovely in the crisp northern air. The shadows of the anchored ships of the Grand Fleet suggested a maritime Valhalla full of ghostlike shapes frozen into a crystal silence in which the leaden water was the only thing that stirred.

The ships were of all sizes, from huge battle cruisers down to destroyers, among them now French ships, and American vessels newly arrived to help defeat the Germans, who twice within forty-five years had thrown Europe into a turmoil with their restless armies. Though Kelly had seen the sight a hundred times since he had rejoined *Mordant* and *Mordant* had rejoined the fleet, it still left him a little awed.

He glanced towards his ship over the lifting bow of the motor boat. The destroyer lay quietly at her buoy. Apart from a period at Rosyth and a long refit to repair the grievous wounds she'd received at Jutland, she'd spent nearly four years at Scapa. And, unlike the big ships, the destroyers had always done long spells at sea, and the morale of their crews was high, despite the damp stickiness of their quarters, the smell of fuel oil and the fear of floating mines that gave them constant nightmares. They felt their sense of responsibility keenly and the bored big ship men had watched them come and go with envy, because to relieve the years-long monotony there had been only collisions on dark nights, fierce northern gales and the holocaust when *Valiant* had blown up to shower the rest of the fleet with debris and mutilated corpses.

As the motor boat approached *Mordant*'s stern, Kelly sat up. The thin November sun had appeared between two banks of cloud over Hoy and had flooded the Flow with light that caught the sides of the destroyer, to exaggerate her slimness and etch the lines of her guns. At Jutland, that scrambled battle in the murk two and a half years before, when they'd failed to annihilate the German High Seas Fleet, she had been left without a single one of them able to fire, and minus her bows and half her crew.

A pair of divers crossed the path of the motor boat, big black birds with outstretched necks, honking as they flew, their heavy bodies undulating to the beat of their wings. Knowing them to be the harbingers of winter, Kelly found himself crossing his fingers in a silent prayer that the promised peace would soon arrive. Another winter with the wind lashing the seas across the

4

Sound so they could neither move nor go ashore, driving the spray in grey sheets over the iron-bound cliffs and bringing darkness in the middle of the afternoon, was almost more than he could bear.

As the boat bumped alongside *Mordant*'s companionway, the sun disappeared again over the hills of Hoy and night came abruptly. The wardroom was gloomy. The signal they'd received that morning that an armistice had been signed with Germany had been cancelled.

'False alarm,' Wellbeloved, the engineer officer said. 'And *I* put up drinks all round on the strength of having won the end-of-the-war sweep.'

Kelly accepted a gin. Wellbeloved had helped him fight the ship back from Jutland, a scarred, charred heap of wreckage on the point of sinking. The only two other surviving officers had long since gone. The Gunner had vanished to a light cruiser and the Sub had been replaced by Seamus Boyle whom Kelly had first met as a newly-joined cadet when he'd dragged him from the sea as the armoured cruiser, *Cressy*, had sunk under them in 1914.

Wellbeloved placed the glass in Kelly's hand. 'It must end *soon*, mustn't it?' he asked.

'It's my earnest prayer,' Kelly said.

As it happened, they hadn't long to wait. Thirty-six hours later the signal came that the Armistice really had been signed. The news was brought by *Mordant*'s captain, Lieutenant-Commander James Peter Orrmont, who had arrived to take the place of the man who had nursed the ship through her refit. He had spent most of the war sunning himself aboard the battleship *Glory* in the Mediterranean and had a somewhat flippant attitude to the North Sea. He was clever and shrewd and was a born staff man, with a sharp appreciation of everything and a manner Kelly knew it would take him, Kelly, years to acquire. He was smooth and confident and, though his ship-handling experience was not extensive and he'd seen little of the war, it was quite clear he didn't expect it to be a drawback since he fully intended his future to be in planning rather than seafaring.

'The party's over,' he said cheerfully. 'The signal's finally arrived and this time the Germans really have thrown in their hand.'

5

The wardroom erupted in a wild cheer and Wellbeloved grinned all over his face. 'Do we break out the champagne, sir?' he asked.

Orrmont smiled. 'We'd better let the ship's company know first,' he said. 'If they don't know already.'

As the lower deck was cleared and the sailors gathered aft in an atmosphere of barely-controlled excitement, Orrmont climbed on to the winch.

'I'm no speechmaker,' he said, 'so I'll just read to you a signal I've this minute received.' He gestured with the sheet of paper. ' "Admiralty General Message: Armistice is signed –" '

There was an immediate yell of delight which died abruptly as Orrmont held up his hand. 'Don't rush it,' he said. 'It gets better as it goes along: "Hostilities are to be suspended forthwith . . . Armistice to be announced at 1100. All general methods of demonstrations to be permitted – and encouraged – including bands." '

Cheering started again but Orrmont held up his hand once more. 'One more thing,' he went on. 'I have also received a signal to the effect that the customary method of celebrating an occasion by splicing the main brace may be carried out at 1900.'

The ship shook under the din, and as it died away they became aware of more cheering coming from other parts of the Flow. Tots of rum, saved specially for the occasion, began to appear below decks, and accordeons, mouth organs and tin whistles were brought out of lockers for an impromptu concert.

That night, as the alcohol began to work, every siren in the harbour screamed and every bell was rung. Rockets crossed the sky, and flares and grenades went up in every direction under the moving searchlights, as each ship and each unit tried to celebrate the occasion in its own way in a pandemonium of noise. The big ships started it with their deep-throated bellows, and quickly every other ship, big and small, took up the racket. A deafening din rose over the flat waters of the Flow which, as though part of the celebrations, were lit by an enormous moon. Steam whistles shrieked, sirens split the air with shrill blasts, and foghorns joined in with their lower-pitched hootings in a tumultuous cacophony. Alternately falling then rising again to tremendous crescendos, the discordance resounded across the

6

shores for three solid uninterrupted hours until 10.p.m., only to start again at midnight, while on deck the sailors danced, sang, shouted and cheered until they were hoarse or exhausted.

From the bridge, surrounded by brilliant stars, Kelly watched in silence. Instinctively his hand went to the pink scar that Jutland had left over his eye. That day the Navy had lost good ships and better men and had suffered a humiliation they hadn't believed possible. At least, he thought, there'd be no more wounds, no more killing, no more grief. Yet, under the elation the thought induced, there was also a strange aching feeling of incompleteness. Despite Jutland, the Navy had won a victory greater than Trafalgar but only by denying the sea to the Germans; because they'd never thrashed them as they'd hoped and expected, the victory was far less spectacular.

'Well, it's over, Number One.'

He turned to find Orrmont standing alongside him.

'Yes, sir,' he said. 'It's over.'

'But I think there's a sense of failure.' Orrmont was clearly thinking the same way as himself. 'An armistice before a Trafalgar's not the same as one afterwards.'

'It'll certainly seem to everybody that it was the army that polished off the Kaiser without us doing much of the fighting,' Kelly agreed.

Orrmont shrugged. 'They'd never have done it without us,' he said. 'They might have given 'em a few black eyes but in the end it wasn't black eyes that finished 'em. It was the blockade and starvation, and it was the Navy that did that.' He pushed his hands into his pockets and leaned on the bridge rail. 'There'll be leave eventually,' he went on. 'I expect you're looking forward to it as much as anyone. Got a girl?'

'Yes, sir.'

'Going to marry her?'

'Eventually, sir.'

'Think she'll wait?'

Kelly smiled. If there was one thing in the world he was sure about it was that. 'Yes, sir,' he said. 'I'm sure.'

Orrmont smiled. 'Well, I suspect you'll have to hang on just a bit longer to see her,' he said. 'We have a job to do first. I gather the German Fleet's coming in to surrender.'

'Think they'll come, sir?'

7

Orrmont smiled again. 'Don't think they have an option,' he said. 'They no longer control their ships. They're being run, it seems, by sailors' soviets and the red flag's flying at all the naval ports. Mutiny's a terrible thing.'

Kelly stared round the assembled ships and the bare lonely shapes of the islands. 'Up here,' he said, 'I often felt like it myself.'

Ten days later the German ships appeared. There had been constant rumours that they might come out for a final battle or would try to get themselves interned in Holland, and even now no one knew how the end would be. Would they surrender tamely or go down with their colours flying in a 'death ride' against the Grand Fleet?

In an atmosphere of excitement and tension, the light forces led the way out, flotilla by flotilla, to meet them. In a tumult of churned water and the hum of boiler room blowers, they passed through the boom one after the other, watched by patrol boats and drifters, one hundred and fifty destroyers all steaming east.

The channel lay by Inch Garvie and Drum Sand. They'd used it many times before, in the dark, past bell and buoy, in fog and under the pale northern stars, clearing for action as they went, as they were cleared now, still prepared to do battle if the Germans decided on a Wagnerian gesture of self-immolation. Every ship in the Royal Navy that could be spared was there – from Dover, Harwich, Scapa and the Channel – three hundred and seventy of them and ninety thousand men, every ship flying as many white ensigns as possible as if they were going into action. Each column consisted of over thirty battleships, battle cruisers and cruisers, with a destroyer abreast each flagship. Heading the line was Beatty's *Queen Elizabeth*, wearing the flag the admiral had flown in *Lion* during the Battle of Jutland.

As the light increased the air seemed to grow cooler. The water, invisible during the night, now became long cold lines of grey movement, and the black loom of ships merged into the pale wash of day. There would be sixty-nine of the Germans, they'd heard – two of them missing because one had engine trouble and another had struck a mine – humiliated ships run by committees of sailors who claimed kinship with the International Proletariat and said they were the brothers of the

8

mutinous men of the Russian Navy. They'd long since lost their fighting potential, because they'd been drained of their best men for the submarines and destroyers, and when the officers had wished to take them to sea in a last desperate attack, the desire for peace had erupted in a revolution and officers had had to escape in cars, on bicycles and on foot to avoid arrest. When *Königsberg* had brought senior naval officers to discuss the terms of surrender they had been accompanied by sailors claiming their admirals were only advisers. Their humiliated officers had had the satisfaction of seeing them told to go to hell.

'Here they are!'

Smoke had appeared on the horizon, then one after the other, they began to pick out the masts and upperworks of the German ships; grey shapes still, but menacing in their blunt outlines. Kelly drew a deep breath. The last time he'd seen these ships, he'd come away from the encounter with a livid wound across his back, a flap of flesh hanging over his eye, a fractured cheekbone and the danger of losing his sight. Wellbeloved was on the deck below him and he saw him also catch at his breath.

'*Friedrich der Grosse* leading,' Kelly pointed out flatly, recognising the outlines he'd been studying in books through four long years. 'I can also see *Seydlitz, Moltke, Derfflinger, Hindenburg* and *Von Der Tann.*'

Orrmont turned. 'How do they look, Number One?'

'A lot tamer than when I last saw them, sir.'

'Bring a lump to your throat?'

'More like a flutter to the heart, sir.'

'Well, you never know. We might still have to sink them. It needs only one chance shot to start the whole thing again.'

Silently, like grey ghosts, the outriders of the two fleets met. In gas masks, asbestos flame helmets, gauntlets and breast shields, the allied crews waited at action stations. But there was no hostility. The Germans were demoralised and they were coming without heroics. As they passed through the line of destroyers Kelly was aware of a deep depression and the aftermath of tension. Had they been held in check all these months by an error of judgement? Had they been deterred only by a myth? Had the threat they'd believed in been merely imaginary?

9

As the Germans approached, the men crowded the main deck and the spaces round the funnels and the gun platforms, pushing among the torpedo tubes and clinging to the boats for a better view. Every ship was stationed on a pre-selected enemy vessel, her guns trained across the narrow stretch of water. On the deck of the ship ahead of *Mordant* film makers were recording the scene, and the German sailors, scowling at the levelled cameras, mimicked the movements of the men cranking the handles and wigwagged unprintable messages in English.

The day was fair now, with a clear blue sky above the thin whiteish mist that shrouded the outlines of masts and hulls and the restless sea swell. As the destroyers hurried by, the ocean was filled with their movement. There seemed no end to them, the air vibrating to their washes and the shudder and hum of machinery. Reaching the end of the German column, with a flutter of flags they wheeled and brought up short abreast the accompanying German destroyers. Three light cruisers, *Cardiff*, *Phaeton* and *Castor*, moved to a position ahead of the Germans. Over *Cardiff* a kite balloon jerked irregularly at its cable, the man in the basket staring through binoculars down at the German ships.

'They look like minnows leading in a lot of whales.' The bearded gunner with the D.S.M. standing below the bridge spoke slowly, wonderingly.

Orrmont smiled. 'They remind *me*,' he said to Kelly, 'for all the world of a herd of bullocks being brought in by a bunch of farm kids.'

The Germans were in single line ahead, nine battleships, five battle cruisers, seven light cruisers and forty-nine destroyers, and the curves of their turrets picked up the sunshine through the mist. Then from *Mordant*'s stern came an unexpected jeering cry and the triumphant sound of one of the cooks beating a wooden spoon on a metal baking tin in a wild tattoo.

'Shut that bloody fool up!' Kelly barked, and the clatter stopped at once.

The solitary celebrant was a man who had recently joined the ship. There was little sign of joy among the other men, especially those who'd survived the hammering they'd received at Jutland, and there was a deep underlying emotion running through the ship so that they were too full for words at the

10

drama of defeat.

'It can't be true. It's against human nature.' The words came this time from Leading Seaman Rumbelo, standing near the forward gun, and as he stared at the phantom ships Kelly saw there was an odd look in his eyes of contempt, pity and mourning.

The German ships were a gloomy sight that Kelly found distasteful – as if he were a part of a crowd assembled for the funeral of some sordid individual who'd been murdered – and he found it incredible, too, that the second naval power in the world could surrender so tamely without attempting to strike a single blow in defence of its honour.

'Anti-climax in large letters,' Orrmont said. 'I never really thought they'd submit. I never dreamed they'd accept disgrace in silence. It's damned hard to find the right words.'

'I expect the Hurrah Departments of the national press will find them for you, sir,' Kelly said dryly.

The main fleet appeared through the mist, looking like huge shadows, silent, stretching for three miles on either hand. With their French and American accompanying units, there were fifty-six dreadnoughts, fifty-six vast ships, the water between their columns stirred to choppy foam as their wakes crossed and re-crossed. As they reached the end of the German line, coloured squares and pennants fluttered aloft, paused, then swept down. The leading ships began to turn outwards sixteen points, moving with elephantine slowness as Beatty reversed course. The manoeuvre was executed with exquisite precision, every ship and every man eager to show what they could do, to prove that the German claim of victory at Jutland had been nonsense from the beginning. The turn had placed Beatty's ship abeam of *Friedrich der Grosse*, and for a while the sea seemed to be full of enormous ships, as the Grand Fleet countermarched to move with the Germans towards the Firth of Forth.

In every vessel, as in *Mordant*, men had been allowed from their action stations to stare at the grey shapes which had been mysterious for so long, grimy stokers shivering as the cold air struck their sweaty bodies. According to the terms of surrender, the Germans had been stripped of powder and shell, of breech mechanisms, sighting instruments and rangefinders. They moved in long lines – *Hindenburg, Derfflinger, Seydlitz, Moltke, Von*

11

der Tann, Bayern, Grosser Kurfürst, Markgraf, Kronprinz Wilhelm, Kaiser, Kaiserin, and many others. The mutinous sailors, Kelly had heard, had wanted to fly the red flag and had only been dissuaded by the information that it was also the flag of piracy and might be fired on, and the old imperial colours were fluttering at the masthead instead. Under their grey clothing, the German ships looked dingy and unkempt, their hulls streaked and rusted, only one, *Derfflinger,* looking as if she had recently been painted.

They cut through the water in a long slow-moving column in the funeral tread of a defeated nation, and as the two fleets approached the Forth, the excitement died. By the time they passed May Island, the reaction had set in, in an overwhelming weariness.

The sun had driven away the mist so that the day was clear, cold and fine and the Firth looked like a vast inland sea. The three parallel lines pressed close together, then the southern line of escorting ships turned once more upon itself and in a long backward sweep fell in behind the Germans. *Cardiff* led to a point halfway between Kirkaldy Bay and Aberlady Bay east of Inch Keith, while the destroyers moved to the Haddington shore by Cockenzie. As the German ships approached their prison anchorage, soldiers from the shore batteries lined the sea's edge, watching, and boats of every description, steamers, row boats and yachts, all packed with civilians, milled about, savouring the triumph.

'I never thought we'd insist on it.' Orrmont still seemed faintly bewildered.

Perhaps, Kelly thought, that was because Orrmont had spent most of his war in the calmer areas of the Mediterranean. The mood of the Grand Fleet had always been grimmer. Despite the feeling of contempt and pity for the Germans, not one of the men who had watched the northern waters round Britain had ever wanted anything but a surrender that was complete and unequivocal. It made up for the harshness of the winters and the toll the North Sea had taken.

As *Queen Elizabeth* passed to her mooring, there was a storm of cheering, and Beatty, standing on the bridge, lifted his cap in acknowledgement. Apart from this, the whole manoeuvre of anchoring was executed in a silence that was almost funereal.

But, as each German ship reached its place and dropped anchor, its bulwarks became crowded at once with men fishing.

'What a way to celebrate *Der Tag*,' Orrmont observed coldly. 'Chucking out a fishing line to catch a herring. Still –' his shoulders moved in a shrug under his bridge coat '– I expect the blockade's been biting and the poor buggers are hungry.'

As the opalescent northern dusk approached, Lipscomb, the yeoman of signals, sang out.

'Signal from flagship, sir,' he said. '"To admiral in command of interned squadron and all German C.O.s and leaders of torpedo boats: The German flag will be hauled down at sunset today, and will not be hoisted again without permission." *Friedrich der Grosse*'s acknowledging.' There was a pause then Lipscomb spoke again. 'There's another, sir. "Flagship to the fleet. It is my intention to hold a service of thanksgiving at 6.p.m. today, for the victory which Almighty God has vouchsafed to His Majesty's arms, and every ship is recommended to do the same."'

Kelly spoke in a voice as flat as a smack across the chops. 'I don't know so much about Almighty God,' he said. 'I always had the impression it was us sitting up here and the pongoes sitting it out in the trenches.'

'Quite so, Number One,' Orrmont said dryly. 'However, I suppose we'd better comply. It seems to be really over at last. Finis. Kaput. End. The war's finally stopped, and we're in for a bit of peace.'

2

The madness that had been in the air at the Armistice had died. By 1919, church bells no longer burst into excited peals, steamers on the Thames no longer hooted at each other as they passed, and the roaring trade the pubs had been doing had subsided. There was no more dancing in the streets and, in the disillusionment that was setting in, bus conductors who had once refused to take money from wounded soldiers were now insisting on their fares. The free drinks and the free kisses were finished and even that most wonderful prize of all to come with the ending of the war – the awareness of simply being alive – was also fading now, because the grim facts of settling down again were being faced by men who for four years had known no such thing as security.

The world was already a poorer place, and among the Australians, Americans and French who crowded London intent on a good time there were still plenty of haunted-eyed young men, veterans of bloody fighting even at nineteen and twenty, boys who'd known no other life but the war since leaving school. Most of them believed in nothing beyond the fact that they had months of living to catch up with, and it was already beginning to occur to some of them that somehow they'd been betrayed and that the ideals that had driven them to the trenches, to sea, and into the air, were being edged aside by hard-eyed politicians interested only in plum jobs and party affairs. Work was clearly going to be difficult to get because, with demobilisation, there was a flood of manpower on the labour market, and doubts about that 'land fit for heroes to live in' that they'd been promised were already beginning to take root; while the flu epidemic which had gripped the whole world was killing off with ease men who'd survived four years of

14

slaughter.

King's Cross Station was full of uniforms, a few heading home to be demobilised, a few still unwillingly joining squadrons, ships or regiments, hump-backed under their kits and enviously eyeing the half-empty compartments reserved for the staff. The platform was full of women, but the crucified look of the war years had gone and they wore instead expressions of relief, though here and there resentful looks flashed from beneath mourning veils and black crêpe.

As his train drew to a stop, Kelly stared from the window, aware of a faint sense of frustration. The German fleet was at Scapa now, sent up there in batches from the Forth, and *Mordant* had gone with them, part of the single unit of battle cruisers and destroyers which were considered sufficient to guard them. Disarmed and humiliated, there was no longer an expectation of defiance.

As he climbed down to the platform, he found himself studying the faces around him. There was doubt, anxiety, even disbelief in them but, thank God, none of he despair he'd seen in the eyes of the Germans.

'Porter, sir?' The man who appeared alongside him was young – different from the old men who had worked the platforms during the war – perhaps some demobilised soldier or sailor happy to return to the humdrum life of peace because of his joy at being alive.

Kelly nodded and indicated his luggage. But his thoughts were still in that curious limbo of bewilderment that had been with him ever since he'd caught the train south at Thurso, the same mixture of pity and contempt for the Germans he'd felt as they'd led them into the Firth of Forth. He'd gone aboard *Grosser Kurfürst* to make it clear that no boats were to be lowered and that wireless was not to be used, and to find out whether the ship might have imported infectious disease into Britain. But the giant vessel had nothing it shouldn't have had beyond the sour smell of unwashed hammocks, blankets and clothing. Its flats were filled with litter which it seemed to be nobody's duty to clear up, and pamphlets were everywhere, while every man seemed to wear a red ribbon on his blouse. The officer who came forward had worn no shoulder straps or imperialist badges.

15

Before he could speak, a sailor had stepped forward. 'I am chairman of the supreme sailors' soviet aboard this ship,' he had announced. 'I am in command here.'

Kelly had stared at him with distaste and turned to the officer. 'Tell the captain I wish to speak to him.'

'The captain has no power.' The sailor had bristled with indignation. 'He is merely a technical adviser. Everything has been changed by the revolution.'

The German officer swallowed, dumb with shame. Kelly stared at him, still ignoring the sailor. 'Well?' he said.

The officer's eyes had flickered to the sailor then he had jerked to life. 'I'll have you escorted below,' he said.

The completeness of their humiliation had been depressing. Inscrutably, Kelly had set about inspecting the ship. The German crew had been ordered on deck, while, with his party of men, he had moved through the deserted lower mazes, searching painstakingly for gun parts, poison gas, bombs, powder and shell. There had been a few brief attempts by the German sailors to make contact with their British counterparts but they had been treated with contempt, the British bluejackets refusing to acknowledge them with a cold aloofness that was shattering.

Even the chilly Orkney landscape must have seemed a smack in the face for the Germans. To men who'd spent most of the war within reach of Kiel's lights, bars and women, Scapa must have seemed desolation itself. The winter had been a bitter one and the Germans, carrying the burden of defeat and the knowledge that their families were hungry and the Fatherland was in chaos, were not even allowed ashore or on board other ships in case the subversive tendencies they had brought with them should inflame the growing discontent that existed in the Royal Navy over pay.

Leading Seaman Rumbelo had expressed it succinctly to Kelly, with the frankness of an old friend who had survived the Dardanelles and Jutland with him, and was married to Kelly's mother's housekeeper.

'There are leading hands in the Fleet, sir,' he had said patiently, 'whose seventeen-year-old daughters working in factories earn more than they do.'

The odd sense of disillusion and frustration was still with

Kelly as he took a taxi to Bessborough Terrace, but the thought of seeing Charley again cheered him considerably. It had been Charlotte Upfold's intention to marry him from the day she'd first met him. They'd grown up together and when, at various times, he'd tried to grab her, he'd never known whether she'd be as lissome as willow and soft as silk, waiting for his kiss with her eyes closed, or whether she'd suddenly develop needle-pointed elbows and knees and burst into breathless laughter. As a schoolboy, he'd regarded it all as a great joke. As an adolescent he'd regarded it as a good friendship, and for a period as a young man even as a nuisance. Finally, however, he had wisely accepted it as something that he wished as much as she did. There was now nothing they didn't know about each other beyond the final consummation of their regard, and their mutual affection was as comfortable as an old coat.

She was in his arms almost before he'd closed the door behind him, her cheek against his in a delirium of delight.

'Oh, Kelly, Kelly, Kelly!' She seemed unable to stop uttering his name.

'Steady on, old thing,' he said. 'You're throttling me.'

'But it's so wonderful! It's all over at last!' She stared at him, noting the slightly hunched way his back wound made him hold his left shoulder, and the pink line of the scar running into the red hair that fell over his eye. He looked so lean, so fit, so capable, and yet somehow so remote with the remoteness that all sea-faring men have and never lose, it almost broke her heart. She seemed to have been waiting all her life for him – certainly ever since she'd known the meaning of the word 'love' – and she'd barely seen him since he'd returned to duty almost two years before.

'Oh, Kelly,' she said again in a tremulous breathy sigh.

'Never mind Kelly,' he replied. 'What about Charley?'

'I'm still nursing.'

'Where?'

'St. George's.'

'Do they give you time off?'

'Not much.'

'The war's over,' he pointed out. 'And I'm on leave, ain't I?'

She gestured. 'There are still a lot of men in there, recovering from wounds.'

17

He grinned. 'It always seemed to me during the war, that when you were free, I wasn't. Now I'm free, you're not. Gives rise to a great deal of ill-will on both sides, that sort of thing.'

She grinned back and hugged him again. 'I expect they'll give me an evening off.'

'An evening? Is that all?'

'There's so much to do and so many girls have already given up nursing now that the war's ended.'

'But not you?'

'I couldn't Kelly. I couldn't.'

He couldn't help but admire her attitude, but he could see that it might lead to a few difficulties while he was on leave. He stood back and looked at her. Her blue eyes were spiky with long lashes, huge underneath the severe fringe of her modern hairstyle, and slightly moist as she stared back at him. All the youthful plumpness he remembered had dropped away from her; her face now had fine lines and her figure was slender and graceful.

'What's the matter?' she asked.

'Nothing. I think you're a corker.'

'How long are you home for?'

'I've got a week. I have to go to Thakeham tomorrow to see my mother but after that the time's my own. How *is* my mother, by the way?'

'She's had flu and so has your grandfather, but they've recovered. Rumbelo's Biddy looked after them. Did you know Biddy was expecting a baby?'

'Rumbelo told me. He tells me a lot my mother forgets. How's *your* mother?'

She gave him a delighted grin. 'Out. At the theatre. So's the cook, who's all the staff the war's left us.'

'That's handy. How about Big Sister Mabel?'

'Also out. With Mother and James Verschoyle.'

Kelly frowned and she looked at him, troubled. 'Isn't that over yet, Kelly?'

Kelly shrugged. He had disliked 'Cruiser' Verschoyle from the day they'd first met as cadets. Verschoyle's bullying had made his life miserable at Dartmouth and there had been nothing since to make him change his mind. Verschoyle was clever and too good-looking by half, and his chief delight for

18

years had lain in tormenting Kelly.

'He did rather well in the end,' Charley said, trying to heal the old enmity. 'He was wounded and got a medal at Zeebrugge.' She touched his breast. 'Though not as big as yours.'

He pushed Verschoyle to the back of his mind and gave her another kiss. 'How about him and Mabel? Think they'll get married? He's wealthy enough.'

She smiled and shook her head. 'He's too wary and Mabel's having too good a time with everybody being demobilised.'

'If she leaves it much longer,' Kelly pointed out, 'she'll be too late. She's getting on.'

'So am I.'

'Barely twenty.'

'It's old enough to be married.'

There was an awkward pause, because this question of marriage was the one difficult problem that lay between them. Though Charley had been waiting all her life for him, the Admiralty disapproved of officers marrying too soon – if at all, Kelly sometimes thought bitterly – and, since they conspicuously failed to give to officers the marriage allowances they gave to ratings, it was difficult to set up home on any pay below a commander's.

'You know what we decided about that, Charley,' he said gruffly. 'We've got to wait.'

Her face wore a stubborn look for a moment, then she thrust the mood aside and pulled him into the kitchen. 'We'd better eat,' she said.

'Out,' Kelly said, thankful that the matter had been dropped so easily.

Her eyes sparkled. 'Can you afford it?'

'No. But we'll go just the same.'

They ate at a little restaurant near Victoria Station that Charley knew. The food was unpretentious but the décor was new and it made them feel they were paying more than they were.

'The last time I came here,' Charley said, 'I was with Albert Kimister.'

A snatch of jealousy seized Kelly. Albert Edward Kimister had been hanging round Charley ever since she'd been taken to

19

Dartmouth by Kelly's mother to see Kelly. He'd fallen in love with her even as she'd fallen in love with Kelly and, like Charley's for Kelly, his affections for her had never wavered.

'When?' he asked.

'Soon after the Armistice.'

'Where is he now?'

'He's in *Queen Elizabeth*. She's going to the Mediterranean.'

'How do you know?'

'He writes to me.'

'Often?'

'All the time.'

'Why?'

She laughed at his expression. 'It's obvious, you idiot! He's potty about me. He even asked me if I'd marry him.'

'When?'

'When we were here. At this very table.'

Kelly stared down at the table as if it were guilty of the basest treachery. 'What did you say?'

'What do you think I said?' She laughed again. 'I haven't been trying to get you all these years to give up now for someone else.'

Kelly swallowed. He felt he had little to offer and he knew Kimister's family had money. 'I couldn't stop you if you wanted to,' he muttered. 'If you wanted Kimister, well – '

He stopped and she put a hand over his. 'Would *you* want me to marry Kimister?'

'No,' he growled. 'You deserve something better than *him*.'

In the taxi back to Bessborough Terrace, he leaned towards her to kiss her. She responded at once, pressing against him. He was startled at the need she showed and responded willingly, roused and eager, ridden full pelt by his desires.

It was raining hard, large drops slapping against the taxi windows. They'd not carried an umbrella and were soaked as they hurried across the pavement into the house. As Kelly shook the water from his cap, he saw that Charley's dress was plastered to her, moulded to the shape of her young body. Immediately, he became aware of the emptiness of the house and the suffocating darkness about them. There wasn't a sound

20

except the beating of rain on the windows. Charley stared at him in an odd way.

'I shall have to change,' she said quietly.

Her voice was low and there was something unexpected in it. He looked at her quickly but she stared back at him, unblinking, so that his heart suddenly thumped and the blood began to course through his veins, as though somebody had opened a sluice gate.

'You'd better take your jacket off,' she said. 'I'll dry it for you. It can go in the airing cupboard. Come upstairs.'

He was looking directly into her face and he knew at once – and knew that she knew, too – that this was the moment towards which the current of their lives together had been moving all the time. She said nothing and slowly began to climb the stairs. Without a word he began to follow her.

Reaching the top step, she didn't pause or look round but moved along the dark landing towards the door of her room. Pushing it open, she stood to one side to let him follow. The bed had a strange menacing look about it that he'd never noticed before in such an ordinary article of furniture.

Charley hadn't moved and he stood behind her, holding his jacket in his hand. As he laid it on the chair, she still didn't move so he stepped up to her from behind, drawing her shoulders back against him and folding his forearms over her breasts. They stood that way for some time, her arms loosely by her side. Then she lifted her hands and put them on his.

'Oh, Kelly,' she sighed.

She still didn't move and he kissed the base of her neck.

'It's all right, Kelly,' she breathed, and he reached over her shoulder and began to undo the buttons of her dress. She stood absolutely still, making no protest, but he found his hands were clumsy because his fingers were trembling. She still didn't say anything until in his confusion he tried to ease the dress down over her hips, then she gave a little sigh.

'The other way,' she said, and lifted her arms.

He drew the dress carefully over her head, anxious not to ruffle her hair, and laid it neatly on a chair. In the light coming through the window her bare shoulders gleamed beneath the straps of the slip she wore. They looked fragile and almost transparent in their whiteness. She still said nothing, waiting,

21

continuing to hold up her arms so that he assumed that the slip was to come off in the same way. He did the job meticulously, as if he might tear it, terrified of touching her. Now that he'd arrived at the critical point in their lifelong affair, he found his courage was barely up to it. Even with his blood hammering in his veins, he felt inexperienced and uncertain.

Her eyes met his and, somehow, what moved him most was the honesty in them. As he began to remove the rest of her clothes, she looked down at him. 'We don't wear as much since the war as we used to,' she whispered.

He was still careful not to touch her skin, but it was difficult because his breathing was quick and shallow and his hands were awkward. As she stepped out of her shoes, he was surprised how small she seemed, standing with her feet flat on the floor, her arms folded across her breasts.

The rain was spattering against the window so that the darkened room, lit only by the street lights outside, seemed to be full of small unspoken urgings. He began to fumble with the buttons of his shirt, tearing one off in his haste. She watched him for a moment then she walked to the bed and sat down, her feet and knees close together, her arms still across her breasts, her eyes on him, solemn and huge. He stared back at her, unable to speak, and she lay back on the counterpane, punctiliously straight, both feet together, her arms by her side, the curve of her breasts catching the light from outside.

There seemed to be a stone in his throat and he swallowed with difficulty, his face as hot as if he'd just returned to his cabin from the bridge on a bitter day at sea. Suddenly he became scared. This was Charley! This was the girl he was going to marry! You didn't do this sort of thing with the girl you were going to marry! This was something you saved until afterwards!

'Charley,' he said hoarsely.

If he'd touched her or if she'd giggled a little or pulled his leg, there would have been no question of hesitation. But she'd been composed, as silent as if she were some sacrifice. Then she lifted her hand to reach out for his and he knew he was lost. All his good intentions went whistling down the wind in a great wave of desire but, as he snatched again at his shirt, he heard a taxi draw up outside with a squeak of brakes and immediately he recognised the sound of Mabel's voice, then her mother's, and finally, worst of all, Verschoyle's.

Charley sat up abruptly. 'They've come back,' she gasped.

For a second they stared at each other, horrified, then she came to life. 'Oh, God!' She was on her feet at once. 'Go to the bathroom. Get dressed there. I'll go down the back stairs to the kitchen.' As she spoke, she was flinging her clothes on as fast as she could. Because they'd not embraced each other, her hair was undisturbed. 'Hurry,' she said, and as she pushed him out of the room he saw there were tears in her eyes.

Furious, frustrated, yet curiously relieved that nothing had happened that they might later regret, when he appeared downstairs she was standing by the range in the kitchen as if nothing had happened and he could hear voices in the drawing room.

'Charley,' he murmured.

She didn't answer and refused to meet his look. She was feeling cheap and tawdry, yet knowing she never would have if what they'd intended had taken place. It was being caught that placed the occurrence in another category altogether – shifty, somehow dirty – and her feeling of guilt caused her to push the blame on Kelly.

He stared at her bewildered. 'Charley,' he tried again.

She lifted her head, her face pink and unhappy. 'Oh, go to the devil,' she snapped. 'Go and talk to them.'

Disconcerted by her reply, he went to the drawing room. Her sister, Mabel, was pouring brandy into goblets. 'Hello, Kelly,' she said, crossing the room to kiss him. 'When did you arrive?'

'Today. We went out for a meal.'

She smiled, friendlier than he'd ever known her. 'Charley's making coffee. *You'd* better have a brandy, too.'

Mrs. Upfold came towards him. She'd always disapproved of him but now, for the first time in his life, she pecked his cheek.

'Kelly,' she said, and he realised that it was also the first time she'd ever called him by his first name since he'd been a boy.

Then he saw Verschoyle. Languid, lean and handsome, he was leaning dramatically on a stick, making the most of his wound. On his chest was the blue and red ribbon of the D.S.O.

'Hello, Maguire,' he said.

23

'Congratulations on the medal, Cruiser,' Kelly said.

Verschoyle touched Kelly's chest. 'That's the one I'd have liked,' he said quietly, his voice tinged with envy.

At that moment, Charley appeared with the coffee, resolutely avoiding Kelly's look. When she finally met his gaze, he saw there was a faint redness about her eyes, but her mother went on chattering happily, unaware of what had happened because the room was lit only by shaded bulbs.

As she handed him his cup, Verschoyle moved alongside him and touched his leg with the walking stick. There was a cynical smile on his face.

'Tie, old boy,' he murmured. 'If I were you I should hoist it up two blocks. Shows what you were up to.'

Kelly had enough control to put his cup down without rattling it and hitch his tie above his stud. Verschoyle watched him and, as he reached for his cup again, he raised his brandy glass.

'That's better, old boy,' he murmured. 'Well done.'

If no one else had guessed what had been happening at the moment of their arrival, Verschoyle had, and in that moment, Kelly decided once again that of everyone he knew Verschoyle was the one person he disliked most.

3

Scapa had a stripped look, as empty as Kelly's emotions.

His leave had not been a great success and for some time Charley had even remained curiously distant, as though she blamed him for the catastrophe at Bessborough Terrace. He'd telephoned her the following day but she'd been at the hospital and it had been Mabel who'd answered instead. She'd seemed to be fishing for an invitation to lunch, and he'd fought her off with difficulty, deciding she went better with Verschoyle.

A gust of wind came across the Flow, blustering against his cheek, and he could feel the touch of rain that denied the late spring. The interned German ships, more depressingly dingy than ever, stretched in a long line to the north and west of Cava, with the destroyers and other small craft moored in pairs in Gutter Sound. He felt strangely glad to be back. There was a rumour that they were due any day for the Mediterranean and he had a feeling that perhaps it would be for the best. The war seemed to have changed more than just the way of living. There was trouble in Ireland and the beginnings of industrial strife, and civilian life seemed a maelstrom of emotions.

When he'd returned from Thakeham to London, Charley had seemed to be hiding from him. In the end, he'd waited outside the hospital for her to appear and whipped her into a taxi, uniform, apron and all, and taken her to the Savoy for tea.

She had managed a little laugh. 'Oh, Kelly, wasn't it awful?' she said. 'What must you have thought of me? Thank Heavens nobody noticed.'

Only Verschoyle, Kelly thought, with his yellow fox's eyes that missed nothing, and his dagger-sharp brain that was able to put two very doubtful twos together and come up with a very certain four. And if Mrs. Upfold hadn't guessed at the time

25

what they'd been up to, she had since and they'd never managed to be entirely alone together after that. Since the weather had precluded any trips into the country, all they'd managed were snatched kisses in the kitchen and a few wild clutches in taxi cabs.

The wind came again across the Flow and this time there was no mistaking the rain in it. Perhaps a foreign station was a good idea, Kelly thought, because something was bound to happen soon between himself and Charley, and despite his wish to consummate his desires, he was still old-fashioned enough to feel that, with the years of waiting the Admiralty forced on him, he might regret it.

Certainly, overseas service wouldn't be difficult because, contrary to the general belief, the war seemed to be far from finished. A civil conflict was going on in Russia and British ships had been despatched to the Baltic, Murmansk, the Black Sea and Vladivostok, and there was a separate flare-up in Asia Minor where the Greeks, encouraged by the Prime Minister, Lloyd George, were stirring up a cauldron of Turkish hatred. The world seemed to be full of places where an ambitious officer might push himself up the ladder.

Kelly frowned. What Charley would say when she learned he'd disappeared again, he could well imagine. But he *was* a naval officer and he could hardly expect to advance his career swinging round a buoy at Scapa.

He stared shorewards. On the curve of the land there was a litter of unoccupied huts and empty concrete gun positions, relics from the war; afloat there seemed only the Germans, and between them and the sea, the solitary battle squadron that supplied the guard, the turgid water patrolled by nothing more dangerous than drifters.

The Germans were model prisoners. They gave no trouble and it seemed that any last chance of defiance had gone when two dirty Hamburg transports had taken away all but skeleton crews. Now there were no more than twenty men to a destroyer and two hundred to a battle cruiser, and their silent hulls were rusted, dirt-streaked and unscrubbed. His own last visit to *Grosser Kurfürst* had left him depressed. Her fires were dead, and the thump and groan of pumps, the hum of blowers and dynamos, the breathing of a living ship, had gone, and his

26

footsteps had rung hollowly in empty steel passages peopled with ghosts.

Three days later, as they'd been half-expecting, *Mordant* received orders for Gibraltar.

'It's Constantinople,' Orrmont said. 'And probably even further. The Greeks and the Turks are at each others' throats, and in Russia the Red Army seems to be knocking hell out of the anti-Bolshevik forces so that they're screaming for assistance.'

That night Kelly sat down in his cabin to write to Charley. Ashore, the islanders were burning the heather and, through the twilit northern darkness, patches of flame flickered on the crofts. Explaining his departure was harder than he'd expected because what he could understand he couldn't expect Charley to understand, and he had an uneasy feeling that somehow, somewhere, an element of unfairness had entered into their relationship. She'd got over the disaster at Bessborough Terrace but she needed reassurance about her future, which he felt he'd signally failed to give. To disappear into the blue might almost be too much.

The next morning was overcast but the cloud was high in a white sky as they passed the hospital ship anchored off Flotta and made a ninety-degree turn into the Pentland Firth.

Their guess that they were due to head further into the Mediterranean than Gibraltar was confirmed as soon as they dropped anchor in the shadow of the Rock, but as they arrived the place was humming not with news of the Middle East but of events at Scapa.

'What the hell have you been doing?' they were asked. 'The German Fleet scuttled itself! Fifteen battleships and forty-six destroyers! The whole bloody guard squadron was at sea and there were only two destroyers, a depot ship and a bunch of drifters to stop them!'

The news was like a blow in the face. The Flow, it seemed, had looked like the aftermath of a great battle, with German ships disappearing in gouts of frothing sea water and escaping steam, watched only by helpless drifter crews and a boatload of children who'd been on a day's excursion round the defeated fleet. All that was left, it seemed, were vast weed-grown

27

bottoms lying on the surface like huge steel whales, and whole trots of destroyers huddled together like sorrowing girls clutching each other in woe.

Two days later they were passed on to Malta and from Malta to Alexandria en route for Constantinople. Kelly's father was there, still a rear admiral. He'd served his whole career in the Navy through the years of Victorian peace without ever hearing a shot fired in anger and had been dragged out in 1914 for a desk job to which he still clung with the tenacity of a leech. He bought Kelly a dinner, introduced him to a few women he appeared to know, asked briefly about his wife, and vanished once more, obviously feeling he'd done his duty.

It was strange once more to see Constantinople through which in 1915 Kelly had marched as a prisoner of war. It was two distinct cities: To the north of the Golden Horn rose Pera, the city of the Christians where the British had established themselves; to the south it was Stambul, the Moslem city, where the French were, and to drive across the harbour by the Galata Bridge was to pass from one period of history to another. With its bright lights, Pera was a city of the present, a curious mixture of the businesslike West and the garishness of the East. With its ridge of domes and minarets, Stambul across the water was a mediaeval area tumbling into decay, a hive where human beings swarmed and lived as they had for centuries.

As they anchored among the British, French, Italian and Greek warships off the Dolma Bagtché, the Sultan's white palace near the Galata Bridge, a lieutenant-commander called Orgill, who'd been at Dartmouth with Orrmont, stepped aboard to escort him to headquarters ashore.

'It's a listless bloody hole here,' he announced heavily. 'Touched with a sense of doom or something. They don't like being defeated and there's no coal to be had. The trams still aren't running properly and the Bosphorus steamers are few and far between. The main streets are only dimly lit and the side streets not at all, so that criminals prosper and nobody moves at night without arms because the police are scarce, corrupt and universally mistrusted. Profiteering's shameless, the currency's valueless and the price of foodstuffs so high the Turks stay in their homes, except to buy bread. Some even pretend they're not Turks at all, shed their fezzes and try to get jobs with us.'

When they went ashore, it was obvious that the difficulties sprang less from Turkish defiance than from Greek bombast. Greeks were everywhere, swaggering through the streets, flaunting their blue and white flag and expecting the Turks to salute it, so that they slunk down the side streets to avoid the shame.

'Old Johnny Turk's bowed under the follies of his rulers,' Orgill said, 'and decayed by misgovernment, beaten in battle and ground down by disastrous wars. But there's been an unexpected germination of nationalist groups recently and, make no mistake, he's still the fighter we knew in the Dardanelles; and if they had a man with some spirit to lead 'em, they could still show both the Greeks and Lloyd George that they can't muck them about as they are doing.'

'And what about us?' Orrmont asked. 'Where do we come in?'

Orgill smiled. 'Lloyd George let the Greeks land twenty thousand troops in Smyrna in May,' he said. 'The Turks would probably have chucked them out again, defeated or not, given the chance, but some yellow-belly in their government told them not to resist and the Greeks went potty. One Turkish colonel, who refused to take his fez off and stamp on it, was shot on the spot, then the Greeks got out of hand and hundreds of Turks were killed. It's quietened down a bit now but it won't be long before the Turks chuck out their present government and start resisting. And when they do, I reckon the Greeks are in for a bit of a shock. *That's* where you come in.'

Mail arrived the following week. There was a letter from Kelly's mother suggesting that only ill health was preventing her return to Dublin, where she'd been born, to take up arms in the struggle for Irish freedom that had broken out, and one from Mabel saying simply and bleakly, 'What in God's name have you done to Charley?' From Charley there was nothing, and her silence left Kelly feeling low. He'd once been told that any girl who fell for a sailor needed a bit of luck, and it occurred to him that perhaps sailors sometimes needed a bit of luck, too.

They awoke the following day to the noise of vehicles grinding through the streets ashore and the baying of an enormous crowd. Sailors had crowded up from below to stare shorewards where they could see thousands of people carrying black flags. They were led by white-turbanned hojas and were surging through the streets to mass near the Chamber of Deputies.

'What in God's name's happening?' Kelly demanded.

They soon found out. The Ottoman Parliament was in a state of collapse and a rebel government set up in Anatolia by a man called Mustafa Kemal had raised guerrilla bands and set fire to the Armenian quarter in Marash. Hundreds of women and children had died, while fanatical Moslems had rampaged round the town slaughtering any who escaped. A French column had already been sent to their relief and the allies were now busy occupying Constantinople to keep the status quo. Armoured cars patrolled the streets, and they could hear the tramp of British troops occupying police stations, military posts and the main public buildings.

Sunset came in a fabulous glow of colour over Stambul and the Golden Horn, with the great dome of St. Sophia and the Seraglio like fairy palaces surrounded by the dark silhouettes of cypresses. The uproar ashore seemed to be over but at midnight they could still see torch-carrying crowds surging down the street of the Sublime Porte to the Ministry of War and the Mosque of Suleimanyi.

Next day's dawn came pearly-white from Angora, the flamboyant beauty softened by a veil of mist low over the land to hide the buildings and blend sea and sky together in an extraordinary opalescence. Though the anger seemed to have died down, there was still a great deal of ill-feeling about and when Orrmont was called on board the flagship that evening they all expected him to bring back orders for an evacuation of Greek civilians from Domlupinu or the Iskenderon Gulf. Instead they were for Sebastopol in South Russia.

'We must be going to support the White Russians,' Kelly decided. '*Marlborough*'s been shelling railways and Bolshevik troop concentrations.'

'I'm not so sure.' Orrmont looked puzzled. 'The admiral didn't seem very interested in the guns. He only asked if the wardroom was well stocked with crockery and if we had plenty of knives and forks.'

The first sight of Russia was provided by the sheer cliffs of

Balaclava where a tug was waiting to put aboard a pilot who was to lead them round Cape Kersonese into Sebastopol. The water was crisped by the breeze blowing into the landlocked harbour where a British squadron lay at anchor under the Ville Civile, and the day was clear, the white houses shining brightly in the sunshine. Across the water bells were ringing lustily on the warm air and, with its tall buildings running up the hill-sides, Sebastopol had about it a faint look of Bath.

The pilot was accompanied by a British lieutenant-commander who jerked a contemptuous hand towards the shore, as if he found the whole business of having to take part in someone else's civil war thoroughly distasteful. 'Personally,' he observed, 'I'd have thought the Russians could manage to choose whatever government they wanted without our help, but it seems we have obligations to a variety of anti-Bolshevik movements. Here it's Cossack Separatism, and it throws up the weirdest chaps. One leader used to be a Caucasian bandmaster and he's given himself a title, a white uniform and a beltful of lethal weapons. Local commander's called Denikin and there's a Military Mission training the troops, though God knows why, because they all desert as soon as they see the enemy.'

It all seemed remarkably casual, and the lieutenant-commander went on cheerfully. 'The French were at Odessa but they made an awful botch of the business and in the end they got out. They managed to evacuate around thirty thousand civilians and ten thousand troops, but they left a hell of a lot behind, too, and whole families committed suicide as the ships pulled away.'

Behind the lieutenant-commander's back, Orrmont's eyes met Kelly's. It seemed they were involved here in a different kind of war.

'Things have picked up a bit since they left,' the lieutenant-commander went on. 'Chap called Wrangel beat the Reds at a place with a name nobody can pronounce and finally got into Tsaritsyn. Denikin's now up near Kharkov, and if we could only get all these blasted White leaders to work together, we could knock out the Bolshies easily.' The lieutenant-commander sighed. 'It's such a bloody uncivil affair,' he said. 'If you'll pardon the pun. Nobody seems to take prisoners. They just line 'em up and shoot 'em. I'd much rather be at

31

home keeping an eye on the Germans. Do you think they'll manage to persuade the Dutch to hand over the Kaiser so we can hang him as everybody seems to want?'

Neither Orrmont nor Kelly bothered to answer because, quite obviously the lieutenant-commander wasn't expecting an answer. He'd been working a long time with the Russian pilots who could only converse in very indifferent French and he was really only concerned with hearing his own voice.

'We shall be putting you in the Southern Harbour,' he said, pointing across the dark waters. 'There's the dockyard, and the Karabelnaia suburbs are just beyond the ravine. Nice park near the Malakov, and there are some good gardens alongside the water to walk a girl.'

The shore seemed to be littered with wrecks, and a three-funnelled destroyer lay canted at an angle on the rocks.

'Captain ordered full astern,' the lieutenant-commander explained, 'and when she went full ahead instead he decided there were Bolshies below so he rushed down and shot the engineer.' He sighed wearily. 'They stuffed him in the furnace. Rather a jolly lot. Officers burned or torn to pieces by their own men; some even chucked overboard with firebars attached to their feet. Have to be pretty careful about swimming, in fact, because occasionally they come to the surface and you find yourself staring one straight in the eye.'

Sebastopol seemed as tense as Constantinople. Fear still overshadowed the streets and the place was said to be swarming with Bolshevik agents. Terrible acts of barbarism had taken place when the Black Sea Fleet had mutinied, and food was difficult to obtain because the country people were fleeing into the city from the Red armies.

When Orrmont reappeared from the flagship, he had a startled look on his face. 'We're to become a private yacht, Number One,' he announced. 'We're to go to Yalta and pick up four members of the Tsar's family who seem to have dodged the general massacre of the Romanovs! Grand Duke Piotr Vjeskov; his grandson, Grand Duke Vissarion; his wife, Grand Duchess Evgenia; and her sister, Grand Duchess Yekaterina Seminov.'

Kelly grinned. 'They *said* Russia was full of beautiful grand

32

duchesses, sir.'

Orrmont sniffed. '*This* grand duke's seventy-eight,' he said. 'And the grand duchesses match. We're taking 'em to Malta or wherever someone will have 'em.'

There was little sign of the civil war in Yalta which still wore the look of a fashionable resort. Only in the gardens near the sea could they see wounded officers and nurses with gay ribbons fluttering from their caps. All the houses seemed to be occupied, and on the heights behind the gardens, magnificent pink-and-white turreted villas perched in terraced vineyards. Cars and carriages moved along the waterfront, many of them containing women carrying parasols.

A pier of booms and a special loading platform were hurriedly put together by the ship's carpenter; and the following day a high-nosed individual in the uniform of a Russian staff captain appeared on board and looked down his nose at the gangway party drawn up on deck. Eventually, as they waited, a fleet of large motor cars appeared and an old man in the uniform of an admiral of the fleet, accompanied by two elderly ladies and one supercilious youngster, tottered up the gangway. Bosuns' whistles twittered and everybody stiffened to attention. As far as the Russians were concerned, they might as well not have been there.

'Where are our quarters?' the young man demanded.

Orrmont's face stiffened. 'There are no quarters, sir,' he pointed out. 'We're only a small ship. You will be very welcome, of course, to use the wardroom.'

The Grand Duke Vissarion looked down his aristocratic nose. 'My great-aunt, the Dowager Empress,' he announced coldly, 'was given a battleship. Very well, you may show us the way.'

As they vanished, Wellbeloved drew in his breath. 'They're treating the Owner as if he were a bloody commissionaire,' he gasped.

More cars began to appear, and luggage was stacked on the loading platform. There were more than two hundred pieces, all unmarked or lettered with unreadable Russian characters, and enough staff to fill a troopship, most of them apparently carrying on waspish feuds with each other.

They managed to stow the important ones away in the

cabins, but it still left a lot without anywhere to go, and bug-eyed seamen in their underwear stared at unseeing parlour-maids passing through their mess flats seeking laundering facilities or hot water for their betters, while elderly ladies-in-waiting in goloshes and mackintoshes and carrying umbrellas climbed leisurely up to the bridge to look at the view. They were all attractive, but they all seemed boneheaded in their inability to accept that their condition had changed.

As Kelly bedded them down in his capacity as major domo, he was informed he was to fill up all spare space with White officers' families and, as they began to appear in cars and carts and carriages and on foot, he pushed them in anywhere he could. The Grand Duke Vissarion clearly didn't approve of sharing the ship with the people whose husbands were fighting to save him, but with the placid stolidity of the British sailor doing one of the multifarious jobs the Navy always had to do, everybody ignored his bleats of protest and they packed aboard old men, women and children, stuffing them below and in and around the torpedo tubes and guns and anywhere else there was room.

As they arrived in Malta after a cold passage across a foggy sea, a signal arrived directing them back to Constantinople at once.

'Get 'em off, Number One,' Orrmont snapped. 'Domlupinu's being attacked by Turkish guerillas and there's battle, murder and sudden death going on!'

Aided by burly seamen, the refugees were bundled ashore, but the Vjeskovs seemed to have no more wish to leave than they had had to come aboard, which, considering how much they'd complained about their quarters, was hard to understand. Startled seamen found themselves the recipients of useless Denikin roubles as tips, sometimes even valuable ikons which left them merely bewildered. Grand Duke Piotr handed out signed portraits of himself to the officers. Grand Duke Vissarion offered nothing. Only the two elderly grand duchesses showed any sign of gratitude and theirs was overwhelming. A handsome pair of diamond cuff links was handed to Orrmont; and Kelly found himself the possessor of a magnificent ruby belonging to the Grand Duchess Evgenia, which he decided ought to make a good engagement ring for Charley when – and if – they finally got around to getting engaged.

They got them all off at last and *Mordant* swung away from the quayside, turbines whining as she headed east. They stopped at Constantinople only long enough to go alongside an oiler and take on mail. Once more, significantly, there was nothing from Charley.

Domlupinu was a warren of mud-brick houses and ruins, huddled lattice to lattice and roof upon roof amid dunghills and winding precipitous lanes. Greek forces, reeling from the Turkish guerillas, had crammed into the town and the cruiser, *Cithara*, was lying offshore with her boats already alongside the sagging wooden jetty which was the place's apology for a quay. Guns and matériel of all descriptions were scattered about amid corpses of exhausted, diseased men and animals, and the stink of unburied carcasses filled the sultry air.

As they stuffed terrified people into the boats, more ships arrived. The French and Italians had done little in the way of making arrangements for their nationals and there was a wail of horror as the news went round that the Turks were on the point of arriving. The decks of the ships in the bay were already covered with weeping women, and bearded bluejackets were nursing screaming babies. Searching the crowded vessels, Kelly found two colliers and began to direct the crowd to them. Within a matter of hours, he had crammed five thousand men, women and children into them and sent them on their way to Mitylene.

The Turks arrived the following morning, their eyes blazing with cold hatred for the Greeks, their swords and bayonets rusty with dried blood. Some of them were drunk, and murder and rape were followed almost at once by smoke as Domlupinu was set on fire. Houses built of lath and plaster took the flames immediately in the growing wind, and looters and Turks anxious to pay off old scores added to the blaze.

Tens of thousands of terrified people crammed the sea front, jumping into the sea or running aimlessly about carrying bundles which were already on fire. Greek churches, mosques and houses were silhouetted against the smoke-filled sky as the sailors struggled to separate British nationals and direct them to *Mordant*'s rescue teams. But it was an impossible task because women were throwing their children into the boats to

35

save them and men were plunging into the water and swimming out to appeal for help. Nobody appeared to have much faith in the Greek navy and they all turned instinctively to the British and American ships. The roar of the flames was deafening and, as darkness came, the sea was like molten copper, with what appeared to be twenty different volcanoes flinging up pyres of jagged flames from the town.

Up to their waists in water, the sailors were handing children into boats while their fathers tried to reach the Greek ships. But there were always too many of them and they seemed to be drowning in dozens. The whole water's edge was littered with corpses and in one spot the bodies of three women who had clearly been raped bobbed against the sea wall, only the seaweed covering their nakedness.

'Good God,' Wellbeloved said grimly as the boats were hoisted in and the ships drew away. 'I hope bloody Lloyd George's happy. You'd have to go a long way to find a worse mess than this.'

They little knew what was round the corner.

4

Still shocked and angry, they headed back to Constantinople. Mail from home awaited them. There was a letter for Rumbelo announcing the birth of a son and a short note from Kelly's mother to say his father had finally returned from the Middle East, but still nothing from Charley.

They had no sooner refuelled when they were ordered to Salonika where vengeful Greeks were forcing out the Turkish population. Since going down to defeat with her German allies, Turkey could no longer support her European possessions and the whole Middle East seemed to be on the move.

Ferrying their unhappy passengers back to Stambul, they rejoined the squadron at Sebastopol and spent the next three weeks crossing and recrossing the Black Sea to Odessa, Batoum and Baku, picking their way through dubiously-charted minefields laid during the war by Turks, Russians, Bulgarians and Rumanians, trying to obtain fixes on lighthouses which functioned only occasionally, if at all, and pick up buoys that no longer existed.

Finally, well into the summer they were ordered to Novorossiisk in South Russia where the anti-Bolshevik campaign seemed to have picked up a little. There was now a clear hope that the three White Army fronts might come together and drive the Reds back into Moscow for Christmas, but of all the confusion in South Russia, that in Novorossiisk was perhaps the worst.

Colourful beneath the onion-shaped domes of its churches, the town was full of penniless refugees and indescribable beggars, and was a hotbed of crime. With the white Army's paper roubles practically valueless, a great deal of speculation in foreign currency was going on, and there was a

37

motley collection of nationalities in the streets – Russians wearing British khaki with epaulettes like planks on their shoulders; foreign entrepreneurs attempting to establish some new base for trade; Levantine merchants; Cossacks in fur caps; women on the make; Jews in shabby frock coats; and dubious Balkan mercenaries, Turks, adventurers, and German and Austrian prisoners of war still awaiting repatriation. In addition, there were also enormous numbers of the old Russian aristocracy, an incredible group, still arrogant and self-satisfied despite the disasters that had struck them, some of the unluckier ones living in tiny cluttered rooms smelling of the creosote with which they tried to discourage the lice that seemed to swarm everywhere in South Russia. Because of the overcrowding, every disease imagineable prospered with ease, smallpox chasing diphtheria, and typhus chasing cholera.

As soon as they appeared alongside, a British naval officer stepped on board.

'Lieutenant-Commander Mawdit,' he announced. 'Naval Mission staff. What have you been sent here for?'

'God knows,' Kelly said, and Mawdit grinned.

'Then it doesn't matter, does it?' he said cheerfully. 'If I were you, I'd suggest to your captain that you leave a responsible officer on board and go ashore and enjoy yourselves. There's a party on at the Smalnovs' tonight, in fact, so I'll pick you up and whizz you along. The Smalnovs like the Navy. Like all the other White Russians, they think they might need it one day.'

The Smalnovs' house was an awesome place surrounded by sweeping flights of marble terraces and mosaic pavements. A buffet supper had been laid out on the terrace, a wide flagged arena reached through a vast room of pink marble sparkling with candelabres. The guests seemed to include half the population of Novorossiisk, and lobster, caviare and chicken were washed down with Crimean wine. Though considering themselves impoverished by the loss of their northern properties in the Revolution, the Smalnovs were still living like princes on what was left, and their attitude was clearly that it was better to die than reduce their standards.

There was a high-ranking R.A.F. officer present and several British army men, including an artillery major called Galt whose mother had been Russian. He was holding forth about the confusion.

'The bloody place has five "times",' he told Kelly. 'Local, ship's time. Petrograd time, the time of the local cement works and British Mission time. There's an hour and a half difference between the fastest and the slowest, so if I were you, I'd put away my watch and just forget it until the war's over.'

The battleship, *Queen Elizabeth*, had just joined the South Russian squadron and almost the first person Kelly met was Kimister.

'Maguire,' he said. 'I heard you were here.'

Kelly noted the disappearance of his Christian name and, already resentful of the fact that Kimister had once proposed to Charley, he remembered the number of fights he'd had at Dartmouth with Verschoyle to protect Kimister from his bullying.

'*How* did you hear?' he asked.

'Charley, of course. Charley Upfold.'

'Oh!' Somewhere along the line, Kelly felt, he'd become second favourite and the betting on Kimister had improved quite considerably. 'See much of her?'

'Well, a bit.' Kimister didn't seem to have changed much. His manner was still uncertain and over the years his round, pale face had lost what character it had ever had and seemed to be devoid of lines, bone structure, everything except soft jowly cheeks.

'I seem to have missed things out here a bit.' He spoke as if he were apologising. 'My father died, and they gave me a long leave to clear up his affairs. He left me pretty well off.'

Kelly grunted. 'More than mine will ever leave me,' he said.

'Heard from Charley?' Kimister went on. 'I had a letter by the last mail.'

Did you, by Christ? Kelly thought savagely. Kimister appeared to be doing well out of his misfortunes. Some people could smell loneliness a mile away and, though he'd never thought Kimister a fast or determined mover, perhaps he'd learned a lot in the last two or three years.

Galt, the artillery major, pulled Kelly away. He was with Orrmont and was talking enthusiastically about the war.

'You interested in guns?' he asked.

'Gunnery officers,' Orrmont pointed out, 'become gunnery

39

officers only so that they don't have to go to sea in the same ship as another gunnery officer.'

Galt frowned. 'A gunnery officer would be a good chap for what we have in mind.'

'What *do* you have in mind?'

'Broneviks – armoured trains. Up to now they've carried only light stuff – field guns and machine guns, that sort of thing – but now we've persuaded your admiral to let us have a naval banger or two so we can indulge in a little decent long-range slogging.'

'What you want,' Orrmont pointed out cheerfully with a sidelong glance at Kelly, 'is a chap who's done a gunnery course, speaks French and is unlikely to panic.'

Galt grinned. 'That's exactly what we want,' he said. 'Know somebody?'

'Indeed I do,' Orrmont said, looking at Kelly again. 'My number One.'

The room seemed to be filled with incredibly beautiful women but the introductions were alarming because the rules of procedure were strict and none of the British spoke Russian. Most of the Russians spoke French, however, and while Kelly, who appeared to be the only Englishman present with any command of the language, was still struggling with protocol, a hand touched his arm and he turned to find a woman in a lavender gown standing alongside him. She had startling topaz eyes that indicated a Tartar ancestry and thick deep-brown hair touched with reddish lights.

'I shall be your friend for the evening,' she announced. 'I am Vera Nikolaevna Brasov. Princess Brasov. Does that worry you?'

'It's not been my good fortune to meet many princesses,' Kelly admitted, 'but the Royal Navy has a self-assurance all its own and isn't likely to be outfaced.'

She gave a tinkling laugh. 'That's a very clever reply, Captain – ?'

'Maguire,' Kelly said. 'George Kelly Maguire. And I'm not a captain, merely a lieutenant. Not really very important.'

She touched his medal ribbons with her gloves. 'My brother had many medals,' she said. 'He was murdered with my mother and father when the Revolution broke out.'

There was an awkward silence. What did one say in reply? Then she gave a short brittle laugh. 'I know exactly whom you should meet,' she said. 'And since the Brasov family is very important, no one will dare to be rude to you with me alongside.'

Her eyes were enormous and she had fine delicate hands, while her English – learned, it seemed, as a small girl at school in England and at the Smolnia, the leading Russian girls' establishment in Petrograd – was as perfect as her figure.

She led him round the room and on to the verandah, introducing him to the other guests – elderly generals, a woman with an eyeglass and a perfect English drawl, her son, a Guards captain educated at Cambridge and now a British liaison officer. None of them seemed to be involved in the fighting.

'What are they all doing?' Kelly asked.

She smiled. 'They are waiting for the end of the world, I think,' she said. 'It isn't very far away.'

An amateur guitarist was playing *The Song of Stenka Razin*, a pretty ballad which had become popular with the officers of the British Mission. Judging by the look of one or two of the Russians, they had been at the abrau durso, the local champagne, and one of them was lying sprawled across the table with his head among the crockery and glasses.

The talk was nostalgic and the women sighed for clothes no longer obtainable in Russia, but everyone was remarkably cheerful, though occasionally there were little gaps in the conversation, hastily covered with a smile, which showed how the circumstances of many of them had changed. Their minds were full of their hopes and fears but they tried hard not to be boring about them, and they were always quick to propose a toast – 'Na Moskvu – To Moscow.'

'I understand you came to Russia to pick up the Vjeskovs,' Princess Brasov said. 'How lucky they are! To be taken somewhere safe with all our belongings is something we all dream about.' She gave her brittle little laugh. 'Let's go into the garden and you can tell me more about yourself.'

The Smalnovs' garden was full of trees and palms, and the paths led to quiet arbours, but, as the evening progressed, a chilly wind came up from the sea, and it emptied abruptly, so that Kelly found himself alone in it with Vera Brasov.

'Are you married, Kelly Georgeivitch?' she asked.

41

'No.'

'Then perhaps you have a fiancée.'

If Charley could still be considered a fiancée, Kelly thought, then, yes, he had, but the gospel according to Kimister seemed to indicate that Charley didn't consider herself in any way spoken for any more.

'No,' he said shortly.

'But you must have a *baryshnia* – a girl.'

'No.'

She glanced about her. 'Then you'd better kiss me now,' she murmured, 'and set your mind at rest.'

Kelly's mind hadn't been particularly uneasy, but Charley seemed to have dropped him and, under the circumstances, he saw no harm. The world appeared to be full of attractive women all itching to get close to a man, and it seemed a pity to waste an opportunity.

The news improved. With the Reds thrown back in confusion on the Tsaritsyn front, Denikin had gone on to the offensive and had taken over two hundred and fifty thousand prisoners and gained a vast stretch of territory, so that his lines now stretched from Poltava in the west through Kharkov and Pavlovsk towards Kamyshin, and he was only three hundred and seventy miles from Moscow. In Siberia, Admiral Kolchak's armies had rallied and also seemed to be headed for the capital, while the Army of the Ukraine, based on Odessa, was advancing with unchallengeable verve, and General Yudenitch in the north-west was said to be within sight of St. Isaac's Cathedral. Lenin, it was gleefully claimed, was waiting in the Kremlin with a train standing by in Moscow station to take him to safety, and it seemed the only thing now needed to make everything right was the elimination of a completely new army which had appeared – the Greens, neither Reds nor Whites and led by a man called Mahkno – who were really only bandits and nothing compared with the defeated Red hordes which had been troubling Holy Russia.

Nobody had taken seriously Orrmont's joke about naval officers on armoured trains, not even Orrmont, but apparently Galt did, and two weeks later a signal was received aboard *Mordant* as she returned from a trip to Yalta, instructing the first lieutenant to repair on board the flagship.

The admiral, a tall, round-faced man peering at a book through horn-rimmed spectacles, looked up as Kelly entered his day cabin.

'Maguire?' he said.

'Yes, sir.'

'Understand you speak French?'

'I took a course after I was wounded at Jutland, sir. I took rather a lot of courses just then.'

'Good.' The admiral nodded approvingly. 'We need French speakers out here. Only way we have of communicating with the Russians. We also need gunners.'

Kelly's heart sank. 'For trains, I suspect, sir.'

The admiral smiled. 'That's right, my boy. How's your gunnery?'

Kelly smiled back. 'That's another of the courses I took, sir.'

'Well, the Royal Artillery are busy training field batteries and they haven't the men to spare for trains. How about you?'

Kelly sighed. 'It's never been my habit to refuse when I've been told to volunteer, sir.'

The admiral's smile grew wider and he rose. 'A very good idea, too,' he said briskly. 'There's a new train just been made up here in the railway yard. There'll be a gunner – I think you've met him – a naval gun's crew with one officer from *Queen Elizabeth* and a squad of Russian infantrymen, strengthened with British. Do you wish to take anybody special with you?'

'Just a chap from my ship, sir. He's served with me before. I know I can trust him.'

The admiral nodded. 'Very well,' he said. 'That can be arranged. You'll be informed when to be at the railway yard.'

That seemed to be that. It took Kelly's breath away.

5

The south Russian summer had come with a vengeance and the days were full of drying heat. With Denikin's advance, the Bolsheviks were nowhere near now but everyone was still in a highly nervous state. Many of them had seen their home towns crowded with mutinous soldiers decked with red ribbons, hundreds had died in organised massacres, and almost everyone you met had lost a husband, son or father. But there was a tremendous optimism about the future now, with large White armies in being, and everybody was beginning to hope for great things.

Protocol and etiquette still filled the Russian minds more than the war, however, and they argued long and earnestly about whether they should propose the toast of the King of England and the Prince of Wales without including the name of the Queen and the Princess Royal, or the order in which the six or seven national anthems of the allies who were supporting them should be played by the Cossack band which was always present at parties.

Outings were laid on which involved drives on vicious mountain roads by chauffeurs who seemed hell-bent on suicide. They visited the battlefield of Inkerman and the scene of the charge of the Light Brigade; and a few startled British officers found themselves the husbands of countesses or even princesses.

'There are going to be a hell of a lot of Boris Albertovitch Smiths and Sergei Angusovitch MacNabs when this is all over,' Wellbeloved grinned.

Among the nightly flirtations which went on under the cypresses, Kimister seemed to be carrying on a hesitant affair with a determined Russian baroness. Though he seemed to spend most of his time backing away at full speed, his devotion ιο Charley didn't seem to put him off entirely and, to Kelly's fury, he still received letters from home which Kelly did not receive.

'Had a line from Charley,' he liked to announce when they met. 'She sends her regards.'

Times were changing, Kelly thought. It used to be her love.

In Novorossiisk the war was clearly nearer than in Sebastopol and the place was full of soldiers all wearing British khaki. The regimental officers were an extraordinary crowd. Dressed in a mixture of uniforms, their badges of rank were often marked on their epaulettes with blue pencil, yet they wore spurs with rowels as big as five shilling pieces that jingled like pebbles in a tin. Generous to the point of absurdity, they were of little use for anything, and they were lazy, arrogant and often cowardly, because they knew their men had no heart for fighting their fellow countrymen.

'The best men vanished in the war against the Germans,' Vera Brasov explained. 'Those who join now are mere ingorotsy or chinoviks – foreigners and petty officials – who enjoy dressing up as officers but have no intention of going near the front.'

Certainly no one at British Mission headquarters had a very high opinion of them, while their soldiers – as often as not country boys recruited by scouting parties – were simple men inclined to put flowers in the muzzles of their rifles and stand in awe at the sight of a train. Among them also, however, were a lot of shifty individuals who'd been taken as prisoners from the Red Army in the skirmishes earlier in the year and given the choice of changing sides or being shot. Not unnaturally, they hadn't hesitated.

'I wouldn't like to be a White officer, standing in front of 'em,' Orrmont observed shrewdly.

'Which suggests, sir, that it might be a good idea to keep an eye on where our own people go when they're ashore,' Kelly said. 'I wouldn't like to think of 'em meeting that lot in bars.'

Orrmont gave him an amused look. 'You expecting bloody revolution to break out aboard, Number One?'

'We saw the Germans at Scapa, sir,' Kelly said. 'And at Sebastopol we were floating above the bodies of a couple of hundred Russian officers, who were chucked overboard with their feet tied to firebars. Their crews gave them the choice of dying hot or dying cold. If they asked for hot, they fed them into the furnaces. If they preferred cold, they went overboard with no chance of swimming.'

How right Kelly was, was proved only a few days later when news found its way south that an Anglo-Slav battalion in North Russia formed from deserters and prison inmates who'd been given their freedom on receipt of a promise to fight against the Reds, had mutinied and murdered three British and four Russian officers and wounded four more. A battalion of Royal Marines sent to stabilise the front where they'd defected had also refused duty and the allied forces had been obliged to retire.

Orrmont was a little shaken and Kelly went ahead hurriedly to organise trips round the Russian museums, and even obtained permission from Vera Brasov to allow him to show a group round the gardens of her family home.

'You'd better make it fast,' Orrmont suggested, tossing a message form across. 'You're to report to the sidings next week.'

The last of the summer warmth had a cloying feel about it now and everybody in the city seemed to be making an effort to get the best out of the weather. Kelly was in a curious state of limbo. He'd still heard nothing from Charley and didn't know where to lay the blame. As he well knew, it lay chiefly with the Navy, and probably with himself, but he suspected, too, that Kimister hadn't been idle.

Mordant's ratings enjoyed themselves at the Brasov Palace because sausages, bread, cheese and a pale soapy liquid which went by the name of beer had been laid on; and a red-haired able seaman called Doncaster stepped forward and insisted on making a ponderous speech of thanks which Kelly translated in his best French.

'I hope you have taken his name, Kelly Georgeivitch,' Vera said quietly. 'In Holy Russia we have discovered that men who make speeches are also the sort who stir up disaffection.'

As the two-horse charabancs arrived to carry the bluejackets back to the ship, she slipped her hand through his arm.

'Why not stay for dinner?' she suggested. 'I think your sailors can take themselves safely back to their ship, can they not?'

They dined on the vast verandah, on a small table laid with spotless linen, the meal served by discreet servants who hovered in the distance.

'Do you trust them?' Kelly asked as they rose.

'Would you?'

'No.'

'Neither would I. But so far, thank God, the Bolsheviki are far away.' She took his hand and led him upstairs. 'We'll use the first floor salon,' she said. 'Here it's like sitting in the middle of the Nevsky Prospekt.'

The salon was a small pink room with armchairs and a chaise longue. The draperies were filmy and smelled of flowers, and a bottle of Russian champagne waited for them. This, Kelly thought, is what Verschoyle does when he invites girls to see his etchings.

She turned to face him. She had sparklingly white teeth, and the oriental opulence about her looks that many of the South Russians had gave her a forthright sexuality she made no attempt to disguise.

She fanned herself and downed a glass of wine. 'The heat can be brutal here,' she said. 'I shouldn't have worn this dress.' She began fumbling with the back of the high neck. 'Would you be shocked if I asked you to unhook me?' She beamed. 'Just the neck, of course.'

Deciding he was becoming expert at this business of undressing females. Kelly stood behind her, his hands under the heavy chignon she wore. Her neck felt hot under his fingers as slowly, methodically, he freed one hook after another.

She made no protest, shivering a little as he touched the skin of her exposed back. It exuded a warm, animal fragrance, and his hand reached inside the thin silk chemise. Abruptly she gave a gasp, turned in his arms to face him and moved her head slightly towards a door at the end of the room.

'In there,' she whispered.

The room contained a bed draped with the same filmy hangings as the salon. She unbuttoned his jacket and began to unfasten his shirt.

'What are we waiting for?' Her voice came as a croak and he saw she had shed all her clothes but the thin chemise and was standing near the bed.

She gave him a twisted smile. 'You are making guesses at why I've brought you here, aren't you, Kelly Georgeivitch? You have heard that Russian girls are trying to find themselves husbands among the British where it is safe, and you think I'm taking out an insurance for my future.'

Kelly said nothing and her face became harder. 'You would be wrong,' she said. 'When the war broke out in 1914, I was twenty-three and engaged to be married. Everybody said it would soon be over so we decided to wait and be married in peacetime. He was killed at Przemyśl. I took a lover after that but he was murdered by the Bolsheviki in 1917. Now I think only of today and what it has to offer. I like my men alive. Please don't stop now.'

It was the beginning of a hectic few days. Whenever he was off duty, Kelly found his way to Vera Brasov's arms. Thinking about Charley, at first he felt guilty, but the feeling soon passed because Kimister seemed to be receiving all the letters that had previously come to him and he had to face the fact that their affair appeared, after a lifetime of taking Charley for granted, to have come to an end.

At a distance of two thousand miles he could hardly blame her and it wasn't hard to put his guilt aside. He was aware that the news of what was happening between himself and Vera Brasov was passing round ihe fleet and he knew that Kimister would inevitably have passed it on to Charley. But in accepting foreign service, he felt he had done no more than any normal naval officer would do and that Charley probably expected too much from him. He suspected it was a shelving of responsibility to salve his own conscience, yet in his heart he also felt he'd been rejected and wasn't entirely to blame.

Vera Brasov made no bones about her pleasure in him. She taught him to call her '*Tsaritsa moyevo serdsta*' – the queen of his heart – and in the mornings across the pillow greeted him in Russian.

'*Dobroye utro*, Kelly Georgeivitch! Oi, *Anglichanie*, you are good in bed!'

She wasn't as sentimental as she pretended, however, and though her love-making was expert, he found her several times watching him with a curious soullessness in her eyes. Despite

48

her denial, he knew she *was* using him as an insurance against the future.

'Make no mistake, Kelly Georgeivitch,' she pointed out coolly,' these armies of ours are not as good as they seem. And at the moment, all is going well because we have broad rivers between us and the Bolsheviki. I don't think anyone here has stopped to think what will happen when the winter comes and they freeze. *Then*, the ice will be thick enough to bear horses and waggons and guns, and the barriers they present will disappear overnight.'

6

Kelly's new command was pulled by a ninety-ton monster of an engine, decorated in red and black and liberally sprinkled with flags. It's name, *Invincible,* was painted in Kyrillic characters along its side and there were more flags on the front and rear of the train and on the corners of every carriage. Living quarters were provided by a coupé for the officers and senior N.C.O.s and two fitted-out cattle trucks called kerplushkas for the men. The rest of the train consisted of the usual armoured repair truck followed by a sandbagged flat car mounted with machine guns, behind which were trucks with a six-inch naval gun and four 12-pounders. Each piece of rolling stock had an iron flap over the buffers so that it was possible to pass from one to the other while the train was in motion.

'Bit tricky in a heavy sea, sir,' Rumbelo grinned.

The living quarters were luxurious, with potted plants, red velvet seats, and gold-framed paintings. As Kelly stared at the picture of a half-clad girl on a leopard skin, the door from the sleeping quarters opened and he was startled to see Kimister.

'What the devil are you doing here?' he demanded.

Kimister gestured. 'New job,' he said. 'They've given me command of the train.' He sounded uneasy and unhappy. 'I've got Russian infantry, a Royal Artillery team, a gun's crew from *Queen Elizabeth*, and another naval officer.'

Kelly grinned. 'Try again, old son,' he said. 'I think you've got it wrong. *I'm* the other naval officer and you certainly haven't got *me.*'

They had expected to move off quietly with nothing more than a send-off from Orrmont, but the Russian authorities had decided otherwise, and three batteries of newly-trained artillery, which were also due to go to the front, had been drawn up alongside the train with a regiment of Cossacks, dramatic, fierce-looking men on small shaggy ponies, with long lovelocks of hair curled Cossack-fashion over their left ears. They had brought their horse-tail regimental standards, and an altar had been erected alongside the railway line. As they waited, a priest in glittering robes and surrounded by acolytes advanced slowly towards them. As he lifted his hand, church bells started.

'Good God,' Kelly said to Galt. 'I think they're going to marry us!'

The solemnity of the service was intensified by huge crucifixes and a choir whose base voices in Gregorian chants competed with the wild pealing of the bells. The Te Deum finished, a Russian officer stepped forward with a silk banner which he handed to Kelly, and there were more muttered prayers, more choral acrobatics and enough holy water flung about to wash the train. As the priest vanished, the artillery clattered past followed by the Cossacks, singing as they went, the music conducted by the officer in front with his whip.

A pale young Russian Guards officer stepped forward.

'Captain Takhatin,' he introduced himself sombrely. 'I am to be your liaison officer. I think perhaps this time they give me an easy job.'

'Wasn't the last one easy?'

The Russian's face stiffened. 'The last time,' he said, 'I am evacuated wounded. But perhaps I am lucky because a week later the others are all murdered.'

It set Kelly back on his heels. It was one of those unexpected anecdotes that always seemed to be turning up in Russia which completely prevented any reply or words of sympathy. They were so common and so terrible there was simply nothing that could be said.

Led by a light train, they set off north. It was sunset as they reached the main ranges of the Caucasus. Rocks, cliffs and pinnacles rose in front with pine forests in a smooth purple plain, and finally a river appeared, rushing from the slopes white with foam.

Kimister carried out his duties nervously so that Kelly wondered if he'd been detached from *Queen Elizabeth* because someone wanted to get rid of him, but the artilleryman, Galt, was

51

everywhere at once, enthusiastically checking rations, ammunition, spare parts and tools. Occasionally they passed other trains waiting in sidings, sometimes full of soldiers docile as sheep, sometimes full of passengers packed into incredibly filthy cattle cars with barely enough room to move. They were even on the roofs and buffers and packing the windows, their pale faces full of resignation. Takhatin watched them gloomily.

'One month ago,' he pointed out, 'they go north. The war goes well and they wish to go home. Now they go south.'

Oh, charming, Kelly thought. Bloody charming! With his usual luck he had found himself in the middle of a lost campaign hundreds of miles from the sea.

After a while the train began to run across a bare treeless countryside as flat as a billiard table. Occasionally they saw groups of mounted men riding alongside the track, tall, well-built men in long grey coats with cartridge belts across their chests and high karakul caps. They seemed to be weighed down with weapons and occasionally one of them fired his rifle in the air in salutation.

They spent the night in a sidings at Ekaterinodar. There seemed a great deal of nervousness about the place but the military maps on the walls showing the White armies' advances appeared to have nothing on them to cause concern, because the whole of the Northern Caucasus seemed to be in Denikin's pocket, while General Wrangel had just liberated the Terek region, and Kolchak, the White leader in Siberia, was advancing towards the Volga in the hope of a link-up.

There were far more troops about in Ekaterinodar even than in Novorossiisk but no less confusion. The soldiers were patient and good-humoured but they seemed to be treated abominably by their officers.

Takhatin shrugged. 'They constantly desert,' he said.

The following morning, as they headed further north towards Tsaritsyn, the steppe seemed more lifeless and depressing than ever. At intervals they passed villages that broke the monotony of empty earth and sky. The houses were all square, mud-brown and thatched, and the entire population, with their cattle and horses, lined the track to watch them pass.

Tsaritsyn was only just beginning to recover from its long occupation by the Bolsheviks. It was said they had murdered thousands of people before it had been recaptured, and their bodies had been placed in the ravines on the outskirts. The information seemed to bother Kimister.

The shops were still empty and the churches desecrated. The population had a shocked look and there were starving children everywhere begging for food. Wrangel's troops were further to the north heading for Saratov as part of Denikin's great plan, but no one seemed to have much enthusiasm for it.

A British Mission officer met them apologetically. 'We're sending you on tomorrow,' he said. 'There's a particularly awkward Bolshie bronevik comes down from Ryazanka and stands off just beyond the River Vilyuj and hammers everything that moves. I think we can knock him out now, though, because he's only got four-inch guns and thanks to the Navy, *we've* got a six-incher. We've arranged for infantry to advance alongside you in carts and for cavalry to spread out to right and left to make sure the area's clear. There's a loop line up there that runs behind a low hill and I thought we might shove you in there to wait for them to arrive.'

'What about our rear?'

'We have a train to follow you up and watch the track at the junction. Can you man it?'

Only too well aware of Kimister's nervousness, Kelly decided that the job was made for him.

Leading the procession was a light engine pulling a truck, followed by the main unit, consisting of the truck carrying the naval six-incher from *Queen Elizabeth*, the first armoured waggon, and a machine gun flat car, pushed by the big locomotive whose boiler in Kelly's eyes appeared to be surprisingly badly protected. Two more armoured waggons were hitched on behind the engine and another open truck full of breakdown equipment brought up the rear. A cord had been strung from a bell in the driver's cabin over the trucks and run through ringbolts.

'To start, we pull the rope,' Galt explained. 'As on a tram. One ting and we stop. Two tings and off we go again.'

There were already alarms in Tsaritsyn as they set off. The Kuban Cossacks had not only failed to take Saratov but had been thrown back as far south as Kamyshin, which only a determined attack by Cossack cavalry had wrested from the Red Army. Despite Wrangel's objections, his orders were to continue pressing towards Saratov.

'There isn't a chance,' the British Mission officer said. 'That bloody armoured train knocks out anything that goes up the line. I think you'd better get moving.'

Leaving the outskirts of the city, they picked up a string of country carts filled with infantry, which jolted and rattled across the steppe on each side of the train. Out in the distance horsemen in long looping lines rode along the crests of low hills. At a village called Sarovkina, as they halted outside the town to eat, barefooted girls harvesting sunflower seeds stopped work to watch them. Bearded men were working little patches of soil along the sandy ground round the village orchards but the burning wind had scorched the earth, putting huge cracks across the dried ruts that stretched across a rolling prairie empty of everything but the shrivelled tawny grass and the clumps of birch and alder. As the afternoon drew to a suffocating close, the girls vanished to the river where they proceeded to bathe mother-naked, to the great delight of the men on the train.

They spent the night at Sarovkina and left the following morning before daylight to pass through the front line, mere groups of badly-equipped men waiting in hollows, mostly without boots or a single machine gun. Their faces, under the covering of wind-blown dust, were blank and haggard and Kelly could see knees and elbows sticking through threadbare uniforms. Some were without shirts and wore only woollen vests, and one or two actually wore the spiked pickelhaubes the German army had left behind at the end of the war.

There was a strange fatalism in their eyes as the train steamed past and one of their officers called out that Wrangel was falling back again towards Tsaritsyn. Just ahead there was another line of men and they could hear rifle and occasional machine gun fire.

'Armoured trains over on our left somewhere, too,' Galt said. 'Indulging in a long-range duel by the method of "chuck and catch it."'

The Whites were holding a hill beyond the far end of the wooden bridge that carried the railway line across the River

Vilyuj, and they were worried sick that the enemy train would appear and cut the bridge behind them. A few peasants were standing near the bridge, watching, apparently quite indifferent as to who won.

With the train stopped, they could hear the unmistakeable sound of 18-pounders firing, and they walked over a rise in the ground to find a battery in action in a cornfield. It didn't seem to be firing very hard and at that moment three of the guns were in difficulty, one with a hopelessly-jammed cartridge which had been thrust into a breech still covered with sand, another with an overrun trigger and the third with such weak springs its crews had to push it by hand into its cradle after every round. The Russians were staring at the silent weapons, their officers wearing woebegone expressions.

Galt looked at Kelly. 'Ever been on a gunnery course?' he asked.

'Whale Island.'

'Well, with the assistance of that leading hand of yours, I think we ought to be able to fix this, don't you?'

They took off their coats and got two of the guns going again almost at once, while the Russian soldiers looked on from behind in amazement at the sight of officers doing manual work.

Crossing the bridge, they left Kimister in the rear train to guard against the line being cut behind them. The infantry and cavalry, well mixed together, were crossing by a wooden foot-bridge alongside. Then the Russian battery they'd helped fired. Its first shell fell harmlessly into the Vilyuj by the far bank, flinging a geyser of black water upwards. The others fell on the bank. Over the steam from the engine it was impossible to hear the shell bursts, and the columns of smoke seemed to rise silently.

They found the loop line and, out of sight behind a slight swelling of the ground, they brought back their scout engine, then Kelly went to the top of the rise with Rumbelo to watch for the Red train on the slow-curving line that came down from the north. As they sat down in the sweet-smelling yellow grass, the loop of the river in the west was picking up the pink evening light like a shining salmon-coloured snake.

'How's the infant, Rumbelo?' Kelly asked, offering his flask.

'Fine, sir. Arrived without any trouble.'

55

'Made a mistake deciding to call him Kelly. He'll regret it all his life.'

'Shouldn't think so, sir. Biddy and me thought you'd like to be godfather, sir.'

Kelly smiled and Rumbelo was just about to say something further when he stopped and gestured. As Kelly turned he saw a column of steam rise beyond a distant slope, then the Bolshevik train appeared over the brow of the hill and slowly began moving down the slope in front of them at a distance of about nine thousand yards.

'Get back to the train, Rumbelo,' Kelly ordered. 'They ought to be able to hit her as she comes round the curve. I'll stick up one arm for a short and two for over, and point for direction. I'll wave both if they're on target.'

'Right, sir.'

Rumbelo started running down the slope towards the railway line while Kelly stretched himself out in the grass, his eyes on the enemy bronevik as it moved slowly forward, stopping occasionally like a great suspicious beast. Through his binoculars he could see a string of Kyrillic letters along the sides of the trucks and a huge number on the engine. He felt as if his heart were in his throat, choking him.

Then, as he waited, he heard the crack of the naval six-incher and almost immediately the whine of the shell and the sound of the explosion. It landed fifty yards short of the curve and he stood up and raised one arm. His breath clutching at his chest, he heard the gun bang a second time, while the gun on the Russian train moved, as though looking for its tormentor. This time the shell fell just beyond the train and he stood up and held up both arms.

'For God's sake,' he muttered to himself. 'Look slippy.'

Then he heard rifle shots and not far away in a dip saw men with horses and realised they were firing at him. Flopping out of sight in the long grass, he peered towards the Bolshevik train. Great jets of steam were coming from it now and through his binoculars he could see it starting to pull back. Then the naval gun fired again and he heard the shell whirr overhead like an underground train and saw the explosion as it hit. A piece of metal went arcing away from near the Bolshevik's front turret to land in the long grass, and a cloud of steam burst from the engine.

'Got the bastard!'

Standing up, he began to wave both arms frantically, then a shower of bullets from the men in the dip made him flop out of sight again. As he lifted his head, he saw a battery of guns thundering up the slope, the weapons bouncing behind the gun carriages, the horses straining at the harness. It seemed to be getting dangerous.

Another shell howled over his head and this time he saw a tremendous explosion just abaft the Bolshevik engine, as though they'd hit the ready-use ammunition, and when the steam and the smoke had cleared he could see the engine distinctly canted to one side and men helping the driver from the cab.

The bullets were coming closer now and he saw a machine gun on a cart rattling out of a dip. It seemed to be time to disappear and he started to run as hard as he could down the slope. As he ran he heard two more shells whirr overhead and after the second one a tremendous explosion beyond the rise. Satisfied that they'd done what they'd come to do, he panted up to the train and scrambled aboard.

'We'd better get out of here,' he yelled to Galt. 'They've got a bettery of guns over there and I wouldn't like 'em to do to us what we've just done to them.'

The train was set in motion by a jerk of the cord to the driver's cab but, to their horror, instead of going backwards, it began to move nearer to the enemy. Galt tugged at the cord until it broke, but the engine continued to move forward.

'I think the driver must be a bloody Bolshy,' Kelly said. 'Come on, Rumbelo!'

Snatching at the door in the front of the truck, they scrambled across the buffers to the machine gun flat car where the Russian soldiers were yelling frantically at the engine's crew. Shoving them aside, Kelly jumped on to the engine's cow catcher and scrambled along the side of the boiler. Rumbelo was behind him and they swung into the cab together. The Russian driver was just about to jump from the train when Rumbelo grabbed him by the shoulder.

'Got you, you bastard,' he roared, slamming him against the tender. The fireman was yelling with fright and Kelly drew his

57

revolver and gestured with it under the driver's nose.

'Back, you sod!' he roared, and the Russian hurriedly reached for his levers and wheels and began to swing on them.

'Faster,' Kelly yelled. 'Faster! How the hell do you say "Faster" in this half-baked language of theirs, Rumbelo?'

'Try "pozhaluista,"sir.'

'What's that mean?'

'"Please." It's the only word I know, sir.'

Kelly shoved the muzzle of the revolver almost up the Russian's nostril and pointed backwards, and eventually the train came to a stop and began to reverse.

'Thank Christ for that,' Kelly said. 'I wouldn't fancy taking tea with the Bolshies after we've just destroyed their Sunday-best train.'

The train was backing out of the loop line on to the main line when they realised that behind them the track was empty.

'Where's Kimister?' Kelly snapped. 'He's supposed to be watching our rear.'

Galt appeared, climbing along the catwalk of the boiler. 'The silly bugger's pulled back across the river!' he yelled, pointing. 'Together with the infantry who're supposed to be supporting us and the bloody guns from the river!'

'Let's hope they haven't cut the bridge,' Kelly snapped. 'Keep your eyes open astern. Rumbelo, get back there and make sure every one of our chaps has a weapon. Even if you have to take it off one of the Russians.'

Rumbelo vanished and, with Kelly still standing with his revolver against the driver's head, Galt hung from the side of the engine.

'There are horsemen on the other side,' he yelled. 'They're coming up the bank. I think they're Red cavalry.'

'Where the hell are *our* cavalry?'

'I think they've bolted.'

The wooden piles of the railway bridge were shaking with the speed of the train as it crossed the river in a mad race to get clear before the approaching horsemen arrived. As they thundered off the bridge and into a shallow gulley leading from the river, they saw overturned carts and dead horses and sprawled figures in the grass, and realised that they were the bodies of the

Russian gunnery officers.

'I think the bastards have mutinied,' Galt yelled.

'Faster,' Kelly roared at the driver and the train hurtled backwards, rocketing round the bends to outstrip the cavalry galloping along the skyline after them. 'Thank God it'll soon be dark.'

Even as he spoke, however, the rear truck carrying the break-down equipment hit a log placed across the track, ran half way over it and fell sideways, flinging steel jacks and khaki-clad figures on to the embankment. The corner of the truck dug into the side of the gulley, throwing stones, clods of earth, torn-off woodwork and pieces of bent metal in all directions. The second truck smashed into the first and the third into that, until the whole train caterpillared and the engine came to a stop, screeching with leaking steam.

As he picked himself up, Kelly saw the engine driver bolting across the steppe and heard the fireman screaming. Hot coals had sprayed from the firebox on to him and his trousers were burning. Beating them out with his cap, he dragged the Russian aside and jumped to the track. The first truck had landed on its side and the next waggon was upside down just behind it.

A few of the bluejackets were scrambling to their feet and Kelly saw Rumbelo snatching them from the wreckage.

'Anybody hurt, Rumbelo?' he yelled.

'Mr. Galt's been knocked out, sir, and a couple of the Russians seemed to have copped it. But none of our lot, though a few of 'em are trapped under the armoured truck.'

'Get the rest up the bank then. We've got to hold these bastards off till dark. Have the machine guns brought up, too.'

A spattering fire was already starting as Kelly went along the train looking for injured. In the overturned truck, he could hear men yelling in the darkness, but he couldn't understand them. He tried to tell them to dig their way out, but as they didn't stop yelling he assumed they'd not been able to hear.

Galt was sprawled by the side of the track, half-conscious, his face covered with blood from a wound in the head. He was clearly in no position to help and Kelly turned to Rumbelo.

'How about the gun, Rumbelo?' he said.

'She's undamaged, sir. And the barrel's just above the top of the bank. We might get off a shell or two.'

'Well, that'll keep the bastards back. Get the crew on it. I'll man the lip of the gulley with the machine guns.'

Takhatin appeared with a sergeant, driving the Russian machine gunners in front of him.

'Flourish your revolver a bit more,' Kelly said. 'They'll take off and bolt if you don't.'

Takhatin gave him a quick smile. 'I think of that already, sir,' he said, pushing at his men until he had them lining the lip.

Behind and above them, the gun's crew were training the gun round and they heard the breech clang shut. The crash of the shot was deafening and as the shell burst just over a mile away the approaching cavalry wrenched at their horses and vanished as if by magic into one of the dips near the river. The second shell was answered by one from the mutineers of the field gun battery and the White Russians lining the lip of the gulley scrambled down out of sight. Kicking them back again with Takhatin, Kelly stared round him. The two derailed trucks had cleared the track and the wheels of the third one had left·the rails and it now lay jamming the track with one end hanging over a small ditch.

'You know,' Kelly said, 'if we could uncouple that bloody truck and throw it over, I think we could take this gun back where it came from. Can you keep these bastards firing?'

'I can try,' Takhatin said.

'Rumbelo,' Kelly yelled. 'Collect a few of the Russians. We're going to need them.'

Working in the growing dusk, they manhandled the jacks from the wreckage of the breakdown truck and with a crowbar managed to force the twisted couplings of the derailed truck from those of the truck next to it.

'Now let's see if we can make this bloody engine go.'

Climbing into the cab, they picked up the burned fireman who was whimpering with pain on the tender and tried to explain what they wanted. He seemed to have given up all hope and Kelly made ferocious signs of throat-cutting and, pointing into the distance to convince him that he'd be safer if he got the engine moving for them, they finally got across their message. He nodded, almost too overcome with pain and terror to understand, and fishing in his pocket, Kelly took out his watch. It was one his grandfather had given him on his twenty-first birthday and he stared at it for a while then solemnly gestured at the fireman, indicating that the watch was his if he did as he was told.

Propping him up in the driver's seat, they tried once more to explain that they wanted the engine to push the derailed truck from their path. It seemed to take hours and, all the time, bullets kept whanging against the boiler or kicking up little spurts of dust from the other side of the gulley. Then the mutineers' gun fired again and earth and stones erupted in a cloud of dust.

Half the Russians lining the lip of the gulley immediately scrambled down and began to climb aboard the train, and Kelly had to go along pushing them off while Takhatin swung from their legs and arms and the seats of their trousers, plucking them away like flies from a fly paper and driving them back up the bank. They were clearly not inclined to take any risks, but at last they managed to convince them that the best thing was to stay where they were until they'd cleared the track.

'Right,' Kelly said. 'Let's go.'

The crash as they hit the rear end of the derailed truck almost shook their teeth loose.

'Again!'

Moaning in pain, the fireman swung on his levers and wheels. The engine drew back, then, getting up steam, rolled towards the truck once more until they crashed into it with a nerve-shattering jolt.

'It's going, sir,' Rumbelo said, his head out.

Immediately, a bullet spanged against the side of the cab and Kelly yanked him back.

'Keep your head down, you ass,' he said. 'I'm supposed to make sure you get back to Biddy and my godson.'

Rumbelo grinned and went to work again by the firebox. As they drew off once more, the gun roared and they saw the shell throw up dust and earth against the lemon-yellow sky. Then one of the 12-pounders came into action with a sharper crack.

'One more go ought to shift it, sir,' Rumbelo yelled.

This time the truck swayed, balanced on its edge then crashed in a cloud of dust into the ditch alongside the track. Immediately, the Russians, terrified of being left behind, abandoned the lip of the gulley and began to scramble aboard. This time Takhatin was well in the lead.

61

'What about the chaps under the truck, sir?' Rumbelo said.

'We'll get 'em out. Keep that gun going.'

Dragging Takhatin and a few of the Russians off the trucks, Kelly thrust spades and pickaxes into their hands and started them digging at the side of the overturned truck. Several times they crept away, and he kicked them back, threatening them with his revolver until eventually the first scared soldier wriggled out through the hole they'd dug. He was one of the British and he gave Kelly a nervous grin.

'Thank Christ for that, sir. I thought we was goners. But you'll have to make that 'ole a bit bigger. The corporal's got a corporation.'

The last man was dragged out, spitting out grit and earth, and pushed with the unconscious Galt aboard the truck.

'Let's go,' Kelly yelled and as the train began to move off, a last despairing shell tore into the wrecked trucks where the train had been standing. Earth, stones, timbers and torn metal flew into the air.

'Talk about the devil looking after his own,' Rumbelo said.

Fishing into his pocket for his watch, Kelly stared at it for a while, then solemnly handed it to the fireman. The Russian stared at it, almost swooning with gratitude, then he took it, strung it across his middle, insisted on shaking hands all round, and, with Rumbelo stuffing logs into the furnace as hard as he could go, he turned to the task of driving them south.

7

'They want to give you another gong,' Orrmont said, handing Kelly a gin. 'The damn things seem to stick to you like burrs to a sheep. There's also mail for you, and one rather tender enquiry from Princess Brasov who left her regards and said she was sorry but she had to go to Odessa.'

The weather changed. The warm summer winds vanished and, with Wrangel giving up Tsaritsyn, *Mordant* was occupied between Novorossiisk, Odessa, Sebastopol, Balaclava and Yalta, running backwards and forwards, occasionally with members of the British Mission heading for some new task, but more often carrying Russian staff officers, decorated with braid and studded with medals, who, if they were actually involved in a job, in fact seemed to be along more for the sea air than anything.

Then, suddenly, the rumours changed and they began to be aware of a new danger in the form of typhus, a disease carried by the lice which swarmed in the overcrowded houses and rooms and the filthy railway carriages and trucks packed with refugees. The hospitals in Tsaritsyn and Novocherkassk were full of victims. And, though Denikin had taken Orel and Novosil, only two hundred miles south of Moscow, the Reds had occupied Kiev and the Saratov front was pulling back. Finally, in the middle of October, the news arrived that Trotsky, the Red Minister of War, had attacked the junction between the Army of the Don and Denikin's Volunteer Army near Kharkov and split it wide open, and the Whites were suddenly evacuating Kursk and Orel in a hurry, and a Red communiqué claimed that Kolchak in Siberia was on the point of rout, that Yudenitch's position was hopeless and that Denikin was about to be crushed.

'What happened to the war?' Wellbeloved bleated.

The news continued to be bad. The entire population of Kotluban were said to have been massacred because the R.A.F. had had its base there and the war maps – those wall posters which had so proudly showed the advances – now showed only ever-narrowing circles of red. It was clear that without more support the Whites could never recover.

Winter had arrived now. Inland it was arctic. Frosts had been coming for some time even in the south and there had been thick mists at night, with occasional breezes to drift away the grey whisps and rattle the dry weeds in the hollows. Yet, despite the horrifying stories of whole regiments dying of typhus; of whole trains pulling into stations with their passengers all dead; of wounded White officers crawling on hands and knees through the mud to the station at Rostov rather than remain behind to be butchered by the Reds; despite all this, Novorossiisk still seemed largely untouched. The cafés were open, the trams running and the theatres doing good business, sometimes with artistes who'd fled south from Moscow and Petrograd. Parties were still held in homes or restaurants, and everybody seemed to be trying, despite the news, to ignore the war.

Kimister appeared occasionally at the gatherings Kelly attended, sometimes nervously in attendance on his voracious Russian baroness. He was inclined to talk less about Charley these days, Kelly noticed, and it appeared that he was writing less letters. They had barely spoken since the train incident by the River Vilyuj. A furious Kelly had demanded an explanation for Kimister's absence and received a vague story of a faulty valve and misunderstood orders that had led him to take his train back to guard the rear. It was totally unsatisfactory and Kelly had itched to put into his report the simpler explanation which he felt sure was responsible for Kimister's absence at the crucial moment. There was something missing in Kimister's make-up and always had been; but the knowledge that Kimister had been his term-mate at Dartmouth, that he'd once relied on Kelly to hold off Verschoyle's bullying and, above all, the uneasy suspicion that he'd suddenly come to mean something to Charley, held Kelly's hand and nothing had been set down.

Nevertheless, he often thought that one of Verschoyle's black eyes might well have put him to rights.

Unhappy without news of Charley and now actively disliking Kimister, he felt he might even have welcomed Verschoyle who, after all, had the courage to be his own man, someone real even if his soul was inclined to a shady tinge of grey.

Christmas came and with it a Christmas card covered with flowers but noticeably without the scrawled Xs with which Charley had once declared her love for him.

Kimister appeared at a party given by the Smalnovs, a little drunk and more uncertain than ever. It was a strange unnerving period because the bottom had unexpectedly fallen out of the White armies and their retreat had become a rout, and now, with the vengeful Reds approaching, the refugee trains were pouring into Novorossiisk full of exhausted men, women and children, all clinging to their last worldly possessions, even the smallest child clutching a package. Every family seemed to have been split up. One had lost its father en route when a train had moved on while he was searching for food, another had had a child swept away in a panic-stricken crush and never found. The station walls were plastered with pathetic little notices: 'Sergei. Your family is in Ekaterinodar.' 'Piotr. Take the children to Odessa.' 'Dear Masha, we are with mother in Novocherkassk.' They were heartbreaking in their simplicity and trust.

The Denikin communiqués no longer seemed to be in the realms of reality and Red propaganda moved freely among the despairing multitudes of people. There was a biting chill in the air and, with the snow now falling in huge feathery flakes, trains, buildings and ships stood out against it in an iron blackness. It was a sad Christmas – for the British full of bewilderment, for the Russians full of nostalgia and a new fearful awe because they all knew Denikin could never regain the initiative. There were still a few parties, but they were smaller now because everybody seemed suddenly to be preoccupied with the need to collect around them all their jewellery and family treasures. The few who still possessed wealth had one last wild fling in their palaces, guessing there would be no more and that from now on they'd be dependent only on what they could carry with them, and women were busy sewing jewellery into their underclothes while men were struggling to find someone who would take them to safety when the time came.

In its own way, the Navy tried to celebrate the season but there was little cheer because it was impossible to be joyful with the wretched multitudes of refugees pouring into Novorossiisk. The youngest rating wore Orrmont's uniform and did the rounds of the ship in his place in the traditional fashion of Christmas inversion, but somehow nobody had the heart for it because every time they went down the gangway they were faced with the sight of gaunt grey-faced people and huge-eyed children begging for bread.

With the New Year the British government lost all interest in the war; and the politicians, at last realising what their folly had let them in for, were back-pedalling as fast as they could go, so that the peace of Europe suddenly depended not on statesmen, but on a handful of professional soldiers and sailors.

'That crafty blighter Lloyd George's behind all this,' Orrmont growled. 'I don't suppose he knows the first thing about it really, and probably even thinks Rostov's a Russian general.'

The Government's about-face was not without its effect and there was a protest meeting on the cruiser, *Coryphée*, about having to fight in somebody else's war, that resulted in a court martial. In *Mordant* three able-seamen who took up the objection were whipped out of the ship at once. There were no punishments but they were sent home without delay.

'In the present climate,' Orrmont said, 'there's no room for people who wish to claim allegiance to the Bolshies.'

With the disappearance of the three culprits, there was a sudden new alertness about *Mordant* that indicated that the short sharp lesson had been a good one, and a lot of innocent expressions about, chief among which Kelly noticed Able Seaman Doncaster's, so that he wondered if they'd punished the wrong men.

With the end of January there was a sudden uneasiness in the city because the Reds were moving so fast now it seemed impossible that anything could ever stop them. Yet, unbelievably, the wealthy still seemed to have their wealth, and the expensive restaurants still stayed open for them.

'I don't think they're real,' Kelly said in bewilderment. 'They still think a miracle's going to save 'em all.'

What he said seemed to be true, because, while White army soldiers starved and tried to fight without weapons or warm clothing, White generals lived in incredible luxury in their train-borne headquarters, surrounded by silver, liveried servants and fur-coated women, seemingly indifferent to the collapse and to the thousands of soldiers and civilians heading south on their own two feet. The railways were chaotic enough to be impossible. Terrified refugees filled every hotel, boarding house and room in the city. Even empty warehouses began to fill up and they slept on the station and in shop doorways, huddled together against the cold.

Then, with the naval squadron waiting for orders to start the evacuation, *Mordant* was sent to pick up a group of Russian naval officers at Sebastopol and transport them to the Russian bases at Odessa and Nikolaev.

They put their ropes ashore in Sebastopol at the Fleet Landing Place on a quay that was dangerous with ice. A car was waiting for them, containing a French diplomat and a British Mission colonel carrying instructions for them to pick up the French consul in Odessa and bring him to safety with his family.

'It's some time since I saw them, you understand,' the Frenchman said, 'but there are four small daughters, I remember.'

As he headed back towards his car, the British colonel moved closer to Orrmont and Kelly.

'The French consul, his family, staff and dependents *only*,' he pointed out quietly. 'We've just received instructions that nobody's to be evacuated but White Russian soldiers and their families, and you won't find many of those because they're being forced further and further east.'

Their Russian naval passengers were nowhere to be seen and they eventually found them in an upper room at Admiralty House enjoying the view towards the sea, less concerned with the state of their defences or even the state of the campaign than with the dislike they felt for the British and the enormous inferiority complex they suffered from before them. They showed no repentance for their lack of effort and concentrated only on making sure their luggage was safely stowed aboard. Considering they were going to war, they seemed to have an enormous amount.

Hauling up the gangway, *Mordant* headed out of the South Harbour and turned north-east past Kalamita Bay and Cape Tarkhan, looking for a light on the point which, it turned out, hadn't worked for some months. The coast seemed bare and empty even of fishing craft, though in the yard in Kherson Bay they saw the hulk of an unfinished battleship, rust-streaked and without even a coat of lead paint.

Odessa looked different from when they'd last been there. The sea was grey now and the trees were leaning away from the wind, while the white buildings beyond the landing steps were dulled by the falling sleet. The place was clearly in a state of panic because, with Kiev and Kharkov gone, pockets of White resistance were crumbling swiftly as the Reds advanced towards the coast, living on the country as they came and driving hordes of refugees before them.

Glad to see the back of the Russian officers, Orrmont called Kelly into his cabin. 'I'm sending you ashore, Number One,' he announced. 'Any objection?'

Kelly shrugged. 'Plenty, sir. But I don't see who else's going to do it.'

'You're the only chap on board who seems to speak decent French, so I can see no alternative.' Orrmont looked apologetic. 'Can I bribe you with a gin?'

Kelly grinned. 'If it's a big one, sir,' he said.

'I suggest you take Boyle and a party of men. Any particular choice?'

'Just Rumbelo. We understand each other. With Boyle to keep an eye on the seaward end and three or four seamen, that should be enough.'

'Contact the British Mission. And you'd better be armed.'

'Not half, sir. With the situation that's developing ashore, I wouldn't trust my own mother behind my back.'

'Good. I have to put the rest of these bloody Russians ashore up the Boug and then I'll come back for you. Three days should be ample. Think you can do it in that time?'

'Good God, yes, sir. It's only a question of getting the consul and his family and traps into the car and running them down to the Fleet Landing Place. Matter of an hour, that's all.'

As it turned out, it took rather more than that.

The Russian telephone and telegraphic system were functioning only fitfully and, with patrols of Bolsheviks within eight miles of the outer suburbs of the Odessa, nobody seemed inclined to be worried about what happened to the French consul. The situation was already nightmarish and even as Kelly stepped ashore the flood of refugees was descending on the city.

It was only when he saw *Mordant*'s stern heading seawards that he realised what he'd let himself in for. Over the slap of the waves behind him, he could hear artillery and, when the wind gusted towards them in flurries of snow, the rattle of rifle and machine gun fire as the Army of the Ukraine faced the Reds beyond the lagoons to the north.

The snow began to fall faster as he stared about him. The Fleet Landing Place seemed to be full of people but none of them seemed to belong to the White Army. Here and there, ill-armed men roamed about, trudging on foot or riding starved horses. Most of them were heading for the sea, and on a corner, a soldier, muffled to the eyes against the weather, was haranguing a group of people who looked black against the snow.

The British Mission had already withdrawn to somewhere in the docks so they decided to look for Base Headquarters. But Base Headquarters were totally deserted and the whole empty place echoed to their voices.

'The buggers have bolted, sir,' Rumbelo said indignantly.

Small tables and palms in tubs in the main hallway showed that, if nothing else, the headquarters staff had not stinted themselves for comfort, but of the inhabitants there was no sign.

'There's a lift!' One of the bluejackets pressed the bell push and looked up the shaft. As the steel rope showed no sign of moving, he turned to his companions with an affected high-nosed stare. 'Damn these lower classes,' he said. 'You can't rely on 'em at all.'

Racing up the curving staircase, they flung open door after door. There were signs of hurried packing everywhere – open cupboard doors and drawers, soiled clothing, a pot of brilliantine, even a pair of corsets.

Through the windows, they could see the opera house opposite, with a poster outside announcing that it would be heated

69

for the next performance, but there was no sign of light, staff, players or audience. From another window, they could see the sea, heavy as lead against a dark sky and the white tip of the snow-covered land. When they all met together in the hall again, Kelly was feeling faintly light-headed. They'd brought rations for three days in their haversacks but he had a sudden ill-omened feeling that their stay could well be longer.

Leading his party outside, he found an eating house. It seemed to have nothing but offal to offer but nobody was arguing. An old lady, wearing a garment cut from a worn carpet, huddled alongside a White officer wearing the board-like Tsarist epaulettes on his shoulders, who was trying to encourage her to eat. Nearby was a mother with two little girls, all neatly dressed, waiting their turn but well aware there were only a few days left at the outside before the Refugee Control Office closed for good.

For the price of an English half-sovereign, Kelly was able to provide his men with a hot meal and wine, and by the grace of God the elderly man who was serving the meal spoke a little French.

'The consulate's in the Kivanov Prospekt,' he told them. 'But nobody's lived there since last year, because the mob got in after the French pulled out. Army headquarters left forty-eight hours ago.'

The eating house had a spare room at the back. It contained nothing but two bare tables and four hard benches, but there was a roof and the draught under the door wasn't quite as arctic as the wind outside. Handing over another half-sovereign, Kelly announced he was commandeering it.

Turning to Boyle, he outlined his plans. 'The chaps can bed down here if necessary,' he said. 'But keep 'em on their toes. I don't know what's going to happen but I don't want to be far from the Fleet Landing Place when *Mordant* comes back.'

Emptying his pockets, he handed over three sovereigns. 'I don't suppose the Admiralty'll ever reimburse me,' he said. 'But that's for food and to keep the owner at bay. What's the rate of exchange?'

'About ten thousand roubles to a Bradbury. And all that buys are two slices of bread and meat.'

'I'm going to find the French Consul. Can you cope?'

Doyle looked at Kelly. He was a slightly-built young man with pale anonymous hair and eyes, and as a cadet in the torpedoed cruiser, *Cressy*, in 1914, had been as near to death as he was ever likely to be when he'd been dragged by Kelly to a raft and pushed aboard. In Boyle's eyes there never was and never would be again anybody quite like Kelly Maguire.

'I'll cope,' he said firmly.

Near Base Headquarters, Kelly found an ancient cab and he and Rumbelo set off for the Kivanov Prospekt. But the French Consulate had clearly been empty for a long time, and they stared blank-eyed at the flat-fronted building, its consular plate askew, its high windows shattered, its rooms in darkness.

'Where are the consular staff now?'

'All left, Monsieur. They were living in a house in Drestrovskiy Street.'

'You'd better take us there.'

Drestrovskiy Street was less important-looking than the Kivanov Prospekt and half the houses seemed to be unoccupied. Telling the cabby to wait, they pushed their way through the open doorway and, striking a match, found a candelabra still containing the stubs of three candles. By their light, they saw more signs of a hurried departure. Books lay scattered everywhere, with papers and scraps of clothing. A trunk standing in the hall was open, its contents draped over the edge. Moving through the empty rooms, they found bedrooms where the bedclothes had been stolen by marauders, and the consul's office with its huge desk, its fireplace full of paper ash as if he'd spent his last hours there burning documents.

'Oh, Christ, Rumbelo,' Kelly said despairingly. 'This is a bloody awful war, and no mistake.'

In the servants' quarters they found an old man, dirty, starved-looking and stinking of booze.

'Perhaps *he*'s the consul,' Rumbelo said and they took refuge in laughter.

Back at the eating house, they found Boyle looking depressed. The room they were occupying had the iron coldness of the inside of a refrigerator. It was hopeless trying to search any further that night and they bedded down on the floor. They were wakened next morning by the owner of the room banging on the door. Behind him was the cab driver

71

they'd used the night before.

'You were looking for the French Consul, Excellency,' he said. 'I've found where they moved to. It's in the Karyetny Ryad.'

With Kelly and three sailors aboard, the cab creaked its way into the town. The place looked arctic now, the buildings black against the snow. A group of men in fur caps and heavy coats watched them from a street corner where they stood around a fire built on the pavement, but there was no attempt to stop them.

The Karyetny Ryad was in an old part of the town, a quiet street lined with bare trees, their branches black against the leaden sky. At a cross-roads at the end, country carts and droshkies laden with refugees were passing in a steady stream. The suburb had been wrecked when the French had evacuated the place the year before and Red sympathisers had moved in to wreak their vengeance on the people who had welcomed them. There was a stark atmosphere of neglect among the houses, with broken windows, and even occasional stone chimneys standing smoke-blackened in the middle of a heap of ruins.

Eventually the carriage slowed to a stop and, peering through the window, Kelly saw a huge gatepost from which hung a rusting wrought-iron gate. Beyond, there were charred trees and bushes in an unweeded garden along a curving gravel drive that was overgrown and neglected.

'This it?'

The coachman shook his head. 'Next door, Monsieur. But if you dismount here, you can get through the garden. It will be better that way. You can't be seen.'

Climbing from the cab, they edged past the empty ruins of the house. The front door, daubed with a red hammer and sickle, stood open, and inside they could see sabre-slashed drapings and broken furniture full of bullet holes. Picking their way past wrecked stables with shattered roofs and charred brickwork, they found themselves in a long sloping garden which had once been terraced, but now consisted of broken walls and rubble.

The next door house was across a muddy lane overhung by gloomy trees. Creeping through the garden, they knocked at a side door and swung on the bell pull. The bell echoed emptily and for a long time there was no sign of life. Then, as Rumbelo and the two sailors began to push their noses against the windows to see if the place was occupied, they heard the sound of bolts being drawn and the door opened.

The man standing in the opening was small, plump and frightened-looking. He opened his mouth to say something then abruptly closed it again.

'This is the British Navy,' Kelly explained. 'We've come to take you to safety.'

The little man continued to gaze at them, his face deathly pale, then his throat worked. 'You had better come in, Monsieur.'

They all crowded inside and the Frenchman closed and bolted the door behind them. They followed him into the hall and, without saying a word, he produced five glasses and a bottle of brandy which he sloshed out with a shaking hand.

The sailors eyed each other sideways and accepted the drinks in the usual unflappable way of all sailors offered free booze. While they were still swallowing it, the little man fished a last sheet from an opened desk crammed with papers, stuffed it in a suitcase and faced them.

'Balustridnyi Ryad,' he said. 'Monsieur Baptiste is there. I am Armande Driand, his secretary. I was collecting papers.' He indicated the suitcase crammed with documents. 'We moved here after the consulate was sacked, but we decided that when White Army headquarters evacuated the city these houses would be the first to be looted. We have all now moved to my house.'

The Balustridnyi Ryad was a quarter of a mile away, and the route they took doubled back and forth several times.

Eventually they found themselves in a narrow road, at the end of which, where it debouched on to a wider, more important street, they could see dark figures against the snow. As they emerged, a shabby hearse, painted white and pulled by two sway-backed knock-kneed greys, plodded past, creaking and rattling over the frozen ruts. The driver was huddled in his seat, smothered in scarves and old coats, and the empty interior was stuffed with withered laurel leaves. A few weeping women trudged behind it, wearing what scraps of black they

73

had managed to find for the obsequies.

'It passes every morning,' Driand said, 'and returns in the evening. It seems to be the only one in this part of the city and there is a lot of work for it.'

He led them down the side of a small mansion set back from the others and, taking a key from his pocket, pushed into a large old kitchen which seemed to be full of drying female underclothes.

As the sailors eyed the underwear with interest, they were surrounded by children who stood in a semi-circle, staring with huge, absorbed eyes. Then a dark, plump man with a doe-like gaze appeared.

'My good Driand,' he said. 'Thank God you're back!'

'This is the British navy, sir,' Driand explained. 'They've been sent from Sebastopol to take us off.'

Baptiste pushed through the children to shake their hands. Rumbelo accepted the greeting with an equanimity which was not shared by the other two sailors, who went pink with embarrassment and turned in preference to the children. Even before the Consul had finished effusing, one of them had a small girl on his shoulders, giggling with laughter.

'You must meet my wife,' Baptiste said. 'Please come this way.'

There were more female clothes piled on every chair and hanging on the banisters as they went upstairs, and Kelly eyed them with alarm, wondering how many people the Consul had collected.

He cleared his throat. 'I ought to point out, sir,' he said, 'that our orders are that no one's to be evacuated except White Russian soldiers and their families, wounded, and non-Russians who need to return to their own countries.'

As he spoke, a pair of double doors opened and what appeared to be hordes of young females poured through. In fact, there were seven but there seemed to be many more and they surrounded Kelly, shaking hands and giggling. Madame Baptiste looked as young as her daughters, who seemed to have grown up a little since they were seen by the man in Sebastopol, and they all seemed to be beautiful in the dark doe-eyed manner of Baptiste himself. Somewhat unexpectedly, Driand's wife was about three times the size of her husband, a statuesque

74

blonde with a bust like the prow of a battleship, but she, too, had clearly once been a beauty, and her daughters, every one of them junoesque and tall, seemed to take after her. The sight of so many pretty girls took Kelly's breath away.

He tried to answer all their questions, but Baptiste flapped his hands and the shrill chatter stopped at once. 'Anne-Marie, the brandy! Pascale, the biscuits! Josephine-Claude, the cigarettes! Angélique, a chair!'

As the hall cleared, Baptiste took Kelly's arm and led him into the salon, a large room with big windows where the curtains had been drawn so that people in the street couldn't see inside. It was full of people and the faces that were turned to Kelly didn't have the consul's beaming confidence.

'General Prince Busukov,' Baptiste introduced. 'The Princess Busukov. Their daughters, the Princesses Svetliana, Nona and Magdalena. Countess Aramitian and her daughter. Madame Mamontov and her two daughters. Madame Valiovski and her daughters. Madame Krosilev and her daughters –'

Kelly was staring at them with dismay. Prince Busukov was plump and pink-faced and looked just what he was – an aristocrat. His wife, a small delicate-looking woman, walked only slowly, leaning on a stick.

'Arthritis,' Baptiste smiled. 'She is very brave.'

'Sir!' Kelly tried to halt the flood of introductions. 'I must remind you of my orders. These people can't *all* be part of your staff.'

'But of course not!' Baptiste beamed. 'They are friends of mine and people who have appealed to me for help.'

'Sir –' Kelly gestured unhappily '– I can't give it! I'm not permitted to. My orders are quite clear and unequivocal. I was expecting perhaps a dozen, but with the children there must be around forty people in this house. I can't take them all.'

'Not even me, Kelly Georgeivitch?'

The voice just behind him made Kelly turn. He knew it at once. Facing him in the doorway, smiling at him, was Vera Brasov.

75

8

The streets of Odessa were deserted.

Not only the wealthy but the white-collar workers and the tradesmen, too, had considered it wiser to disappear from sight. Dock labourers, drunk on stolen vodka, were seeking out everybody who didn't earn their living with manual toil; while others, affected by drugs from looted shops, were rampaging through the streets and welcoming the Bolsheviks as they emerged from their hiding places armed with stolen weapons.

Leaving Rumbelo in charge and wearing Baptiste's civilian coat and hat, Kelly set off back to the Fleet Landing Place to warn Boyle.

'Keep the shutters closed, Rumbelo,' he advised. 'And keep everybody out of sight. If anybody tries to get in, deal with 'em.'

'Aye aye, sir.' Rumbelo smiled. 'There's a couple of funny-looking blokes down the road been watching this place for a bit already.'

The same funeral hearse they'd seen the previous day was moving down the street again, its chipped white paint curiously diminished by the icy silver of the snow. This time there was a rough coffin inside, covered by branches of laurel, alongside it two women. Behind walked a procession of shabby people.

'Don't they ever stop it?' Kelly asked.

'There's not much loot in a coffin, Monsieur,' Driand said with a wry smile. 'And there are so many funerals these days. I believe it even has a laissez-passer.'

As Kelly left, a few threadbare White troops were retreating through the city towards the sea, passing in long lines, dark against the snow. They were joined occasionally by a few terrified bourgeoisie who had taken refuge from the mob among the ancient hovels behind their homes, most of them clad in

76

patched, greasy clothes which they'd begged, borrowed or stolen to hide their identities. Most of the soldiers were either wounded or stumbling with hunger, and among them were the remnants of the cadets from the city's military schools and colleges, who'd been called out in a last desperate attempt to stem the Red advance, callow boys, deathly pale and staggering with wounds, their faces taut with exhaustion. Bolshevik sympathisers, knowing the Red army would soon be in the city, were growing bolder now and were taking pot shots at them as they passed.

Boyle was still in the room at the back of the eating house. With the skill of all sailors, he and his party had made it surprisingly comfortable and had even made a fire which, though it filled the place with smoke, at least gave it a vestige of warmth.

He greeted Kelly with relief. 'I thought we'd lost you,' he said.

Kelly grinned. 'Not me, Seamus. Any sign of *Mordant?*'

'Nothing.' Boyle's face grew bleak. 'We've heard that Nikolaev's worse than was thought. *Mordant* might be there for some time.'

'I hope not because this place's going to fall apart any day now. We've got to find somewhere to shelter until the ships come.'

'There's an empty place along the street.' Boyle gestured with his hand. 'Hotel Alexander I. It's boarded up but I got inside and there are beds. I suspect they're full of bedbugs but it's bigger than this and we could make it our headquarters.'

Kelly nodded. 'Move in there,' he said briskly. 'If you can get in through a back window and keep the front closed, so much the better. I've collected around forty-odd people. Seen any sign of that cab we used?'

Boyle frowned. 'I gather he's gone out of business rather abruptly,' he pointed out. 'His horse was stolen by the army.'

Kelly frowned. 'Damn!' he said. 'I was hoping to use him. We've got a chestful of cash, a case of papers, an old dear who can't walk and a bloody Russian general who's not only a prince but looks like one.'

Before he set off back towards the Balustridnyi Ryad, Boyle was already pushing one of his seamen through a rear window of the hotel, a shabby building that belied its resounding name.

The paint was peeling from the portico and more than one of the window panes was broken, while the inside was bleak, threadbare and comfortless. But at least it was shelter from the icy blast that came from the north and Kelly was thinking of the large-eyed children in the Balustridnyi Ryad.

As he headed back into the suburbs, he noticed that the sound of gunfire to the north had grown nearer and the city seemed to have changed, and he realised that the outer suburbs had been given up and there were no longer any of the weary columns trudging south. It was growing dark when he reached the Balustridnyi Ryad and he could see the glow of fires in several places. The streets were full of excited men and boys eager to start trouble and a few houses were being looted nearby, so that he could see open doorways with men and women running in and out with silver, vases, linen and clothing. The same dingy hearse was just returning in the dusk with its shabby procession of mourners and he reflected they must have had a long day.

Rumbelo was looking anxious as he let him in through the back door. 'Them two buggers we saw have been sniffing around again, sir,' he said. 'But I'm keeping 'em all quiet. It's a bit of a job with the kids, but we made it into a sort of game. The first one to make a noise has to pay a forfeit.'

As the day drew to a close in a bleak grey-black evening, with the snow sharply white against the lowering sky, Vera Brasov caught Kelly on the back stairs and pulled him into the dark deserted kitchen among the strings of drying undergarments.

'Kelly Georgeivitch – ' she whispered as she clung to him in the shadows, her mouth searching for his ' – where have you been?'

It seemed no time for hole-in-the-corner love affairs and he pushed her away roughly. 'Somebody'll come,' he warned.

'I don't care. I love you, Kelly Georgeivitch.'

'You know damn well you don't!' Kelly snapped.

She stared at him with bright, calculating eyes. She was nervous and concerned for her future, but she was warm and beautiful and he was terribly aware of her sexuality.

'I gave myself to you, Kelly Georgeivitch,' she pointed out.

'You threw yourself at me, Vera Nikolaevna.'

She laughed. 'What's the difference? Now you must get me

away from Odessa. I do not intend to disappear like the rest of my family. I am a survivor and Russian girls who've survived this far will never take "no" for an answer. Klaudia Pepelyaev even married a Red commissar to survive. Nina Dimitrievna Crosov did better. She allied herself to a French general and went to Paris. Perhaps Svetliana Dukhonin did the best of all. She married a British colonel who is a nobleman and now has a passport and a coat of arms.'

Kelly grinned. '*She* ought to be all right.'

'But there were others.' Her voice was hard and her eyes were glowing with anger. 'Irene Vietrovna Borisov worked in a cabaret in Ekaterinodar and had to allow herself to be pawed by the customers. Olga Biorko gave herself to a Greek ship's captain. She's in Athens now but she's only a Greek ship's captain's wife. Her sister sold herself to raise money for a fare to Constantinople and when she discovered that she needed still more to provide food because food was not provided aboard, she hanged herself.' She shrugged. 'The Biorkos were all fools,' she ended coldly. 'Every one of them.'

She put her arms round his neck again, and was just trying to manoeuvre him into a corner when he stiffened. A shoe had scraped outside the door and he could hear voices muttering.

'Belay that bloody nonsense, Vera,' he whispered. 'There's somebody trying to break in.'

He was just looking round for a weapon when there was a single tremendous crash on the lock of the door and it burst open. Outside, outlined against the snow, he saw two men wearing long leather coats, shaggy fur caps and mufflers. One of them held a club and the other was just lowering the sledge hammer with which he'd forced the lock. Vera gave a gasp of terror from the shadows, high-pitched, agonised and feminine, and the man with the sledge grinned and pushed inside.

'Chto takoe?' he said. 'Women? Tsarist women? Officers' women?'

As Kelly's fist closed over the handle of an iron cooking pot which stood on the sink, the man with the sledge saw him. As he turned, Kelly swung at him with the heavy pot and the Russian dropped the hammer with a yell and staggered against the wall. Immediately, the other man, a giant with a red beard, pushed through the door after him, swinging his club. It struck Kelly a

79

glancing blow on the shoulder, but it was enough to paralyse his arm and he clung to the Russian one-handed, catching a whiff of stinking breath and the smell of grease from his clothes. In the struggle, the Russian dropped his club, the lines of washing snapped and they rolled on the floor, tangled in cord and damp linen. With the Russian's hands on his throat, Kelly's fingers fell on the club the Russian had dropped and he thrust it upwards with all his strength into the Russian's open mouth. He felt teeth break and, as the Russian fell back, gagging on his scream, Kelly scrambled to his knees, hammering at the giant's head with every ounce of strength he possessed.

As the Russian became silent, he dragged himself to his feet still entangled in cord and underclothing, then he realised that the man with the sledge hammer seemed to have vanished. Looking round, wondering why the heavy hammer hadn't cracked his skull, he saw Vera Brasov standing transfixed, her back to the wall, one hand over her mouth to choke back a scream. The Russian was lying on his face at her feet, his arms spreadeagled. Then he saw that in her other hand she was clutching a carving knife and that the blood on it was staining the front of her dress.

As he looked at her, she seemed to realise for the first time what she'd done and dropped the knife as if it had been red-hot. As it clattered to the floor, Kelly kicked the door to.

'I hope to God they haven't got any pals waiting for them outside,' he said. 'Go upstairs and send Rumbelo down.'

When Rumbelo appeared, they dragged the bodies outside and left them under the bushes down the garden, returning to the house with two ragged fur caps and an armful of mufflers, jackets and leather coats which they'd decided might make useful disguises. They were just mopping up the blood from the kitchen floor when Vera Brasov reappeared. She had changed her dress and, although she was pale, she seemed calm and well in control of herself.

She gave a harsh laugh at Kelly's expression. 'Cheer up, Kelly Georgeivitch,' she said. 'In Russia today, murder is no more than a daily hazard and, on reflection, I think it was the most satisfying thing I've done since the Revolution.'

The problem of how to get their charges to the Fleet Landing

Place grew rather than diminished and, with the deaths of the two intruders, became much more urgent. The city was full of people who would gladly have used the incident to butcher them, British or not. But Baptiste had no intention of leaving the Consulate money behind and Princess Busukov could hardly be carried, while her husband was demanding that he be allowed to leave in full uniform wearing his decorations.

'I have been an Imperial officer all my life,' he pointed out. 'If I am to die, then I will die like one.'

Kelly felt like hitting him with something.

As he watched the shabby hearse trundle down the street next morning with its daily load of sorrow, he wondered how in God's name he was going to get his awkward squad of women and children to the shore. The crowd at the end of the street opened to allow the hearse to pass and he wistfully watched it turn the corner and vanish towards the cemetery, his mind full of his problems. The two bodies outside worried him most. Sooner or later, some prowler would stumble on them because they were still unburied.

Unburied! His head lifted and his eyes brightened. Unburied, by God!

'Rumbelo!' he yelled.

When the hearse came back at dusk, Kelly and his seamen were waiting just inside the gate. The crowd at the end of the street had disappeared and, as it came abreast the house, they were out and surrounding it at once. Rumbelo was on the box and the shabby conveyance had been swung into the drive and round the back of the house before anybody had noticed. Before the driver knew where he was, he had been bundled into the kitchen and pushed into a chair, still croaking his protests.

'Tell him he's hired for tomorrow morning,' Kelly told Driand.

The Frenchman spoke in Russian to the driver who shook his head and gabbled back at him.

'He says he has to pick up two bodies in the morning,' Driand said. 'There are two families waiting and they have paid him in advance to make sure he turns up.'

'Not this time,' Kelly said. 'Tell him we want him instead.'

Driand produced several gold pieces from Baptiste's funds as he talked. The driver stared at them, his eyes bulging.

81

'Da, Gospodin,' he said excitedly. 'Da, da!'

He seemed to accept the decision philosophically, and Madame Driand began to cut bread and cheese and lay it on the table in front of him. Leaving one of the sailors with a revolver to watch him, Kelly and Rumbelo went outside to unharness the horses and tie them securely inside the stables.

'Now we want a coffin, Rumbelo,' Kelly said. 'Big enough for two corpses.'

Before dawn the next morning, they mustered Baptiste and his charges in the salon. They all wore their oldest clothes and as much black as they could raise between them. Behind the house, the horses had been put back in the shafts of the ancient hearse, and a large double wardrobe with holes punched in the door had been manhandled on its back inside.

Baptiste and Prince Busukov – wearing his uniform and all his decorations – were pushed inside the wardrobe and the door shut, and the withered laurel branches piled over it. Sitting alongside in the hearse were Princess Busukov and the smallest children, with strict instructions to keep silent. Rumbelo seemed to have a gift for handling them, and though he couldn't speak a word of their language, he had persuaded them it was a game, and they sat silent and large-eyed hoping to win the prize he'd promised them.

'I hope we can find one, sir,' he said.

'Life itself wouldn't be a bad one,' Kelly pointed out grimly.

They shared the stinking articles of clothing from the corpses in the garden, and rugs and small carpets were cut into smock-like garments with holes for necks and donned by the girls to hide their figures.

'Tell 'em handkerchieves – dirty ones – to faces,' Kelly instructed Driand. 'They've got to look as though they've been bereaved.'

Baptiste's hoard of funds and his papers had been stuffed in the wardrobe with him and Prince Busukov, and other small items of luggage were hidden under the laurel leaves, the coats of the children and the skirts of Madame Baptiste. The rest carried nothing but what could be concealed about their clothing and they had been up half the night sewing jewels into their corsets and silverware under their skirts. There had been a lot of

82

giggling and a lot of heartsearching, but Vera Brasov, calm and apparently unmoved by the murders in the kitchen, carried only a muff concealing a heavy candelabra which she claimed could also be used as a bludgeon if necessary. Every scrap of jewellery she'd been able to carry away from the Brasov estates was hidden about her person.

'And I am wearing at least three of everything except shoes,' she said. 'God help anyone who feels gallant enough to try to carry me aboard.'

The rumble of guns to the north was more pronounced now, with faint screams and the noise of bloody little affrays as the Bolsheviks pressed deeper into the city. As they moved down the stairway to the kitchen, they could hear the smashing of glass and occasional shouts, and a baying sound like a pack of hounds. The hearse turned out of the drive, the nervous driver clutching the reins in mittened fingers. Rumbelo sat alongside him, wearing an old top hat of Driand's and a ragged jacket from the corpse in the garden which concealed the revolver that was jammed into the driver's side. Behind the hearse marched the two other sailors, unshaven and looking like anything but naval personnel. In his enthusiasm, one of them wore a voluminous black coat of Madame Driand's which he'd had to split across the shoulders to get on his broad frame, but it was vast enough to allow him to carry a rifle underneath. The other weapons were within easy reach inside the hearse.

They looked a shabby procession as they stumbled down the street. The girls were acting the part well, sniffing into handkerchieves and pretending to weep, with Vera Brasov the most enthusiastic of all, howling from time to time and helped along by Kelly who walked with one hand supporting her round the waist, the other hand jammed in his pocket with his revolver.

A sleety snow was drifting down, wet and freezing so that the crowd at the end of the street was thin. It opened to let them through without question. The hearse had passed that way every morning and only a few incurious eyes watched them. Vera Brasov set up a new wail of anguish and Kelly's hand tightened on her waist.

'For God's sake,' he breathed, 'don't make a meal of it!'

Fires were raging everywhere in the city now and Red infantry was pouring into the suburbs. Down the Kiev road Red

83

cavalry was clattering towards the Nikolaevsky Boulevard, searching the hospitals for helpless White officers. A wind of arctic bitterness was blowing and in almost every street they saw bodies, some of them coatless and bootless, stiff and blue with the cold.

Then they heard the rattle of small arms fire and Driand held up his hand.

'The mob is moving down the Shevchenko Boulevard,' he said. 'And we have passed the cemetery long since. It is imperative that we get rid of the hearse.'

At a signal to Rumbelo, the vehicle swung into the drive of a deserted house under the trees. The two old men, stiff and half-frozen, were helped out of the improvised coffin, and Madame Driand slung a length of carpeting over Prince Busukov's shoulders. He shrugged it off immediately.

'I prefer to die like a Russian prince,' he said.

Growing sick of the whole performance, Kelly drew his revolver and stuck it under the old man's nose.

'Take off your jacket and cap,' he ordered. 'You've made a token escape in full uniform and decorations. Let it be enough.'

The old man was too startled to argue. As he stripped off his tunic, Kelly helped him into his own stinking leather overcoat and slammed a fur cap on his head. The medals were thrust into the Princess's handbag and the tunic turned inside out and placed round one of the older children. At the sight, Vera Brasov's funereal wails changed into a gust of laughter and the Driand girls began to collapse into helpless giggling.

'Dry up!' Kelly snapped and they stopped with an abruptness that indicated there had been more than a little hysteria in it, and one of them began to sob.

The driver was touching Kelly's arm. 'Gospodin –'

'Pay him, Driand!' Kelly said. 'Then lock him in the hearse, Rumbelo, and take the horses out of the shafts and tie 'em up somewhere. That ought to stop him raising the alarm before we're clear.'

Pushing the women and children before them, the sailors huddled them together in the ruined garden. As the mob drew nearer rifle bolts clicked. But the crowd swept past, filling the street and ignoring the shadows. One or two of the smaller children began to wail with hunger and their mothers and older sisters clutched them to them, whispering urgently to them to be quiet, trying to instil their own fears into minds too young to be aware of danger. For an hour the mob swirled up and down beyond the garden wall and they could hear the crashing of glass and yells and occasional shots, and once they heard the most appalling screams as though some wretched girl had been discovered hiding in an attic or a cellar and been dragged out to be raped by her tormentors. As the racking screams rang out again and again, Vera Brasov clapped her hands over her ears, her face agonised, and buried her face in Kelly's coat.

'We cannot stay here,' Driand told Kelly. 'They have never forgotten that the French came to the assistance of the Whites last year. They would kill the consul. I'll go ahead and find a safe route.'

Shuddering with fear, he slipped out of the garden into the darkness. It was cold under the trees and the children were whimpering with the icy wind, and Kelly was just wondering how in God's name they were going to move Busukov's wife when Driand returned. He was pushing a wheelbarrow.

'I doubt if she'll argue about the transport,' he said. 'And I have found a route.'

Leading them from the garden in the shadow of the trees, he dived down a narrow alley so suddenly they almost lost him. The whole city seemed to be awake now and, with two of the seamen carrying the money and Rumbelo wheeling the barrow containing the old woman, they began to move past the backs of shabby houses that grew smaller with every step. The barrow wheel shrieked like a pig in torment and, underfoot, the paving stones gave way to cobbles, then to slush that crept up to their ankles and splashed skirts and trousers. Finally they found themselves creeping past middens and back alleys until they reached the waterfront at last, and headed for the area of the Fleet Landing Place.

Occasionally, soldiers waved them past, giving them snippets of news as they went. To the north typhus was raging everywhere and the White medical services had broken down completely. Desolation and anguish gripped the countryside and thousands of wounded died untended as hospitals were evacuated. Horses, waggons and guns were being abandoned, and the Greens under Mahkno were looting what the

85

Bolsheviks hadn't already taken, while the Reds were capturing whole strings of stranded trains full of sick and starving women and children. Any White officer who was found was murdered on the spot in front of his family, and the frozen bodies lay in piles on every station, neatly stacked like the wood they used in the engine furnaces, grey-white and stiff, and naked because their clothes had been stripped off for the living.

Boyle was tense and nervous as a kitten but he had the little hotel well guarded, with men in the upstairs windows. Food had been found and there was even a large pot full of hot soup with black bread. With the children sleeping in their arms, the women sat around the shabby lounge on chairs and settees from which the stuffing had been removed by rats and mice to make nests.

They spent the whole of the next day in the deserted hotel. No one came near them except a small group of people who discovered the broken back window, and climbed inside to find the place already occupied. By some strange alchemy of physical attraction, Boyle and the eldest of the Baptiste daughters, Anne-Marie, decided in their moment of strain that they were soul-mates and spent their time whispering in a corner when Boyle wasn't dodging out to find out how the land lay.

They could see several huge fires close by, one of them filling the sky with flying sparks.

'The Hotel Besserabia,' Driand reported, returning from one of his forays into the darkness. 'It was packed with refugees.'

There was no water in the Tsar Alexander I and no sanitary arrangements, and they were beginning to grow hungry by the next evening when the darkened rooms were suddenly flooded with light. Peering through a crack in the boarded-up windows, they saw a dazzling blue-white beam from the sea moving slowly across the town to the snow-clad hills beyond.

'Searchlights, sir!' Rumbelo breathed. 'That can only mean one thing.'

When Boyle reappeared from one of his prowls along the waterfront, his face was alight with relief.

'The Navy's here!' he announced. 'I didn't see *Mordant*, but I saw what looks like *Queen Elizabeth* and a cruiser. There are also one or two transports and passenger vessels and a few small coasters flying Greek and Turkish flags.'

In the relief that flooded over him, it suddenly occurred to Kelly that neither he nor Rumbelo had been to sleep for three nights.

As they woke the others the next morning, they could hear shots and cries of anguish as the town fell into a final reign of terror, with robbery, murder and rape as hourly occurrences. With daylight they made their way past the deserted inner basins of the harbour to the moles. *Queen Elizabeth* had started lobbing ten-inch shells over the city on to the approach roads being used by the Reds, her big guns booming with the monotony of a tolling bell. But by now an avalanche of refugees was filling the city so that it had become a vast camp of starving people desperate after their long trek from the north. Many of them were too weak and too disheartened to help themselves, however, and those who were still capable were surrounded by a sea of sick.

The streets, full of boarded shop windows, were thronged with carts, perambulators and barrows and they had to push past desperate merchants trying to get their remaining goods to the wharves in the hope of starting their businesses again elsewhere. There were even still a few lost troops, cutting off their shoulder straps and seeking scraps of red cloth with which they might hide among the advancing Bolsheviks; while officers were wrenching off their epaulettes, because the Communists had an obsession about these symbols of privilege and liked to indulge in the pleasant habit of stripping their captives naked and nailing them to their shoulders.

The only way out of Odessa now was by barge, launch, tugboat, a Mediterranean tramp or a military transport or man-o'-war. In every street lay bodies, their clothing stirred by the piercing wind that had got up. It was freezingly cold and petrified the starving scarecrows among whom the typhus was already reaping a terrible harvest. People who had once lived in great houses were now existing in squalid cellars so that the whole city seemed to be overwhelmed with despair. Though more ships were appearing all the time and the Italian Lloyd Line offices had opened, the city was in terror because organised bands of criminals looting the northern suburbs were only held back from the waterfront by the guns of British ships. The Reds were in no hurry, however, quite content to wait until the

87

warships had gone, because only a few outposts of White volunteers still guarded the hills, and infiltrators were in the streets, bold and unafraid.

As the grey-black sea rolled against the frost-bound shores of the bay, the rigging of the ships sparkled with icicles. A group of boys dressed in rags were doggedly stoning a few seabirds trapped in an area of thin ice. As one of the birds was hit, it lay helpless, its head bloodied, one wing dangling, squawking feebly, then the boys saw Kelly's party and swarmed round them at once, crying out 'Mister! Mister! Bread!'

A Refugee Control Office had been opened near the new Mission Headquarters but it was drowning under a tide of frantic people. Fighting his way through desperate men and women, Kelly had his orders made clear to him.

'No civilians. Only Mission troops, soldiers of the Volunteer Army and their families. The Control Commission will be vetting everybody who steps aboard.'

As he left, the city rocked under a tremendous explosion as the port's petrol tanks were fired. The shooting sounded closer and the union jack over Mission Headquarters came down in jerks. Lighters, launches and small Levantine transports, their owners making fortunes from the last agony of the White armies, were already crammed to capacity, but people who could find the money were still joining them, packing on to vessels that were already criminally overcrowded and devoid of the simplest means of sanitation or feeding. But, while sobbing women and their screaming children were being put back ashore because they couldn't pay, the possessions of the wealthy were still being dragged up the gangplanks, and a heavy Stutz motor car and a grand piano were lifted aboard near the petroleum harbour, watched by a man in a fur cap and coat, a cigar in his mouth.

The moles were black with shivering human beings. Some of them, still haughty and high-nosed, wore furs and stood optimistically among piles of trunks, but there were others petrified with cold who wore only a coat over their night attire. Every refugee in the city, knowing what awaited them when the last of the ships left, was on the quay now, and heavy guards were posted on the gangways of all the warships to prevent them swarming aboard. They were camped in thousands, clutching their belongings and warming themselves round bonfires they'd lit. Occasionally, a desperate young man jumped into the icy sea and swam to a ship, only to be plucked from the water, dried off, and returned to the shore. Fat merchants offered suitcases full of valueless paper roubles and young girls frantically offered themselves in the hope of earning enough to pay their passage to safety.

The place was sick, desperate and terrified, with people surging in huge crowds to any point they thought might give them a better chance of safety, pushing between horses and waggons to crowd the waterfront and plead with shipmasters, knowing their only alternative was death under the sabres of the Bolshevik cavalry.

The big guns of *Queen Elizabeth* boomed again as Kelly's party made their way through lines of abandoned field pieces, ammunition, supplies and equipment, and along the treacherously iced planks of a board walk to the quayside. The ships against the wharves were so packed with desperate human beings not another soul could be squeezed aboard, and here and there panicking seamen cut loose from time to time with machine guns over the heads of the mob to keep them at bay. Then, beyond the Volnolum breakwater, they saw the slim lines of a destroyer anchored in the bay and Rumbelo touched Kelly's arm.

'There she is, sir,' he said. 'I've looked on her drunk and sober, and I'd never mistake her.'

The heavy guns of *Queen Elizabeth* roared again and the air quivered like jelly under the blast as the huge projectiles thundered over the town. An area had been roped off and reinforced with barrels, carts and spars to make a clear space by the landing steps where boats were gathered, and a British naval officer with a straggly beard like a rather tatty rat was watching the only entrance with a group of seamen armed to the teeth and stopping anybody who tried to pass. As Rumbelo put down the handles of the wheelbarrow containing Princess Busukov, it dawned on Kelly that the officer was Kimister, and he gestured to his party to move ahead.

But as Rumbelo moved forward, Kimister signed to his men and two of them stepped into the breach with fixed bayonets.

'You asking for a punch up the nostrils?' Rumbelo asked

them quietly.

Startled by the words that came unexpectedly from the big man in the ragged coat, the sailors looked at Kimister who stepped forward, stroking his beard.

'Who's this?' he demanded.

'Rumbelo, you bloody fool,' Kelly snapped at him from under his shaggy fur cap. 'And I'm Kelly Maguire. If your eyes weren't full of that bloody bum-fuzz you've grown on your face, you'd recognise us.'

Kimister stared uncertainly at him and Kelly glared back, red-eyed and quick-tempered with sleeplessness, his unshaven face dark and angry.

'If I'm not Kelly Maguire, you ass,' he snorted, 'who do you suppose I am? Czar Nicholas in disguise or something? Don't be a damn' fool, Kimister! I've got kids here who are exhausted and women who are half-starved, one of 'em probably dying. Stop arguing and let us through.'

Kimister backed away, then he gestured nervously at the women and children behind Kelly. 'My instructions are that no one but White officers and their families, British officers and their wives, and White troops and wounded are to be taken aboard.'

'A bit of Nelson's blind eye never hurt the Navy,' Kelly snapped.

Still Kimister hesitated and Kelly gestured at Baptiste. 'That's the French Consul,' he said.

'They said he was dead.'

'He's been resurrected,' Kelly retorted. 'Coffin yawned and out he came. Now, for Christ's sake, get out of the way! I was sent here to bring him out and I'm bringing him out. His family's alongside him. Next to him's his secretary, but for whose guts probably none of us would have got out. The rest are the families of staff and servants and White Russian officers.'

'All of them?'

'They have big families.'

Kimister was staring at Vera Brasov who had moved closer to Kelly, her eyes burning in her pale face. He had clearly recognised her.

'And this one?' he asked.

Kelly stared him down.

90

'My wife,' he said. 'Now get out of my bloody way or I'll shove you in the sea! We're coming through! All of us!'

As Kimister swallowed his pride and waved them past, Kelly stalked by him, gaunt, dirty and bearded, followed by the whole untidy string of women and children.

Orrmont welcomed them on board with a grin of relief. 'I thought we'd lost you, Number One.' He stared at the party filing below. 'Were *all* that lot connected with the French Consul?'

'Every one, sir.'

'Even Princess Brasov?'

Kelly grinned. 'Particularly Princess Brasov, sir.'

Orrmont didn't argue. 'Get 'em tucked in. None of 'em are allowed back ashore. Quite apart from murder there's the danger of disease. Transports that have already left are being held in Levantine ports under quarantine and the bloody people aboard 'em are dying like flies. We've got sentries posted at the gangways and machine guns manned and men at all points of the ship in case the buggers try to board from the sea. Nothing's to be put over the side that might help 'em climb aboard and no boats are to be lowered without my orders.'

Below, where the women were crowded into the mess flats with the children, Baptiste embraced Kelly, kissing him on both cheeks to the delight of the lower deck, and every one of his daughters flung her arms round him and hugged him warmly.

Vera Brasov rose as he approached. 'I am grateful, Kelly Georgeivitch,' she said quietly. 'I shall never forget.'

As he returned to the deck, a platoon of soldiers began to file aboard, followed by instructors of the British Mission. Next to them a steamer was loading White cavalry, and rather than have their horses fall into the hands of the Reds, the soldiers were shooting them, or pushing them into the harbour to drown, so that the animals were swimming between the ships, whinnying with terror. Then, as a mob of desperate refugees rushed the gangplank, a machine gun opened up from an Italian ship in the next berth and men and women fell.

'For Christ's sake,' Kelly yelled in fury. 'Stop that bloody shooting!'

A Greek destroyer went astern from the quayside in a panic, then, as though at a signal, other ships began to leave. Weeping

91

women with children waylaid the last naval and military officers and Orrmont ordered Kelly to break out the rum and pass it ashore.

'Better to die drunk than sober,' he said.

From *Mordant*'s bridge the red flags of the Bolsheviks could be seen at the street ends, waiting for the moment to sweep to the water's edge, and Red snipers on the rooftops began firing on the crowds which surged and heaved, trying to escape as people fell. Not far away an ancient paddlesteamer, her starboard paddle smashed, was struggling to leave. Then on a nearby mole, they heard a full-throated scream and, swinging round, saw that the Red horsemen had broken out and were driving among the unarmed men, women and children along the quay, their sickle-like sabres swinging.

Wordless and sick, they stared at the carnage. Then Orrmont's commands broke through the screaming. 'Have the gangway taken in,' he said.

Seamen with bleak faces carried out the orders without a word.

'Springs!'

As the ropes were hauled aboard, Orrmont stared about him, trying not to see the agonised looks on the faces of the people still on the quay or their arms lifted in wordless appeal.

Mordant's thin plates began to pulsate and her guard rails quivered.

'Let go forrard! Half astern port.'

The big guns of *Queen Elizabeth* lobbed a last salvo over the city, then, as *Mordant* began to swing, they saw the battleship moving, too.

'There's nothing to stop them now,' Boyle said wretchedly, and as *Mordant* drew away a vast high-pitched wail went up, chilling their hearts so that, unable to look back at the land, they had to stare fixedly at the open sea, their eyes bleak and empty and cold.

Part Two

1

Britain was no place to return to after a long commission abroad.

The Russian Civil War was over, but Boyle had only just taken a sentimental parting of Anne-Marie Baptiste in Constantinople and Kelly a rather more earthy one from Vera Brasov when the Middle East turmoil boiled up again. The arrival of Admiral Sir Reginald Tyrwhitt with the Third Light Cruiser Squadron from Malta had snatched Kelly off *Mordant* for a trip in *Cardiff* as a French-speaking aide to the port of Constanza and a long trip by train through the war-devastated areas of Rumania to Bucharest. The journey was slow and uncomfortable and even in their reserved coach all the seats had been stripped of their cushions, while most of the windows lacked glass and were boarded up to combat the cold.

At the Danube, they were obliged to get out and walk a quarter of a mile through ankle-deep mud to a bridge of boats, then another quarter of a mile on the other side to a waiting train. The journey's only compensation was a lunch with the King and Queen of Rumania and the offer of the royal train for the return. Within a week of reappearing in Constantinople, they had hurried off to Batoum to help bring back thousands more White Russians to join those already driving cabs and opening restaurants in the Turkish capital, and from there to Chanak to support a British army eyeball-to-eyeball with victorious Turks anxious to cross into Europe and win back all they'd lost.

From the other end of the Mediterranean England had seemed like a haven of peace, but *Mordant*'s homecoming had an empty feeling about it. They were sent to Port Edgar on the south side of the Firth of Forth, upstream of the bridge and

95

close to South Queensferry. It had originally been a small fishing port, little more than an area of mud which dried out at low water, but it had been taken over by the Admiralty as a destroyer base, and though the little harbour had been dredged and wooden jetties erected for the accomodation of ships, there was little to interest their crews.

There was time to think on the long journey south, and for the first time in his life for Kelly there was a faint unwillingness to seek out Charley. There had been a slight recovery in his fortunes while Kimister had been involved with his Russian baroness but nothing had come of it in the end and, before *Mordant* had left Constantinople for good, he had gathered from Kimister that he and Charley were in touch with each other again.

The idea of marriage must by now be firmly fixed in her mind, he knew, and he felt he could hardly blame her, because she'd been waiting ever since 1918 for him to make up his mind. Though he could still claim poverty, he could no longer plead she was too young and, despite a bank account that showed more red than black, he couldn't even claim lack of rank against the Admiralty's entrenched ideas that naval officers ought to be wedded only to the Service, because his promotion to lieutenant-commander had come through and his next appointment might even be to a command of his own.

The country seemed to be in a strange despairing mood that was doubly noticeable after being away from it for so long. There was an air of neglect and decay everywhere because industry, which had grown and expanded in the previous century, had suddenly become out-of-date. The country needed new methods and new machinery, yet the loss of foreign markets had so impoverished the City it could not afford to provide them, and the greatest effect had been in shipping. Even the Navy was in danger because the Americans were insisting on equality of tonnage and ships and, to get it, were demanding that Britain should pare down her fleet.

At Euston, as Kelly walked alongside the porter pushing his gear on a barrow, a hand fell on his shoulder and he turned to see Kimister standing beside him dressed in mufti.

Kelly stared at him with little warmth. It was hard to forget that Kimister, for reasons best known to himself, had left him in

96

the lurch on the wrong side of the River Vilyuj, and harder still to feel that while he, Kelly, was out on his ear as far as Charley was concerned, Kimister could do no wrong.

Kimister smiled, unaware of Kelly's dislike. 'At least, you're still in the Navy,' he said. 'And that's something. That damned man, Geddes, that they appointed to look into the economy, uprooted a devil of a lot of junior officers and chucked 'em on the labour market with only a small gratuity and a smaller pension.'

Kelly looked at Kimister's civilian clothes. 'You safe?'

Kimister gave a shy self-effacing smile. 'I scraped through.'

'Verschoyle?'

'Naturally. He got his half-stripe in the same gazette as you. He's at the Admiralty. I saw a chap called Poade the other day, though. Said he knew you. He's going in for farming and not much looking forward to it. Felt he'd been betrayed. So does everybody come to that. Even the lower deck.'

Kelly was in no mood to discuss the Navy's troubles. He was as well aware of them as Kimister. The shortage of men had caused time ashore to be so reduced that the old naval prayer about returning to enjoy the blessings of the land had become nothing but a mockery, and crews returning from commissions in the Middle East were finding themselves drafted immediately into ships headed for Singapore.

'Things are different these days,' Kimister said. 'The new intakes are bitter because they've been forced in by the absence of work and, since a lot of them have been members of unions, they're a bit inclined to air their grievances.' He paused. 'Seeing Charley?'

'Of course.'

'Oh!, Kimister smiled. 'I've seen her once or twice.'

'Oh?, It was Kelly's turn to be non-committal. In his nervous way, Kimister seemed to be warning him off.

'I've been doing a stint at Chatham,' he said, 'so I've been able to slip up easily. She was pretty lonely.'

And a prey to smooth operators who could smell loneliness at a distance of five miles, Kelly thought, to say nothing of sad cases like Kimister who attracted soft-hearted females by nothing else but their own helplessness. How Kimister had dodged the Geddes axe he couldn't imagine.

Kimister blushed.'Saw her a couple of nights ago, as a matter of fact,' he went on offhandedly. 'Verschoyle and I took her and Mabel to the theatre.'

Kelly's head jerked up. 'New line for you, isn't it?' he said. 'Allied to Verschoyle.'

Kimister shrugged. 'We're not midshipmen now.'

Kelly didn't answer. His own attitudes were still more black and white than grey. Verschoyle was the enemy and had been ever since he'd first met him at Dartmouth, and he couldn't ever imagine joining him for a theatre party.

He was glad to be rid of Kimister because he hadn't progressed much either as an officer or as a human being. Dumping his gear at the Junior United Service Club and taking a cab to the Admiralty, he was shown into Verschoyle in the Second Sea Lord's office. Verschoyle greeted him cheerfully even if warily and, to his surprise, Kelly found him a pleasant change from Kimister. As he'd decided long ago, at least Verschoyle had the courage to be something definite, even if it was only a cad.

'Back again,' Verschoyle smiled. 'Turning up like the proverbial bad penny. Ginger Maguire, the most decorated man in the Navy next to Evans of the *Broke*. And what, might one ask, are you hoping for next time?'

'My own ship,' Kelly said shortly.

Verschoyle shrugged. 'You'll be damn lucky,' he said bluntly. 'These days our political overlords aren't sure whether officers should be fighting to get a ship or ships should be fighting to get officers. It's a rough old Navy these days, old son.'

'Is it really as bad as I've heard?'

Verschoyle's face, plumper with good living than Kelly remembered, changed.

'Well,' he said, 'the quarrel as to which gets most money, the Navy or the Air Force, has quietened down now and so has the Anglo-American naval building race. But the results rouse no great enthusiasm in the Board of Admiralty, because they wanted more capital ships and they're distinctly cool to the Frock Coats. Since then, of course, Lloyd George's gone and we now have Stanley Baldwin, and everybody's gone peace-minded so that it's considered much more moral these days to kill people with small guns than big ones.' He sat back and

98

looked at Kelly. The old snub-nosed, urchin-face, red-haired young man he'd been in the habit of bullying was gone. In his place was a strong-featured, unhandsome yet not unattractive man who was as certain of his future as he was that the sun would rise the next morning. To Verschoyle, far from lacking in ability and self-assurance himself, it was something he could understand.

'Since they merged the Naval Air Service with the Flying Corps to form the Air Force,' he went on, 'a few people turned in that direction, feeling there might be a future in it, but it militates against the efficiency of the Navy, and you can bet those buggers in the Commons will cut the air estimates if only because they haven't the foggiest idea what air power is. Nobody these days knows whether he's on his arse or his elbow.'

Verschoyle had lost none of his gift for seeing things clearly, or for putting them in a nutshell.

'I bet *you* know,' Kelly said.

Verschoyle looked as if butter wouldn't melt in his mouth. 'James Caspar Verschoyle always knows which way up he is,' he agreed. 'Actually, I'm very much a man of the people these days. After all, we expect to have a Labour government any time now and the chap in the cloth cap standing next to you in a bus queue might well be your boss tomorrow. I'm a great one for humanity. It's people I don't like very much.'

Kelly laughed, strangely at ease with the man he'd always considered his deadliest enemy. 'You don't change much,' he said.

'That's always been a family boast.' Verschoyle gestured with his cigarette. 'I often wonder how it was that nobody in my family ever managed to acquire a title. I think there must have been a great deal of carelessness somewhere.'

'How's Mabel?'

'Inclined to be clinging these days.' Verschoyle flicked a scrap of dust from his sleeve. 'Beginning to worry she's going to be left on the shelf. Always game for a laugh, of course, but somehow getting left behind a little. After all, she's older than your Little 'Un and even your Little 'Un's beginning to consider herself growing a little long in the tooth.'

'She's only twenty-three.

'Twenty-four, old boy. I know because Mabel's twenty-seven

and always bemoaning the fact. Going to pop the question this time?'

Kelly didn't answer and Verschoyle grinned.

'I know the feeling,' he said. 'You're too young to die.'

Esher didn't look very different, though Kelly noticed new houses going up everywhere in the building burst that had started since the war. What had been a village was now rapidly growing into a township.

Rumbelo's wife, Bridget, greeted him at the door. Her face lit up at the sight of him, and she pushed a small boy forward. 'You'd better say hello to your godson, Master Kelly,' she said.

'This child needs a father who's a petty officer,' Kelly said as he bent to shake hands with the solemn red-haired child clinging to her legs. 'I'm going to see that your husband gets his fore-and-aft as soon as I can, Biddy.'

'Thanks, Master Kelly, He'll be pleased. Will it mean him going overseas again?'

'Bound to, Biddy. Same as me.'

'He isn't home much, Master Kelly. He thinks it'll be China next time. A gunboat, he says.' She sighed, then she managed a smile. 'I'm glad I'm here, Master Kelly. It's better than being in rooms in Portsmouth. The wages he gets wouldn't provide us with much, and at least I don't get lonely when he's away.'

Kelly's mother looked smaller and older and he realised how much she'd changed since he'd left England for the Mediterranean. The lines on her face were deeper but she still possessed the same doggedly cheerful air.

'Still handling horses,' she admitted. 'Money's tight these days and I'm afraid your father doesn't help. He seems to spend all his time at his club and he always did get through money far too quickly. You goin' to see the Upfolds?'

'I suppose so, Mother.'

'Aren't you as keen as you were?'

Kelly shrugged. 'It's a bit of a problem, ain't it? Marriage's not something to rush into if you're not certain.'

'One's married a long time, Kelly. And sometimes it can be very lonely. Especially married to a sailor.'

'I always thought Charley had that sorted out,' Kelly admitted. 'She always said she'd wait.'

'She was a bit younger then.' His mother sighed. 'She's probably afraid now that she ought to be getting on with it, because they're not as well off as they were.'

Borrowing the old car his mother used, Kelly drove the mile or two from Thakeham to the Upfolds. The house seemed to contribute to the general air of shabbiness and despair he'd noticed about the country. The drive was unweeded and the paint was fading.

Charley was thinner and, he noticed, much more attractive with the sort of beauty that didn't come simply from youth. She stared at him for a fraction of a second then her eyes filled with tears and she flung herself at him, clutching him tightly, her face in the curve of his neck. Her voice came to him muffled from the region of his ear. 'I thought you'd gone for ever.'

He was so pleased at her reaction he couldn't stop grinning.

'Not me,' he said. 'Verschoyle says I'm like the proverbial bad penny.'

'Have you seen him?'

'Yes. At the Admiralty. I went to see what was in store for me.'

Her arms slackened at once and she released him to stand back and stare at him.

'Already? Before you've even been home?'

He was aware of an immediate chilliness. 'You have to look ahead,' he said.

'To the next trip abroad?'

He found himself on the defensive. 'To the next step in promotion,' he said. 'Promotionitis, like piles, seems to be an occupational hazard in the Navy.'

Her voice seemed suddenly cold. 'What *is* the next step?'

He realised he might be wise to tread warily but he was in no mood to be cautious. 'Well, it's not due for some time,' he pointed out. 'I've only just had one. But you can get another within four years if you're lucky with your appointment. Then it means six years' hard labour as a commander, followed by promotion to captain, which is twelve years' solitary confinement.'

She looked at him uncertainly, not sure that she knew him any more. There was a grim look about him these days and he was thin and taut, as if his temper weren't far below the surface.

A bleak expression behind his eyes suggested that he'd seen things she couldn't even imagine, and he seemed more laconic, too, and unwilling to explain. Even as she doubted him, her heart went out to him.

She paused, her face serious. 'And where do I fit into the scheme of things, Kelly?'

He found himself stuck for words. Thanks to the diehard admirals who believed there were already too many married officers in the Navy, there was always a chronic shortage of cash among those who'd had the nerve to take themselves a wife. More than one he'd known had resigned his commission because he couldn't make ends meet and was now in a job in the City he detested. He didn't fancy doing that. He was a naval officer, had known no other life and didn't think with his qualifications that he even stood much chance as a civilian.

He was just going to answer when she spoke again. 'Albert says – '

'Albert?'

'Albert Kimister. He says you have a Russian wife.'

Kelly smiled, glad to change the subject. 'Just shows what a fathead he is.'

'There *was* a girl?'

'Nothing to write home about,' Kelly said, praying silently that he wouldn't be struck by lightning for the lie. 'And why not? You could hardly say I was being encouraged from this end, could you? I notice Albert Kimister didn't feel so neglected.'

There was a long silence that grew uncomfortable, then she drew a deep breath.

'You haven't answered my question yet, Kelly,' she said. 'Where do I fit into the scheme of things?'

He stiffened, feeling goaded. 'Charley,' he said, more bluntly than he'd intended. 'I can't afford to get married yet. I haven't a bean beyond my pay.'

'I see. When *would* you be able to marry?'

He was about to say 'Captain's rank' but he bit it back. 'When I'm a commander,' he said.

'In another four years? At the very least?'

He nodded.

For a long time she said nothing, sitting on the settee playing

102

with the fringe of her sleeve.

'I'm nearly twenty-four, Kelly. I went back to the solicitors' office in Esher when I stopped nursing. It's stale and dusty and he tries to paw me when he gets the chance.'

She spoke matter-of-factly in a way that left him without an answer. He could only try to beg for understanding.

'Charley, I can only ask you to wait. I have no money of my own.'

'Albert Kimister has.'

The words were spoken quietly but defiantly. He sighed.

'I can't compete with Kimister, Charley.'

She was silent again for a moment. 'I think the Navy expects too much of its officers.'

'It always did. But so does tram conducting if you're going to be a good tram conductor.'

'Tram conductors get home to their wives at night,' she retorted. 'Have you ever thought of resigning?'

'No,' he snapped. 'I haven't'

'Other people have.'

'*I*'m not going to, Charley,' he said firmly. 'Being poor's the price we pay for holding the King's Commission. I don't agree with it but I can't change it. Not until I become an admiral, anyway. And I'll never become an admiral if I resign my commission now.'

She said nothing for a while. She seemed to be weighing up the pros and cons, and he found himself watching her closely. Longing to take her in his arms again, he fought off the wish because he knew he had no right to, and he came to the conclusion that he was growing old and cynical. A man who could weigh his career against marriage must be.

'It's hard to stay at home all the time, Kelly,' she whispered eventually.

'I can't expect you to, Charley. In fact, I suspect I've kept you chained to me for far too long. Perhaps you ought to consider yourself a free agent.'

'Albert Kimister asked me to marry him again.'

'What did you say?'

'I didn't even consider it. But that was a long time ago, too, now.' She drew a deep breath. Kelly looked so clean-cut and so responsible, she thought, with none of Kimister's doubts and

103

uncertainties. But she *was* nearly twenty-four now, and it seemed he was asking her to wait another four years without any guarantee, even then. Though her heart ached for him to put his arms round her, commonsense warned her to walk warily.

'I've been waiting a long time, Kelly,' she said. 'There was a time when I never had any doubts about it at all. I even believed you and I were intended for each other. I felt that from the day I first met you. But now – ' she sighed ' – well – '

She left the sentence unfinished, blinked the tears back and sat up straight, struggling to force a smile. 'Now you're home, Kelly, what shall we do?'

'We can enjoy ourselves, Charley. We used to.'

She stared at him, her eyes huge and full of unhappiness, then her face crumpled and she flung herself into his arms. 'Oh, Kelly,' she wailed.

He was just gently kissing the top of her head, when the door opened and Mabel appeared. She was wearing a shapeless dress that seemed to be made of fringes. Its hem was high above her knees, and a string of amber beads hung to her waist. Her mouth was a slash of red and her hair, which had been cut short with two large kiss curls on her cheeks, was waved until it looked as if it had been fried.

'Ooops, dears!' she said. 'Didn't know we had guests.' Then she stared and smiled. 'Well, well,' she said, 'if it isn't Kelly Maguire! God bless you, children. I now pronounce you man and wife.'

There was a harder look about her, Kelly noticed as he stood up, and a calculating expression round her eyes.

'Do we name the date this time?' she asked.

'No,' Charley snapped.

'Sorry!' Mabel swung her beads. 'Trust me to put my big foot in it. Off again, Kelly? The way you get around, it's a wonder anybody ever manages to keep track of you. James Verschoyle doesn't seem to wander far, I notice. Come to that, neither does Willie Kimister.'

Charley's head came up. 'His name's not Willie,' she snapped and it dawned on Kelly that she had to put up with a certain amount of derision from Mabel.

Mabel smiled, crossed to Kelly and kissed him on the cheek.

104

'At least you *look* like a naval officer,' she said. 'Pity you haven't more money. I might have made eyes at you myself. And now if you'll excuse me —'

She picked up a cigarette case and lighter and turned to the door. In the entrance she turned. 'Toodleoo. I know just how you feel, Charley dear. I've been trying to get James Verschoyle to the post for years.'

2

They tried to enjoy themselves but something was missing, and it occurred to Kelley that perhaps it was trust. For the first time in their lives, neither of them quite believed the other, and neither of them was being entirely honest.

He didn't want to get married yet. His career was in the balance and he felt he daren't take a chance. He knew he still loved Charley but he couldn't ask her to marry him and live in the sort of genteel poverty the Board of Admiralty seemed to feel ought to be the lot of officers who had the courage to defy them. And, while Charley couldn't bring herself to admit outright that she was dissatisfied with the arrangement, circumstances had forced her into considering Kimister, whose family was far from short of money. Because of other people, they were both having to hedge their bets.

They went to the theatre together occasionally, bumping into an embarrassed Admiral Maguire at Drury Lane with a girl on his arm as young as Charley. They went sailing in the Solent in a borrowed boat, and racing at Sandown and Ascot, Kelly in the full fig of a hired suit. They occasionally even clutched each other despairingly, kissing each other wildly, but somehow there was no truth in it. Kelly knew he should have been able to take her without asking, and one night when they were alone in the house he very nearly did. But she pushed him away angrily, pulling her dress straight and patting her hair into place.

'Why not, Charley?' he demanded. 'Once you were all for it.'

'Well, now I'm not sure.'

'Not sure about what?'

'Us.'

Frustrated, feeling as virile as a bull, he forced himself to understand. Since he couldn't ask her to marry him, the faint vestige of decency that he felt still remained in him told him that he should hold back if she were contemplating marriage to someone else. In the world of the Twenties inhabited by Mabel and 'Cruiser' Verschoyle, it was perhaps an old-fashioned idea, but he decided he *was* old-fashioned and he felt that Charley was, too.

They tried hard to pretend things were the same as they always had been but Kelly knew he'd taken too much advantage of Charley's faithfulness and been too long away from her. It had been none of his doing, but other men – Kimister for one – had wangled their way home early, and despite everything, despite Domlupinu, despite Odessa, he had always preferred service abroad to service in England.

In the end there were gaps when they didn't even bother to see each other or telephone and he knew she was seeing Kimister who was now at Devonport, had even been to stay with his mother who'd taken a house near St. Germans to be near her son. To his bewilderment, he found that when she wasn't around he missed her, yet he knew that if she'd not disappeared to Cornwall they'd have found it more and more difficult to be happy. He wasn't sorry when a telegram arrived from Verschoyle asking him to call and see him.

'Not much of an appointment for a dashing two-and-a-halfer,' Verschoyle admitted. 'Exec in *Karachi*. The captain's one of the old school but she's a cruiser and fairly new. It's only for a year, of course, because the job really belongs to Toady Gresham but he's in dock at Haslar having a boiler clean. Appendicitis or something. The Owner says he wants somebody to take his place and that he wants somebody lively. I can't imagine anyone more lively than you.'

Despite their long-standing antagonism towards each other, Kelly could have kissed Verschoyle.

Karachi was at Portsmouth and, so great was the popularity of the North America and West Indies station, three or four times the number of men required had come forward to man her. Her captain, Charles Denham Davidge, was not an easy man, however. He had a face like a collapsed tent and an exaggeratedly upper class voice, and clearly considered himself in the running

107

for flag rank.

Bermuda was uncomfortably hot when they arrived and there were more than a few who had volunteered who began to regret their haste. Their duties consisted of showing the flag, answering calls from any of the West Indian islands that were suffering enough from the heat to indulge in civil disturbances, and keeping in touch with the Royal Canadian Navy.

Montreal, known as the sailors' Mecca, was a place where every member of the ship's company seemed to have a hatpeg with some family ashore, and *Karachi*'s officers became honorary members of every club in the vicinity. Kelly was seized on by a voracious girl who was so affected by his full dress uniform he came to the conclusion she was either a nymphomaniac or not quite compos mentis. He might have felt guilty but for the apparent indifference shown at home to the letters he wrote.

The visit was without any untoward incident except when the ship's fishing club visited a nearby river after salmon and one of the midshipmen fell in and was only rescued with difficulty from drowning. A complaint arrived from the chaplain that the paymaster – whom he disliked – had declined to help. 'I was into a fish at the time,' the paymaster retorted. 'And everybody knows that a salmon's worth more than a midshipman.'

There were a few odd jobs to do. British residents were complaining that the wreck of a destroyer which had run aground during the war on an island off Newfoundland was causing derision among Americans, so Kelly went ashore with an unlimited amount of depth charges and an explosive expert and reduced it to rubble. The explosion was a most satisfying affair, and almost removed the island, too, while the people who'd complained originally now complained of smashed windows and frightened cattle.

They did a few night defence exercises – what Kelly claimed were the quickest and surest way of catching pneumonia known to mankind – and that best imitation of a cloudburst yet invented, fire stations. Finally, they hurried south to put a party ashore in the warm silk Caribbean air of Antigua where plantation workers, deciding they were underpaid, underprivileged and undermanned, had started a riot. Armed sailors and Marines glared at them from behind rolls of barbed wire and endured a hail of brickbats in an atmosphere of tension and bad

108

feeling until the matter was cleared up. It was just another one of the jobs the Navy had to undertake, but most of what they had to do still seemed to consist of drinking, paying court to important elderly ladies and eager young ones, and playing football against the other ships with such skill and determination they won the Admiral's cup.

For the second time he received no letters from Charley and he began to consider that somewhere along the line he'd made a mistake over her. She'd been part of his life for so long her coolness to him before he'd left had shaken him. It was like trying to live with only one leg or deprived of the use of his right hand. He could still get by, but it felt wrong and awkward. Then, back in Bermuda, he found a letter waiting for him, totally unexpected but bearing writing that made his heart leap.

He snatched it from the rack and vanished to his cabin, aware once again that they'd been apart of each other's life too long to be easily put aside. Charley was unexpectedly humble and he knew at once she was lonely and missed him, and was pouring out her fears and woes in the hope of making up their quarrel. Her letter was simple, pleading for understanding, and he made up his mind there and then that as soon as he returned to England he'd marry her and damn the Admiralty. She knew what a naval officer's wife had to do, had known it all her life, and he knew she'd never mind so long as she could share his existence and not merely be left at home full of uncertainty.

He started to write back to her, his words full of promises, saying things with a feeling he'd never expected. He'd always previously been cautious in what he wrote, even to Charley. 'Say it with chocolates,' Verschoyle had once warned him. 'Say it with mink. Say it with flowers. But never with ink.'

There was a tap on his door. Deep in the letter, he resented the interruption.

'Yes? What is it?'

It was one of the midshipmen. 'Meteorological report, sir,' he said. 'There's a hurricane in the West Indies moving for the coast of Florida. It's expected to pass the coast of Bermuda tomorrow.'

'And?'

'It seems to be turning north earlier than expected, sir. They think it's due here tomorrow.'

109

Kelly laid down his pen. 'We're supposed to be sailing for Nassau, tomorrow. Does the captain know?'

'Yes, sir. He's been in touch with the captain of *Katmandu*. He thinks we shall be clear before it arrives.'

'I'd better see him.'

When he reached his cabin, Captain Davidge had just returned on board after spending the afternoon at Admiralty House.

'Ah, Maguire! You look as if you've heard of the hurricane?'

'Yes, sir. I've had a word with the master-attendant of the dockyard. He seems to think we're going to get the full force of it here.'

Davidge shrugged. 'I spoke to *Katmandu*'s captain and the squadron navigating officer. They've had reports from Washington, and they judge the centre will pass three hundred miles north tomorrow afternoon. There'll be strong gales but no cause for alarm. We should be clear before then.'

'The master-attendant of the dockyard doesn't think so, sir.'

'He's a lieutenant-commander passed over for promotion.'

Kelly frowned. 'He's a good navigator of excellent judgement who's been here a long time, sir,' he insisted. 'And he has a reputation as a meteorologist. He thinks it'll strike Bermuda.'

Davidge gestured. 'I think we'll abide by the decision of the two seniors,' he said flatly.

There was a strange stillness about the air as *Karachi* left Hamilton. There was no morning sparkle and low down on the horizon a thin layer of dark cloud lay like a range of mountains out to sea. The water looked dark and the atmosphere had become so heavy even the palm fronds seemed to be weighted.

Huge silky swells were moving from the end of the bay, long, leaden and slow. They looked smooth but they were the colour of steel and Kelly noticed there were no boats about. The bright hues of the island seemed to have been dulled by a strange light beyond the haze, and the thin skin of cloud that had been low down on the horizon was beginning to spread quickly and widen. People on the waterfront were staring at the horizon and he could see men working over the lines of small boats, while the barometer had become erratic and had suddenly dropped towards twenty-nine and was still falling.

As they left the harbour, the daylight had become a curious grey-yellow and the sea was gurgling and bubbling along the quays. It started to rain, stopped abruptly, then started again, as if someone were turning a tap on and off, but the air was like the inside of a steam laundry, and to the south purple-grey masses of cloud were gathering. Even over the sound of the waves, they could hear a queer roaring that didn't seem to come with the wind.

Kelly stared out to sea, still firmly of the conviction that the captain and the experts were wrong and that the master-attendant was right, and he hoped they'd be well clear before the wind really struck. As they put the island behind them, through his glasses he could see people lashing down hencoops and nailing up shutters, showered all the time by palm fronds torn from the trees. Then, as they left the shelter of the land, the wind, which seemed to have sprung from nowhere in a second, struck the ship with brutal violence and water poured across the deck. Men struggling to lash things down leaned against the gale.

The sky had an eerie light that was reflected in a purple glow along the lines of the guns and the upperworks, and the sea seemed stirred from its depths so that it was filled with grey-yellow mud. There was reassurance from the roaring of the engine room fans and the seagoing smell of hot oil and salt, but the wind struck them with increased force as they reached the open sea, heeling the ship well over; then a wave broke over the bow in a great cloud of spray that reached half as high as the mast. Kelly had been in dirty weather before around the fringes of hurricanes, and Atlantic gales were nothing, but somehow a deep-seated feeling of unease told him that this time it was different.

The navigating officer tapped the chart. 'Barometer's dropped fourteen points, sir, and the wind's shifting all the time. It's force seven at the moment.'

During the morning the wind grew worse. In the dismal yellowish light the sea was heaving like grey treacle, white streaks of foam laying along the deep troughs, and the wind was strong enough now to tug at Kelly's eyelids and drive at his cheeks. All round them there were only ridges and valleys of water. The forecastle was inches deep in it and foam boiled

111

along the deck, piled against the bridgehouse and sloshed over the side. Dark grey clouds tumbled overhead and the deck went up and down like a lift.

'What's the barometer reading?'

'Twenty-nine point four-oh, sir.'

Glancing about him, Kelly drew assurance from the stolid faces of the helmsman and the quartermasters who clung expressionlessly to the wheel or engine room telegraphs, clearly aware that the responsibility was not theirs but the captain's. In the moment of drowning, he wondered, would they still not worry because that wasn't their responsibility either?

When he returned to the bridge after eating, the wind had increased again and there was a deep hollow whine in it now that seemed to come out of the bowels of the sea in a ghostly echoing note as it howled across the vast miles of the ocean. He no longer had any doubt that the master-attendant of the dockyard had been right. They were beset by a hurricane.

Davidge clearly thought so too. He was uneasy and frowning heavily, clinging to the chart table in the lurching chartroom. He pushed a signal across. 'To all ships: There will be no tennis at Admiralty House today.'

'Oh, charming, sir,' Kelly said cheerfully. 'I like to see things done in their proper order.'

The sea was a dull pewter colour now and the ship was groaning in every plate and nut and bolt in protest.

'Better warn the head quack to be prepared for emergencies, Davidge suggested. 'There are bound to be some accidents.'

The ship was shovelling grey seas over the bows, and the water was careering across the forecastle to send up gouts of spray sixty or seventy feet high. Below, conditions were nauseating. With everything battened down, there was no air and the decks were slippery with moisture and stank of human excrement and vomit. Hardened sailors were lolling about in acute discomfort among the creaking and vibration in a fug of cigarette smoke and thick heads.

The day seemed to have disappeared and they were surrounded by a close gagging darkness like the inside of a sack. With the fading of the light, all they could see of the ocean was an occasional flash of racing foam from the wash alongside as the ship dragged herself up the steep slopes and slid wildly

112

down the other side.

'Centre's a hundred and fifty miles away, due east, sir.' The navigating officer jabbed at the chart with his dividers as Kelly returned to the bridge. 'I'll be glad to see the sun again.'

There were loud smashing sounds from below as if someone was playing quoits with whole cartloads of crockery and, by now, with the wind abeam, the ship was remaining at a slant. The wardroom was already a wreck, with smashed chairs and tables tangled with broken glass, newspapers, magazines, cushions and spilt food. Then the ship soared up, as though lifted by a giant hand, rolled over to starboard, crushing a wave of foaming water that was fiery with phosphorescence, and reeled back again as if she were falling into a great pit. On the horizon there was a flash of purple lightning that lit up the heaving ocean in a tumbling plain of grey-mauve water rising and falling in ghostly mountains, then the ship crashed into a trough like a pole-axed ox and the whole interior shuddered and rattled as the water boiled across the deck.

The waves now were taller than anything Kelly had ever seen, huge as blocks of buildings marching by, majestic and rhythmic, so that *Karachi* rose and fell like a scrap of wood in the swell running up a beach. Then she rolled again in a terrifyingly sharp lurch and the wind came out of the sky in a deep gloomy whine above the crashing of the waves. The barometer read 29.29.

The wind was already force nine and *Karachi* was smashing into the sea with a desperate doggedness. With her head to the storm, she was riding well but the pitching of the ship was enough to make the most experienced sailors feel queasy. The barometer had dropped to 29.20 and was still falling.

Even the blank-faced quartermasters had a worried look behind their eyes now. Their age and experience did not allow them to show anxiety but it was there, nevertheless, if only in the way their eyes moved. The chief yeoman's expression was more forthright and he was staring at the endless procession of waves blundering down on them out of the horizon with dilated eyes.

'Jesus,' he said suddenly.

There was something in the simple unexcited way he spoke that snatched at their attention and, as they stared in the

113

direction he was looking, they saw an enormous wave, a gigantic freak-wave dwarfing all the others, a hundred feet high, its crest torn by the wind.

As it broke over the ship it flung hundreds of tons of water across the hull to sweep in a grey-yellow foaming stream the whole length of the deck, smashing boats and twisting iron stanchions into knots. The ship heaved, shuddering, lurching over on her side as the battering ram of water swept across her, carrying away everything in its path and filling their nostrils with the rough salt smell of drowning. Then, slowly she began to lift, crawling slowly out of the depths, the water pouring from her scuppers in a solid stream. As she lay in the water like a floating log, to his horror Kelly saw that the barometer had dropped below twenty-nine.

Aerials were down and boat davits had been buckled, while below decks was a shambles of smashed dishes, chairs, bottles, small instruments and stores tumbled helter-skelter out of lockers. Tons of water sloshed about the alleyways, filthy brown and dirty.

A report arrived from the galley to say the meal that had been cooking was no longer a meal under preparation but cold, salt-washed meat and congealed fat spattered along the bulkheads, and that potatoes flung across the galley were spluttering and crackling on the hotplates. But that was the lot. They accepted philosophically the cold bully beef and biscuits that appeared, aware that the worst of the hurricane was passing. Though the motion was still wearying and violent, the rain had stopped and in the murk along the horizon there was a suggestion of brightness once more.

As he went below to rescue some of his belongings, Kelly caught a glimpse of the ship's cat stepping daintily through a flood of debris, condensed milk, flour and sugar towards the miniature hammock it occupied in the petty officers' flat. It sprang to a table and from there to an empty bunk, stepping unsteadily to the swing of the ship, then a big roll followed and it missed its jump, fell into the water, and charged through a door spitting and shrieking as if demented.

He found his cabin awash, with clothing and blankets floating in a swill of sea water. With them was the letter he'd been writing to Charley, half the ink washed off it, and he picked it

114

up and tossed it into the waste paper basket, deciding that if nothing else she deserved something that was clean and neat. It had been a good letter and he could set it all down again as soon as he had time.

They had been lucky. Even the ships in harbour had been driven against the jetties and had stove in their plates, and the anemometer ashore had registered 138 miles an hour before disappearing at full speed itself into the murk. Moorings had snapped and bollards had been torn away; and two ships, one of them a single-screw sloop, had vanished, never to be seen again. Because of the damage she'd suffered and a new problem of condenseritis that had arisen, *Karachi* sailed for home a week later. There were so many smaller ships filling the repair yards, it was felt that she was big enough to make it across the Atlantic to have her scars healed in a British shipyard.

There was so much to clear up aboard, it was days before Kelly got down to writing to Charley again and, when he did, somehow all the fine words he'd put in his first letter had gone. It had been a letter full of spontaneous feeling and somehow he couldn't remember how he'd expressed it. In the end he decided instead to write when he got home.

They docked in Liverpool on the second day of May to find the country in the grip of a general strike. Inefficiency among the mine-owners had started it with one more of the interminable disputes that had taken place between them and the miners for years. Hit by rising prices, they were backing out of agreements they'd made, the government was demanding a reorganisation of the industry, and the miners were demanding nationalisation as the only cure. The headlines were black with mourning announcements. 'Agreement must be reached between owners and workers,' they announced.

'They've a hope.' The gunnery officer was cynical. 'They haven't agreed on a damn thing for years.'

Hard-faced politicians who had never ventured further north of London than Berkshire were demanding wage reductions and, when the owners had thrown their weight behind the idea, the miners had refused to accept. Now, with the sympathy of the whole of the working classes behind them, the country had awakened to find the railways closed and buses and taxis off the streets.

115

'What a bloody homecoming,' the gunnery officer complained.

Transport was almost entirely suspended and those who still wished to work had to make their way there in the best manner they could. A few volunteers, many of them university students prompted less by politics than by their willingness to indulge in a lark, were trying with more enthusiasm than skill to drive buses and trains. There were no newspapers and all the information they received was second-hand. Anxious to head south, Kelly fretted aboard ship. It was pointless trying to write to Charley because there was no post and the telegraph wasn't working.

Towards the end of the week, *Karachi* was ordered to supply a party of fifty men to guard stores near the docks, and they marched from the ship led by Kelly and accompanied by the navigating officer and two petty officers.

The stores were inside a wire-netting compound which didn't look strong enough to keep a rabbit at bay. Across the road on a patch of waste ground dockers were staring at the place, looking as if they were ready at any moment to break in.

There were a few policemen under an inspector standing by, but they were behaving very circumspectly, because incidents were liable to break out elsewhere at any time and they were thin on the ground.

'Think they'll try anything?' Kelly asked the inspector.

The policeman shrugged. 'They'd like to, sir. Have you brought arms?'

'No, by God,' Kelly said. 'And if we had, I wouldn't ask my chaps to start shooting at people who might well be their brothers and fathers and cousins.'

The policeman smiled. 'I think Winston favours drastic action, sir.'

'Well, if he thinks *I*'m going in for it, he's got another think coming.'

The following day, they were settled into a warehouse, the sailors, with the skill of their kind, comfortable on crates and packing cases, their blankets on straw and shavings they'd found, their only complaint that the rats and mice took up almost as much space as they did. Food came in a lorry twice a day and for the rest of the time they stood by the wire netting

116

fence warily watching the sullen strikers.

By the next morning, Kelly had had enough.

'I think we can do better than this,' he argued. 'Surely to God we can come to some agreement with those chaps out there. I don't suppose they want to set about us any more than we want to set about them. If we can get that across to each other, at least we can spend the strike in peace.'

The police inspector was dubious. 'How're you going to do it, sir?'

Kelly grinned. 'How about playing 'em at football?' he said.

The strikers were as bored as the bluejackets and, picking his most able petty officer as a go-between, Kelly soon found they'd have been willing to while away the time even with a game of ludo.

The police inspector offered to act as referee and, before the match, Kelly drew his team on one side. 'Just make it a good game,' he said. 'And no dirty play. And one more thing – *they win!*'

There was a growl of dissent and he grinned. 'We all know you're the best footballers in the West Indian Squadron, but those chaps across there need something to bolster up their pride. They haven't fed as well as you gannets feed either, so go easy with 'em and see they pull it off.'

The match was a great success. The news had sped round the neighbouring area like wildfire and an enormous crowd of men, women and small boys turned up. The two captains shook hands warily but the game was hard, though with both sides inclined at first to be cautious, as if wondering what to expect. When the strikers had scored three goals without reply at half time, Kelly got his team on one side.

'For God's sake,' he said. 'I told you to let 'em win, not murder you!'

Karachi's team scored two goals in the second half to growing excitement among the crowd, and finally drew level just before the end. It seemed a most satisfactory result and when one of the ordinary seamen, overcome by excitement and opportunity, stood with the ball facing an open goal, the situation was saved only by one of the petty officers sweeping his feet from under him in what was intended for – but didn't look like – a mistaken tackle. The yell of laughter that went up stopped the game and when the police inspector's whistle went two minutes later, everybody on both sides, both supporters and teams, heaved a sigh of relief.

The good will was clinched by four crates of beer paid for by Kelly and the navigating officer, which arrived from a pub across the patch of waste ground. Though it was out of licensed hours, the inspector not only turned a blind eye but had a bottle himself. The resentment had vanished completely and from then until the strike ended three days later, *Karachi*'s men were even the recipients of fruit pies, tea and sandwiches from the houses nearby.

'Seems to me,' Kelly said, 'That it was a method we might well have used in Antigua.'

3

When Kelly returned aboard, there were two things waiting for him – Lieutenant-Commander Gresham, who had turned up at last, cured and recuperated and ready to take over his duties, and a telegram from the Second Sea Lord's office telling him to report there.

He shook hands with Gresham and accepted a drink in payment for holding the job down, then returned to his cabin to stare at the telegram. He knew what it meant. Somebody had found a job for him, and for once he wasn't sure he wanted one.

He had telegraphed Charley from Bermuda telling her he was on his way home and had framed it in enthusiastic terms so that he knew she'd be waiting for him. He wasn't sure that he was eager to disappear into the blue again. If the job didn't suit, he decided he'd accept half-pay until something turned up that did.

There was also a letter from his mother saying that Biddy's Rumbelo had been posted to the Yangtze gunboat flotilla and one from Charley in much the same vein as the one he'd received in Bermuda. He left for London after a heavy night out in Liverpool, and slept most of the way south. Remembering what had happened last time, he was on the point of going to see Charley first and then to the Admiralty, but curiosity got the better of him and he decided to arrive on the doorstep with the news that he'd been offered a job and turned it down for her sake.

For the first time in his life he *felt* like getting married. The wardroom was no substitute for a home of his own. Even the house at Thakeham reflected his mother's personality, not his, and he felt suddenly that he'd reached the time of life when he needed somewhere to put his feet up.

Once more it was Verschoyle who greeted him.

'Just the thing for you, old boy,' he said. 'I always used to say I'd look forward to seeing you posted to the ends of the earth, but oddly enough I think this is made for you.'

'I'm not interested unless it's in this country,' Kelly said. 'I'm going to get married.'

'To the Little 'Un?'

'Who else?'

Verschoyle smiled. 'Mabel's more to my taste,' he said. 'But things are harder than they were and the Verschoyle fortune ain't what it used to be. When I marry, I'm marrying an heiress, and poor old Mabel's got nothing in the form of a dowry. The Upfolds are on their uppers.'

'I don't believe it!'

'True, old man. Got it from Kimister.'

Kelly scowled. 'What's he know about it?'

'What do you think he's been doing all the time you've been winning fame and fortune across the Atlantic? He ain't exactly been twiddling his thumbs down in Devonport, y'know.'

Kelly's scowl grew deeper. Charley's letters had never mentioned Kimister still waiting in the wings, and a niggling uncertainty started in his mind.

'What are you offering me?' he asked.

'Tyrwhitt's asked for you on his staff.'

'Tyrwhitt!'

More than any other sailor, Sir Reginald Tyrwhitt had come out of the war with an unsullied record, and had been the only man who had held the same command through the whole four years of hostilities without a breath of criticism.

'He's got a reputation second to none,' Verschoyle pointed out earnestly. 'With him, you've got somebody worth having behind you.'

Kelly drew a deep breath, aware of a sense of guilt. 'Where is he?' he asked.

'In this country at the moment.' Verschoyle smiled. 'But he won't be for long. He's got the China Station.'

Kelly's face fell. 'I'm not interested,' he said.

Verschoyle sighed. 'For God's sake, you make me tired! You want to be an admiral, don't you? I've seen some of your reports: "Has on one occasion after another acted with

120

unfailing promptitude." "Has proved himself an officer of exceptional value and unerring decision." ' He gestured angrily. 'You'll never become an admiral salt-horsing the seven seas. You might win a lot of gongs, but that's all. You've either got to take the senior officers' war course, run one of the manning depots, or appear on somebody's staff. I know these things.'

It was true enough, Kelly thought. Trust Verschoyle to know the score. He'd had his finger on the nerve centres of the Navy ever since Kelly had known him, full of gossip, sure of his facts, always certain how to move to his own advantage.

'When?' he asked slowly, his heart thumping suddenly. 'When must I leave?'

'At once. Tyrwhitt leaves later but he wants somebody in Shanghai ahead of him to do a bit of tact-finding and be ready to brief him when he arrives. There's an RAF experimental flight on its way tomorrow. They're setting up a new route to prove then can reinforce foreign stations quicker than we can and they've got room for a passenger. You'll pick up a ship in Calcutta. For a chap with your go-ahead attitude, an insight into how the other services operate might well be very useful.'

It was an exciting and tempting prospect. Kelly thought of his letter to Charley, wished for a moment he'd been to see her first and fixed up the wedding date, then changed his mind again.

'Couldn't it wait for a week?'

Verschoyle looked up. 'Worried the Little 'Un'll up and marry somebody else?' His smile was cynical but there was also an unexpected trace of sympathy in it.

'Yes,' Kelly said.

'Why not get her to follow you and marry her out there? Fleet Chaplain. Ceremony on the quarterdeck. All the usual fuss. She'd love it. Get it fixed. That ass Kimister's beginning to be a bit insidious and you've landed on your feet, if you only knew it. So don't be bloody naïve and turn it down. Tyrwhitt knows you've just arrived back in this country and, with the Navy List cut to ribbons by that idiot, Geddes, it doesn't pay anybody to turn things down. Not even me. And I'm filthy rich. *Still.*'

Kelly nodded. What Verschoyle said was true. There were too many cold-eyed politicians eager to reduce the navy to impotence.

121

'I'll take it,' he said abruptly.

Verschoyle smiled. 'Tyrwhitt'll be pleased,' he said. 'What about your personal affairs?'

'The only personal affairs I have are in my sea chest.'

'I was thinking of the Little 'Un.'

'Oh!' Kelly smiled ruefully. 'I'd better get over there now and make things right. She'll want to know.'

'Don't forget the Fleet Chaplain and the quarterdeck ceremony. I'm told you can have a wonderful honeymoon at Wei-Hai-Wei. I might even call in and have a glass of champagne with you. I'm heading that way myself. They've given me the destroyer, *Wanderer* – or rather I've made sure they've given me *Wanderer*. And, believe it or not – ' Verschoyle's smile widened – ' – that ass Kimister's going too!'

Charley greeted Kelly ecstatically. His telegrams had clearly delighted her and set her mind at rest, but she seemed more wary than in the past and, after kissing him solemnly, she stood back at arm's length to stare at him.

'You're thinner, Kelly,' she said.

'Hungry, perhaps.'

'And there's some grey in your hair.'

'That hurricane frightened the life out of me.'

She smiled. 'It makes you realise how long we've known each other.'

She took his hand and led him into the morning room, and though she said no more he knew very well what she was implying. This time, she was telling him, is *it*.

But she avoided the subject and gave him a drink. As he waited for her to pour it, he glanced about him, noticing the room looked a little shabbier, as though curtains and covers needed replacing. And on the wall over the fireplace, there was a small painting surrounded by the darker hue of a square of wallpaper, as though a larger painting had been taken down.

She saw his eyes on it. 'We sold it,' she said frankly. 'It was worth a lot of money.'

He took the drink and sat with her on the settee. 'Are things bad, Charley?'

She gave him a little smile. 'My father's pension doesn't provide for everything, you know, and I'm afraid he invested badly.

122

He had his money in coal and you know what's happened there. We shall be selling the house soon. Mother's going to live with her sister in Dorset. She's a widow, too.'

'And you and Mabel?'

'Mabel's running a dress shop in Knightsbridge.'

'Running a shop?'

'It's different these days, Kelly, and actually she's rather good at it. She never thought about anything but clothes, as you know, and perhaps it's just as well, because what she learned is standing her in good stead. I still have the job at Esher, but I don't want to stay there for the rest of my life.'

'You won't,' he promised.

She looked at him without speaking and it wrenched at his heart to see the doubt in her eyes. Then she smiled, making an effort.

'But they've given me a week off while you're home,' she said. 'I thought we could do a few things together.'

He drew a deep breath, hating himself. 'Tomorrow,' he said in a rush, 'I have to report to RAF, Hendon. I'm leaving the following day by air for China.'

The silence that followed his words was painful. She didn't raise her eyes.

'I see,' she said at last. 'And me?'

'It makes no difference.'

She looked up at last. 'But it does, Kelly,' she said quietly. 'It makes a lot of difference. I've been waiting for you to crook your finger for a long time now. I think I'm tired of waiting. I'm sorry, because – because – ' she looked at him, trying to say that she'd always loved him and still did, but she couldn't manage to make the words surface. 'I'm not like Peter Ibbetsen's girl friend, you know.'

Kelly frowned. 'I don't know him. What ship's he in?'

She gave him an angry look. 'He's a character in one of George du Maurier's novels,' she explained sharply. 'They were separated for most of their lives but they still managed to remain in love. I got into the habit of reading things like that. I thought they'd sustain me. But in the end I found them hard to believe. You're no good to me in China. Letters are a poor substitute for a warm body alongside you in bed.'

Her bluntness startled him and for the first time he realised

123

she was a grown woman with a woman's instincts, no longer a young girl to be treated with care. He groaned inwardly. He'd already accepted the appointment and he knew he couldn't back out of it now. He tried to make her understand that he hadn't overlooked her part in it.

'Actually, it makes things easier,' he said. 'It's a staff appointment. With Tyrwhitt.'

'No! No, Kelly!'

'Look, Charley, listen –'

'I'm tired of listening, Kelly.'

'For god's sake, Charley, hear me out –!'

'Kelly –' her eyes were blazing now ' – I've been hearing you out since I was seventeen. Too much water's passed under the bridge. Mabel's missed her chance and, if I'm not careful, I shall too. Do you think I enjoy working in that solicitor's office? It's dusty and it's fusty and I think he fancies getting me into bed. No, Kelly! No! No! No!'

Her refusal to listen made him angry. 'There were things I'd hoped to talk to you about,' he said stiffly. 'That's why I came here. But I'm in the Navy, and I not only have to do my duty, I also have to take my chances or get left behind. This is a chance and I've got to grab it with both hands. Nobody gets very far without influence or patronage. Jacky Fisher said patronage was a damn good thing, in fact –'

'Damn Jacky Fisher! I think I've lived with Jacky Fisher all my life!'

Her face was pink with anger and her eyes were blazing. He stepped forward and reached for her hand. If she was a woman – the thought flashed through his mind – then he'd better treat her like a woman and not like a little girl. Perhaps the best way to shut her up was to push her down on the settee and make love to her there and then. His mind was still working as her hand came round unexpectedly and the whack as it struck his cheek sounded like a pistol shot in the room.

He dropped her fingers as if they were red hot. He had reached the end of the line at last and he knew it. Without saying a word, he picked up his hat and stalked out, his face pale, the red wheal where her fingers had caught his cheek startlingly bright on his skin.

Charley was still huddled on the settee when Kimister arrived. With the maid long since dispensed with, there was no one to answer the door and he pushed inside to find her curled up, dry-eyed, among the cushions.

She'd longed for Kelly's return. Her life since his departure had been a series of torments, with her at one moment bitterly resenting his professional life apart from her, hating the Navy, hating his ship, even at times hating Kelly; yet the next swearing she'd try to understand and not expect to share that other esoteric existence of which she knew so little. But somehow, somewhere, it had gone wrong and, sick with disappointment and disgust at herself, she could only go over it all again and again, dissecting it, pulling it apart strand by strand like a scrap of tapestry, to try to discover where the weave had gone awry.

Kimister sat down alongside her quietly.

'Charley! What's happened?'

She didn't reply then, as he put his hand out to touch her, she suddenly flung herself into his arms and began to sob on his chest.

Kimister was startled. She'd never before encouraged him to hold her and his adoration had been mostly muted and uncertain. He lifted her face and, taking the opportunity that was presented with a boldness that surprised him, kissed her on the lips. She didn't resist, but there was no encouragement either, then, unexpectedly, he found her clutching him more tightly.

He had no idea what he owed his luck to, but he'd learned a lot from his Russian baroness in Novorossiisk and he didn't argue. What he didn't know was that jealousy, envy, a sense of being left out, all combined to make her impulsively anxious to hurt Kelly.

'Mabel's in London,' she murmured. 'And Mother's in Dorset.' She knew she was behaving like an idiot but, surging up inside her now, sweeping her along with it, was a growing anger, a sense of having been used and dropped.

Kimister was still eyeing her uneasily. 'Charley –'

'Oh, for Heaven's sake – ' her voice became harsh ' – use your sense, Albert.'

'Charley –'

'Stop saying "Charley," like that. Do you want me or don't you?'

125

For a moment Kimister was speechless. He'd arrived to bewail his appointment to the Far East and, despite her apparent and inexplicable fury that didn't seem to go with what she was offering, he was receiving an unexpected consolation prize.

He swallowed. 'I'd marry you tomorrow if you'd have me.'

It was dusk outside, dark earlier than normal after a grey and cloudy day. Charley rose abruptly and, going to the hall turned the key in the front door. To Kimister, unaware of her agony, she looked defiant rather than loving.

She stared at him with steady eyes and he had an uncomfortable feeling that he was staring at someone who was offering herself as a sacrifice.

'I wasn't talking of marriage,' she said.

4

They knew they were approaching the Yangtze miles before they saw land. The water became grey-yellow and oozy, and the brown patched sails of junks stood out on the horizon like drab moths. The mouth of the river was thirty miles wide with only a thin purple line in the distance to show where China lay.

Calcutta had been followed by Colombo, Penang and Singapore, and then Hong Kong with its mats of bobbing junks, and still troubled, still hurt by Charley's attitude, Kelly had found the only cause for joy in the whole trip had been the appearace on board of Lieutenant-Commander Archibald Fanshawe, with whom he'd served in the cruiser, *Clarendon*, before the war. Fanshawe hadn't changed with the years and was the same cheerful, cynical soul he'd been in 1914. Like Kelly, he couldn't afford to marry nor take a chance with his career, but unlike Kelly, he was already an old China hand.

The Whangpoo, where the ship dropped anchor, was a yellow-brown stream twelve miles up the Yangtze, teeming with sampans that swarmed about like drab water beetles. Tugs fussed round vessels anchored in midstream; and river steamers, their tiers of decks making them look top-heavy, slid between the straying junks that manoeuvred clumsily on the strong tide.

'What's it like, Fan?'

'China?' Fanshawe shrugged. 'Well, things are what you might call in a state of flux just now. The place's full of foreign concessions and treaty ports set up in Victoria's Happy and Glorious, but they continue to exist at the moment only by courtesy of the gunboat flotillas, because nobody loves us any more. In addition, there's a nationalist uprising going on which doesn't help matters, with one government in Canton trying to

127

overthrow another in Peking. You might say it's a bit of a lottery these days.'

He paused to watch a junk slide past, ghostly against the lights, so close they could see its red-brown sail was webbed like a bat's wing and decorated with patches. The rhythmic chant of the crew straining at the huge stern oar came across the water with the nauseating smell that passed with it.

'Foo-foo barge,' Fanshawe explained. 'Contains what's delicately known to the British as night soil. It's a pong you'll come across all over China.'

He leaned on the rail and squinted at the city of Shanghai, an odd mixture of East and West with its electric signs, brash advertisements and big square hotels. There seemed to be more cars even than in London and trams groaning round every corner, dragging trailers packed with coolies, vegetables and live poultry.

'The government in Canton,' he went on, 'was run until his death by a left-wing intellectual called Sun Yat-Sen, but another chap called Chiang K'Ai-Shek's beginning to gather all the bits together now and starting to move north. He's expected here any day.'

As the ship edged alongside next morning, blue-clad coolies swarmed over the bund and across the junks that covered the water in a heaving carpet. The din was appalling, with the honking of horns overlaid by the perpetual high-pitched yelling of the Chinese labourers and street traders. Even the coolies unloading sacks of rice from a river steamer, the bony fans of their ribs showing as they worked, sang all the time as they trotted up and down the gangways, a rising and falling song of two notes that added to the racket which came from the waterfront.

'Don't let it panic you,' Fanhawe advised. 'We're well established here and there's plenty of fun. Girls come out from home on every ship that arrives, to stay with relatives and find a husband. And if they don't please, you have what's ashore to choose from: Chinese, French and American, and Russian princesses by the dozen who came down from Vladivostock to escape the revolution.'

They moved through the crowded lounge packed with porters holding baggage, the stiff farewells of the old China hands,

and the multitude of chirruping Chinese clerks and shore workers who had swarmed over the ship. The din was deafening and
they had to shout to make themselves heard.

'You'll get used to it in time,' Fanshawe said. 'It's not real, of
course. Everywhere else in the world, the British male served
through the war. Out here, they just enjoyed it and did their bit
by making fortunes and building bloody great places for themselves in the Bubbling Well Road. To them, all Chinese are
idle, thriftless, filthy and full of squeeze, and the Country
Club's like a Bournemouth hydro on a wet Sunday afternoon.'

Shanghai's importance lay in the two foreign enclaves, the
International Settlement and the French Concession, and
towering buildings lifted above streets where human beings
swarmed like ants, mere beasts of burden weighed down with
poverty, the contrast as sharp as that between the British and
American warships in the river and the swarming Chinese
junks and sampans. At that moment, however, Western arro-
gance was tempered a little by apprehension, because of the approach of the Cantonese armies, and the extremities of the
Anglo-American-French city were guarded by sailors and soldiers, and bayonets glinted above piled sandbags.

They took a taxi out to the Majestic Hotel, a luxurious establishment in the middle of vast green gardens along the Bubbling
Well Road, a splendid empty palace of too much luxury.

'Only alternative to the Astor House,' Fanshawe explained.
'That's always full of newspaper correspondents and old
China hands, all expounding their theory of *Gott Strafe China.*'
Besides, it's quiet. Few too many servants and really far too
expensive for ordinary sailormen, but it's only for one night
and you can't hear the noise of the streets and what you
might call the uproar of the hatred the Chinese have for us.'

That night Fanshawe showed Kelly round Shanghai. It
was a Western city surrounded by an Eastern one, prosperity
beset by the encroachment of poverty, a nervous city surrounded by hatred. It seemed to have nothing but its wealth
and its fear of losing it, with most of its inhabitants waiting
nervously behind the barricades, where slovenly Spanish sailors, who had nothing to do with the situation, helped to
search the patient Chinese. In its apprehension and uncertainty, it seemed to exhibit human nature without dignity

and entirely without compassion.

An assistant to the senior officer of the gunboat flotilla, Fanshawe lived aboard an old paddle boat moored opposite the Chinese town of Pootung. Near it lay two Insect class gunboats, odd-looking craft with low freeboards painted white with yellow funnels and covered almost entirely with awnings.

'Carry two officers, six P.O.s and leading seamen, and seventeen able seamen,' Fanshawe explained as they made their way alongside by means of a sampan handled by a girl, whose crew consisted of a baby and a farmyard complement of chickens. 'In addition there's an official Chinese crew of five. But each one has his makee-learn and apprentices who keep the brightwork nice and tiddly and work simply for food and board. God knows how many there really are because they come out of the cracks like cockroaches at times. They all live in the tiller flat aft because there's no accommodation allowance for them, yet they still think they're well off. We maintain smartness, put down riots and try to avoid being drowned by the river or shot at by bandits, Communists or disbanded soldiery who have a nasty habit of removing beacons and buoys and waiting to loot the first ship that runs aground.'

'What about the other nations?'

'Don't count the French. Never have, of course. The Americans are inclined to a devil-may-care attitude. As for us, we're taut, with upper lips stiff as usual. Relations between us aren't always as cordial as they might be, because the French never did like us and the American admiral's an anglophobe.'

'You've got a chap called Rumbelo in the flotilla, I believe.'

'Petty officer?'

'Yes.'

'In *Spider*. At the moment she's upriver near Kiang Yin. Know him?'

'Very well. How's he enjoying life?'

'They *all* enjoy it. Not much to do except keep the paint blinding white and maintain the guns, which usually date back to 1898 and have never been seen outside a museum. The river's always difficult, of course, but there are a thousand miles of marshy reaches with the best rough shooting in the world, together with the usual bawdy delights of the oldest profession, to which you might ally the wives of taipans, to whom anything fresh out from England is a godsend.'

Headquarters' view of the situation seemed a little less ebullient than Fanshawe's. Shanghai was surrounded by the cancerous growths of Chinese towns, all of which, with corruption and bribery rampant, were examples of how towns should not be run. The streets reeked at night with opium fumes and the pungent scents of singsong girls and Russian streetwalkers, and police officers automatically took their pistols off the safety catch when going on duty. Though it was the centre of all Christian missionary effort in the country, it was also the centre of slavery, piracy and drugs. Every kind of currency was available and the city's constitution seemed to be founded on laissez-faire and little else.

There had been trouble in Wahnsien, followed by riots at Wuhan; and in an attempt to get it clear in his mind, Kelly took to sitting in his room in the evening with the army liaison officer and a glass of whisky, trying to find out all that was known of the situation. It was enough to confuse anybody.

'It's got to come soon,' the army officer said. 'The Chinese are beginning to realise that if it comes to the pinch we haven't a chance, and we wouldn't dare make a war of it, because world opinion's too much against us.'

Tyrwhitt arrived soon afterwards and Kelly met him in Hong Kong. He'd been inclined towards retirement and wasn't looking forward to his new job. He'd arrived at a bad time, too, because only three days before Kelly went on board *S.S.Moorea* to greet him a Chinese mob had attempted to enter the British Concession at Hankow and had only been kept out by a cordon of Marines and naval ratings. There had been no shooting but two days later, when the defence of the Settlement had been entrusted to Chinese troops, the mob had forced an entrance and most of the European women and children had had to be evacuated by river boat the same evening. The following day a similar crisis had occurred at Kiukiang, and though, in this case, the British women and children had already been cleared, the China Command was faced with the difficult task of trying both to follow up the British government's new policy of conciliatory negotiation and to take the necessary steps to protect British lives and property – particularly in Shanghai, the focus of international trade and one of the world's principal ports.

131

'You'd better brief me,' Tyrwhitt said, his heavy black eyebrows down as he glanced over his spectacles at the sheaf of signals with which Kelly had greeted him.

Kelly drew a deep breath. 'As C.-in-C., sir, you have the yacht, *Petersfield*, at your disposal and I suggest you transfer your family aboard as soon as possible. The destroyer *Despatch*'s standing by to take you to Shanghai.'

Tyrwhitt gestured angrily. 'I don't mean my own comforts, dammit! I mean the situation here.'

Kelly smiled. 'It's impossible to describe what it's like sir,' he said. 'Because it's impossible to describe chaos. Trouble for us has been going on since 1923 on and off. The old China hands seemed to do nothing but hoot their rage and disgust, but since many of them have been here all their lives and can't imagine being anywhere else, their attitude's less patriotic than selfish. They're expecting you to put things right.'

'Go on,' Tyrwhitt said bleakly.

'There's a ghost of a government in Peking clanking its chains,' Kelly went on. 'But no one takes any notice because another government in Canton passes bills and makes laws without reference to them. The only real source of money to either government's the Customs, which is run by the British, and the only stable thing seems to be the Chinese peasant who goes on working his plot of soil, raising his family, celebrating his festivals and trying to avoid starvation.'

Tyrwhitt pulled a face.

'The Yangtze's navigable,' Kelly continued. 'As far as Hankow for ocean-going ships – including destroyers – during the summer months when it's swollen by rainfall and the melting of the snow in Tibet, and for smaller craft at all times.' He handed over lists of gunboats, destroyers and cruisers. 'In addition to those, there's an aircraft carrier, twelve submarines and auxiliary vessels. The cruisers are due to be reinforced, three here at Hong Kong and five at Shanghai. The International Settlement has a police force and a volunteer corps, which is equipped with armoured cars, artillery and machine guns, but it's far too small for the situation now confronting it. This, sir, is rather an over-simplification but it puts the picture in a nutshell.'

'Well, I've been primed by all the various departmental views

132

of China already,' Tyrwhitt growled. 'Foreign Office. Admiralty. War Office. The lot. But I find it damned difficult to put them all in one bag. My brain's like a badly mixed pudding. It seems to me that what we want is not more ships but more men.'

'I think that sums it up exactly, sir.'

'Perhaps even a movable force of Marines.' Tyrwhitt's heavy eyebrows jerked. 'I'll transfer my family to the commander-in-chief's yacht and go to Shanghai. What's the situation there at the moment?'

'The Nationalists – that's the southern government's forces – are now advancing towards it, sir. Their policy's "Out with the foreigners" and they've sworn to take the concessions back, so that European fugitives are pouring into Shanghai from the upper Yangtze.'

Tyrwhitt sighed. 'I wish I knew what I was in for, my boy. Thank God you've been doing your homework.'

'Thank you, sir. The trouble in the Yangtze gorges at Wahnsien started when a Butterfield and Swire ship was boarded by armed soldiers. There was a bit of to-ing and fro-ing and Rear Admiral, Yangtze, commandeered a Jardine Mathieson ship to take up a naval party under the command of a Commander Darley. Unfortunately, Darley wasn't experienced on the river and the affair ended up as rather a shambles. Three officers and four ratings were killed, the naval party had to retire and the Chinese ran riot through the place when they'd gone.'

'Good God!'

'That's Hankow, sir. A mob attacked the settlement, but Marine and naval parties were put ashore to help the local volunteer force. They were obliged to fire into the crowd. The crowd ran away.'

'I'm surprised *our* chaps didn't run away What about Hankow now?'

'Cantonese army soldiers broke into the Hankow Race Club and picked all the flowers.'

'They did *what*?'

Kelly grinned. 'In any other country it would have been ridiculous but, in fact, it was a calculated defiance of the British, who regard it as their personal property. Marines were landed, barbed wire was erected and the crowd tried to rush it. Stones were thrown and a sailor was wounded and a rifle lost. Order was restored by the local police and the Chinese army. There was another riot the following day, started by students, but heavy rain damped their ardour a bit. Marines were landed again but three were wounded by missiles. It was like the Boxer Rising all over again.'

Tyrwhitt's eyes became bleak and Kelly hurried to reassure him. 'It's all right at the moment, sir,' he said. 'The students are busy with exams just now. But these riots are becoming different and I gather there's more trouble today at Kiukiang and they're expecting to have to abandon the concession.'

Tyrwhitt's great eyebrows worked again and Kelly found himself being studied beneath the corner of one of them. 'You been upriver yet, boy?' Tyrwhitt asked.

'No, sir. I've hardly had the time.'

Tyrwhitt grunted. 'Then you'd better pack a bag,' he said, 'because that's the first thing we're going to do.'

By the time they reached Shanghai, things had changed again. There seemed nothing now that could stop the advance of the Cantonese army, and the volunteer force in the city was clearly inadequate for its defence without reinforcement. The first thing Tyrwhitt did on arrival was to request a fully-equipped division at once before the Cantonese forces arrived.

'The alternatives,' he growled, 'seem to me to be evacuation peacefully at an early date or under fire later. The Consul-General's in entire agreement. I wish to God I'd never come, my boy, but thanks to you I'm beginning at last to grasp what's going on'

Moorea had also brought Verschoyle and Kimister, Kimister for a shore appointment, Verschoyle for command of *Wanderer*. Kelly met them in the Astor Hotel and bought them drinks, Verschoyle seemed to be in great form and was looking forward to whatever came along. Kimister, as uncertain as ever, was strangely smug, and not at all keen to be involved in massacre.

'Might not come to massacre,' Verschoyle said cheerfully. 'They might not kill *everybody*. Just you.'

There was a letter from Charley waiting for Kelly when he returned to headquarters. She seemed to have changed her mind again, and her words showed her indecision — as if, despite her doubts, she still couldn't throw off the habit of a lifetime. The shock came in the tail.

'I'm coming out to China in the *Carantic* to stay with the Belfrages,' she said. 'They're old friends of Mother's and they're bankers in Shanghai. Mabel's coming, too. She sold her share in the dress shop to pay the fare.'

To his surprise, because he'd thought he'd managed to forget her, Kelly found his heart thumping again and that same evening he went round to see the Fleet Chaplain. Over a gin and without naming names, he pumped him gently about marriage. The Fleet Chaplain had been at the game too long to be fooled.

'How long have you known the girl, my boy?' he asked.

Kelly gestured. 'It's not me.'

'No?'

'No. Chap I know on the staff. Too shy about the whole thing to make enquiries himself.'

The Chaplain laid a hand on Kelly's arm. 'Just don't worry, my boy. After all these years, we can guarantee that it will be absolutely painless.'

The following morning, Tyrwhitt started upriver for Hankow in the destroyer *Veteran*. At first the channel was marked by buoys and the shore on either side danced in a shimmering haze, but later the flat ground began to rise and from the destroyer's bridge it was possible to see dykes and scenes like ancient Chinese paintings. Then what had seemed at first to be an empty countryside began to come alive, and what had looked like a patch of dried-up earth began to seethe with blue-clad ants. Every now and then, curving roofs lifted over the banks of the river, some with tiles, others of tattered rush matting, then, as the bank dipped again, they could see into paddy fields where women in cotton clothes splashed through the muddy water to transplant the tender shoots.

Strings of pack horses headed upriver, flicking their ears and tails against the flies, then a wheelbarrow bus passed loaded with girls all giggling and laughing under sunshades. A sail had even been spread on it and the sweating coolie was loping along in a long-strided jog. As the bund dipped again, the destroyer's wash swilled through the open door of a hut, bringing out excited dogs, pigs and an angry woman hobbling on tiny bound

135

feet.

Finally the river became a ribbon of reddish-brown fringed by dark green, with rocks and banks hidden under surging waters, and they anchored at sunset with a falling breeze so that the heat stood in the corners of the ship as menacing as an assassin. It was a relief when the sun disappeared and the twilight descended in wide violet shadows.

The lights attracted insects by the million and Kelly had to wrap himself in a sheet to escape them when he went to bed. When a moth got inside his pyjama jacket, he sat up to avoid the stuffy mattress and lit a cigarette to keep the mosquitoes away but, as he reached for a glass of water, he saw his eye was already closed by a bite and he was finally driven on deck to get some air.

The shore had a mysterious look, all looming shapes pinpricked by small yellow lights, and overside he could hear the lap and gurgle of the river. The petty officer by the watchkeeper's compartment was staring at the shore. 'What do you make of it, Quartermaster?' Kelly asked.

The petty officer smiled. 'Chinese are all right, sir,' he said. 'Like everywhere else, it's the politicians that cause the trouble.'

Kelly smiled back. 'And how would *you* handle it?'

The petty officer's smile grew wider. 'Like a lover with all the night before him, sir – I wouldn't rush it.'

As they up-anchored the next morning, wooded mountains were visible, purple in the morning mist. Small hills ran down to meet the river, sometimes surmounted by a crumbling fort or a pagoda among the trees.

Chinkiang was the first of the treaty ports they came to and it looked like a miniature Shanghai. A union jack flew from the consulate flagstaff and there were cool-looking houses and gardens and a neat stretch of bund was completed by a club and tennis courts, tidy, sanitary and surrounded on three sides by a wall beyond which was the Chinese city. The consul came aboard to meet them, full of a story about one of the river boats which had been wrecked by the removal of a buoy. As it had struck, it had canted over and, with all its lower ports open, many Chinese had been drowned.

After a short briefing, the admiral transferred with his staff

136

aboard the gunboat, *Cockroach*, whose captain, Lieutenant Arthur Smart, was a shrewd young man who clearly enjoyed the river.

'It's a good life,' he said. 'There are always canteens for the troops where we stop – short on entertainment but long on beer – and we all have concert parties and perform when we take over from another ship. Same old jokes, of course, but so long as the faces are different it doesn't seem to matter. People are always glad to see us. The representatives of Butterfield and Swire, Jardine Mathieson, Clemo-Oriental and British-American Tobacco, which are the companies that really matter up here, lead a pretty monotonous life and, with the clubs pretty claustrophobic, they fight to get us to dinner.'

A junk they were following cut across their bows. It seemed like bad pilotage but the junk's crew seemed delighted with their daring and began to beat gongs and let off firecrackers. Smart was unmoved. 'If your bows are crossed,' he explained, 'you collect demons from the ship in front, and they've just got rid of their lot to us, and the crackers are because demons are a bit dim and don't like noise.' He looked at Kelly grinned. 'If I were you, sir, I'd keep my hat on. Demons have red hair and blue eyes and they're repulsive to Chinese.'

'They've been a bit repulsive in their time to a few Europeans,' Kelly said, thinking of his parting from Charley.

As they progressed further they met junks, foreign gunboats and river steamers full of refugees, then a huge raft of floating logs complete with people, dogs and huts steered downriver by sea anchors. Great flocks of ducks filled the sky as they passed through a series of lakes, then round a bend, Hankow came into sight, a large city with the tanks of the oil companies darkening the flat shores. There was an ocean-going cargo ship anchored offshore and, beyond the tall buildings of the bund, the smoky haze of the Chinese city. Even from midstream, they could see the façade of the Hong Kong and Shanghai Bank, strikingly modern in white stone, but there was only a road separating the British concession from the Chinese city, on one side of it Sikh police, sanitation and traffic regulations, on the other teeming life, humour and a reckless sprawling vitality.

There was still a lot of commotion going on in the town so that two British destroyers, a sloop and two gunboats were

137

lying alongside, and the Counsellor of the British Legation came aboard to report on discussions he'd been having with the Foreign Secretary of the Cantonese Government.

'The missionaries from the interior have been rounded up,' he told Tyrwhitt. 'But it's a bit of a thankless task because none of them wish to leave and I think some of them secretly relish martyrdom.'

'We want no shooting,' Tyrwhitt growled.

The Counsellor smiled. 'Oh, we've had that,' he pointed out cheerfully. 'But fortunately, there weren't many casualties because of the rotten aim of the Chinese and the home-made shells they use. Most of the abuse's directed at the British, of course.'

'Can't it be stopped?'

'We have to walk carefully. We don't use force because that's just what the Chinese want. The crowds are led by students who try to provoke us. If we react, they stop yelling and accuse us of bullying innocent people.'

With Smart to show him the ropes, Kelly went ashore near a building crowded with British and American sailors that carried a sign over the dark entrance – ENGLIƧH BEER. GIN. WIƧKY. GIRLƧ FOR ƧAILORƧ.

'The beer's lukewarm, of course,' Smart said. 'But the girls are pretty cool. Let's visit the other concessions. It'll give you an idea what it's like and you'll be lucky to get a rickshaw next time you come up. There's talk of a strike against the foreigners and even the prostitutes are threatening to join in.'

The French concession was guarded by small Annamite soldiers, and seemed to be marked by the smell of cooking, coffee and Caporal cigarettes. Next door, the houses had the barbaric splendour of Czarist Russia but the paint was peeling and the few Russians still living there dreamed only of the past. The German concession, now taken over by the Japanese, had the old German bombast about it, but the street was full of life and noise like the Chinese streets, though tawdry and somehow lacking stability, and an officious little officer in glasses demanded to know who they were.

'Aelwyn Urquhart MacGillicuddie,' Smart said. 'From Crossmichaels Loch, Kircudbrightshire. This is Llewellyn ap Gruffydd, from Pwlleli, Caernarvon.'

138

The Japanese officer struggled for a while to set the names down in a notebook but in the end he gave up in disgust and waved them on.

'Always foxes 'em,' Smart said cheerfully. 'They're such self-important little beasts, y'see, and we're going to have trouble with 'em before long.'

5

Tyrwhitt's trip upriver produced little beyond a clearer view of his command, while the negotiations at Hankow resulted only in the transfer of the Hankow and Kiukiang concessions to the Chinese and a resultant wail from the foreign communities who felt they'd been let down.

'They'll quieten down, sir, when the river allows us to send something big up to keep an eye on 'em,' Kelly pointed out.

'Better be *Vindictive* and *Carlisle*,' Tyrwhitt said. '*They* ought to make the Chinese think a bit. In the meantime, we just go on biting our nails until the troops we asked for arrive. They're giving us all we want. Three infantry brigades, two from Britain or the Med and one from India. There's also a battalion of Marines on its way, and a Punjabi battalion due for Hong Kong.'

'First Cruiser Squadron's also due for Hong Kong next month, sir.'

'I'd prefer it here. But at present it'd just be in the way. Besides – ' Tyrwhitt smiled ' – I'm not sure I want a second flag officer at my elbow. He's a bit of a fire-eater, and I gather he'd like to bombard Canton.'

Tyrwhitt's flagship, *Hawkins*, arrived soon afterwards. Tyrwhitt didn't like her very much. 'She's damn' wet,' he complained, 'and she vibrates badly at speed.' With her arrived more foreign warships as the nations lined up for the confrontation with the Chinese Nationalists. During February, the total in Shanghai rose from twenty-one to thirty-five, representing seven navies.

'Pity we can't manage to co-operate,' Kelly said to Verschoyle when they met in the Grips bar. 'But the French are being difficult and the Americans' orders are that if the

140

Nationalists arrive they're to embark their men, not fight. I think the whole trouble is that everybody resents the British Empire and wants to see us cut down to size.'

They ordered another drink and began to discuss Kimister.

'Saw him today,' Verschoyle said. 'Looked like a bird dog that had lost its bird.' He frowned. 'What *is* it about him? Sometimes he's enough to curdle milk, and he's about as good at his job as my grandmother's Pekingese is at rounding up sheep.'

'He's not so bloody inefficient at chasing Charley,' Kelly growled. 'Where's that damned drink?'

It was brought eventually by one of the under-managers. 'A little trouble with the Chinese staff,' he explained. 'They seem to have disappeared.'

When they left to return to the waterfront, they found it was not only the bar staff that had disappeared. There were no taxis or rickshaws to be seen and an army officer standing by the door with a hopeful expression informed them that they'd gone on strike.

The following day the strike had spread. Banners were being paraded, slogans chanted and windows smashed, while agitators whispered in the teashops, along the wharves and in the godowns, and orators ranted at the crowds on every street corner. Then reports came in of more unrest at Hankow. A Japanese sailor had been stabbed, and the Japanese had opened fire and killed a few labourers, but the malice was still directed not at them but at the British.

'We've got the wrong coloured skin for this part of the world,' Kelly observed.

'Have no fear,' Verschoyle smiled. 'Our turn'll come. Boil a merchant in oil or decapitate a missionary or two, and there'll be only dignified protests, notes and demands for satisfaction. But one day some white woman will be stripped to the buff and then – *then!* – you'll see us rise in wrath. Parliament will stand on the seats in the Commons, the British army will be mobilised and Tyrwhitt'll lead the battle fleet upriver to bombard the Nationalists with everything we've got.'

Despite Verschoyle's flippancy, the tension was marked. It seemed like a coiled spring and, with more trouble clearly brewing, plans were put in shape for the possible evacuation of all British and foreign nationals from upriver. Then, however, twenty-four hours earlier than expected, the first of the troopships from India arrived and the two British battalions clanked through the town, to the relieved cheers of the British population and the muttered resentment of the Chinese.

Tyrwhitt was in a better mood that evening. 'Seems to have done the trick,' he said. 'The Italians are now going to send troops, too, and I've just been informed that the Japanese also have men standing by ready to join us if necessary.'

The Punjabi battalion arrived the following week, strong, brawny men, heavily bearded with dark gleaming eyes. But the sporadic strikes grew worse. One day it was the dock labourers, next day the rickshaw men, the following day the taxi drivers or the tramway workers. The actions were deliberate and well organised so that the city was never able to function properly. The day after the arrival of the Punjabi battalion, there was a complete shut-down. Shops closed. Trams stopped. Taxis and rickshaws disappeared and the idle labourers from the docks hung about the street corners in threatening crowds, staring bitterly at the troops manning the essential services.

Units of the Shanghai Defence Force, supported by Italian Marines, moved out to form a cordon round the International Settlement, but when the new commanding general appeared on board *Hawkins* to meet Tyrwhitt, it appeared he intended to tread carefully and use words rather than firearms.

'Chief of staff seems able enough, though,' Kelly said. 'Viscount or something called Gort.'

'Met him.' Verschoyle, of course, knew everybody who mattered. 'Quite a soldier, I hear, but I'd have thought a bit intense for peacetime. Might be the result of his domestic troubles, of course. Wife left him. Spartan type. 'You'll probably find he likes to sleep on a bed of concrete hosed down nightly with cold water.'

By this time, Shanghai was so crowded with troops it was difficult to move without falling over them. There were eight British battalions, as well as Italians, Japanese and Americans, and a week later two more British battalions and another contingent of American Marines arrived. There was no unified command, however, and only the French had agreed to act in concert with the British in the event of trouble.

The retreat of the beaten Chinese northern army through the area bordering the foreign cordon took place without serious trouble. The soldiers were ragged, jaded and often bootless, their uniforms hanging off their lean bodies in folds, while their horses were nothing but skin and bone and their guns battered and dusty. Almost as they disappeared to the north, the Nationalists arrived, halting with their sun banners not far from the British lines. They looked confident, fit and well equipped, and the British stared at them curiously, trying to weigh them up. There were no incidents, however. The British had been warned by friendly Chinese what to expect and the city was an armed camp, with infantry and even artillery on high buildings, and armoured cars on regular patrols up and down the outlying roads where foreigners had their homes. On the only occasion when the Nationalists tried to enter the Settlement they were firmly turned back and the incident seemed to rouse not only the Americans, who sent Marines to assist, but also the municipal council, who allowed armed posts to be stationed outside the cordon to guard foreign properties beyond the settlement boundaries.

Watching the reports, Kelly found himself debating what to do about Charley. With each day, Shanghai seemed less and less a place to bring women to, and he sent a message via the shipping office in Hong Kong that they should disembark and remain in safety there for the time being. A message back informed him that *Carantic* had already left and as he returned aboard the flagship, another general strike was announced for the next day.

The following morning Nationalist troops broke through the cordon on the north of the settlement but were driven out by machine gun fire from two British armoured cars at the cost of four British casualties and an unknown number of Chinese. Another clash occurred soon afterwards at the station yard in Chapei, just outside the settlement, where sixty Chinese were killed or wounded, but the Nationalists seemed to be well in control and most of the trouble appeared to be stirred up by the Chinese Communist Party. Murders were being committed regularly, however, and sniping by Communist gunmen was taking place all the time, and five Punjabi soldiers were hit.

Carantic was due to arrive in two days' time and Kelly found

143

himself in a tizzy of nervousness. By this time, he'd made up his mind he'd pop the question before Charley could change her mind. She seemed in the mood to listen again and he knew it was now or never. It might even be a good idea, he decided, full of lust, to get her into bed somehow and seal the contract that way. That afternoon, however, reports arrived of trouble at Nanking. With *Wanderer* involved in a minor collision with another ship, which had scraped her paint, Verschoyle was aboard the flagship when the news came in.

'Who's Lord Clemo?' Kelly asked him.

'Uses the same club as my Old Man,' Verschoyle said. 'Claims to be a socialist thinker, though how he equates that with the money he's got I'm buggered if I know. He's Clemo-Oriental.'

'That's what I thought. How about Arthur Withinshawe? Know him?'

Verschoyle shrugged. 'Son-in-law. Rather a wet like Kimister. Clemo's daughter Christina's a bit of a cock-teaser. Know her well. Does a marvellous tango.'

'For God's sake man, keep to the point!'

Verschoyle smiled. 'Married him after she dropped George Ames. Found out he'd been tupping Nancy Averleigh and she chucked him in a rage and married her father's London under-manager, Withinshawe. Poor man never knew what hit him. I heard they were out here.'

'They are,' Kelly said flatly. 'At Nanking. And the buggers are missing.'

Tyrwhitt didn't receive the news of the new trouble cheerfully. He was quite clearly unhappy in China, and with one group of advisers itching to set about the Chinese in the old Victorian gunboat manner and the other terrified of losing lives, trade and possessions, he was torn two ways.

'This damn place's enough to drive a man mad,' he said.

'I'm afraid there's more, sir,' Kelly pointed out. 'There's trouble at Nanking. The Nationalists went in on the heels of the retreating northern army and ran wild, killing, looting and raping. Six non-Chinese – including the British harbourmaster, a French and an Italian priest, and a seaman from *Emerald* – have been murdered. The British consul-general, an officer of the Shanghai Defence Force, an American and several Japanese have been wounded, and houses have been looted and individuals stripped of their valuables and even their clothes. White women have been subjected to attempts to rape them.'

'What's been done?'

'*Emerald* and several American destroyers opened fire. They were firing for about seventy minutes according to the report. Various estimates on Chinese casualties. The rioting and shooting's stopped.'

'Go on.'

'The evacuation of foreigners is reported complete but it seems we had to threaten another bombardment before the Nationalist general would allow them to be brought to the waterfront. Foreign property's still being looted, and there are also attacks on property downriver at other places. They want to retaliate with another bombardment.'

'No!' Tyrwhitt's voice came in a bark of anger. 'Make a signal to *Emerald*. If the damn' man insists, I'll relieve him.'

'There's one other point, sir.'

'Go on.'

'It seems that, despite the report that all foreigners have been evacuated, some British nationals have *not*, in fact, been brought out. We have lists of names and there are some not among them. Chiefly a Mr. Arthur Withinshawe and his wife. She's the only daughter of Lord Clemo.'

'Who the devil's Lord Clemo?'

'Clemo-Oriental, sir. Big man in petrol. I understand from Lieutenant-Commander Verschoyle, who appears to know everybody worth knowing, that he has the ear of the Prime Minister and is a personal friend of the First Lord.'

Tyrwhitt turned, his eyes angry. 'Meaning that if I don't do something about it I'm likely to be in trouble. Do we know where they are?'

'It seems they were last heard of in Wu-Pi, sir. That's a small town further upriver. A non-treaty town, sir, recently captured by Nationalists. They have a house there.'

'Why the devil can't they stay where they can be protected? What do you suggest?'

'It seems to indicate someone going up to look for 'em, sir. I gather the Clemo-Oriental ship, *Swei-Fan*, was despatched to

145

bring 'em downriver but at some point during the night the Chinese boarded her, killed the captain and locked the rest of the white officers below. As far as I can make out, the Withinshawes are still trapped in their house further upriver. Lord Clemo's cutting up a little rough.'

'Is he, by God? Does he expect us to send the Marines in to fetch 'em out?'

'I suspect so, sir, but we have no rights there. It's officially Chinese territory.'

Tyrwhitt gestured angrily. 'Then surely we can't be held responsible for these damn people, can we?'

'I understand Lord Clemo thinks we can, sir.'

Tyrwhitt scowled. 'Go on.'

'I think it's got to be a small party, sir.'

'How small?'

'Two or three. No more. With one of them an expert Chinese speaker.'

Tyrwhitt stared at Kelly for a moment. 'Only one man I'd chance for this,' he said.

'Who, sir?'

'You.'

Despite Kelly's protests, Tyrwhitt was adamant.

'But, sir!' Kelly's voice became a bleat. 'I have my fiancée arriving in the next day or two.'

Tyrwhitt swung round to face him. 'Surely to God she can wait, boy?'

'I'm not so sure she can, sir.'

Tyrwhitt glared. 'Then you'd better delegate one of your friends to keep her entertained until you return. I want someone up at Nanking who knows exactly how I feel.'

Kelly drew a deep breath. 'Very well, sir.'

'And there's no need for heavy breathing. It's got to be done. Who're you taking?'

Kelly didn't hesitate. Rumbelo was in *Spider*, he knew, and *Spider* was near Kiang Yin. 'Just one good interpreter, sir. For the rest I can draw on the crews up there.'

Tyrwhitt waved a hand. 'Very well. Get on with it. *Wanderer*'s due to relieve *Opal* at Kiukiang so you'd better make the passage in her.'

The problem of what to do about Charley worried Kelly. Oddly enough, he felt he might have entrusted her to Verschoyle, who seemed to have a soft spot for her, but Verschoyle would be upriver, too, and Fanshawe was due to follow them. It only seemed to leave Kimister.

As he outlined what he had in his mind, Kimister said nothing. He'd heard of Charley's visit from his mother and, though her last letter had given him little encouragement, he fully intended to see her.

'Leave it to me,' he said.

The interpreter who'd been assigned to the project was a man called Balodin, the son of an Anglo-Russian father and a Chinese mother. He was a sturdy, intelligent-looking man with the jet black hair and lemon skin of a Chinese, and he showed Kelly where he could obtain a twelve-shot Luger to match his own.

On board *Wanderer*, Verschoyle led Kelly to his cabin. 'Who's going to look after the Little 'Un while you're away?' he asked.

'Kimister,' Kelly said, and to his surprise Verschoyle's smile died.

For a moment he said nothing, then, hoisting his glass, he spoke with forced cheerfulness. 'Here's to success,' he said.

Kelly frowned. 'Are you getting at something?' he demanded.

'Why should I?' Verschoyle was all innocence.

'There's something on your mind. You always were a dirty dog, Cruiser.'

'Well, it's true, I always did believe in trampling on the silly little skulls of smaller men to make my way to the top. But not you. Not you, old boy. I saw you come back from Jutland, remember? That's where it stopped.'

'Then, for God's sake, say what you're thinking.'

'Look – ' for the first time in his life Kelly saw Verschoyle looking uncomfortable ' – leave it alone. It's nothing.'

'It must be something. Or you wouldn't have said "It's nothing."'

Verschoyle frowned. 'I didn't say a word. Only "Here's to success."'

Kelly was beginning to lose his temper. 'There was a lot you

147

didn't say!'

'For God's sake man,' Verschoyle snapped. 'It's none of my damn business!'

'What isn't?'

'Look, I don't want to cause trouble, but I think it's a pity you can't find someone other than bloody Kimister to meet your Little 'Un.'

'Why *not* Kimister?'

'I wouldn't trust him, that's all. You forget Sister Mabel and I are like that.' Verschoyle held up two fingers close together. 'Always mentally and very often physically. Mabel's a bit of a shyster like me. But she's got her sister's welfare at heart. She always thought she needed her head examining to feel the way she did about someone like you who's spent most of his career trying to get himself killed. But, in the perverse way of women, she also wants the Little 'Un to get you to the post.'

Kelly stared. 'What are you getting at?'

'Girls weep on their sisters' shoulders. And then the sisters weep on their boy friends'. Mabel doesn't like Kimister.'

'Why not?'

'It seems that when you moved out, he moved in.'

'Moved in?'

'For God's sake, perhaps she got it wrong.' Verschoyle sounded harassed and unhappy. 'Perhaps there's nothing in it. You know what Mabel's like.'

'Yes, I do. What was she suggesting? That Charley and Kimister – ?'

'I wish to God I'd kept out of this.' Verschoyle sighed and nodded. 'Yes,' he said.

Kelly stared at him, shocked and bewildered. After a lifetime of certainty, he'd been shaken to discover that Charley could give him marching orders, but to find that she could turn to Kimister for satisfaction shook him to the core.

'You mean – ?'

Verschoyle nodded.

'The whole bloody hog?'

'Oh, Christ! Yes! That's what Mabel said! But, for God's sake, take no notice! Even if it's right, perhaps the poor girl got a bit sick of waiting for you. You weren't exactly home much. And she didn't ask what *you'd* been up to, I'll be bound. Surely you're adult enough to accept it.'

Kelly wasn't sure he was. He'd seen a few idols toppled in his life, but there'd never been such a resounding crash as this time. He felt resentful, cheated and, remembering Charley's letters, bitter.

'How about me putting you ashore to find someone else?' Verschoyle suggested.

'No!' Kelly's face was sullen. 'If it's Albert Kimister she wants, then it had better be Albert Bloody Kimister.'

'I think you're making a damn great mistake.'

'I shall know that when I return.'

Verschoyle sighed and shrugged. 'Have it your own way. There's nothing so blasted stubborn as an honourable man who sees honour go astray in his friends. I think you're a bloody fool.'

Ten minutes later, still scowling, still shaken, still uncertain, Kelly joined Balodin on *Wanderer*'s stern and spent half an hour near the A.P.C. wharf as the ship oiled, shooting at rubbish in the harbour to check how the Luger threw its bullets.

A P. and O. boat downriver gave a gloomy hoot as it prepared to sail and Verschoyle appeared on the bridge. 'Firing practice finished?' he asked blandly. He appeared to have forgotten their argument.

'Yes,' Kelly snapped.

'Right. Well, we have the "go ahead" from the flagship, so I think it's time we were off.' Verschoyle stared forward. 'All ready on the forecastle?'

'All ready, sir!'

'Slip!' As the buoy cable clattered free, Verschoyle turned to the officer of the watch. 'Half ahead together. Take her away, Coxswain.'

6

They ran into the first refugees at Kiang Yin downriver from Nanking. They were boarding a river steamer with all their belongings and were in no mood to be helpful. They'd lost practically everything they possessed and considered the British government – with whom they lumped the navy, the army and the air force – had let them down. The consul-general's assistant, who appeared with the Senior Naval Officer, a lieutenant-commander from the gunboat flotilla, talked to Kelly in his cabin – and none too willingly because he shared the general view.

'Things had quietened down,' he complained. 'And some of those people who'd refugeed had returned. Then the Nationalists arrived and they were cock-a-hoop and thought they could carry everything before them. We took refuge in a B. and S. hulk in the river and buildings outside the walls.'

'An attempt was made to land Marines.' The naval officer took up the chant. 'But the Chinese had armed sentries at the city gate. We got 'em in by sending 'em through three at a time by taxi.'

'Nobody expected trouble,' the consul's assistant joined in again. 'In the end we decided that complete evacuation was the best.'

'It was bloody hard getting our Marines out again, too.' The lieutenant commander seemed to think they'd been let down. 'And one seaman was shot dead by a sniper. The consulate was looted, and the consul-general was wounded and held to ransom with his wife and the female staff. They were in the building for thirty-one hours and the women were subjected to the grossest indignities. They also tried to loot the American consulate, but the Americans, of course, bought them off with

150

money.'

He sounded almost as if he resented the Americans' wealth and Kelly wondered why the British hadn't thought of that simple solution.

'What about Wu-Pi?'

The lieutenant-commander looked startled. 'Wu-Pi's nothing to do with us.'

'It is with *me*,' Kelly said. 'I'm looking for Mr. and Mrs. Withinshawe.'

'That woman!' The consul's secretary looked bitter. 'They were warned to head for Nanking and the Consulate but they didn't come. Now I hear they've lost the *Swei-Fan*. If you're thinking of trying to get 'em out, you'll never do it. The mob's out up there and the Nationalists are on the rampage.'

At Nanking feelings were running even higher. The river seemed to be full of warships, from a cruiser down to the little flatiron-like gunboats, and the S.N.O., the captain of the cruiser, *Coronet*, was suffering from a great deal of anxiety because of the disappearance of the Withinshawes and the reported arrival in the vicinity of a string of missionaries and their families from up-country who'd got lost. He had sent the gunboat, *Spider*, up the previous afternoon to find them and bring them off, but the decision had been promptly slammed back in his face, because *Spider* was now trapped and aground just beyond Wu-Pi with her captain, coxswain and one rating killed by a shell, and four more men wounded, two of them seriously.

Kelly frowned, thinking of Rumbelo. 'Names, sir?'

The S.N.O. shook his head. 'No names yet,' he said. 'Apart from the captain. I'm considering sending *Emerald* up to fetch her out, but they've got a battery on the point, and I'm still trying to decide the best way to go about it?'

'Think the operation could be delayed for a while, sir?'

'Why?'

'I'd like to be put aboard *Spider*. I've been sent up to find the Withinshawes, and I might also turn up your lost missionaries.'

The S.N.O. eyed Kelly dubiously. He was itching to do someone some damage, 'It might be possible,' he agreed. 'They're letting us send a surgeon up to *Spider's* wounded, and I can get *Centipede* up to the bend under a white flag. We can put the doctor aboard *Spider* by motor boat. How many of you are there?'

'Two.'

The S.N.O. nodded. 'You'll have to hide under a tarpaulin. We'll do the job at dusk and put you aboard near the hatch on the side away from the shore. We're sending extra blankets up so we'll get the crew to stand by to take them aboard. You ought to be able to slip among 'em in the confusion.'

The surgeon, a lieutenant called Chadwick, seemed frighteningly young, as though he were just out of medical school, but he was quite calm and entirely unperturbable.

'Get hold of the Sub,' Kelly instructed him as *Centipede*'s boat drew away. 'Tell him you want every man on deck, because they'll be watching from the shore with binoculars.'

Spider lay with her bows on the mud, opposite a barrier of oil drums, logs and overturned carts the Chinese had erected on the bund, a blackened scorch mark just behind the bridge where the shell which had killed her captain had burst. No attempt had been made to clean up the decks and they could see the wreckage still alongside the wheelhouse.

Just below her downstream, the Clemo-Oriental ship, *Swei-Fan*, a medium-sized cargo vessel, lay in midstream. Occasionally a Chinese soldier moved along the deck but otherwise she looked deserted, one of her davits empty as if the boat had been stolen. The town was ominously quiet, though occasionally they heard yells from the mob still prowling the streets, and there were several columns of smoke from burning houses lifting slowly into the sky.

As they arrived alongside *Spider*, a youthful-looking sub-lieutenant, who seemed to be scared stiff, appeared from below.

'Better hurry,' he urged.

'Get your men on deck, Sub,' Chadwick said. 'We have blankets.'

'Push 'em up. I'll get a couple of chaps.'

'Turn 'em all out. Those are my instructions.'

'Just for a pile of blankets and medical supplies?'

Kelly pushed his head out from under the tarpaulin. 'For Christ's sake, Sub, do as you're told!'

The sub-lieutenant jumped and a few minutes later two

152

dozen men were assembled on the deck, none of them Rumbelo, Kelly noticed. There were a few uncomplimentary comments about the number it had been necessary to turn out for so few supplies and Kelly's head appeared once more.

'Shut your rattle,' he snapped. 'And stay in a bunch! Hop aboard, Balodin, and get out of sight!'

As the interpreter vanished among the crowded sailors, Kelly turned to the doctor. 'Right, Doc, it's all yours. Make as much fuss about your blankets as possible so they can see 'em from the shore.'

As Chadwick nodded, he dived between the groups of sailors and vanished below. Balodin was waiting in the alleyway leading to the captain's cabin, being greeted by the ship's dog.

'At least one of 'em's got his tail up,' he observed.

The Sub, a youngster called Gregory, looked as though he'd only just passed his examinations and, with three bodies awaiting burial and four wounded men whose condition was growing more and more distressing, he was white and strained.

There had been no sign of Rumbelo and Kelly was growing anxious. 'Let's go and see the wounded,' he said.

The four injured men, all punctured by shell splinters and in great pain, were in the wardroom where an emergency dressing station had been set up. Outside the door, twisted metal and shattered glass littered the alley and water from burst pipes swilled about. There was a stink of blocked heads and ether from the wrecked sick bay, but the burly figure bending over one of the injured men with a needle and gut was familiar and Kelly breathed a sigh of relief. As he entered, the figure straightened up, and a face as featureless as a potato stared at Kelly then broke into a wide grin.

'Mr. Kelly, sir!' Rumbelo said. 'This is a surprise, and no mistake.'

Kelly handed out the chocolate and cigarettes he'd brought with him and in the faces of the injured men there was a look of mingled gratitude, relief and reassurance.

'We'll soon have you out of here,' he said.

Outside Rumbelo was waiting for him. The long years of intelligent discipline, experience, humour and pride in the Service to which he'd devoted his life had left their traces in a self-confident unflapability.

'The engines are all right, sir,' he said. 'And the steering's all right, too. No reason at all why we shouldn't get off here under our own steam.'

Kelly smiled. 'That's what I like to hear, Rumbelo. How badly are we aground?'

'Held by the bows, sir. But there's plenty of water round us if we can only reach it. We only draw four and a half feet.'

'How about the hull?'

'Leaks a bit, sir. A few holes. But nothing to worry about.'

'Right. Let's have 'em plugged with hammocks and bedding and shored up with mess tables and timber.'

Heading for the bridge, Kelly found the Sub waiting for him. He was nervous and worried. 'The Chinese crew all jumped overboard and left us,' he announced.

'Dry your tears, Sub,' Kelly snapped. 'We ran ships without Chinese before. We're going to take *Spider* out of here.'

Gregory seemed inconsolable. 'There's no chart, sir, and we're short of men.'

'And the ship's covered with rubbish, broken glass and debris!' Kelly retorted. 'To say nothing of blood everywhere! I think you should pull yourself together and get her cleaned up! Let's have a start made as soon as possible. In the meantime, I'd like to see the Chief.'

'Chief E.R.A. Dover, sir. I'll take you to him.'

'No, you won't! You'll bring him to *me*. I'll be in the captain's cabin.'

'I'll go and fetch him.'

'For God's sake, Sub,' Kelly snapped. 'Pull yourself together! Until I came you were captain of this bloody ship! The captain doesn't run messages. Send someone.'

Chief E.R.A. Dover was a tall black-browed man who seemed to dislike the sub-lieutenant. He gave a brief factual report that bore out what Rumbelo had said.

'How about pumps?' Kelly asked.

'Damaged, sir. But they'll be working again any time. There's also been a lot of damage to the electrics and with engines shut down there's no power available. Some of the lights, ventilators, and other gear aren't working either, because we haven't enough insulating tape on board to cover the damage to cables and some of the repairs'll have to be left bare.'

'What about radio?'

'Out, sir. Wireless office smashed. Wireless operator among the dead.'

'Right.' Kelly slapped at a mosquito and looked at Gregory. 'There seems to be a lot of animal life aboard, Sub. Can we do anything about it?'

'We have Flit sprays, sir.'

'Break 'em out. How about rats?'

'All ships have rats, sir.'

'We have a dog. See he earns his keep. How about fans, Chief? It's hot on board.'

'The shell did a lot of damage, sir, but I'll have 'em working soon.'

'Right. Well, we're going to take her off as soon as I've finished what I have to do ashore. So we'll make a start by having the boilers flashed up. As soon as it's dusk, Sub, get the bamboos out and sound round the ship. We'll also have the bows lightened. Everything that can be moved aft's to be moved. But it's to be done after dark so those buggers ashore suspect nothing. I also want the anchor cables prepared so we can slip 'em in a hurry if we need to lighten the bows further at the last minute. How about drinking water?'

'Going down, sir.'

'Ration it. A pint a day per man. How does that sound?'

Dover grinned. 'We'll arrive home ponging a bit, sir.'

'So long as we arrive home, I don't think anybody'll complain.'

As it grew dusk, the bamboo poles appeared and Rumbelo found a depth of three and a half feet round the bows and four feet in other places, though in one patch on the port side the water barely covered the tip of the pole.

'Looks like we're 'ere for keeps,' the seaman who was doing the sounding said gloomily.

'Don't you believe it,' Kelly snapped. 'Get the sampan lowered and let's have some soundings away from the ship.'

The sampan soundings showed deep water running out to midstream along a narrow channel, and Kelly turned to Gregory. 'Shove a kedge on a three-and-a-half wire hawser out into midstream along that channel so we can haul off when we're

155

ready. Get it done before daylight, and keep the cables slack enough to be out of sight below water.'

'Aye aye, sir.'

'And let's have the chap in my cabin who runs the ship's concert party.'

The sailor who ran the concert part was a grizzled little man with a creased neck and a nutcracker face.

'Able Seamen Donkin, sir. I'm the resident comic. I do a soft shoe shuffle to *Japanese Sandman*. It goes down well.'

'I've no doubt. Well, we might want the use of your props. Got any greasepaint?'

'Plenty, sir. We put on a neat little cross-talk act between a chap dressed as an officer and a Chinese makee-washee man. The officer's laundry's gone missing.'

'I bet it's killing,' Kelly said dryly. 'Got enough for three people to be made up like Chinese?'

'Oh, yes, sir. We having a show?'

'No, you bloody idiot! I want to go ashore.'

The ship lay in silence. Beyond the bund was China proper, not the veneer of Shanghai or even Hankow. The looting and raping were still going on, but the worst was over and the town looked as dirty as it smelled, a bouquet of open sewers and the rotting corpses of dogs, cats and abandoned female infants. It was raining and the people moving up and down the bund carried umbrellas of bamboo and oiled paper, and there were none of the taipans in private rickshaws or elegant ladies carried on the shoulders of bearers. Here it was only sweating coolies, carrying loads on springy poles which raised orange-sized callouses on their bare shoulders, gaping soldiers in ill-fitting uniforms, and occasionally some wretched man pursued by a screaming mob hurling abuse, dung and stones.

Watching the nervous crowds moving agitatedly along the shore, their eyes on the stranded ship, Kelly arranged for the machine guns to be quietly mounted and unobtrusively manned.

'We'd best take no chances, Sub,' he warned. 'When I go ashore, you'll be in charge, so keep your head and let's have no shooting. I don't want to stir the bloody place up, I want to calm it down. Can the battery touch us here?'

156

'No, sir. The bank hides us. They'll be after us if we try to move downriver, though.'

The rain stopped and the sun raced up, a blinding glare on the water. The heat shimmered over the land and the mountain behind the town reared like a blue shadow out of the plain. There were still yells from the town and men with rifles patrolled the shore. At midday, along the roadway opposite the ship where the town's refuse was dumped, the crowd began to thicken and the stream of coolies came to a stop.

'Now what?'

'Executions,' Gregory said in a strained voice.

'Of whom?'

'Chinese, sir, who've been working for the British.' Gregory looked shaken. 'This is the second time they've done it.'

Soldiers appeared and began to push the crowd back, and one of them began to place nine stones in a row along the flat stretch of the foreshore near the barrier of carts and drums. Through the line of spectators, two men were pushed. They were fat and their wrists were bound cruelly behind their backs to their ankles so that they had to walk with bent knees. They were forced to kneel by the end stones, which had been placed directly opposite the ship, then seven more men appeared at intervals, all dressed in white, one man to each of the remaining stones. More soldiers arrived, escorting a tall man dressed in the blue denim of a coolie, who carried a huge two-handed sword decorated with tassles.

'Oh, Christ,' Donkin murmured. ' 'Ere we go again.'

There was a hush as the escorting soldiers stepped back. The nine men in white didn't move. Then an officer stepped forward and, drawing a heavy revolver from his holster he walked up to the nearest man and placed the muzzle to the back of his head. As the shot rang out, the man's skull seemed to burst apart and the body was flung forward across the stone. There was no sound from the crowd as the officer walked along the line, solemnly shooting five more of the men. At the sixth, he handed the revolver to a sergeant who exchanged it for another and the seventh man was despatched.

They watched from *Spider* with angry eyes. Then the man with the sword stepped up to the two fat men, the sun glinting on the metal.

157

'The last bribe is to the officer,' Balodin said. 'So they can die with the dignity of a beheading.'

As the escorting soldiers stepped out of the way, the big coolie spat on his hands, and the whirling sword flashed as the sun caught it. Then, measuring the distance, the coolie rushed forward with a scream. Automatically, it seemed, the kneeling man inclined his head to one side, and as the sword swept down there was a loud snick that came across the water quite clearly, and the head hurtled yards from the trunk to come to rest on a pile of rubbish, the eyes still blinking, the mouth still twitching. Spurting blood, the body remained kneeling for a second then it overbalanced. The last man's head landed at the foot of a soldier who indifferently kicked it aside.

As the ninth man toppled forward, the crowd began to disperse and the soldiers and executioners moved away. The procession of coolies started again, passing the bodies without even looking at them. For a while everything was quiet, then wailing women appeared, and, picking up the heads, began to sew them back on the bodies.

'Can't face their ancestors without their heads,' Balodin said dryly. 'They'd lose face.' He gave a stiff smile. 'No pun intended, of course.'

As coolies appeared with coffins, they all retreated below deck again, keeping out of sight. When it was dark, Kelly moved quietly round the stern, checking the kedges that had been put out. Then he called Gregory, the Chief E.R.A. and Rumbelo to the captain's cabin.

'What we're going to do has got to be fast,' he said. 'I'm taking Petty Officer Rumbelo and Mr. Balodin with me and I hope to be back tonight or tomorrow night. If I'm not, you'll just have to sit tight. I shan't be wanting to move except after dark, so see you have steam for a quick take-off, Chief, whatever night it is. Right?'

'Right, sir.'

'In the meantime, Sub, we'll have screens placed along the deck ready to be raised after dark, to give us a more solid look. Like a three-tiered passenger ship, for instance. Gunboats look like gunboats in anybody's language.'

It was after midnight when Kelly, Rumbelo and Balodin, dressed in Donkin's concert party rigs and with their faces daubed with mud, clambered over the bow and hurried up the bank. There was no movement along the bund but there were fires where coolies slept, and here and there the plink-plonk of a stringed instrument and the breathy whistle of a flute or the thump of a gong; further along the dim glow of a lantern showed where the sentries waited by the barrier.

A thin sliver of moon was picking up the squares of the paddy fields and they could see the rushes stark against the water. Over the centre of the town there was a glow in the sky where fires lit three days before were burning themselves out, and occasionally they heard a howl from the mob prowling about the streets.

Nationalist shells had smashed the great studded gate in the river wall and, groping their way over the stones by the light of a hanging lantern, they skirted the houses and broken-down hovels, to scramble over a cascade of bricks and head down an alley, hardly daring to breathe. The place was ominously quiet and every door and window was shuttered and barred, the inhabitants out of sight and praying for daylight.

The sound of the mob still rose and fell in the distance as they splashed through stinking patches of water, holding their breath at the smell of sewage, ordure and years-old rotting rubbish. A puddle reflected the moon and the shape of houses in silhouette, then they were stumbling in and out of ditches and falling over broken masonry and charred beams back to the bund beyond the barrier. There was a smell of burning everywhere and a stink of death from the rubble, and several times they heard rats squeaking and the scrape of their claws over the stones.

The Withinshawe house was outside the town and close to the river. Weeping willows overhung the stone banks and they could hear the water lapping alongside. Occasionally a dog barked and once a whole lot of wild ducks started honking loudly. Here, the path was muddy, and night birds swooped about seeking the mosquitoes, passing close to their heads with the whirr of wings.

Then they saw a pagoda-like building with decorative gardens now trampled by dozens of feet, and as they reached it they saw a faint glimmer of light through the windows. As they tapped on the door there was a scream from inside.

159

'Open up!' Kelly said quietly. 'It's the Navy!'

There was a long silence then they heard bolts being drawn. As they stepped inside, Kelly became aware at once not of one or two people but of many. A curtain was put across the windows and a wick in a saucer of bean oil was lit. By its light he saw the room had been wrecked and the windows smashed by looters. It seemed to be full of men, women and children, most of them dressed like himself in the padded clothes of coolies.

'Who the devil are you?' Kelly asked.

A tall man with a red face and mad blue eyes rose from his knees. 'I'm the Reverend Donald MacIntyre,' he announced in a strong Scottish accent. 'Presbyterian Foreign Bible Society. My wife an' bairn are here, too, and two American families. There's also a Dutch family and two Irish nuns. Seventeen souls. There are also eleven Chinese converts. We cannae leave them behind. They'll be murdered.'

'Where are the people who own this house?'

MacIntyre didn't seem to think it was any part of his duty to worry about the safety of anybody else, but somebody plucked at Kelly's sleeve and an old Chinese, bent and yellow, a whisp of white beard on his chin, looked up at him with slant black eyes. He whispered something Kelly didn't catch.

'What's he say?'

'He says he's the gardener,' Balodin translated, 'and that Withinshawe was beaten to death by Nationalist soldiers. Mrs. Withinshawe, her small son and two more British who came to persuade her to leave are in the *Swei-Fan*. He carried their things aboard. They were expecting to leave at first light the following morning, but that night the Chinese boarded her.'

Things seemed to be growing complicated, and Kelly saw that his simple plan for rescue was going to need amending. Plucking people from a captured ship was a very different kettle of fish from leading them to safety along the river bank.

He drew a deep breath and looked at Balodin.

'Are they, by God,' he said. 'Well, that makes things a bit bloody awkward, doesn't it?'

7

The noise in the town seemed to have died down during the night and the mob appeared to have dispersed.

As soon as it was daylight, Kelly began studying the river through the closed shutters. He could just see *Spider* to his left wedged on the mud. Beyond her downstream was *Swei-Fan*, desolate-looking and deserted except for one man who was lounging in the sun, shaded by an umbrella. Later during the morning a few Chinese soldiers in grey uniforms and bus conductor's hats appeared, but there seemed to be no discipline and no look-outs. Whatever other men were on board, they were certainly not very obvious and he hoped they'd found the ship's liquor stores and were drunk.

'See any Europeans?' he asked Rumbelo.

'No, sir. Just the slopehead on the stern with the sunshade.'

'Let's hope he sleeps deeply.'

Clouds formed around noon and during the afternoon it began to rain heavily.

'Just what we need,' Balodin said. 'It'll keep people away from the bund.'

They called the missionaries together and told them to gather their belongings, and Rumbelo vanished into the rain as dusk fell. He was back within two hours with three of *Spider's* seamen, all complaining less about the danger than about the weather. They were led by Able Seaman Donkin, looking vaguely like Mr. Punch, and all carried rifles and were dressed to kill in gaiters, bandoleers and bayonets, with that portion of the day's rations that orders insisted they should carry when away on duty from the ship.

'Screens ready to go up round the fore and after decks, sir,' Donkin reported. 'Christ knows what the slopeheads'll think

161

we are if they see us. Probably the Gosport ferry.'

'Right,' Kelly said. 'Get this lot formed up, Donkin, and lead off with Mr. Balodin. I'll bring up the rear with Petty Officer Rumbelo.'

Led by Donkin, the procession moved off. It wasn't easy getting the missionaries across the mud and up *Spider*'s side. They were an unhandy lot with their bags and Bibles, and fell over things as they climbed aboard; and there was one sudden affronted silence as Donkin jerked his foot away from MacIntyre's boot.

'That's my fucking toe!' he complained.

They got them all aboard at last, more or less in silence. Chief E.R.A. Dover was waiting in the rain with Gregory as Kelly appeared.

'All ready, sir,' he announced.

'Good. This has got to be fast, Chief. Is there steam on the winches?'

'As much as you need, sir.'

Kelly peered through the rain at the dark shape of *Swei-Fan*.

'Right,' he said. 'I want an armed party, Sub. It seems the people we came for are aboard *Swei-Fan*. It looks as if we've got to board her.'

Gregory's face changed, but he said nothing and Kelly went on quietly.

'Make it as many men as we can spare. Break out all the cutlasses and revolvers we've got. After that, pick handles, because, for what we're going to do, rifles'll be a bit unhandy. How many men can we manage?'

Gregory looked at Dover then back at Kelly. 'Sixteen, sir? Perhaps eighteen. That just leaves the engine room crew and the party on the bow.'

'Good. I'm going alongside. Any idea how many Chinese there are?'

'Thirty-odd, I reckon, sir,' Gregory said. 'We've seen no more go aboard.'

'We can handle that lot, I think. This rain ought to keep 'em below. When I've got her, I'm going to tow her away alongside. I'll want warps ready to go across at once, and it'll have to be done while the boarding party's still chasing out the Chinese. As soon as they're in place, I'm going to slip her cable and take her downstream with us. It's only a couple of miles to the corner and once round we're safe. As soon as we're aboard I hope to be able to release the officers and any of the crew who're left. To get off the mud, I shall go full astern and have the winches hauling at the same time. Petty Officer Rumbelo will look after the kedges. Any obstructions in midstream, Sub?'

'None on the chart, sir.'

'Right. Rumbelo, pick your men and get aft. And when you go aboard *Swei-Fan*, for God's sake be careful. If anything happens to you I've got to face Biddy. Sub, let's have the guns manned. If they spot us, they might just try to board us. We'll have the passengers below. And make 'em be quiet. No lights. No hymn singing. No praying. I think the Almighty'll forgive 'em just this once.'

The rain was falling in torrents as Kelly climbed to the bridge with Gregory. He had changed back into uniform and wore a steel helmet and the Luger. Spitting the rain from his lips, he stared at the compass and bridge telegraphs.

'Everybody in his place, Sub?'

'Yes, sir. Everybody's ready?'

Drawing a deep breath, Kelly looked round him. 'Slow astern both, Sub.'

There was the low thump of machinery and, as the gush of the water boiling under the stern came to him, he heard the capstan clank and Rumbelo call out softly.

The telegraph clanged. The thump of the engines grew faster and the clatter of the capstan increased. The bight of the hawser leading to the kedge leapt out of the water with a spatter of drops and a loud twang as the strain came on. The engines were going full astern now and a dirty grey-looking froth floated forward as the screws churned uselessly at the mud.

'Stop both!' A bell tinkled and the vibration ceased. Gregory peered over the side. 'Cut-off's going to be all silted up, sir.'

'Never mind that,' Kelly said. 'Get a sounding aft.'

As Gregory vanished he heard Rumbelo's voice giving quiet orders. 'Get them bamboos out.'

The sounding showed no result and Kelly frowned.

'We'll have another go,' he said. 'And let's hope she unsticks this time. They'll be waking up ashore soon.'

163

As the engines thumped again the capstan began to groan. The wire tautened slowly once more then whipped out of the water, vibrating madly. Lights appeared in the darkness on the bund.

'Machine gunner, watch those lights.' Kelly called out. 'Don't shoot yet. Just report what's happening.'

'Aye aye, sir.'

'Stand by, Quartermaster.'

'Stand by, sir.'

'Full astern, Sub.'

Watching the mud alongside, Kelly held his breath. Would the wire part or would the ship move?

The capstan groaned and coughed.

'More steam.'

'Got all I dare give her, sir,' the stoker at the capstan valve said.

'We'll take a chance. Give her the lot.'

The splice in the end of the hawser began to twist and turn; then the wire became a thin steel bar, humming and singing. The gunboat trembled and smoke poured from the funnel in black greasy clouds, curling like snakes. The water from the stern raced along the side as if she were moving, rushing and boiling as it surged forward.

'How's it going, Sub?'

'No movement yet, sir.'

Kelly put his head over the edge of the bridge. 'Come on, you bastard,' he muttered. He'd look a proper fool if she didn't move and they were still there in the morning.

'Let go the anchors!'

There was a sharp clang as the man with the sledge swung at the pin of the shackle holding the port anchor cable, then a splash and a roar as the cable ran out through the hawse-hole. The sound was repeated for the starboard anchor and they felt the bow lift as it was relieved of the weight.

'She's moving, sir!' Rumbelo's voice came hoarsely along the deck and Kelly's heart leapt. Then there was a different shiver from the ship. The hawser dipped suddenly, splashing into the water with a loud thwack, then leapt out again.

'Haul it in,' Rumbelo yelled. 'She's moving! Have it out of the way of the screws!'

'Half astern!' Kelly shouted. 'Keep those winches going, Rumbelo! Let me know when we're clear, Sub.'

Spider was moving quite distinctly now, sliding off the mud, still slowly but gathering speed all the time. Then suddenly she seemed to settle herself comfortably like a duck taking to the water, until finally she was afloat and swinging round, alive once more, a ship. A faint cheer came from aft.

'I thought we'd pull the bloody capstan out of the deck, sir,' Dover said with a sigh of relief.

Kelly grinned. 'Let's hope we don't need it again. We've probably wrecked it. Port a fraction, Q.M. Keep us facing upstream. I'm going to let the current take us down.'

'Aye aye, sir. Upstream.'

'Kedges aweigh, sir,' Rumbelo called.

'Make 'em fast. They can stay where they are until we've time to get 'em inboard. Stop both.'

Watching, Kelly waited a second then turned to the quartermaster. 'Can you see what you're doing, Q.M.?'

Peering from under the lip of his steel helmet, the quartermaster nodded. 'More or less, sir. The rain's blurring things a bit.'

'It's got to be better than that. Make it slow ahead.' Kelly pushed his head out of the wheelhouse window. 'No shooting,' he ordered. 'The quieter we are, the safer we are. And stand by the searchlight. I want to see what we're doing.'

They could see *Swei-Fan*'s bulk close astern of them now, like a house-side and growing bigger all the time as she came up fast. Then as she slipped past, a bulky shadow in the darkness, Kelly turned.

'Half ahead both!'

Both ships were facing the current, *Swei-Fan* held by her anchor, *Spider* just beginning to halt her rearwards drift as her propellers bit. Then, slowly, the way went off the gunboat and she began to move ahead into the current, pulling up towards *Swei-Fan*'s stern. There was still no sign of life aboard the freighter and no sounds of alarm from ashore.

'Searchlight!'

As the light came on, the blue-white beam leapt across the black water, turning *Swei-Fan*'s hull to silver.

'Stand by, Q.M. Starboard side to, and it's got to be first

time. Think you can do it?'

'If you don't mind a bit of scraped paint, sir.'

'We'll worry about that later. Sub, tell the boarding party to stand by. I want a wire across to *Swei-Fan*'s bow. The current'll swing us in.'

Kelly's heart was thumping. They were about to take on the whole Nationalist army with twenty-odd men. If they pulled it off, he'd be a marked man. If he failed, he'd be on the beach looking for a job as a wine shipper or a dockyard manager.

'Stop both!'

'Stop both, sir!'

'Starboard twenty. Deck lights!'

As the decklights came on, there was a clang and a grinding of steel as *Spider*'s bow thumped against *Swei-Fan*. Kelly was handling the gunboat with the technique of an over-enthusiastic midshipman with a pinnace; and a steel rail, caught by a projection on *Spider*'s waist, buckled, was torn off, and leapt into the air with a clatter of steel on steel, curled like a petrified caterpillar. Gregory appeared on the bridge, panting, as *Spider* came to a stop alongside the bigger ship.

'Right, Rumbelo,' Kelly yelled. 'Now!'

'Get that wire across,' Rumbelo's voice came out of the wet darkness, and Kelly leapt from the wheelhouse.

'Keep her at slow ahead, Sub,' he said. 'She's all yours. Let's go!'

Running the length of the ship, he found Rumbelo already on *Swei-Fan*'s deck, making a wire rope fast round a bitt.

'Let's have another at the stern,' he yelled.

The crash of the two ships colliding seemed to have wakened the Chinese on board and they came tumbling out of a hatchway as *Spider* swung heavily alongside in the current. They held rifles but they were jacketless, some of them even shirtless, their eyes wild, their mouths cages of teeth. As the first man appeared, Rumbelo kicked him in the chest and he fell back on the others in a tangle of arms and legs, and for a moment there was sufficient respite to get another wire across amidships.

'Watch the other side!' Kelly directed, and two seamen hurtled round *Swei-Fan*'s stern.

A Chinese soldier's head poked through a doorway and Kelly

166

fired. The face seemed to burst like a smashed melon, blood spattering the white paint. Another took its place immediately but, as one of the seamen swung his pick shaft, it vanished again just as quickly. Bullets were coming from forward now and Kelly dashed off along the deck, to find himself face to face with what appeared to be millions of Chinese tumbling down from the bridge. He shot one and kicked the feet from under another. But more appeared and he was surrounded. Just when he thought he'd seen the last of life, Donkin appeared alongside him, his face almost obscured by an enormous steel helmet, using a revolver as if he were at target practice. In the wet roaring darkness, Kelly found himself struggling with an enormous Chinaman who stank of stale sweat, but he brought his knee up and, as the Chinamen yelled and doubled up, he clubbed him at the back of the head with the pistol.

Gathering his party round him, he led the way forward in a rush to the centrecastle where the officers' quarters were. Another bunch of Chinese appeared, bursting out of a doorway with what seemed like a hedge of steel below yelling yellow faces. Lifting his pistol, Kelly was just about to fire when he slipped on the rain-wet deck and went down on his knees. Looking up, he saw a man standing over him with a rusty spear in his hands. God, he thought in horror, fancy dying with a foot of rusty steel in your guts! As he shoved the pistol into the bare belly above him and pulled the trigger, the Chinaman gave a howl and fell across him, screaming, and the spear clattered across them both and fell to the deck. Warm blood pumping into his face, blinding him, he struggled free to find the deck empty of living Chinese.

'Where've they gone?'

'Over the side, sir,' Donkin panted.

'Thank God for that! Stand by the wheel, Donkin. Rumbelo, see what you can do about *Swei-Fan*'s anchor.'

Darting below, he started yelling. '*Swei-Fan*, it's the Navy! Anybody about?'

A yell came from one of the cabins and he blew the lock off. Four men fell out at his feet as the door burst open.

'Archer,' one of them said. 'Second officer. That's Mr. Smith, Third; Mr. Collins, Chief Engineer; and Chief Steward Watercorn.'

'Go forward, Mr. Archer,' Kelly said. 'Help my chaps to slip your cable. Fast as you can. We're towing you away.'

'Are you, by Christ? Right.'

'On the bridge, Mr. Smith! Mr. Collins, have you any firemen?'

'Three. One hurt.'

'Get the others below. We'll need your engines as soon as possible. Where are your passengers, Mr. Watercorn.'

'Cabin. Upper deck.'

'Stand by. I'll need you to show me the way when we're clear.'

Leading the Chief Steward in the scramble to the deck, Kelly heard the anchor cable go and yelled across to *Spider*. 'Slow ahead, Sub. Starboard helm. The current'll swing us round.'

Still covered with blood, he scrambled back aboard *Spider* and up to the bridge. As he did so, a bullet struck the wheelhouse roof and whined away, and they heard the flat report of a rifle.

'Do we fire back, sir?' Gregory asked, like himself yelling with excitement.

'Not yet.'

Catching the greater bulk of *Swei-Fan*, the current slowly swung them right round so that they faced downstream. The town was sliding back behind them and now another scattering of shots struck the wheelhouse and made them duck.

'Machine-gunner, can you make 'em keep their heads down?'

'Yes, sir.'

'Go ahead.'

The ancient maxim rattled in slow time and the shooting from the shore stopped at once.

'Dead ahead, sir,' Rumbelo's voice warned from near the gun on the bow. 'There's a lighter in the way!'

'Full ahead both, Sub, and let's hope to Christ *Swei-Fan*'s weight don't take us into it.'

Holding his breath, Kelly stared into the darkness. The sheer effrontery of what he'd done occurred to him for the first time and it took his breath away. Maguire, he thought, it's a bloody good job you never stop to think.

As they slid past the lighter, an anchored passenger ship,

168

three tiers high, loomed up ahead. *Spider* swept past, almost brushing her stern as she was carried downstream by the current, and they saw startled faces caught by the deck lights staring down at the little gunboat with the bulk of *Swei-Fan* lashed alongside. Then the passenger ship's siren bellowed to draw attention to the escaping vessels and immediately other sirens followed and a flare went up from the shore.

'Where's that bloody bend, Sub?'

'Coming up now, sir.'

'Well, we shan't need any rudder. *Swei-Fan*'ll do it for us. Make it full astern both.'

As *Spider*'s screws churned the water and she slowed, the weight of the big freighter swung them both round until they had changed direction by forty-five degrees.

'Half ahead both. Steady on that light on the hill, Quartermaster. See it?'

Another flare rose into the sky, illuminating the gunboat and her bulky companion, and a machine gun started to fire from the shore. The bullets clattered against *Swei-Fan*'s bows.

'This is the nasty bit,' Gregory said. 'This is where the batteries are.'

'Tell everybody to keep their heads down, Sub,' Kelly ordered. 'Then go below and make sure the passengers are lying down.'

There was an acid-white flash from one of the hills and a six-inch shell screamed overhead to explode in the river beyond them. In a flare of flame, a second hit the passenger ship they'd just passed. Immediately every gun ashore, mistaking her for *Spider*, opened up on her so that the night seemed to be full of orange flashes and the swift flow of red tracer.

'How much longer, Sub, before we're clear?'

'Few minutes, sir. No more. There's another bend.'

'Same way?'

'Yes, sir.'

'Good. Same tactics. Let *Swei-Fan* take us round.'

As Kelly spoke there was a crash astern and a flash that lit their faces. Yells and women's screams came from below where the missionaries and their families were cowering.

'Find out what's happened, Sub!'

Gregory reappeared two minutes later. He was grinning. 'I

169

think we've lost the kedges, sir.'

'Both of 'em?'

'It hit the winch, sir. It parted the hawsers and they've both gone.'

'No injuries?'

'None, sir. Though we have one man with a nasty cut from a sword. The doc's got him. We're probably clear now.'

'Right, I think I'll take a look round *Swei-Fan* now and sort out Mrs. Bloody Withinshawe before she starts laying a complaint against me to the Admiralty. Come on, Mr. Watercorn.'

They found half a dozen Chinese soldiers in the freighter's saloon just recovering from a drunken stupor. They were surrounded by bottles and the place stank of human excrement.

'Have 'em over the side,' Kelly said.

Reaching the passenger cabins, he began kicking on the doors until he heard a voice inside. Kicking the door open, he found himself facing a man standing by a table with a bulbous-looking blonde who looked as if she'd been poured into her dress and left to set. An amah huddled in a corner clutching a small boy.

As she saw Kelly's blood-soaked whites, the woman gasped. 'Oh, God,' she said.

'We're not the Kuomintang,' Kelly announced. 'We're the Navy. Are you Mrs. Withinshawe?'

'No,' a cold voice behind him said. '*I*'m Mrs. Withinshawe. That's George and Agnes Rowntree. Who're you?'

As he turned, he saw another woman standing behind the door. She was in her middle twenties, a tall slender woman with dark hair and brilliant green eyes. Despite the dirt on her face and the fact that her hair was awry, it was clear she was a beauty.

'Lieutenant-Commander Maguire, Madam,' he introduced himself. 'I've come to take you off.'

8

Christina Withinshawe stepped forward, proud, erect and contemptuous.

'You've been a long time,' she said.

Kelly smiled, indifferent in the success of the venture to her annoyance. 'We've been rather occupied,' he pointed out.

He felt it was the sort of casual indifference people liked to hear from the Navy, but she seemed unimpressed.

'I thought you'd never come. They raped me, did you know? They stripped me naked and raped me.'

Kelly's smile died and, for a moment, he didn't know what to say. What *did* you say to a woman who'd been violated?

'In front of my own husband and son. They murdered my husband. They shot him.'

'I thought he'd been –'

'They shot him,' she insisted. Despite her fury, he was aware that her eyes were sizing him up. She seemed remarkably in control of herself for a woman who'd recently been assaulted by Chinese soldiers and he decided she was lying to impress him.

'How long before we shall be in Shanghai?' The words were less a question than a command to get moving.

Kelly felt he had her measure now. 'That depends on the Senior Naval Officer,' he said.

'I'll have you know I'm Lord Clemo's daughter and I don't wait for some piffling individual with gold rings on his sleeve to decide when *I* can go home.'

'I think this time you'll have to,' Kelly retorted. 'And now, since we have things to do, we'd better move you and your belongings over to *Spider* until we've cleaned this tip up.'

He reached for a fur coat that lay on the bunk to help her, but she immediately rounded on him.

171

'You keep your damned paws off my clothes,' she snapped. 'God knows where you'll have them next. I know sailors. More than one of them's eyed me as if he'd like to throw me across my own bed.'

In *Spider*'s wardroom, the missionaries and their children seemed to be having a prayer meeting, breathing heavily and uttering occasional loud 'Hallelujahs', their fervour darkening the deep red of MacIntyre's face. Her head erect, unmoved and remarkably unemotional for a woman who claimed to have just suffered rape, Christina Withinshawe stared coldly at them, her nose in the air.

'Who *are* these people?' she said.

'Refugees, like yourself,' Kelly explained.

'Surely I don't have to share the place with *them*. Is there nothing else?'

'There's the first lieutenant's quarters.'

She peered into Gregory's cabin and sniffed. 'Is this the biggest there is?'

'The captain's is bigger.'

'Why can't I have that?'

'Because,' Kelly said, 'it's become a nursery for the babies and their mothers.'

'You have a sick bay or something don't you? Why can't I have that?'

'Because there are four wounded men in there.' Kelly's helpful expression had vanished. 'Five now. They were hurt coming to your rescue. There are also three dead in the tiller flat – to say nothing of around a couple of dozen Chinese we had to kill.'

Leaving her sitting disgustedly in Gregory's cabin, Kelly hurried to the bridge. The darkness was giving way by now to the misty greyness of dawn. They were well out of danger by this time except for stray batteries along the shore, which persisted in dropping shells in their wake. Then, round a corner of the river in the growing light, moving up from Nanking, they saw the grey shape of a destroyer. The forward gun cracked and they saw a puff of dust on the hillside near a particularly troublesome field piece, and a scurrying of ant-like figures up the slope.

'I think, sir,' Rumbelo observed, 'that it's *Wanderer*.'

'Destroyer signalling, sir,' the yeoman of signals yelled out.

172

'She says "Fancy meeting you," sir.'

'I suppose we ought to reply with something clever and fitting,' Kelly said. 'Make it "The pleasure's all mine."'

By the following day they were well clear of Wu-Pi and, though Christina Withinshawe's attitude to the missionaries remained barely civil, with Kelly it took a marked turn for the better.

'Afraid I put up a few blacks last night,' she apologised brusquely. 'I'm sorry.'

She produced a small pistol. 'I was just getting ready to use this when you arrived,' she went on. 'I don't suppose it would have stopped a charging buffalo but it might have made a coolie yell a bit if I'd hit him in the family jewels.'

Her bluntness made Kelly grin. During the trip downriver, he'd noticed she had never been far from his side as he moved about the ship, surprisingly informative about the currents and clearly no fool. Then she followed her first climb-down with another. 'It might interest you, Commander,' she said, 'to know that you look a lot better now you've wiped all that blood off your face. And I also have to admit on second thoughts that your accommodation is better than it seemed. If I'd known I might have left before. My husband was all in favour.'

Kelly studied her. 'What *about* your husband, Mrs. Withinshawe?' he asked.

'What about him? He was properly buried. I've no doubt it wasn't Anglican rites and probably his ancestors are spinning in their graves because the gardener burned joss over him. But I'm not sentimental about death.'

'What about his family?'

'He gave them up when he married me. My father fixed it. I never met them.'

'Seems a funny way of being married.'

'It *was* a funny way of being married. In fact, I'm damned if I know how he ever managed to make me pregnant.'

She stared with interest at the missionaries who were kneeling in groups near the forward gun, gazing at them as if they were some strange breed of zoo animal. 'Do they always go on like this?' she asked.

'I believe so, Mrs. Withinshawe.'

'Oh, for goodness sake, call me Christina! *I'm* not a

missionary and neither are you. Under normal circumstances we might well be at the same cocktail party. You must forgive me for last night. I was a little distraught. I was worried for my son. He's only seven.'

'I see.' So far Kelly hadn't seen her show the child the slightest sign of interest.

'I've been talking to your sergeant.'

'Petty officer, Mrs. Withinshawe.'

'Christina.'

'Very well: Christina.'

'He has a great admiration for you. He tells me you're a very brave man.'

'Perhaps he knows something about it. He's pretty brave, too.'

'He says you've been decorated several times. During the war and since.'

He began to see the reason for her new interest. She'd probably never come into close contact with a naval man before in the narrow business circle she and her husband had inhabited and it was a new experience.

'You seem to be very much the strong silent type, Commander.'

'It's a strong silent service, Mrs. Withinshawe.'

'How are we getting downstream?'

'At Nanking we shall transfer you to a passenger ship where there'll be more comfort. Probably *Swei-Fan* herself if she's not needed.'

She gazed at him and he decided she had the greenest eyes he'd ever seen, bright and enigmatic like a cat's.

'Are you married, Commander?' she asked.

'No.'

'Surely somebody's got their eye on you.'

He thought for a moment of Charley. She'd have arrived in Shanghai by now and would probably be jumping into bed with Kimister. 'No,' he said. 'No one.'

She stared at him, bold and calculating. 'I think somebody slipped up badly. You haven't any strange habits, have you? One hears odd things about sailors.'

The sheer effrontery of it made him laugh. 'No, by God,' he said. 'Nothing like that.'

'Then I can't understand why you're not married.'

He stared back at her, finding to his surprise that he was enjoying himself. 'Couldn't ever afford it, Mrs. Withinshawe.'

'Christina.' She was determined to get him on to first name terms. 'You should find yourself an heiress. It's done in all the best circles.'

With *Swei-Fan* manned by a scratch crew from *Spider* and *Wanderer* bringing up the rear, they progressed slowly downstream. *Spider* was still crowded and Christina Withinshawe clearly detested both MacIntyre and his mousy little wife and thoroughly enjoyed playing for them the role of a French aristocrat who'd just escaped the guillotine. Kelly watched with amusement as she pressed drinks on them from an enormous flask, so that MacIntyre, who'd fawned round her from the minute he'd become aware of her title, found it hard to refuse. Oh, you bitch, you wicked mischievous bitch, he thought as he watched her deliberately forcing them to break their own rigid code. Somehow, she reminded him of Verschoyle – arrogant, indifferent to others, coolly certain of herself and her background.

As they dropped anchor at Nanking, the Senior Naval Officer stepped aboard.

'You're to continue on down to Shanghai,' he said. 'The Admiral wants you back and *Spider* needs a new captain. *Cockchafer*'s relieving you.'

'And the people on board, sir?'

'You'd better keep them with you as far as Chinkiang. There's a passenger ship there clearing what's left of the Europeans because the bloody Nationalists are kicking up trouble again. We'll take over *Swei-Fan* and supply you with extra blankets, palliasses and stores for your passengers. Can you handle 'em?'

'Most of 'em, sir,' Kelly said, thinking of Christina Withinshawe.

Now that they were safe, the rival sects of missionaries, camped out on the afterdeck on strips of coconut matting, were jealously keeping themselves to themselves and trying to entice the crew to their meetings. MacIntyre, his pale eyes wild, his thin hair on end, approached Kelly.

175

'We would like tae hold a service o' thanksgiving tae the Lord for our safety,' he said.

'There's nothing to stop you,' Kelly pointed out, thinking that the Lord hadn't had half as much to do with their safety as the crew of *Spider*.

'We would like your men tae be present.'

'I think they'd prefer to make up their own minds, Mr. MacIntyre. You have my permission to inform them that there'll be a service and to let them know what denomination it'll be. Any man of that denomination who wishes to attend and who is not on duty will be free to do so if he wishes. You will *not* be allowed to canvas them and you will *not* be allowed to preach at them unless they ask you to. The Navy looks after its own religious affairs.'

'You're preventing us doin' the work o' God!'

'You may do the work of God any way you wish, Mr. MacIntyre, but you will *not* harass my sailors.'

'You're being gey obstructive, I think, and I can complain tae your admiral, y'know.'

Kelly smiled. 'And I, Mr. MacIntyre,' he pointed out, 'can put you in jug if I feel it necessary. I have the authority in this ship.'

As MacIntyre vanished, grumbling, Kelly saw the Withinshawe child on the afterdeck with the other children, sitting on a swing rigged up by the crew. His mother was in her cabin, with the door open as if she were waiting for Kelly to appear. She had contrived to do her hair and apply make-up.

She gave him a wide smile as he appeared.

'You should do that more often,' he said. 'It suits you. You're to be put aboard a passenger steamer at Chinkiang.'

'And you?'

'I'm taking *Spider* down.'

She gave him a broad grin. 'I'd like to repay your hospitality, Commander. It isn't every day one's rescued by a handsome man, and I'm very much in your debt.'

She moved to him and kissed him unexpectedly on the cheek.

'Mere gratitude, I hope,' he said.

'More than that.' She pushed the door to and put her arms round his neck.

As he disentangled himself gently and opened the door

again, she stared at him, clearly disappointed. 'Are all naval officers so aloof?'

'We're noted for our detachment.'

'Aren't you interested in me?'

'Very much. But it's a bit soon after your husband was killed, isn't it? Were you really raped?'

She shrugged. 'One of them manhandled me. He tore my dress and I fell down. When I got up I punched him on the nose and the others started laughing. I think that's what saved me.'

'I'm told it often does.'

'Come and see me in Shanghai,' she begged. 'I have a house there.'

For a moment Kelly hesitated, then he gave way. 'I'd be delighted to,' he said. 'How about you? Aren't you a bit scared now you're on your own?'

'The Clemos are never afraid.'

'You've lost everything.'

She shrugged. 'There's plenty more where that came from,' she pointed out. 'I ought, in fact, to be able to dine out on this for months.' She looked up at him, oozing sex appeal in waves. 'It's still beyond me,' she said, 'how a man who looks and behaves like you has managed to remain single all these years.'

Chinkiang was in the throes of a riot when they arrived, and the captain of *Coronet* stepped aboard as soon as they made fast alongside his ship.

'I've got to hold you for a couple of days,' he said. 'These bloody Nationalists are creating merry hell ashore and I need your men. We'll have your passengers transferred to *E-Wo*. She's a B. and S. freighter and she's downstream where it's safer.'

Christina Withinshawe was surprisingly pliable. 'When do we leave?' she asked.

'Boats will ferry you down,' Kelly said. 'You have to be ready in one hour. I'm taking a party of men ashore.'

She listened to the sound of screaming as the mob rampaged through the city. Through the scuttle she could see a huge crowd swarming along the bund, whacking in windows with carrying poles.

'To face that lot?'

177

'I expect we'll manage.'

She slammed the door to and flung herself into his arms. 'Damn your bloody navy stand-offishness,' she said. 'I don't want you to!'

He kissed her gently and was kissed back fiercely. He gently detached her and opened the door.

'There'll be time for that later,' he said. 'The Sub will be staying aboard with the engine room crew. He'll see you all into the boats. Now I must go.'

As they were put ashore, the drums and the gongs and the yelling seemed to increase in tempo, and sporadic shooting came on the wind with a thin high baying from the town that filtered between the houses. Here and there bodies lay in flattened heaps along the bund where Chinese merchants who'd done business with the British had been dragged out of their homes by the nationalist mob and battered to death. Groups of sailors were escorting women and children to where *Coronet*'s boats were gathered, and Kelly's party joined that of a midshipman who was holding the crowd back from the end of the jetty.

The midshipman was a round-cheeked youngster who looked no more than a schoolboy. Erect in front of his men, he had a black eye from a brickbat and was wearing a fixed grin to show he wasn't afraid, standing motionless and unflinching while the filth and the brickbats bounced off him and his little party. Spat at, covered with ordure, the little group of sailors waited with their rifles at the ready, not threatening, but also not budging.

'Nice to see you, sir,' the midshipman said out of the corner of his mouth, without taking his eyes off the mob. 'William Latimer. I was getting a bit worried.'

'Kelly Maguire. What's it like, Mid?'

'I'm terrified, sir.'

'You'd never know it.'

'*I* would, sir. I know they say that midshipmen are bipeds of extraordinary stupidity used as a medium of personal abuse between two persons of unequal superiority, but there's more to it than that. We breathe, sir, we think. Like that chap in *Merchant of Venice*, we have eyes, hands, organs, dimensions, affections, passions. If you prick us we bleed.'

'By God, Mid, you know your Shakespeare better than I do.'

178

'Habit of mine, sir. Rather like the old Bard. How long shall we be here?'

'I gather they're bringing the last of them along now.'

'Thank God for that, sir. If it goes on much longer, I'm afraid I'll cut and run.'

'You look as though you're rooted to the ground.'

'If I am, sir, it's with sheer funk.'

The wet streets were full of smoke and soggy ashes. The mob had quietened a little by this time and they could hear outbreaks of firing from small groups of soldiers dodging between the houses. Idols and dragon symbols were being carried through the streets and further along the bund coolies were making messy sacrifices with chickens and goats. British, American, French and Japanese flags had been torn down and a crowd of students were earnestly burning pictures of King George and President Coolidge.

Small groups of Europeans, their shoulders bowed, their faces grey with strain, their children wailing with terror, kept appearing, escorted by small parties of bluejackets armed to the teeth. They moved falteringly along the rubbish-littered bund, watched by defiant-looking Chinese militiamen, students and coolies. Beyond the mob telegraph wires looped above pavements strewn with broken glass, stones, paper and blowing chaff, and further back still a burning car sent a black pyre of smoke curling up like a plume against the sky.

The evacuation took longer than they'd expected and the last people to arrive were being carried on stretchers. As they approached, the mob pressed closer.

'Stand by, Mid,' Kelly said.

As the Chinese advanced, a line of young girls, their slant eyes narrowed, their faces contorted with hatred, pushed in front and, wrenching at their skirts and blouses, exposed their yellow bodies to the sailors.

'Out, King George!' they screeched. 'Shoot, white pigs! Shoot!'

Peering from under the lips of their steel helmets, the sailors' faces remained expressionless, but Kelly heard a small united gasp of appreciation as they stared at the slim yellow bodies naked to the waist, and the row of bobbing young breasts.

'Christ –' the voice was Donkin's '– just take a dekko at them knockers.'

'Stop that talking,' Kelly rapped. 'And keep your eyes where they ought to be.'

' 'Arder than you'd think,' Donkin murmured.

The line of rifles lifted and the sailors gritted their teeth to stand immoveable under the handfuls of dung and decaying vegetable matter.

'I've heard of showers of shit,' one of them muttered. 'But this is fucking well *it*.'

As the mob came closer, swarming over the gardens and smooth lawns of the nearby houses, the few Sikh policemen backed nearer to the sailors. Behind them, the crowd surged like water running from a burst river bank to join those already shouting abuse, while more behind pushed forward, waving carrying poles and sticks and forcing the front ranks forward until they were only a few feet from Kelly's nose. The barrier of sailors was forced back a few steps and the struggling line of refugees came to a standstill.

'Do they pay your pension to your mother, sir?' Latimer asked sideways as a brawny coolie stripped to the waist brandished his pole under his nose.

'So I'm told,' Kelly said.

'Tell her I died doing my duty, sir. Head erect. Face to the foe.'

'And covered all over from head to foot –' the voice behind them broke into a popular bawdy song '– covered all over in – Sweet Vi-olets –'

Latimer grinned. 'At least the troops are in good heart, sir.'

The crowd had halted now, bewildered by the calmness of the foreign devils, wondering what they had up their sleeves and just when the order to fire would be given.

'I think we're winning,' Kelly said.

Those at the back of the crowd, safe against disaster, were still yelling and screaming, and a stone coming over the heads, hit Kelly at the side of the face. Latimer unbuckled his holster and the crowd edged backwards a fraction. Kelly had gone down on one knee but he rose, shoved his helmet straight, and stood upright, a thin trickle of blood oozing from his cheek.

'Keep that thing in its holster, Mid. You know what they say about revolvers: It's easier to blow your own foot off than hit

180

what you're aiming at.'

The stones continued to fly and a sailor's helmet was knocked off, then the burly coolie turned to address the crowd, obviously proud of his physique. The yelling died as he began to lash himself into a fury against the Whites. The hail of stones continued, the small boys hurling pony droppings; then, as the coolie prepared for a final tirade, a handful of manure hit him full in the teeth just when his mouth was wide open. As he staggered back, raging and spitting, Kelly grinned and a small Chinese boy fell to the ground, spluttering with delight. The next minute there was a yell of laughter from the crowd.

'I think this might be the moment, Mid,' Kelly said. 'Let's move forward. Use your rifle butts on their bare toes.'

As the line of blue-uniformed men advanced slowly, tapping gently at bare feet, the crowd began to back away. People drifted down alleys, trying to look unconcerned, then the edges crumbled and finally the centre began to melt. When there were only a few left, the last of them hitched at their blue cotton pants and, with their poles over their shoulders, sauntered off.

The Woodbines came out. The casualties had not been high, and at once the parties of white men and women pushed forward again to the jetty. As the last of them arrived, a harassed-looking consul in yesterday's whites appeared. Behind him there was an officer, carrying the union jack from the consulate flagstaff.

'I think we can go now,' Kelly said.

Back aboard *Spider*, Kelly went below to the captain's cabin to clean himself up. The missionaries seemed to have left all their discarded clothing lying around, together with torn paper, a few Mission pamphlets and a dog-eared Bible. He turned to the sailor who had followed him below to take his filthy clothes.

'I always thought cleanliness was next to Godliness,' he growled. 'Let's get this bloody lot cleared up.'

He found a bottle of whisky and, filling a tumbler, stood drinking it, his jacket in one hand, as the sailor gathered up the lost belongings and vanished. As he sank the last of the whisky, there was a tap on the door. As it opened, he saw Christina Withinshawe outside, smiling at him.

'What the devil are you doing here?' he snapped.

'I didn't leave with the others.'

'Why the devil not?'

She blinked at his anger. 'Don't shout at me, Commander! I didn't wish to, that's why. A squabble broke out between the Total Immersionists and the Seventh Day Adventists, or whatever they call themselves, with the Catholics in between holding them apart. Nobody noticed I wasn't there.'

'Didn't they check the cabin?'

'I was inside with the door locked. They didn't break it down. Perhaps it isn't done in the Navy to break doors down.' She gazed at his cheek. 'You seem to need attention. That's a nasty cut.'

'I'll get the surgeon.'

'There isn't one. He went with the wounded to *E-Wo*, if you remember. But I did a bit of nursing during the recent hurly-burly with the Germans – mostly holding the hands of titled officers at my mother's convalescent home in Norfolk.'

He poured himself another whisky while she vanished to the wardroom to search among the bandages the doctor had left behind. As she reappeared, he sat down on the bunk and she produced water and a piece of lint and began to dab at the cut on his cheek.

'I don't think this does much good,' she pointed out. 'But it looks terribly efficient and the patient always seems to enjoy it.'

She bent and kissed him gently on the forehead, then she dabbed iodine on the cut and put a strip of sticking plaster over it.

'Fit to meet the ladies,' she said.

He rose and she straightened up close to him, her eyes on his, daring him.

He smiled. 'Now we'll have you taken to *E-Wo*,' he said. 'And this time I'll come myself to see you get there.'

9

Tyrwhitt was delighted to see Kelly back and to have *Spider* safe and reasonably sound.

'Pity we didn't get up there in time to save Withinshawe,' he said. 'But I gather Lord Clemo won't argue with his daughter back in the fold. I've been bombarded with congratulatory telegrams. How did you find her?'

'Highly delectable, sir,' Kelly said briskly. 'She's a brave intelligent woman – even if a little self-willed.'

Tyrwhitt's heavy eyebrows shot up. 'Well,' he said, 'I suppose you'll be wanting to see that girl of yours now, won't you? I gather she's been well looked after and that the Belfrages have taken her to Hong Kong.'

It was not news to Kelly because he'd already enquired. 'Indeed, sir?'

'I'd like to send you after her,' Tyrwhitt went on, 'but I'm afraid you'll have to wait just a little while longer because things are still sticky here. Think you can hang on a little while?'

With Christina Withinshawe in the Bubbling Well Road, Kelly decided with a surprisingly small amount of guilt that he could. He'd learned very quickly about Charley's trip to Hong Kong with Mabel and the Belfrages, and a further discreet enquiry had revealed, not entirely surprisingly, that Kimister had suddenly found he was needed there, too.

'The bugger's learning quickly, ain't he?' he observed to Verschoyle.

There was a letter for him from Charley to say she was sorry he'd not been able to meet her, but there was a curious indifference about it, and between the lines he could read her annoyance that he'd not been there when she stepped ashore. A

183

discreet enquiry to a friend in Hong Kong revealed that she was far from lonely and that Kimister was entertaining her round the hotels and floating restaurants and, instead of telegraphing Hong Kong as he might have done, he telephoned Christina Withinshawe's house in the Bubbling Well Road instead. She seemed to be well on form.

'I've been checking up on you,' she said at once. 'I've learned that your father's an admiral and that you're the heir to a baronetcy.'

'You've been quick,' Kelly observed.

'In the Clemo empire we employ people to find out things like that.'

'I see. Does this put me in your class?'

He heard her chuckle. 'Very definitely in the running. But what about that little English girl who's come all the way out here to see you? I've heard about her. Is she pretty?'

Yes, Kelly thought bitterly, she is. 'Not as beautiful as you,' he said.

'I like to hear that sort of thing.' The voice over the telephone was smooth and happy. 'Work it into any conversation you like. Come and see me.'

She remained in his mind, lying alongside the anger he felt about Charley. Tyrwhitt was busy with commissions of enquiry into the outrages upriver, struggling with Chiang K'Ai Shek's Foreign Secretary, who was claiming that the trouble lay entirely with the Western Powers' insistence on maintaining the treaties which benefited them without benefiting the Chinese; and, feeling vaguely relieved of guilt by the demand that he remain in Shanghai, Kelly put on a civilian suit, called a taxi, and set out for the Bubbling Well Road, determined to find out where his affections really lay. When he was announced by a Chinese maid, Christina appeared wearing a close-fitting, high-necked cheongsam of fine silk that showed every line of her body, her slender throat accentuated by its high neck. She'd done her hair in a bun on top of her head and her pallor was enhanced by the make-up she wore. It was typical of her, he thought, to defy all the British matrons in their cotton and pearls and wear something Chinese.

'I think you're the most beautiful woman I've ever met,' he said.

184

She smiled. 'You took a long time to get here.'

'I've been busy. The admiral's going off his head. He's not the diplomatic type and he'd much rather set about the Chinese and beat them hip and thigh. I spend most of my time hanging on to his coat tails to hold him back.'

She smiled. 'I think he's getting on top of you a bit.'

'At times.'

'Nobody's been getting on top of me lately. Certainly not you.'

He grinned at her lusty vulgarity. With her wealth and background, she could get away with things other women would never dare say. 'He has enough here to drive the average man crazy,' he pointed out 'Fortunately, things are quietening down a bit now and the government's decided to send out another brigade.'

'There'll be so many soldiers here soon,' she said, 'they'll be elbowing each other into the river.'

She moved to him and he took her in his arms and kissed her without embarrassment. She returned the embrace quite naturally, as though they'd known each other for years.

'We'll dine out,' she said. 'Thank God there's still plenty going on. We can come back here for coffee.'

The restaurant was crowded, with an orchestra of Philippino musicians playing the sort of music for dancing you could hear at the Savoy. Despite the Chinese reputation for inscrutability, they were taking to Western jazz with a vengeance, and slant-eyed girls with flimsy chiffon dresses were hard at it dancing the Charleston.

Christina looked a knockout in a daringly low-cut evening dress that dragged every eye to her at once.

'What keeps it up?' Kelly asked.

'Hope and holding my breath.'

After eating they danced, and, in that dress, holding her was like clutching someone unclothed. There were only a few people on the balcony of the hotel and because it was cold in the breeze coming from the sea, she moved closer to him. As he put his arm round her, he felt her shiver under his hand. He knew her interest in him was purely predatory, but he was young enough not to be indifferent to having alongside him an attractive woman in a dress so staggeringly brief she might have been

185

naked.

'The Shanghai matrons don't approve of me,' she said. 'But I don't approve of them much either. No wonder the Chinese want to throw them out. Let's go home.'

The house was silent and the street roar was subsiding. Dim yellow lights showed from the sea. As the door shut, Christina turned. 'What in God's name did I do before you arrived?' she asked.

Drowzily, as though the action were instinctive, she lifted her arms and put them round his neck. For a moment she clung to him like that, his hand moving on the bare flesh above her dress at the base of her spine.

'It unfastens,' she said quietly.

He unhooked the dress without speaking. She didn't take her eyes off his, her face as pale and smooth as marble.

'This is an age when morals don't seem to matter much,' she said. 'It's still too soon after the war and the world's falling apart at the seams a bit. I always thought it best to take an easy-going attitude towards it. I'm in love with you, did you know?'

She released him and turned away to walk through the lounge to the stairs. Kelly followed. At the top, she turned and took his hand.

'I'll spare you the thought of sleeping in Arthur's bed,' she said. 'We'll use the spare room.'

She slipped out of the dress and let it fall at her feet. As she stepped out of her shoes, he moved towards her and she sat down on the bed and looked up at him, her face pale. Then, breaking into an unexpected cascade of laughter, she made a grab for him and he fell across her, cracking his skull on the headboard and almost knocking himself silly. As she squirmed under him, he felt her fingers tearing at his shirt. A button shot across the room and she laughed, wriggling out of the remains of her clothes.

'*It broke the old Duke's heart* – ' she burst into a gay chirrup of song '– *when Lady Jane became a tart*. The properly constituted female always likes to clutch at the staunch male breast, you know, and I'm a properly constituted female. I feel like a properly constituted female, anyway, and I suspect you're a properly constituted male. At the moment you *certainly* feel like one. I think you're as randy as a bull mastiff.'

186

'Yes I am,' Kelly panted, 'because I *am* a properly constituted male. And you're quite a dish, with or without clothes.'

'Hand on heart?'

'You'd stir a bishop.'

She laughed in his face and he laughed back at her. Then, suddenly, abruptly, they stopped, staring at each other, and in one moment, as though they were both activated by the same strings, their smiles died and they reached out for each other, their hands desperate in their urgency.

Aboard the flagship, Kelly found Tyrwhitt fretting over the minor tension of Wei-Hai-Wei. It was a neat harbour, almost entirely landlocked, to the north of Shanghai where the navy used the island of Liu-Kung-Tao as a leave centre for its men. With the tension high in Shanghai, British civilians were asking if it would be safe to take their usual summer holidays there, and Lady Tyrwhitt was anxious to go there with her family.

'Write her for me, Kelly,' Tyrwhitt said. 'It'll sound better coming from you. Explain that if *she* goes, everybody here will start saying I've guaranteed its safety. And that's not true. It's all right for naval personnel and families because we could evacuate them in no time if necessary. It's different for civilians.'

Kelly wrote the letter carefully, but his mind was less on Tyrwhitt's problems than on his own. Another letter had arrived from Charley asking when he was going to Hong Kong. It was far more pleading this time and he wrote back explaining what was happening and said – quite honestly, he was pleased to feel – that he couldn't leave. But, as he wrote, his mind was on the sight of Christina Withinshawe sitting on the side of her bed that morning, wrapped in a sheet that barely covered her, one slim naked arm outside it, watching him as she served him tea and toast. They had awakened to plunge into a new wave of urgent love-making that had ended with them exhausted in a tangle of tortured bed clothes.

'You look like a cat that's been at the cream,' she had said, smiling at him. Then she had picked up her ring from the dressing table and slipped it on his little finger.

'With this ring I thee wed,' she said. 'With my body I thee worship.'

187

'No need to shout,' Kelly grinned.

'I want to shout.' She had sat up and yelled. '*With my body I thee worship!*' She beamed at him. 'I hope you were careful last night because it was fun, and we mustn't spoil it with anything silly like babies.' She paused. 'What about that little girl of yours in Hong Kong, though?'

What indeed about the little girl in Hong Kong? Staring at the sheet of notepaper. Kelly decided he was a heel, but he had managed to console himself within ten minutes that, with Kimister in Hong Kong, too, and with what had happened in England after he'd left he had a right to be.

When he went ashore that night they made no pretence and went to bed together as if they'd been doing it for years.

By now, everybody in Shanghai was living in a state of virtual siege. What had seemed at first to be only a vast indisciplined anarchy had jelled into a great campaign of detestation against the Western powers. The whole of South China seemed to be on the march, each uprising against the hated foreigners starting another in a chain reaction. Millions of pounds worth of property was being abandoned without even a backward glance, its owners glad to be escaping with their lives.

Beyond the safety of Shanghai, the Westerners had been humbled. They had found suddenly that the Chinese would not even offer them their rickshaws to the waterfront because there had been too many beatings with bicycle chains and too many rickshaws burned, and they had to go on foot to the ships and always in groups for safety – humiliated, cowed, sometimes even bloodstained – through the shouting, spitting mobs. For generations the Chinese had accepted their inferiority without question but now they'd become a nation simply by joining hands and marching together. Nothing mattered any more – neither treaties nor flags nor guns – only victory; and the Whites had grown shabbier and dirtier every day as they'd waited for rescue. The days of the treaty powers were numbered. American and British consulates were being wrecked, and every vessel in China seemed to be somewhere up the Yangtze doing the same job of evacuation. By now almost every woman and child had been lifted to safety and their men were living on the river banks ready to leave at a moment's notice.

'The damned river's in a state of chaos,' Tyrwhitt grumbled.

By the end of the week, when Kelly was wondering what excuses he could offer for not going down to Hong Kong, he announced that he was going upriver again on a tour of inspection and that they were taking Lord Gort as a guest. Hurrying ashore that night, Kelly made his farewells with Christina clinging to him and weeping.

'Oh, come on,' he urged. '*You're* not a weeper.'

'I am now,' she sniffed. 'I shall miss you.'

'With fifteen thousand troops in the place? – every one of 'em willing to give his right arm to get a look at you.'

She gazed at him, her eyes big and bright and calculating. 'Why don't you marry me, Kelly?' she asked.

He smiled. 'Because it wouldn't work.'

'It did with Arthur Withinshawe. Well, after a fashion, it did.'

'I'm not Arthur Withinshawe,' he pointed out. 'And never likely to be. Besides, I can't afford it.'

'*I* can. Plenty of impoverished soldiers and sailors have made their name by managing to catch an heiress. Don't you love me or something?'

'Yes.' But he wasn't sure it was true and there was still a nagging feeling of guilt about Charley.

She looked at him shrewdly, calculatingly. 'Once upon a time, you'd have *had* to marry me – if only to make me an honest woman.'

'Honest be damned!' He gave a bark of laughter. 'You'd always be devious.'

'I'll be waiting for you when you come back. And if you don't pop the question then, *I* will. I'm getting old.'

'You'll never grow old.'

'I'll soon be too old to stagger into church. I'm twenty-seven. That's old for a woman without a husband.'

She opened a bottle of champagne and they took it upstairs with them. Their love-making was violent and he crept away in the early hours of the morning, unclenching her fingers from behind his neck as he backed from the bed.

They left Shanghai in *Hawkins* and headed upriver. The situation didn't seem to have improved, and at every town and village there were mobs of people along the bank and groups of soldiers riding on shaggy ponies. There seemed to be fires everywhere, where the homes and offices of the British and Americans and the Chinese businessmen who'd worked with them had been set alight, and it seemed to be as common a practice now for the Nationalist batteries to fire on them as it was to fire back.

As they stopped for two hours at Kiukiang, the consul came aboard to meet Tyrwhitt, a tired harassed-looking man who was trying to look after British interests under enormous difficulties because the British settlement these days consisted chiefly of sand-bagged gunposts. Though the treaty powers' flags flew alongside the company flags over the office buildings to put on a show, they seemed pathetically few against the enormous number of Kuomintang banners.

At Hankow, a new storm was brewing. The imposing marble of the Hong Kong and Shanghai Bank still stood, but it had a shabbier look now and there was a huge scorch mark near the front door where someone had tried to set it on fire.

The stay was short and they dined wherever anyone wanted them to put on a show, all of them doing their best to cheer up worried businessmen in danger of losing everything. Despite his reputation for going baldheaded at the enemy, everybody seemed pleased with the restraint with which Tyrwhitt was handling the situation.

'Thank God this is our last job,' he announced as they headed downstream. 'When I leave China, I don't want another. I've never stopped since 1914. When we get back, I'm taking my family to Wei-Hai-Wei, tension or no tension, and I advise you, my boy, to slip down to Hong Kong and tie things up with that girl of yours before someone else does it for you.'

What he'd suggested had been in Kelly's mind throughout the trip. Christina's words were still in his ears. She was beautiful, intelligent and exciting, but he had a suspicion that her interest in him might soon pall and, with her wealth and her energy for enjoying herself, his career could well be hampered rather than helped. He could hardly imagine her sitting at home while he served abroad or packing up an empty house to follow him to some foreign station. With Christina there would certainly be no rented rooms and hired houses, and he'd never be able to trust her, he knew. Somehow, he felt, he *must* go to

190

Hong Kong and see Charley. There'd been too many misunderstandings and failed meetings, and perhaps it would all be different if he did.

As the ship dropped anchor again at Shanghai, Tyrwhitt gestured. 'I'm off,' he said. 'I need a break from all the conundrums. You clever young chaps are quite splendid but it's a bit of a strain to live up to you, you know. You'd better get off to Hong Kong as fast as you can.'

But when Kelly went to the club for luggage he'd left there, there was a message from Christina and, far from unwillingly, he swallowed his gin and took a cab along the Bubbling Well Road.

She was dressed in red and her green eyes flashed as she clung to him, kissing him fiercely.

'Steady on, old thing,' he pleaded.

'I don't want to "steady on",' she said. 'You're mine, aren't you?'

'Am I?'

'Surely you're not thinking of bolting to Hong Kong to see that muddle-headed little creature down there, are you?'

Kelly was indignant. He'd never heard Charley called a muddle-headed little creature.

'I had thought so,' he said stiffly.

'Well, you can unthink,' she said. 'I have news for you. I've cabled my father. We're getting married.'

'Are we, by God?' Kelly snorted. 'I don't recall popping the question.'

'You don't have to.'

'It's normal.'

'Not this time. Haven't you noticed anything about me?'

'You're beautiful. And that dress suits you. The red's like blood. It makes you look more like a man-eater than ever.'

'I didn't mean that. I've lost weight. Know why?'

'Father telegraphed back to say "Nothing doing"?'

'No. He telegraphed to say he was delighted.'

'It's a pity he didn't ask *me* what *I* felt about it.'

'Don't you *want* to marry me?'

Suddenly Kelly knew he didn't. No, something inside him shouted. No! No! No! By Christ, No! Suddenly he realised he'd got into something that was going to be difficult to get out of.

191

She stared at him, smiling. 'I've lost weight because I've been worried,' she said. 'You weren't careful enough, my love. You *have* to marry me. You've made me pregnant.'

Kelly had been on the point of drinking, and the gin blew from his mouth in a shower as he choked on it. '*What!*'

She gave a hoot of laughter and slipped easily into his arms to kiss him. 'I'm going to have a baby.'

He stared at her, his jaw dropped open. 'Mine?'

'Who else's would it be? After the way we've been going at it.'

'Is this true?'

'What do you expect? You could never keep your hands off me.'

He stared at her. 'By God, you were as quick off the mark at that as everything else.'

She kissed him again. 'You sound alarmed.'

'Of course I'm alarmed. A man don't go rushing off marrying a woman who's only been widowed a couple of months.'

She smiled. 'Oh, it doesn't show yet,' she said. 'We can leave it for another couple of months. Then it ought to be all right. Rather romantic and all that, in fact. You saving my life and so on. I can be very decorous. You can invite the Admiral if you like.'

'But the baby! What happens when *that* arrives in six months time?'

Her smile widened into a grin. 'Really, Kelly, you're so old-fashioned. After the wedding, I shall hurry home to see my family. They might even give *you* leave, too, under the circumstances. But *I* shall stay in England and the baby will arrive quietly in the depths of the family estate in Norfolk. Nobody will ever know until I choose to let them.'

'I bet somebody will find out,' Kelly said gloomily.

'You worrying about your career?'

'Of course.'

'Well, stop as from this moment. I have plenty of cash and you don't even need a career married to me. I'm a one and only, and everything my father possesses comes to me eventually. Especially married to someone he approves of. There's a lot of land in Norfolk, a house in London, and a shooting box in Scotland, to say nothing of the house here and one in Bermuda. You'd look rather well as landed gentry.'

Charley's letter of congratulation was short, stiff and formal, and it contained a sting in the tail.

'It seems we've both deluded ourselves for years,' she said coldly. 'Because I've got engaged to Albert Kimister and I'm very happy.'

She didn't sound it.

Oh, Christ, Kelly thought, almost in tears at the way things had turned out. Not *Kimister*!

Tyrwhitt seemed surprised at Kelly's news and not particularly pleased, while Verschoyle, back from Nanking in *Wanderer*, gave him a sad look.

For the first time in his life, he noted, Kelly seemed uncertain of himself. Damn all women, he thought, damn all faithful, loving women who wanted husbands. He himself had always refused to allow himself to be tied, not even to Mabel who, God knows, was not only highly delectable and very experienced but was as subtle as a hunting cat.

'You know, old man,' he said slowly, choosing his words with care. 'I've been a bastard all my life and there was a time when I'd have howled with delight at this. But this time I think you've picked the wrong 'un. Can't you get out of it?'

'I don't want to,' Kelly snapped.

'I don't believe you,' Verschoyle snapped back. 'And what in God's name happened to the Little 'Un?'

'She didn't want me. She decided to marry Kimister.'

Verschoyle's face fell. 'Oh, my God! What a rotten bloody mix-up.' He studied Kelly over his glass. 'Need someone to give the bride away?'

'The Far East Manager of Clemo-Oriental's doing that. He's a fat pompous bastard with an office in Shanghai.'

'My, aren't we bitter? Need a best man?'

Kelly lifted his head and stared at Verschoyle. There'd been a time once when he'd have felt that Verschoyle was the last person in the world he'd want at his wedding. But somehow he seemed to go with Christina, even – because he knew what made her tick – seemed a form of defence against her.

'I'd be grateful,' he said.

The situation didn't improve. Tyrwhitt had started to send

aircraft over the fortified districts where fighting between the Chinese armies was taking place, feeling they might add to his information, and when a British DH9A made a forced landing outside the Settlement boundaries, the unarmed party that was sent out to retrieve it came back only with the engine and fuselage, but not the wings, pilot, or observer.

There was a great deal of back and forth and, in retaliation, the Shanghai–Hankow and Shanghai–Nanking Railways were cut, which affected the Nationalists' lines of communications; and eventually the airmen and the wings were released. There was another hurried trip upriver to land Marines at Nanking and call at Kiukiang, but the lack of progress depressed Tyrwhitt. It was like trying to plug a leak while thousands of others appeared. No matter what they did, no matter what methods they used, the Chinese were quite intractible and far too numerous to defeat.

By this time, however, the situation in Shanghai itself seemed to have quietened down, and Kelly was married at the end of August. His guests included Verschoyle and the Tyrwhitts. Christina's seemed to be chiefly Shanghai business associates of her father's, hard-headed types who didn't fit in among the naval uniforms, any more than the naval uniforms fitted in among them. Since he'd known her so long, Kelly sent an invitation to Charley, certain she wouldn't turn up; but, probably for the same reason, she did, looking like a ghost at the feast. Their greetings were as stiff and formal as their mutual congratulations.

'Kimister's a lucky man,' Kelly said.

She gave him a small twisted smile. 'Your wife's lucky, too. I always thought –'

She stopped, pecked his cheek and moved away hurriedly so that he shouldn't see the moisture in her eyes. Kelly's congratulations to Kimister were blunt, insincere and almost rude.

'Why *that* bloody man?' he hissed to Verschoyle.

Verschoyle shrugged. 'There's nothing,' he said, 'that defies explanation so much as the attraction for each other of two apparently unattracted people.'

Mabel was there, too, her mouth a vivid slash, and Kelly noticed that she and Verschoyle were preparing to vanish even as he and Christina headed for the taxi on the journey that was

194

to end at Hong Kong where, it seemed, the Clemo family owned yet another house on the Peak. He'd also hoped to have Rumbelo at the wedding but Rumbelo was clearly on Charley's side and was red-faced and uncomfortable as he stumbled out a feeble excuse about being on duty.

Hong Kong compared favourably with anywhere else in the world and at night beat them all, with the Peak sparkling with light and the illuminations reflected in the black water where an unending procession of ferries and native vessels plied from the island to the mainland. It was full of the wives of Shanghai taipans, all of them revelling in the enormous numbers of unattached young men the crisis had brought to the east.

While they were there, Lord Clemo arrived, flown out in easy stages to Singapore, from where he'd taken a coastal steamer to Hong Kong. He was a long lean man like a greyhound with the same pale face and black hair that Christina had, the same sharp wit, the same diamond-like mind.

'What do you intend to do now you're married to my daughter?' he asked Kelly. 'Get yourself a decent job in the city?'

It sounded like a euphemism for a living death and Kelly answered shortly. 'No, sir,' he said. 'I'll do the same as I've always done. Follow my profession.'

Clemo didn't seem to think much of the idea. 'Not much future in that, is there?' he said. 'The way everybody's cutting down the armed forces. Chances are that you'll be out on the street without a job. Your admiral, too, come to that.'

There was noticeably no reference to children and Kelly guessed that Christina hadn't told her father the circumstances of their marriage.

From Hong Kong they went to Wei-Hai-Wei where the mountains inland looked like a background for a film. The island was wooded and beautiful and was set in a burnished sea, a mass of acacia and pomegranate rich with scarlet blooms. The naval establishments were housed in pagodas with eaves winged against the activities of devils, and the sailors' canteen was in a temple. There was no traffic but rickshaws, and no sound but the metallic evening concert of the cicadas and the chatter of sailors strolling past the row of shops on the waterfront, staring with wistful eyes at the jade and soapstone, and the shantung they couldn't afford to buy for their wives.

195

They had a bungalow with a garden full of snapdragons, zinnias, sunflowers and sweet williams, doubtless planted by some earlier naval wife, and they could hear only the twitter of birds and the mad calling of a cuckoo. Kelly thought it was beautiful but Christina complained that it was too small and too dull and Wei-Hai-Wei too humid, with mildew that was likely to spoil her clothes, and they left just before a typhoon piled junks and sampans on the rocks and left a mat of drowned Chinese in the shallows.

They arrived back in Shanghai to find the place seething with news of a coming clash between the Chinese Communists and the Nationalists, and nobody very pleased that the army had lost two of its battalions and that Tyrwhitt had released the Second Cruiser Squadron for the Mediterranean. The warships had moved up opposite the bund beneath the façade of banks and the high gold dome of the Cathay Hotel, and the place seemed to be living at a feverish pace with the knowledge of a coming Armageddon with standards haywire and delirium in the air.

It was easy to fit into the life again. There wasn't even any need to look for a house because they already had the one in the Bubbling Well Road, heavily staffed with Chinese servants who made entertaining easy. Verschoyle came often to dinner or for drinks, accompanied usually by Mabel. They were quite obviously deep in an affair.

Charley was married to Kimister in October, Kimister eager to bind her securely captive to him while he could. The invitations included one for Kelly and his wife, and Christina spent so much time preparing for it he knew it was for no other reason than that she wanted to outshine Charley.

This time it was a naval wedding with uniforms, frock coats, epaulettes and an archway of swords that drew only contempt from Christina. Belfrage gave away the bride and the best man was a fat little lieutenant-commander called Nyland who'd been in the same term at Dartmouth as Kelly, Kimister and Verschoyle and was as dull as Kimister. Inevitably Kimister's adoring mother arrived, like Kimister overfed, pale and characterless. 'So bloody ordinary,' Verschoyle said, 'She gives you a headache.' The speeches were formal and Charley looked like a sacrificial lamb. Kelly's heart bled for her.

'Why Kimister?' he asked himself again. 'Why bloody Kimister?'

Mabel supplied the answer. 'Because he was *there*,' she said bluntly. 'And you weren't. I did my best to keep the little toad at arm's length, but it was too late by then. The poor kid didn't stop crying for two days. If you ask me, you played her a damned dirty trick because she was always convinced she was going to marry you from the first time she hit you over the head with her doll. However –' she flashed her scarlet smile at him '–that's the way it goes, isn't it? Look at me. I've been engaged twice and they both escaped.'

As the year approached its end, the situation in Shanghai grew tenser. They knew the clash between the Nationalists and the Communists was coming and they were worried about how it would affect the city and the foreign residents. Occasional rescue parties were ordered out. Priests and nuns from an Italian mission on the coast eighty miles away were taken prisoner, and a destroyer put a landing party ashore to bring back the captives in a horrifying state of dirt and starvation.

The expected upheaval came at last. The Communists made an attempt at a coup but, as the Nationalists hit back, they were swept out of the city in a series of bloody reprisals that did little harm to the Westerners, though a lot of damage was done to buildings, and the ensuing work left Kelly in no mood to chase his wife round the night-spots with her friends. Somehow, despite the social life of the Navy, he'd always suspected in an old-fashioned way that evenings ought occasionally to be spent together at home, reading or knitting or something, with short ecstatic passages in bed which ended up by producing the usual family. Visiting friends, dining, dancing – chiefly with business taipans and their plump wives who didn't even speak the same language – didn't quite seem to fit the bill, and a suspicion was growing in Kelly's mind which he finally blurted out one evening as they prepared to go out.

'When's the baby due?' he demanded.

Christina turned. She had just emerged from the bathroom and was standing stark naked by the mirror holding a towel in front of her.

'What's that?' she asked.

'For God's sake put something on and listen to me!'

'I don't have to wear clothes to listen to you,' she said coolly. 'And I am listening. What did you say?'

'I said. "When's the baby due?" I thought you were going home to have it.'

'Ah!' She smiled at him under a fringe of dark hair. 'Well, now I'm not.'

'You know damn well you can't have it out here! The bloody word will be round the fleet in no time!'

She leaned over to him and kissed him. 'You do worry about that silly old career of yours a lot, don't you?' she said.

'It's the only one I've got.'

'Well, try not to do it too much in front of me, there's a dear.'

'I asked you a question.'

'What was it?'

She seemed quite unwilling to pay attention and, in a rage, brought on by tiredness and concern, he snatched her wrist and swung her round.

'Why aren't you going home?' he snapped.

She stared back at him coolly. 'Because it's no longer necessary,' she said.

'Do you mean you're not having a baby?'

'Exactly.'

'Did you get rid of it?'

There was a momentary pause before she answered. 'Yes.'

He didn't believe her and in that moment he knew he'd *never* be able to believe her. She'd played him like an angler with a trout and had finally landed him. She'd wanted him and, because she'd never been denied anything in all her life, she'd cheated him with the oldest trick in the world.

'You were never having one,' he accused. 'You were lying as usual.'

She smiled and he went on angrily. 'You've got so much bloody money you think you can behave just as you like! You thought you could get me the same way!'

Her smile grew wider, triumphant and delighted. '*I got you,*' she pointed out.

'I ought to walk out on you.'

'You wouldn't dare.' She beamed at him, quite unperturbed. 'Think what your precious Navy would say: Walked out on his wife after only a few months' marriage. Tut tut! Demote him.

Keelhaul him. Hang him from the yardarm, or wherever it is they hang them from. And now you'd better hurry and dress. We're dining at the Rowntrees'.'

Kelly glared at her, '*I'm* not.'

'I've accepted.'

'To hell with the bloody Rowntrees!'

'They're father's friends – mine too, for that matter – and very influential.'

'I don't give a damn!'

She stared at him, her eyes hot. 'You're a fool, Kelly,' she snapped.

'And you're a liar!'

As her hand came round to hit him, he grabbed her wrist and wrestled with her. As they fell across the bed, her heard her chuckle unexpectedly and, to show he meant what he'd said, he snatched at the towel she wore.

'I say,' she said gaily. 'Steady on!'

'Damn you,' Kelly snarled. 'I'll show you whether we're going out or not.'

Afterwards, with her lying alongside him. Kelly found himself frowning with disgust at himself.

'You know,' she said quietly, 'that was rape.'

'It'll make up for the time when you *weren't* raped.'

There was a long silence.

'Actually, you know –' her voice was dreamy '– you were rather good – though there's no coming back for seconds – not tonight, anyway, because you've tired me out and the Rowntrees, as you say, can go to hell.'

As she turned and pulled the sheet over her, Kelly, lying alongside her, straight-limbed and angry, stared at the ceiling. There was only one thing in his mind: Clear as a blinding light, he knew, after only a few short months, that he wasn't in love with his wife and never would be.

Part Three

1

Gashed with red lead and festooned with wire hawsers and ropes, the battle cruiser, *Rebuke*, looked like a vast steel fortress, a man-made mastodon against the graceful lines and spars of Nelson's flagship, *Victory,* resting in her new concrete dock not far away. The R Class ships had none of the elegance or symmetry of *Hood*, which in comparison looked more like a yacht, and in her square lines and ugly turrets there was an awkward look of aggression. The great guns pointing fore and aft were an indication of her power, and her high sides and towering bridge an indication of her size. Commander Kelly Maguire disliked her on sight.

She was obsolete and, though she was just finishing a refit, he knew as well as every man aboard her that she was years out of date, a monument to the creed of the big gun and the dead belief in the power of the great capital ship, which even its creator, Jacky Fisher had repudiated before his death.

As he climbed from the taxi that had dropped him alongside, the Marine sentry rattled his rifle butt on the concrete, and he noticed with approval that the side party was already appearing at the top of the gangway. As he stared up at the ship, towering and monstrous in her iron-grey paint and representing over thirty-thousand tons of expensive equipment, he knew full well that, in spite of her cost, she was not of great value.

Like everybody else first joining a capital ship, he was taken aback by her sheer size. It had become an old joke that every new officer exploring her inside tied a thread to the handle of the wardroom door to guide him back, and his heart sank as he studied her. He didn't like big ships. Remembering the war years at Scapa when he'd watched them swinging at anchor for month after month, their crews staring wistfully at the destroyers rushing past about their everlasting business with the sea, he had long since come to the conclusion that battleships were an expensive luxury, too slow to do much damage yet too valuable to be risked, expensive monuments to the idea of a fleet in being that had held sway throughout the Great War. There was no feeling of belonging among their crew, too much specialisation and little idea of what was going on. He'd once met a junior officer who'd been in one of them at the rear of the fleet at Jutland, who'd had no idea there'd been a battle until he'd read the papers on his return to Rosyth.

As executive officer, his duties were going to cause him a great deal of thought, and what he was going to do with the thirteen hundred men of her crew in peace time when there was nothing much to hold their attention and no excitement beyond holystoning and painting he couldn't imagine.

He climbed the gangway and saluted the quarterdeck. Despite himself, despite his dislike of *Rebuke*, he couldn't help but feel the old surge of pride in the Navy as he felt her size beneath his feet and caught the hum of ventilating machinery that provided the background to all the other noises of a living ship.

As he acknowledged the officer of the day, he saw a familiar face among the men lined up behind him.

'I know you, don't I?'

The leading seaman he addressed, a big red-haired man with a washtub belly, grinned. 'Yes, sir. Leading Seaman Doncaster.'

'*Mordant*. Novorossiisk, 1919.'

'That's right, sir. We was sorting out the Russkies. You took us to a garden party at a house belonging to some Russian princess, sir.'

And you made a speech, Kelly thought to himself, and that same Russian princess warned me to keep an eye on you.

As he saw his black tin trunks being put down in his cabin and watched Corporal O'Hara, the elderly Marine who was to look after him, begin to unpack them, he decided it was going to take him weeks even to get to know half the people aboard. It seemed important that he had a link with the lower deck and it crossed his mind at once that Petty Officer Rumbelo was just the man. It wouldn't be difficult to have him drafted to *Rebuke* and, while Rumbelo had been somewhat distant since Kelly's marriage, he was still entirely loyal.

'Do you 'ave photographs, sir?' O'Hara asked.

'Photographs?'

'Children, sir. Your lady wife. Most of the officers like to have 'em about. I'll stick 'em around for you.'

'No,' Kelly said. 'No photographs. Don't believe in 'em.'

It was a lie. Photographs in the bare steel cabins, even if they didn't give the place a homely aspect, at least allowed a man to think of home. He preferred not to.

Home, to Kelly Maguire, was still the old house at Thakeham, efficiently run, between looking after her children, by Rumbelo's wife, Bridget. Kelly's mother had moved out to a cottage at the end of the lane so that Kelly and Christina could take it over, and there had been no objection from his father who, in any case, rarely appeared from his London club. It had not come to much, however. Christina had never liked the country and rarely went there.

'I don't intend to moulder quietly away in this bloody place,' she had announced firmly as she had stood staring round her in the hall on their return from China. 'Not with you away all the time in your ridiculous ships. It might be all right for some people but I'm not cut out for that sort of thing. Naval wives are almost a biological sub-species, and I'm not one.'

It was true that naval wives had tended to come in batches of a dozen – service background, unimaginative and able to hold their own in their husband's struggle for promotion – but post-war generations were learning to marry healthy, unembarrassed middle-class girls who possessed the gift of being good letter-writers, and in the absence of their husbands at sea could handle the tradesmen, the children and quick-witted estate agents while pursueing the everlasting chore of house-hunting.

Kelly frowned. The first year of his marriage had seemed normal enough and, with no knowledge of what a happy marriage ought to be, to Kelly it had even appeared that his own was jogging along contentedly enough despite his doubts. But Christina had never enjoyed playing second fiddle to a ship and her first glamorous view of the navy had quickly changed. It soon became obvious that she was not prepared to play the role he expected of her, and by the end of the second year the melting away of trust between them had started. Now, beyond the physical attraction which still undoubtedly existed, there was nothing to admire but her sharp wit and efficiency and her shrewd ability to handle her own affairs.

She'd done all the right things, of course. Her father, making sure his bread was buttered on both sides, had a minor position in the government – not big enough for him to be associated with failure if things went wrong but sufficient to be associated with success if the government pulled things off – and he *made sure* that she did the right things. The house had been redecorated and improved throughout so that Bridget no longer had to get up early to clean out the kitchen range but had instead a vast electric cooker she detested, and for shopping a car in the garage that she drove in a state of mortal terror when Rumbelo himself wasn't home to do it for her.

Staring round him, Kelly decided that *Rebuke* was a bit like his marriage: Involving too many people to handle successfully but too big, important and expensive to be put aside.

At least, he thought, there was no longer any worry about money. Christina never asked him for any and what he drew as naval pay was entirely his own, but she also never asked his views on how to behave. She had a house in Mayfair and spent most of her time there in the company of a set of people – mostly business tycoons or hothouse intellectuals – whom Kelly didn't understand and couldn't bear.

The marriage had staled even before they'd left China, and she had disappeared to her father's estate in Norfolk long before his tour had come to an end. He had accompanied Tyrwhitt on a circuit of the whole China Station, and when he'd returned the house in the Bubbling Well Road had been closed and she'd left him a letter which showed how much she'd inherited her father's shrewdness. With the Shanghai taipans still considering there was a future for them in China, she'd cut her losses early and sold the house while it was possible to do so without too much suffering.

A visit to Japan with Tyrwhitt with *Kent, Suffolk* and *Berwick*, to attend the naval review that had followed the coronation of the new Emperor, Hirohito, took away some of the unpleasantness of suddenly finding himself alone. They had visited Shinzu and Fujiyama, and the endless round of salutes and calls had kept him too busy to think. The lines of anchored ships were not so different from those he'd seen off Portland, and they'd all been introduced to the Emperor, each of them clutching a small basket wrapped in a silk cloth and containing a piece of fish, a piece of pie, an apple, an orange, a piece of cake and a box of sweets. It was only when he'd made considerable inroads on the contents that he'd learned the correct procedure was to take out only a little and use the rest to distribute among his friends. He'd met Admiral Togo, victor of Tsu-Shima, danced at the British Embassy with Princess Chichebu, who spoke perfect English and seemed a vast improvement on the diamond hardness of Christina, then Tyrwhitt had left for England ahead of him at a time when it was becoming clear that Britain's interests in China were going to have to be confined to Shanghai and Hong Kong, and there was even a doubt about those.

A spell at home, when the marriage had appeared to pick up a little had been followed by a tour in the Mediterranean in command of a destroyer. For that, Christina had condescended to appear at Malta. She had taken a house on Piéta Hill, not among the other lieutenant-commanders but in that part known as Snob Street because the illustrious and wealthy had taken mansions there. It had not been a successful commission, either from the point of view of his marriage or from the point of view of his career.

Somehow, Roger Keyes, the commander-in-chief, had not come up to his expectations. Polo seemed to matter most and to someone like Kelly, whose only connection with a horse was falling off it, the whole place smelled of privilege. A roll call of the staff in the flagship sounded like a court circular, and officers were said to be reporting for duty with a pair of polo mallets and a copy of Debrett's under their arm. What was worse, he had had nothing to do. Under Keyes, orders were so intricate, detailed, and prepared so far in advance, a ship's captain could use his initiative only to arrange the time when he wanted calling in the morning. The Mediterranean, those disgruntled officers who were not favoured claimed, had become not the Italians' Mare Nostrum but Keyes' Mare Meum, and manoeuvres were nothing but waterborne square dances.

Christina had loved the excitement and the glitter that went with the social season surrounding the flagship, but had not been impressed by the pink glow of mighty fortifications in the world's most magnificent naval shelter, and still less by the great grey warships. She had quite failed to sense the atmosphere in Grand Harbour, and was unmoved by the things that touched Kelly's heart – the dghaisas swaying alongside to ferry ships' complements, the shouted orders you could hear from on shore, the clank of anchor cables, the charging of submarines' batteries and the sad sweet notes of the Last Post across the water at night. They had meant absolutely nothing to her and, while Kelly had seethed at the lack of personal command, she had noticed only the fashionable people who followed the fleet.

It had all come to an abrupt end with the cataclysm known as the *Royal Oak* Affair, when a cause célèbre rose from the unfortunately close proximity in the same ship of a choleric squadron admiral, a dogmatic flag captain and a neurotic commander. When Keyes had misjudged the situation, the result had been that the Navy had made a fool of itself, and the odium that had rubbed off had ruined Keyes' chances of becoming First Lord. Kelly had gone to the Mediterranean looking forward to his own command – and in a destroyer, too! – but he'd been glad in the end to leave for England, only to find command of a shore station was one degree worse.

He sighed at the disappearance of so many hopes and went to seek out *Rebuke*'s key officers and ratings. These were the men he would come to know individually as the ship settled down, the men on whom the ship and his own reputation would ultimately depend. It seemed wiser to put the past firmly behind him and try to make something of the present.

When he arrived on board to take command – immaculate in full fig of sword and frock coat – Captain George Major Mason Harrison turned out to be a dark lean saturnine individual not unlike Tyrwhitt in looks but by no means blessed with Tyrwhitt's keen commonsense.

The officers were drawn up on the quarter deck, the key ratings standing behind. The new captain shook hands with them all as Kelly introduced them, but only as though it were a chore he had to get through quickly. To the Heads of Department, it seemed as if he were already looking for faults in them, and his first walk round the ship was done at the gallop because he was clearly more eager to get Kelly alone in his cabin to make his attitude to command plain at once.

'I like discipline,' he announced in a high-pitched aloof voice that was already beginning to grate on Kelly's nerves. 'And I'm fussy about the honours done to visitors by the side parties. I've already – even in so short a time – noticed a great many errors and omissions and from now on I'd like to meet every new officer immediately he comes aboard.'

He stared coldly at Kelly. 'I notice you wear a medal we all cherish, but I'd have you know, Commander, that it's no answer to slackness. Too many people have won that medal by being brave in the heat of the moment and have had no further success in their career because they've not had the staying power to be courageous when there's no danger. Do I make myself clear?'

Kelly said nothing because Harrison obviously didn't expect an answer. There was nothing like a new broom, he thought.

'I'd be glad if you'd inform those of the ship's company who're already on board,' Harrison went on, brushing invisible fluff from his spotless sleeve, 'that I prefer to have things done by the book. It saves a great deal of trouble later.'

'Indeed, sir,' Kelly agreed.

'I expect both officers and men to be in the correct rig of the day at all times – and I expect it to be immaculate. I shall also check my predecessor's order books as soon as possible, because I feel sure there will be items I'd prefer changed. Orders will remain as they are, however, until I've considered them, and I'd be grateful if you could make time as soon as possible to meet me here and discuss the changes I'd like made.'

Kelly made his escape hurriedly. Harrison seemed to be a glutton for protocol and as pernickity about behaviour as he was about dress. He'd met his type before. The captain of his first ship had been exactly the same, with every man in his place and knowing his place, and woe betide anybody who tried to step out of it. His written orders would cover every eventuality – chiefly as a means of clearing his own yard arm if things went wrong – a bureaucratic system which, to Kelly, seemed to show a lack of self-confidence and a penchant a mile wide for old-womanhood. That's how the Good Book says it should be done, he thought, and that was how it was going to be done. It was going to provide some sticky moments in the wardroom, he felt sure, and a great deal of tooth-sucking below decks; in his experience there had always been and always would be moments that were quite definitely not covered by the Good Book. But perhaps George Major Mason Harrison's career had run so far either on oiled wheels or in the more sober backwaters of the Service where everything could be relied on to be covered by orders. He decided he wasn't going to enjoy *Rebuke*.

In his office, to his surprise he found Seamus Boyle, wearing spectacles and with white between his gold stripes.

'Seamus! What are you doing here? Last time I saw you was in Russia.'

Boyle jumped to his feet, smiling. 'Transferred to Paymaster Branch, sir. Started having a bit of trouble with my eyes and it seemed the best thing to do because I didn't wish to leave the Navy. I came aboard just behind the captain.'

'I remember you were all dewy-eyed over the Baptiste girl – what was her name?'

'Anne-Marie, sir.'

'What happened to her?'

Boyle grinned. 'I married her, sir. Three years ago.'

Kelly laughed, feeling that he had at least one ally on board who would understand him. 'Well, that's wonderful!' he said. 'And for me, too, to have you aboard. Are you getting the hang of everything?'

'Just taking a look at the order book, sir.' Boyle cleared his throat. 'I gather from your writer that the captain doesn't approve of orders as they stand.'

'I think you'll be working on them a great deal before you've finished.'

It was a pleasure to see a familiar face, but *Rebuke* herself didn't fool Kelly. As he and everybody else with any sense knew, she belonged to a fleet that was becoming rapidly out of date. Battleships no longer had a place in a modern world and, though everybody had them still and the Germans were reported even to be planning new ones, the Americans had proved years before that bombs from an aircraft could sink them without a great deal of difficulty, and since a youngster called Lindbergh had proved the potential of the aeroplane by

210

flying the Atlantic non-stop and alone while Kelly was still in Shanghai, the world's navies were beginning to take heed and were thinking of weighing down their great ships with an enormous amount of anti-aircraft guns and an armoured deck.

'Thinking' was the operative word, Kelly knew, because it hadn't taken him long to notice that, despite her long refit, *Rebuke* still had the great defect of a lack of strengthened steel on her upper decks. She had been laid down before Jutland where three British battle cruisers had been destroyed in seconds by heavy German shells, which had plunged vertically down on them to explode their magazines. Though all big ships built since had strengthened decks, in the financial and international crises of the years since the war, with *Rebuke* they had never quite got around to it. She even had little or no defence against submarines, despite the vast torpedo bulges which had added to her already enormous girth and reduced her speed still further. And, while the new streamlined funnel made the ship look new, no one aboard was kidded that the millions of pounds which had been spent on her modernisation had made her anything else but a done-up battlewaggon.

Like an old tart with new false teeth, Kelly thought.

Harrison made no objection to Kelly's request for Rumbelo, who arrived within a fortnight. He stared around him and sniffed.

'Big,' he observed, and that was all he said.

Christina showed roughly the same amount of approval.

'And where are *you* going to live?' she demanded.

'On board.'

'And me?'

'Wherever it suits you.'

'I'm certainly not going to camp out at the Keppel's Head on Portsmouth Hard,' she announced firmly. 'I tried it once, and it's not a hotel for my fastidious taste.'

'I could get a house,' Kelly suggested.

'Buy one?'

'Naval officers don't buy houses because they never live in them.'

'Well, *I* don't intend to live in a rented maisonette, with intimidating brown walls, an aspidistra and brown furniture with the stuffing oozing out; any more than in a basement flat

211

looking at other people's ankles. It's a pity you haven't noticed yet that there are plenty of other jobs far better paid.'

Kelly frowned. 'I've been in the Navy too long to want a change,' he said. 'It wouldn't be easy now to take to another life or, for that matter, find another job.'

'My father could fit you up with an excellent job.'

'I prefer to stay in the Navy.'

She looked at him coolly. 'Suffering from promotionitis all the way. A very prevalent complaint, it seems, because those stupid idiots who run the show consider naval officers don't need wives or children.'

'*We* don't have any children,' Kelly pointed out.

'*I* do.'

In fact, one of the few joys of Kelly's life was Christina's son, Hugh. A dark-eyed shy boy, rather in awe of his mother, his habit was to turn to Kelly when in trouble. He was at a preparatory school in Sussex, a thin child half-swamped in the red cap and blazer he had to wear. Since the school was handier for Portsmouth than for London, invariably the visits he received were from Kelly.

'*In a hurry,*' a note would come from Christina. '*See Hugh for me, there's a dear.*'

Kelly knew perfectly well that she simply had no interest in the boy. He looked like Withinshawe, and for Withinshawe she'd had nothing but contempt and simply couldn't be bothered to interrupt the life she was leading in London to spend what was inevitably a dull week-end taking the boy to the cinema, to the beach or to restaurants, watching him eat with all the silent gluttony of all small and growing boys.

The year 1930 ended in a strange sort of gloom. The Navy was not the sharp-edged instrument it had been, and though Britain had won the war it had lost the peace. There had been a reaction everywhere against huge fleets and America had emerged from the manoeuvrings as the major power. She had started building to produce fifty-one first-line capital ships while Britain had ended the war with only forty-two, thirteen of them obsolete and all of doubtful value. At the end of the naval conferences, twenty more ships had been listed for scrapping and four partly-built battle cruisers had been demolished, so that that navy in which Kelly had grown up had been reduced

212

to a skeleton of its former pride. The panache had gone and the Geddes axe which had carved ruthlessly into the Navy List had destroyed confidence; while, because the country was in the middle of its worst-ever financial crisis, the ratings who were joining now were all too often only avoiding unemployment.

Everywhere there was a feeling of resentment and disappointment. The high social and ceremonial factors of naval life had gone, with the brilliantly-uniformed etiquette, the shining brass, the spit and polish; yet nothing had taken its place, and England was no place to enjoy the blessings of the shore. The country had avoided the political upheavals that had followed the war in Russia and Germany, but there had been seven governments in power since 1918, and with hostilities abroad never really ceasing, there was a crescendo of industrial action.

There had also been the most awful financial crash in the United States and Kelly had heard that it had hit Kimister, whose father, fearing a financial crash in England, had invested heavily across the Atlantic. Out of the three of them, only Verschoyle seemed to be content with his lot. Now back in London and on the staff of the Third Sea Lord, he seemed entirely untouched by the crisis. His family, with the cool cunning and experience of their kind, had not only kept their fortune but, with wages dropping everywhere and prices dropping to keep them company, were actually better off. It was from Verschoyle that Kelly learned what Christina did in London, because it seemed their paths crossed from time to time as they moved among the same set of people.

It was early in the year and the week-ends in the ship were cold and uncomfortable. Most of the officers and ship's company had not yet joined and the great vessel was still more than half empty. Many of her messdecks were uninhabited and her long passageways were unheated. There were only skeleton staffs on duty and the hot water supply, heated by steam from two donkey-boilers on the jetty, was often only lukewarm or dried up altogether, while electric power, supplied by cables from the dockyard, fluctuated erratically, and lights and fires frequently went out without warning. The men on board behaved like arctic explorers – inhabiting isolated colonies of

213

light and warmth about the ship.

Steaming trials passed without too much dissatisfaction though Kelly noticed that, like Tyrwhitt's *Hawkins*, *Rebuke* was wet; her funnel, despite the money and effort spent on streamlining it, still threw out boiler fumes which obscured her spotting top; and at high speed she seemed to suffer from an acute form of St. Vitus' dance. The engineer commander, a small, uncertain angry man who had the shrunken look of something that had been too frequently laundered, was on edge throughout the whole business in case any of the dozens of sea-connections which could cause flooding had been left open. Dockyard workers weren't known for their sense of responsibility and, since they weren't likely to be on board if the ship filled with water and sank, they didn't have the same feeling for leaky steam joints, untightened nuts or bilges choked with cotton waste, fag ends and lunch paper. The skeleton crew with which the steaming trials were completed were also hardly to be recommended, and with *Rebuke* part of the Atlantic Fleet and due to sail with them in the summer, Kelly went to the commodore in charge of the port establishment to demand that when the proper crew arrived it should contain at least a nucleus of good men.

The drafting commander was sympathetic but unable to help much. 'You know what they're like,' he pointed out. 'They're not exactly enamoured of the Navy these days.'

Verschoyle filled him in on the facts.

'Now we have a Labour Government,' he explained bluntly, 'they prefer the socialist method of approach. They know the ways of the Admiralty are as tortuous as Hampton Court maze and that any request to them can disappear from sight, never to be seen again, so if they don't like something, instead of going to their officer, they go to the dockyard M.P., who's usually a Socialist and it's brought up in Parliament. It induces what you might call a slow erosion of confidence both ways.'

'Can't you lot at the Admiralty do anything?' Kelly demanded. '*You*'ve been here long enough to put down roots.'

Verschoyle smiled. 'My dear chap, I'm just one more bottleneck in the stream of papers passing round.' He paused. 'Seen the Little 'Un lately?'

Kelly shrugged. 'Not since Shanghai.'

'I saw Kimister.' Verschoyle smiled. 'He's in the minelaying cruiser, *Advance*. Said it was nice to have the Three Musketeers back in England.'

'Three Musketeers?'

'You, me and him. I asked him what made him think *he* could ever be a Musketeer. He'd probably shoot his own foot off.'

Kelly laughed. It was cruel but no less than the truth.

'Heard they had to give up that house in Wales they had,' Verschoyle went on. 'He lost all his money.'

Kelly pretended disinterest but he was overwhelmed by a feeling of sadness. Everything seemed to have happened to Charley.

'They're living entirely on Kimister's pay now,' Verschoyle said, 'and he hasn't the guts or the brains to get on or get out. I reckon that at the next counting of heads he's due to be tossed out on his ear.'

Only once did Kelly meet Charley. He stopped in the Keppel's Head for a meal before catching the train to London and she was waiting there for Kimister. She didn't seem much older and, with her dark hair and blue eyes, there was a strange sort of calm about her.

'How's Albert?' Kelly asked.

'Oh, he's all right!' Her greeting was warm because she couldn't remember a time when she hadn't been in love with him and, despite everything, she still was. 'He's not too happy in *Advance* but he doesn't see any alternative. He says he's been in the Navy too long to look for a job outside.'

'I think we all have, Charley. How about Mabel?'

She shrugged and gave another little smile. 'Running a dress shop again.'

'Married?'

'Not yet. She seems to have accepted now that she won't be. She's very cheerful.'

'And you?'

'Times aren't quite what they used to be, are they, Kelly?'

'No, not quite the same.'

'I see Christina's picture occasionally in *The Tatler* or *The Sketch*.'

'Yes,' Kelly said bleakly. 'She gets around quite a bit.'

So bloody fast, he thought, he never managed to catch up

215

with her. He'd suspected for some time that she'd already taken to having men friends who were rather more intimate than they need have been and he'd been reminded several times of the captain of *Clarendon*, in which he'd been serving when war had broken out in 1914. He'd married some tart while on the China Station who'd turned out to be the daughter of a third-rate entrepreneur in Shanghai, and they'd all laughed at him because Chinasides was noted for what it did to men's reputations, sending them back drunks, corrupt or married to someone they wouldn't normally have looked at. Well, he was an old China hand himself now and he'd suffered in the same way.

He started back to the present. 'How about you, Charley?' he asked.

'Poor Albert's finding things a bit difficult at the moment.'

'And you?'

'Me, too.' She smiled. 'But we all have to furrow our own row, don't we? Albert tries very hard.'

'Sometimes I think—'

She put a hand on his quickly. 'It probably wouldn't have worked, Kelly,' she said in a breathless little rush. 'It often doesn't with people you've known all your lives, you know.'

He had a feeling that it would always have worked with Charley if he'd given it a chance. It was working even now, he felt bitterly, reaching out to him in a way that nothing about Christina ever did, despite her sex and her money.

Christina was already dressing to go out when he arrived at the house in Carlton Terrace.

'Not again, for God's sake,' he said angrily.

She was in full warpaint and she smiled at him, everlastingly cheerful and completely indifferent to his distaste.

'We're going to the Carters',' she said. 'There'll be a lot of Germans there from the Embassy. I'm told they're a very interesting lot.'

'I don't like the bloody Germans,' Kelly snapped. 'I spent four years of my life disliking them. It's not easy to start doing the other thing now.'

She turned from the mirror. 'You really are narrow-minded, aren't you?' she said. 'There are things *happening* in Germany,

216

you know. This chap Hitler's going to make the place hum.'
She dabbed at her nose with her powder puff. 'Looks a bit like
Charlie Chaplin, of course, but he's the head of a large party
and he knows what to do about the economic crisis.'

Kelly scowled. 'Do we *have* to go?'

'Yes, old thing. It's for charity.'

'These bloody parties for charity that everybody gives these
days seem to consist of a great deal of junketing and bloody
little charity.'

She stared at him coldly. In her sophisticated world, following the rules and dictates of the shallow society in which she
moved, she'd once considered herself too clever for him. He was
an extrovert individual, normally happy, brisk and full of an
energy that seemed to suggest he rarely thought deeply. But she
was astute enough to acknowledge that, though she disliked the
Navy, it demanded at least that a rising young officer should be
intelligent, too, and she often suspected he was sneering at her,
because he had acquired a disconcerting habit of hiding behind
his own face so that she didn't know what he was thinking.

'You sound like a bosun's mate or something, not a commander,' she said. 'The industrialists are supporting Hitler
more and more. He's found the answer to all the unrest we
suffer. Pity a few of our own lot can't set up someone like him
here. Somebody like Oswald Mosley. Father says that if a few of
the troublemakers had the stuffing knocked out of 'em as
they're having it knocked out in Germany, it might be a bit
easier to run things.'

'Your father,' Kelly said deliberately, 'is a bloody funny
Socialist.'

Unwillingly, he changed into evening dress. 'I hope we shan't
be late,' he said.

Christina was indifferent. 'These things always go on a bit.'

'Then I shall have to leave early. We're commissioning on
Monday.'

'Doesn't mean a thing.'

Kelly's scowl deepened. 'It means that it's taken three weeks
of careful planning with a list of twelve hundred ratings and seventy officers. Every department has to be manned and it's my
job to see to it.'

She dabbed at her nose once more. 'See Hugh?' she asked.

217

He might just as well have been commenting on the colour of the carpet for all the interest she showed in his problems.

'Yes,' he snapped.

'How was he?'

'Wanting to see his mother.'

'I don't believe you. He'd much rather see you. Told me so last time I went down, in fact. Bit off-putting, I thought. Decided the little beast could fish the next time there was a weekend out. In any case, I hate that bloody town where the school is as much as he hates London. He'd much rather look over one of your ships or something or go sailing with you in the Solent.'

The party seemed to consist of all the same faces he'd seen a hundred times a year since they'd returned to England. He had a feeling that after the years in the Far East and the Mediterranean, he was out of touch, and that the people he met in England were a cleverer lot who could tie him in knots. The fact that it wasn't true made no difference and he still felt lost for words in their company. Fortunately, Verschoyle was there, bland, amused and casual.

'How's that monstrous monument to Jacky Fisher you're in?' he asked.

'Coming to be known as *Rebuilt*.'

Verschoyle looked about him. 'Odd things, these charity functions,' he observed. 'Be much easier if we just turned over the money we spend to the poor and went out and had a drink at a pub. By the way, there's someone over there who claims she knows you. She's the wife of Count von Schwerin, one of the German attachés, and she said she knew a few naval people from after the war. Yours seemed to be the name she dwelt on most.'

The German attaché was a middle-aged man with a bald head, a monocle and a face like a borzoi. His wife had her back to them but Kelly knew at once who she was.

She turned eventually and he saw a pair of slanting topaz eyes smiling as she raised her glass to him. '*Za vashe zdorovye*, Kelly Georgeivitch,' she said. 'Your good health.'

'Vera Nikolaevna, as I live and breathe! What in God's name are you doing here?'

Vera von Schwerin smiled. She looked in command of herself, poised, wealthy and enjoying a far better life than when

218

he'd last seen her in Odessa.

'Germany's full of Prussian junkers who married Russian princesses,' she said. 'Half the Russian nobility was German in origin, anyway. If nothing else, we taught them how to behave like gentlemen and not aggressive boors.'

She didn't appear to have changed much and Kelly's instinct was to back away. She didn't fail to notice his hesitation.

'You remember me with warmth, I hope?' she said.

'Of course. And your husband?'

She gave him a cool look. 'When I met him, all he had to be proud of was the fact that he'd been a captain in the Death's Head Hussars. Now he's a colonel in the reconstituted German army. I told you I would survive, Kelly Georgeivitch. I married him in 1923 in Berlin where I went from Constantinople.' She fished in her bag and slipped a square of pasteboard into his pocket. 'That's my telephone number,' she murmured. 'A fortnight from today, my husband has to report back to Berlin for a week. I shall be alone. We could meet again and talk about old times.'

Verschoyle was just putting the telephone down in the hall when he escaped.

'You off, old boy?' he asked.

'I've had enough of this bloody place,' Kelly said.

'You always were one for salty language. What about Christina?'

'She has the car. I'll take a taxi.'

Verschoyle gestured. 'Take the car. I'll see her home for you. Where did you pick up the beauteous countess?'

'Novorossiisk, 1919.' Kelly was still a little shaken by the meeting. 'What we got up to was nobody's business.'

'Better not get up to it again, old son. Not just now, anyway. Things are happening.'

'What sort of things?'

'Mutiny, old lad. Submarine depot ship, *Lucia*. Chaps refusing to obey orders. She was converted from a captured German freighter, so perhaps some of the ghosts of the High Seas Fleet are still hanging around her holds.'

2

The whole fleet and all the dockyards were talking about *Lucia*, and the whisper was already running through *Rebuke*'s skeleton crew.

Lucia had been an unhappy vessel with a long record of trouble, and because of the dirty state of her decks after coaling ship, week-end leave had been cancelled by a choleric first lieutenant. Nothing had been said about the crew not being allowed ashore for the normal Sunday afternoon leave, however, and when the duty watch were ordered to fall in, they had remained sullenly on the mess deck until marched off under close arrest. There had been no trouble, only a protest.

More news came in later in the day along the invisible grapevine that carried titbits from one port to another, and they arrived in the wardroom unadorned.

'First lieutenant's got as much tact as a bull in a china shop,' the engineer commander said bluntly. 'I was in *Caerhays* with him and he couldn't organise a whelk stall.'

Kelly had long since put the final touches to *Rebuke*'s watch and station bill, the key to every ship's organisation, and with the manning of every branch from Signals to Stores worked out days before, Captain Harrison was anxious that commissioning day should go well.

'I want only men of the highest integrity for the ship's police,' he pointed out.

'That goes without saying, sir,' Kelly said. Harrison seemed to be trying to teach his grandmother to suck eggs.

'There's to be nobody who's likely to take a bribe to let a man ashore when he's not entitled to go. And inform the Paymaster that I want the same thing for the officers' stewards. There was a case of thieving in *Royal Oak* last year. And, although we use

220

the older Marines for the wardroom, make sure we don't get them hamfisted with six thumbs. There's more to it than freedom from drills and awkward duties. I expect to be visited by the commander-in-chief and commanding officers from other ships, and I shall expect them to carry out their duties not only with decorum but also with efficiency. I also want the Paymaster to make sure the first day's food is hot and at its best.' The nagging check on things Kelly could have attended to in his sleep stopped abruptly. 'Have you organised the petty officers and leading hands?'

'I have, sir.'

'Can't have twelve hundred men stumbling about the ship trying to find where they're supposed to go. Midshipmen arrived?'

'They're already beginning to throw their weight about and suck sweets when they shouldn't, sir.'

The great day arrived bright and clear. Petty officers and midshipmen had been well instructed in their duties and, as Kelly appeared on deck, lorries began to arrive, piled high with kitbags, hammocks and sailors hampered by raincoats and attaché cases. As they tossed the gear into chalked squares that had been prepared, the sound of drums and fifes was heard in the distance and a blue snake appeared round the corner of a shed. The barracks bluejackets band was pounding away to the best of its ability but the snake was so long those farthest from the music could hear it only as they turned corners, and seemed to be advancing in a series of hops, skips and jumps as they constantly changed step.

'You've heard of the military two-step, Seamus,' Kelly said to Boyle. 'This is the naval version.'

The midshipmen with the commissioning cards were in place as the column crashed to a stop. Immediately there was a buzz of chattering. 'Captain's messenger. That'll be nice.' ''Oo's the Bloke? Maguire of *Mordant*? They say 'e's a bit regimental, don't they?'

The Marine detachment arrived soon afterwards, their band playing 'Hearts of Oak', rifles, packs and white helmets squared off to a T, and as everybody scrambled aboard to stow bags and hammocks and snatch the best places below decks – leading hands near to the ventilators, newly-joined ordinary seamen squeezed into the alleyways – it was obvious they all knew what had happened at Devonport. 'Lucia!' 'Lucia!' 'Lucia!' The word intruded again and again in a low buzz and Kelly found himself on the look-out for any of *Rebuke*'s officers who might be inclined the same way as the first lieutenant of the guilty vessel.

They got the ship clear at last of what the dockyard mateys had left around – the rejected machine parts, the firebricks from the boiler room furnaces, the coke braziers on which they'd brewed their tea, the miles of air hoses and electric cable, the old lunch packets, newspapers and fag-ends, and started to set about the muddy footprints and the gulls' droppings she'd accumulated during her long stay alongside. A farewell dance was held in the Guildhall for the crew, and a cocktail party on board for the officers and their wives, and eventually the great ship left for her final drills, damage control exercises, full power trials, and anything else that occurred to them. To Kelly, who had never assisted in the departure of anything bigger than a light cruiser, *Rebuke* seemed enormous. With her strange bridge arrangements, peering down towards old Portsmouth as she left harbour was like staring down from Blackpool Tower. There also seemed an extraordinary remoteness between stem and stern and she had a majestic sluggishness in answering her helm and propellers, but Captain Harrison – or Gorgeous George, as he had come to be known not only to the lower deck but also to the Wardroom – knew exactly what he was doing.

The ship's company were experienced, though they were a mixed lot. Portsmouth crews were always an unknown factor. Chatham crews were always easiest because they were largely Londoners with a helpful Cockney wit, while Devonport crews – largely West Countrymen with a scattering of unemployed Welsh miners – though slow on the uptake, were as solid in behaviour as they were in thought. Crews from Pompey, however, came from everywhere in the British Isles and it was necessary to feel your way with them. There was always a large proportion of Scots – because there was no manning port north of the Tweed – and many Midlanders, both of whom suffered at leave time from being a long way from home and were inclined to be bloody-minded.

Even the officers, Kelly found for the first time in his life,

222

needed watching. They had already been severely shaken by the Geddes Axe, which had seen the abrupt departure from the Navy of twelve hundred lieutenants and lieutenant-commanders and a further six hundred officers at other levels, and in the Atlantic Fleet, to which *Rebuke* belonged, they were so often changed nobody ever got a chance to settle down and work as a team. In addition, with no fewer than nineteen lieutenant-commanders on board, work that should have been done by a midshipman or a petty officer was consigned to a lieutenant, while men in lower ranks had no chance of exercising responsibility and most of them had little practice in watch-keeping at sea.

Captain Harrison didn't make life any easier. He was a rigid disciplinarian punctilious about side parties and greetings and, a man of private means, it was his delight to point out to Kelly that, unlike most married officers, he preferred not to spend too much time ashore. 'I've been married thirteen years,' he liked to say, 'but my wife has learned to do without me.'

'Perhaps she prefers it that way,' was the first lieutenant's opinion.

Fortunately, with hot food, Captain Harrison also believed firmly in that rare and precious herb that rarely grew in home waters, leave – as much as possible and whenever possible – though for Kelly it provided little joy because it was always difficult even to find Christina. The ship spent a month in and out of Portland and, as they returned to Pompey, Harrison decreed leave for half the ship's company. Long refits, like Heaven, were always a long way off and since they'd only just emerged from one they had to be thankful for the one sane element in Harrison's make-up. As they came alongside there was a telegram waiting for Kelly – 'At Thakeham. Must talk' – and he set off, hopefully expecting that at last Christina had begun to see sense and decided to abandon what he considered a half-witted existence in London for the more mature life of the country. When he arrived at Thakeham, however, the place was empty as usual, and Bridget met him with a worried look on her face.

'I thought you were meeting Mrs. Maguire in London, Master Kelly,' she said.

'Is that where she is, Biddy?' He saw Bridget give him a side-long glance and hurried on. 'Business, I expect. When did she leave?'

Bridget looked puzzled. 'Master Kelly, sir, she never came.'

Furiously angry, Kelly caught the late train to London but even in the house in Carlton Terrace there was no indication of where his wife had gone. Without success, he telephoned a few friends who might have been able to tell him where she was and in the end headed for his club for a meal. Verschoyle was in the bar in evening dress, knocking back a pink gin.

'Hello,' he said. 'What are you doing in London?'

'Looking for my wife chiefly,' Kelly growled. 'What are you up to in your glad rags?'

'Dining out.'

'Who is it this time?'

Verschoyle shrugged. 'Old acquaintance. Known her for years. Met her in somebody's bed. Bored with her husband, I'm afraid.' He took a sip at his drink. 'I see our political masters have reduced the sentences on *Lucia*'s guilty men. Considering they didn't hesitate to put the captain and first lieutenant on half pay, it smacks of politics rather than discipline. All the same – ' Verschoyle shrugged ' – I can't imagine it attracting much attention in the turgid atmosphere in the world outside. Not with two million unemployed and no one with any ideas about how to find jobs for them. What's of more concern is this talk about reducing the 1919 rates of pay to effect economies.'

It came as no surprise. Everybody knew the country was in a mess and sacrifices were inevitable.

'So long as they're all the same,' Kelly said, 'I can't imagine anybody grumbling.'

'It'll cause a lot of ill-feeling,' Verschoyle pointed out. 'Chaps who joined before 1925 consider themselves privileged. They think they've got a contract that their pay can't be touched.' He gestured with his glass. 'But they haven't, you know. The act states quite categorically that they're not entitled to claim a right to any rate of pay or any other emolument under existing scales in the event of reduced scales being introduced.'

'The small print?'

'I looked it up.'

'These chaps are seasoned men.'

Verschoyle shrugged. 'They're also the chaps who're married and have the heaviest travel expenses. Their marriage allowances have never met reality.'

Kelly frowned. 'I hope those bloody fools in Parliament have enough sense to tread warily,' he growled. 'I don't suppose they've noticed that the Russian revolution of 1905 started in the navy, and the German revolution of 1918 in the High Seas Fleet.'

Verschoyle shrugged. 'I think they're so bloody besotted with socialist idealism,' he observed, 'they don't notice anything at all. But I can't really see 'em staying in power much longer, can you? The Budget admitted a deficit of twenty-three million and it's well known it's nearer thirty-eight. They've got to reduce it and I've heard that the remedies they're suggesting are explosive.'

There was a nervous air about the club. The financial position *was* unstable. Abroad it was even impossible and everybody was waiting to see the Labour Government collapse under the weight of its own problems.

The talk at the bar was bitter. Naval training and staff courses were still unreal and nobody could see where they were heading. Kelly finished his drink, anxious to get away from the atmosphere of dissatisfaction and complaint. He was bored with London and angry with Christina. All in all, he was dissatisfied with a lot of things. He didn't like *Rebuke* and he didn't like Captain Harrison, but as a naval officer that was something he was expected to handle without resentment, and after all, *Rebuke* was a great deal more exciting than the shore station to which he'd been condemned for eighteen months on returning from the Med. At least she was a ship, and she hummed with activity. The officers on the whole were rather too comfortable, but the younger lieutenants were lively enough, devoid of inferiority complexes, quick-witted, arrogant, lusty, apt to drink more than they should, yet never missing a watch or a duty despite the hangovers they suffered. It wasn't the ship, he knew. The mystique was still there, as it always would be, but there was a sense of disillusionment, an awareness of the Navy being led by old heroes who were no longer right.

He frowned, trying to see into his wife's mind. Christina had never been hypnotised by the Navy and her only comment on being shown round naval museums had been 'I'm sick of the death of bloody Nelson.' The awe of uniforms and medals, with which she'd first been overwhelmed, had long since gone and she'd grown tired of having a husband who would not come to heel.

He moved restlessly. The thought of going back to Thakeham didn't interest him, yet the idea of spending a week-end in London appalled, and in the end he asked for the telephone and dialled a Belgravia number. Vera von Schwerin's voice answered, and there was a little laugh down the telephone as she recognised his voice.

'Kelly Georgeivitch! You must come. My husband's in Germany and likely to be for a long time yet. Things are beginning to move in the Reich. Adolf Hitler's become a power at last.'

She greeted him at the door wearing a dress that had been chosen less for what it concealed than for what it revealed, and she informed him immediately that the servants were all out.

'You don't change much, Vera Nikolaevna,' he said.

She smiled. 'In Berlin, unfaithfulness doesn't worry people any more, and morals have a new look. Berlin's lost its conscience and everything's permissible there. Even meetings between old lovers, and you and I will always be a special case. We once committed murder together and that forges a link that's difficult to break.'

They dined at a restaurant along the river and drove back in the dusk into the city. As they opened the door to her house, she took his hand and pulled him after her towards the stairs, kicking off her shoes and flinging her handbag and fur stole to the floor as she went.

He had known all evening what was in her mind and he didn't back away. Christina's sexuality had been the only strong link between them, and at that moment he couldn't remember when he'd last been in her bed.

Vera was glancing backwards at him from the bedroom door, and she shrugged herself out of her dress as easily as if it had been a cloak.

'For God's sake,' Kelly said. 'Are you trying to set a record?'

'Oi, my husband is a bore who considers bed is only for sleeping in.'

For Kelly there was a strange absence of satisfaction in their

226

love-making. It made him feel like a devious schoolboy, but he never knew these days what Christina was up to, and Vera von Schwerin, with the brash indifference to morals that appeared to be the thing these days in Berlin, asked no questions.

'It's odd to find you a German,' he said.

Her shoulders moved in an indifferent shrug. 'There are White Russians in France, Turkey, China and America,' she said. 'Everywhere except Russia. Soon, however – very soon – we shall be back in Moscow. Can you imagine Adolf Hitler and the Bolshevik commissars ever seeing eye to eye.'

'Are you a National Socialist?' Kelly asked.

She indicated a photograph on the dressing table and he saw a dank forelock and ridiculous moustache and a pair of hypnotic eyes. He felt they were making love under the gaze of an arbiter of morals.

'Many people are Nazis,' she said. 'But so far they do not all admit it. And there are thousands more in Holy Russia – ex-Czarists, just waiting for Adolf Hitler to come to power.'

'I think you're being bloody optimistic,' Kelly said.

She gave him an enigmatic smile. 'That's because you're British and the British have consistently underestimated Hitler.'

He returned to the house in Carlton Terrace long after midnight, drawing at his cigarette until the smoke was in danger of coming out of his ears and down his sleeves. As the taxi drew to a stop, he climbed out and paid off the driver. The air was chilly and there was a hint of rain about, so that he paused, enjoying the coolness after the hothouse atmosphere of the Von Schwerin house. He walked down the road for a few minutes, still smoking, trying to organise his thoughts, then he threw away his cigarette and walked briskly back. As he opened the door, he saw Christina in the lounge drinking whisky with a young man who was so put out by Kelly's expression he hurriedly emptied his glass and vanished.

'Now look what you've done,' she said in mock complaint. 'He was such a nice young man. He's desperately in love with me, did you know?'

'The young puppy needs his arse kicking,' Kelly growled.

She laughed and he realised she was tipsy. 'We are in a bad temper, aren't we?'

'Is he the makee-learn gigolo who's taking you around?'

She laughed again. 'That? Oh, do try to be serious. He tags along, that's all.'

'I arrived home to find the house empty as usual. Where were you?'

She shrugged. 'It'd be equally to the point to ask where *you*'ve been?'

'At the club.'

'Until nearly one o'clock?'

'I didn't fancy coming home to an empty house.' He hated the lies that passed between them and remembered how he'd once sworn that he'd never behave like this. He'd imagined then that *his* marriage would be straightforward and honest, but that had been in the days when he'd expected his wife to be Charley. It was different now. He saw Christina looking at him quizzically and decided attack was the best form of defence.

'Where were you?' he asked again.

'Dining out?'

'Where, for God's sake?'

'The Jenners'. You know the Jenners. They're that couple who asked us to Cannes. We didn't go, of course, because you were in a foul mood and had to go to that stupid ship –'

'To hell with the Jenners!' Kelly snapped. 'Why did you tell me you'd be at Thakeham?'

'Well, I *was* going to be. But then I had this invitation.'

'You might have informed me.'

She was unmoved by his rage. 'You wouldn't have turned up. And, in any case, I didn't know you were coming on leave.'

'I'm not on leave. I have the week-end.'

'There you are! You don't expect me to send you a stream of notes down to Portsmouth in case you decide to come home, do you? "I'm going out for drinks with the Playfairs," "I'm dining at the Joneses'." "I'm going over to Le Touquet for golf." The crew would think I'd gone mad.'

'You said you wanted to talk. What about?'

She smiled. 'You know, I've completely forgotten.'

He didn't believe her. She'd simply changed her mind. 'It's not much fun,' he growled, 'when I come and haven't the fog-giest idea where you are.'

She shrugged. 'You can always resign your commission.'

'That's a bloody silly thing to say,' he shouted in sudden fury, 'when I'm on the brink of high rank!'

She laughed. '*You*'ll never reach high rank, my love. Very soon there won't be a navy because we shan't be able to afford one. Father says that this government's precious deficit isn't twenty-three million, or even thirty-eight million, as some people are saying; it's a hundred and twenty million. He got it from a member of the May Committee and since they were appointed to enquire into the country's financial situation, the chances are that he's right.'

'So what will he do?' Kelly growled. 'Juggle a few investments to make up for any losses *he* might incur?'

She smiled. '*His* finances'll be all right,' she said. 'Don't worry.'

The following day's newspapers were full of the May Committee's report. What Lord Clemo had said was true. The country's real deficit was over a hundred and twenty million pounds and the remedies they suggested were explosive. Unemployment benefit should be reduced, they claimed, weekly contributions increased and a means test introduced. In addition, the salaries of teachers, police and service personnel should be docked by ten per cent.

'Ten per cent!' Kelly snorted. 'Good God, the troops barely get a living wage as it is!'

'Can't see why you're worrying,' Christina said. 'Not with all the money *we* have behind us. Anyway, it'll be the holiday season before long and everybody'll soon forget all about it digging sand pies and bathing and buying the kids ice cream.'

Kelly glared at her over the paper. 'There'll be a lot of people who won't be able to afford ice cream,' he snapped. 'Including a lot of people in my ship!'

The news made depressing reading. Despite the Labour Party's promise at the last election to reduce unemployment, it had now reached the unprecedented figure of two and a half million and all the boasted schemes of public works had come to nothing. The nation's morale seemed to be declining rapidly, in some parts of the country four men seeking every available job. Unemployment had become a social problem, and even emigration didn't help much because the dominions were

229

in equally difficult straits. Only those who were already wealthy seemed untouched and the politicians seemed to be entirely devoid of vision.

'Up the revolution,' Christina said gaily. 'Bring your own bombs. If we're all going to end up in the tumbrils, I'm certainly going to have a good time first. I'm not staying in listening to the gloom on the wireless. I've arranged to go to Norfolk. Father's giving a house party. Are you coming?'

Kelly stared at her bitterly. He couldn't imagine a revolution for the simple reason that the country seemed to be swamped in apathetic misery.

'No, I'm not,' he snapped. 'And I don't suppose it occurs to you that since I only manage to get home rarely, it might be a good idea if we spent the time together.'

She beamed at him. 'As a matter of fact,' she said, 'no, it doesn't occur to me. It never has. In any case, we'd only spend all our time slinging insults at each other, so we might just as well go our own way.'

'Then don't blame me if I don't bother to make a point of coming to London!'

She was maddeningly cheerful. 'Oh, I *don't* blame you,' she pointed out. 'After all, I've made it very clear that *I'm* not going to suck up to the Admiralty, and I'm certainly not going to drop on one knee to the captain of your ship like everybody else in the Navy. It's the most sanctimonious outfit I've ever come across. Nobody has the courage to answer back to a senior officer in case it causes a bad mark against his name. They're the worst lot of toadies I've ever come across.'

Kelly glared, doubly furious because what she said was true. Since promotion depended on a good report from a commanding officer, the Navy was full of tensions as everybody jockeyed for appointments. Simply by getting one in a fleet flagship in home waters, officers could gain seniority; and their wives were equally involved in the rat race, because no one dared put a foot wrong in case they were damned forever.

'I don't suppose I'll be back before you return to your ridiculous ship,' Christina went on.

'You're *never* here,' Kelly snorted.

She was quite unruffled. 'Thinking of seeking a divorce on the grounds of desertion?' she asked. 'Because it won't work, you know. My father doesn't believe in it. That's why I had to stay married to Arthur Withinshawe. It offends his sense of what's right. He was brought up a churchman, you see, and although he didn't hesitate to drive my mother to an early grave, he wouldn't have dreamed of divorcing her. If I divorced you, old thing, I'd find myself cut off without a penny. Makes for marital fidelity.'

'And extra-marital activities!'

She beamed, quite unmoved by the accusation. 'Shall I give your love to my father?' she asked.

'You can tell your father to go to the devil,' he snorted.

They spent the day in the house together but rarely in each other's company. At lunch time, they ate at opposite ends of the table, but Kelly read a report he had to work through and Christina huddled over the newspaper.

'Country's losing gold,' she announced.

'Oh?'

'This damn May report. It was a stupid time to publish it now. It's convinced everybody abroad that the country's insecure. They're all starting to withdraw their money. Somebody'll have to do something to prop up our credit.'

It was largely gibberish to Kelly. He'd never had enough money to worry about.

'You're in a foul temper,' Christina observed.

'Of course I'm in a foul temper! The bloody government wants to cut the matelots' pay.'

'Steady on, old thing,' she warned. 'You're talking about my father. *He*'s government.'

'Then it's a pity he can't use his influence to help my poor bloody men. The buggers want to take even more from a 1919 man.'

'What in Heaven's name is a 1919 man?'

He tried to explain. 'Men who joined the Navy after 1925 got less pay and now those bastards in the government – including your bloody father, I expect! – not only want to cut pay but they also want to make pay equal *first* for the men who joined before.'

She gestured. 'Well, if one man can manage on three bob a day, why can't another?'

'Because, for God's sake,' Kelly shouted, 'the man on three bob a day's usually unmarried with no commitments! The man

231

on four's an older man with a home and a family and more than likely hire purchase commitments!'

'If they can't afford these things, they shouldn't go in for them.'

Kelly felt desperate as he tried to explain. 'How the hell do they provide a home for their wives and kids *without* hire purchase?' he snarled.

During the afternoon, Christina slept in preparation for her departure to Norfolk, while Kelly moved about the house, bored. In the evening, she appeared in the hall, dressed to kill and with the maid behind her holding a suitcase.

'Call me a taxi, there's a dear,' she said.

He called the taxi with bad grace. As she left, she pecked his cheek. He was well aware that with the money she provided he was hardly in a position to complain and he felt he was selling his soul.

The evening paper was full of gloom again. The gold losses that day had risen to over two million and it was prophesied there would be more the following day.

'What the hell's wrong with the bloody country?' he demanded out loud to the empty room.

He flung the paper aside in disgust. The evening stretched ahead of him in a defeating emptiness. He could go back to his ship but he suspected already that the story of his marriage had got around and there were whispers about its lack of success circulating round the wardroom.

In the end, he picked up the telephone and dialled Vera von Schwerin again.

232

3

The country continued to stagger from one crisis to another. Unimaginative politicians offered schemes which were worthless and, as far as the poor were concerned, entirely surgical, cold-blooded and inhuman, and still there remained the firm prophecy that the following year, despite everything that was tried, there would be a deficit of a hundred and seventy million. The run on gold continued so fast that a loan the government had negotiated abroad was draining away more quickly than it was arriving. Cuts in pay seemed to be drawing nearer with every day.

'Think they'll do it?' Kelly asked Verschoyle.

'Bound to,' Verschoyle said. 'They're going to cut unemployment benefits and *they* affect nearly three million voters. Service cuts affect less than a third of a million, not all on the electoral role either. Of course they'll cut.'

'It won't be worth staying in. People will resign.'

'That'd be a pity,' Verschoyle said shrewdly. 'Because, after the Geddes Axe, survival alone's a recommendation. You're either bloody clever or bloody crafty, and either way that's a useful thing to be if a war should come; and if that bastard Hitler gets power in Germany, it might. Much better to go on leave as I'm going to do. Everybody else in this ridiculous hierarchy's going. The whole Admiralty Board for a start. Not that they're what you'd call a strong board. The First Sea Lord's got a prodigious memory for names and he's a member of the Magic Circle, but he shows no talent for producing miracles.'

With the increasing tension and the drain on gold, a further international loan was negotiated but it soon became clear that unless the government showed itself willing to do something

233

about the financial crisis, nobody was going to throw good money after bad, yet the May Committee's suggestions were still unpalatable and suddenly, towards the end of August, the country found its rulers had changed.

The Prime Minister had not resigned. When the split in his government had shattered the Labour Party with the thunder of a breaking sea wall, he had simply remained in office and agreed with the Conservatives and Liberals to form a coalition. Only nine members of the Parliamentary Labour Party followed him and Lord Clemo was out of office.

'Well, that's a remarkable effort if you like,' Harrison observed to Kelly. 'A Prime Minister without a party and a second-in-command who leads the largest group in the House. The only thing you can say about it is that the world's financiers seem pleased and the drain on gold's been halted. Perhaps it's all over.'

'I doubt it, sir,' Kelly said dryly. 'There's a quote in *The Fleet* that might be of interest.'

'That's a socialist rag,' Harrison said sharply.

Kelly stood his ground. 'It's still correct, sir.' He started to read from a sheet of paper Boyle had typed out for him. 'It's supposed to have been written by a chap in the Mediterranean. He says "God knows how any Royal Commission came to the conclusion that the poor misused matloe's pay can be reduced. They might have been expert economists but never, surely, humanists. Did any of the commissioners visit a sailor's home to see how his money is spent? Did they ever live with sailors in small ships to see how it's earned?"'

Harrison frowned. To him, the Bible and the Navy were the two greatest forces for good in the British Isles and he had no time for anyone who tried to tamper with them.

Kelly went on earnestly. 'There's a loss of confidence between officer and man I don't like, sir,' he said.

Harrison gazed coldly at him. 'The Navy will loyally accept the sacrifices,' he observed, 'if equivalent reductions are made throughout the public services and in unemployment pay. The Admiralty Board have said as much. Anyway, we're due for Scotland on September 7th. That ought to keep everybody busy.'

The opinion of the lower deck was different. Rumbelo put it

234

plainly. 'Pay cuts for the 1919 men'll mean 25 per cent less, sir. I'm one and it affects me, but, thanks to you, sir, it won't hurt too much. But some of 'em have hire purchase commitments they're not going to be able to keep up, and they're scared they'll lose their homes.'

Kelly gave a wry smile. 'There hasn't been much security for officers either, Rumbelo, since the war.'

As the month drew to a close, he heard over the wardroom wireless of the sudden death of Lord Clemo. It was a heart attack brought on, the announcer said, by the unexpected collapse of his party. The announcement was repeated in the newspaper the following morning, and as he stared at it propped up on the wardroom table in front of his toast and marmalade, Kelly half-expected there'd be a telegram from Christina.

But nothing came and he could only assume that she preferred to handle things on her own. She was tough-minded and capable of handling her father's affairs and he assumed she intended to do so without his help.

He was still worried by the uneasiness he felt about him. Somehow in the big ships, the two halves of the navy seemed to have lost touch with each other. In the destroyers there was no sign of the problems, but in *Rebuke* the officers seemed to be too immersed in matériel and were neglecting the human factor, and he was aware of a distinct parallel with the Navy of 1914 when too much thought had been given to ships and not enough to the crews who manned them.

As the month drew to an end, he went to London. There was no sign of Christina and no hint as to where she was. Assuming she was in Norfolk, he simply rang up Vera von Schwerin.

The following day, he met Verschoyle at his club. 'It's coming,' Verschoyle announced grimly. 'There's to be a signal to all commanders-in-chief that we've got to toe the line and take cuts like everybody else. Men on the 1919 pay scales will also have to accept the 1925 rates. Officers lose eleven per cent. There'll also be reductions in kit upkeep, grog money and a few other things. The signal's prepared.'

Kelly scowled at his drink. 'I think they're asking too much,' he said. 'It's bloody dangerous. Some of the older chaps were in Russian ports during the Civil War and some have been into

Kiel. Somebody on the Board of Admiralty should bear all that in mind.'

Verschoyle lifted a cynical eyebrow. 'They should indeed,' he said. 'But they won't. There are strong boards and weak boards. This one's just a bad one.'

London seemed to be recovering from its upset of the spring and even the financial crisis seemed to have settled down a little. Yet there were uneasy stirrings in the air. At the beginning of the month, the Chilean fleet had mutinied and it was now being claimed by the Chilean government that the deep-rooted cause of it was the fact that their ships had been refitted at Devonport where the crews had acquired attitudes prevalent in British dockyards.

Travelling by train to Esher, Kelly was conscious of a deep-seated restlessness. He was married yet he never saw his wife. In the Navy this could hardly be called unusual, but most married men were aware of a settled existence somewhere back in the shadows, and they had homes and the blessings of the shore when they went on leave. He seemed to have grown used in the last two years to empty houses and a total absence of family.

To his surprise, the first person he saw when he reached his mother's cottage was his father. He looked considerably younger than his wife and even seemed to be thriving. He was now almost eighty but he didn't seem to have changed a scrap.

'What in God's name are you up to?' he snorted. 'All this talk of unrest in the fleet! We never had anything like that in my day.'

Kelly's mother tried to keep the peace. 'Don't take too much notice of your father, Kelly,' she advised quietly.

'I never did,' Kelly said sharply.

The first thing he saw when he opened the door of the big house was a fur coat belonging to Christina lying across a chair. It was worth a fortune but had been tossed down as indifferently as if it had been rabbit.

'My wife at home, Biddy?' he asked.

Bridget shrugged. 'No, Master Kelly. She came two days ago but she didn't stay.'

'Did she say where she was going?'

'No, Master Kelly. I thought she was going to Norfolk, but I

236

don't think she did.'

'Why not?'

'Well, there were labels on the luggage, Master Kelly. She wouldn't want labels on the luggage if she were only going to Norfolk, would she?'

Almost the first people he met on the station platform on his return to Portsmouth were Kimister and Charley. Charley greeted him warily. In uniform he seemed to blaze alongside Kimister with his medal ribbons and the gold on his cap. Kimister seemed irritated and restless. He was going bald, Kelly noticed and, alongside Kelly, seemed to diminish rather than increase as he grew more mature. He was worried about his ship and was convinced the Navy's present troubles could all be laid at the door of the Communists.

As he went to organise his baggage, Kelly found himself alone with Charley. He was ill at ease, but she made no mention of the past and talked cheerfully only of the future.

'Come and see us, Kelly,' she suggested. 'When the exercises are over and we're home.'

He was not entirely willing because it would remind him too much of what had vanished. 'I'll try,' he promised. 'In fact, my stepson might enjoy coming with me for tea. He might also enjoy meeting you.'

She was silent for a moment then she raised her eyes to his, clear and honest and forthright.

'Do you think there'll be trouble with the fleet, Kelly?' she asked.

He shook his head but he wasn't sure. The evening paper had been full of the proposed wages cuts; the teachers, the police, the post office workers and the unemployed were seething with discontent; and there were reports of mass meetings and clashes between police and demonstrators.

Kimister looked pale and harried as he returned and, his stomach knotting in agony as he saw Charley's unhappiness, Kelly longed to shake him. Kimister was a failure, and she knew it now. He wasn't even one of those officers who, even if they always appeared at a tragic disadvantage before their senior officers, could at least appear at their best before their men. There was nothing there and never had been.

237

The following week-end Hugh was free from school and, on an impulse, taking advantage of what Charley had offered, Kelly took him along to where she lived to the east of Portsmouth. The house Kimister had acquired was a typical rented residence, with all the hallmarks of other people's lives about it. There seemed to be nothing in it of Charley, but she was calm and, although the boy was puzzled by the house's smallness and the lack of the luxuries he was used to at Thakeham and Carlton Terrace, he was soon at ease. They took him to the beach at Hayling Island where they all swam together. As they left the water, Kelly found himself gazing at Charley. She seemed younger somehow with him than she did with Kimister and still had the same youthful figure she'd always had.

As she saw him staring at her, her smile died and for the rest of the afternoon she was silent. He drove her home and they talked quietly of inconsequentials as Hugh waded through an enormous tea, then, still awkward, they said goodbye and he took the boy back to school.

The following morning's mail brought him four letters – all from women. One was from his mother thanking him for visiting her; one was from Charley asking him to take Hugh again; one was from Vera von Schwerin asking where he'd got to; and one was from Christina which, he noticed, carried a French stamp and the postmark, 'Cannes'.

He left it until last, reading the others as he ate his toast and marmalade.

The first lieutenant was complaining from the other side of the table about his egg. 'If this had come from Russia,' he was saying, 'the man who provided it would have been arrested for making bombs. Let's have a fresh one, steward.'

The steward removed the egg silently but, in his glance, Kelly caught a faint flicker of annoyance and he resolved to have a word with the first lieutenant. Just now didn't seem to be the time for clever sarcasm.

Finishing his coffee, he took his mail to his cabin to read Christina's letter. He had a feeling it contained something momentous. He wasn't disappointed.

'It's all grown so silly,' she wrote with her usual brisk clarity. 'You with your ridiculous ships living a monastic life afloat and me doing the same in London. I never see you and, when I do,

238

you have no time for what I want to do. Now that my father's wishes no longer have to be considered, I think it would be better if we just quietly terminated everything in friendly fashion. I shan't be returning to Thakeham, but I shall not be keeping the house in London. I shall therefore be glad if you'd remove your possessions, as I've instructed my solicitors to sell it. I'd also be glad if you'd ask Bridget to pack up my belongings at Thakeham and have them sent to Norfolk.'

He sat back, staring at the letter. Well, he thought, *that* was short and bloody sweet.

4

Embarkation of stores for the Atlantic Fleet's summer cruise started. With the economic situation, there was to be no voyage to the Mediterranean and the plan was to head for Scapa, Rosyth or Invergordon for practice firing.

After the stores, the ammunition was embarked from lighters. Since the missiles for the big guns weighed around a ton each, there was always a danger and signals had to be given with care, and Kelly found himself putting two men on the captain's report for trying to snatch a quick puff at a cigarette when nobody was looking. It was symbolic of the attitude of the new navy. It would never have happened in the days when loyalty was secure and worked both up and down. But things were different now and he even had to lecture the officers on the importance of their communications with the unseen capstan operators, particularly when cordite was hoisted aboard.

With the storing finished, the ship had to be cleaned. Stages were slung overside and hundreds of brushes, pots and hoists arranged for the application of grey paint. Kelly threw himself into the work, absorbed and occupied, because it stopped him thinking. He didn't believe in friendly divorces and felt that in something as cataclysmic as a final separation between a man and his wife there ought to be blows, bad temper and a little crockery throwing. But, examining his feelings, he realised he didn't feel hurt enough for that. Now that she'd inherited her father's fortune, Christina could do as she wished and, since she clearly wished to be free, he had accepted her decision as a *fait accompli*. He couldn't imagine her ever rushing back to him and, taking the view that it would be quite pointless, he had no intention of chasing down to Cannes to fetch her back by the scruff of her neck. Her letter had been closely followed by a second from

240

a solicitor who had set out quite clearly what she wanted and what she had no objection to him retaining. It was all quite cold-blooded.

Pity she didn't go into politics, he thought. She'd have been perfect on the May Committtee.

He found he was quite calm and quite indifferent to what had happened. The whole four years had been a mistake. She was used to getting what she wanted and when he'd fished her out of Wu-Pi where her own intransigeance had placed her, she'd wished to have a much-decorated young naval officer first as a lover then as a husband. But the demands of the service had been too strong and she'd found he was not willing, as Withinshawe had been willing, to fall in with her wishes.

He felt no enmity, no hatred, just a sad acceptance that she'd ruined not only his life but probably Charley's also. Or *he* had. He was not unaware of his own guilt and didn't back away from it. He'd been too quick to judge, too unwilling to allow for loneliness.

There was a letter from Hugh from the Hotel Majestic in Cannes that was heart breaking in its simplicity. 'Dear Uncle Kelly,' he wrote. 'Here with Mum. She says I am not going back to schole in Sussex. Mum says I am going to schole in France. I don't want to. I am sorry I didn't see your ship. I enjoyed our day out and I like your friend Charlie. Yours truly, Hugh Withinshawe.'

There was also a note of warning from Verschoyle, like Verschoyle clear and to the point. 'Cuts a *fait accompli*,' he wrote. 'Signal will be sent to all commands. Don't expect any help from the Board. Those who aren't on leave aren't capable of it, anyway.'

Fortunately the crowding in of events took Kelly's mind off his own troubles. Already the flat outside his cabin, marshalled by Corporal O'Hara, was filled regularly with men wishing to see him. They were always older men who felt themselves the victims of a breach of contract. They had served ever since the war and sometimes before, and it was hopeless trying to explain to them, because there'd been no lead either from the Admiralty or Parliament and, so far, the only comment Kelly had heard from anybody in authority had come from a bored politician who could say only that the two scales of pay were

241

'an inconvenience.'

'Sir –' Leading Seaman Doncaster's beefy red face was angry – 'them people on that committee don't have any idea how we live! Nobody's bothered to ask, as far as I know, either. Even on the 1919 rates, with kids there isn't much between making both ends meet and getting into debt.'

'I entered hire purchase agreements,' another man announced, 'on the understanding I'd be paid the 1919 rates. If I'm not, sir, and they take back me furniture, what's me wife supposed to do? Rents are hard enough in Pompey at any time – even for the sort of accommodation we've got. There are plenty of people glad to make a living out of us, and *they* don't conform to the cuts.'

It was a hopeless situation. The only way to avoid trouble was to encourage them to bring their difficulties to their officers, but the officers were as well aware as they were that nobody took any notice these days of requests made through the proper channels, because nine times out of ten they were lost in a welter of paperwork presided over by admirals and civil servants in no danger of suffering much themselves.

The week-end before they were due to sail north, Kelly went to London to see his solicitors and arrange his part of the divorce. He took a room at the club and went to a show at Drury Lane. By sheer chance, Vera von Schwerin was there with a pale young man whose picture he had often seen in the glossy magazines.

'He wants to be a Nazi,' she whispered as they stood together at the bar between acts. 'I must arrange for him to visit Berlin. He might have influential friends.' She brushed his arm with her programme. 'He's very sweet, but he touches me as if he were handling a flower, so I'll tell him I have a headache.'

They took a taxi to her home and immediately they were inside she took his hand and pulled him towards the bedroom.

'You don't waste time, do you?' he said.

'Oi, there is no time to waste, Kelly Georgeivitch,' she retorted. 'That's one thing we've learned in Berlin. Life's too short – physically, morally, politically. What has to be done must be done at once, without consideration for others.'

With cynical detachment he unfastened his tie and began to unbutton his jacket. Then, as he laid his jacket down, he saw

242

the photograph on the dressing table again, complete with black moustache and pale intense eyes staring at him. Reaching out, he placed it face-down.

'I bet he doesn't go in for this sort of thing,' he observed.

Their love-making was swift and devoid of passion. Vera had grown older in a harsh world and he was reminded all the time of the cold hidden eyes of Hitler staring across the bedroom at him.

He saw her studying him from the pillows. 'Where have you been for so long?' she asked. 'Concerned with your country's financial troubles?'

'I suppose so. You'll know what they mean.'

'*I* shall pull through,' she said soberly. 'After Odessa I swore I would be rich again and there are men in Germany who know what to do. Government funds don't always pay for portraits of President Hindenburg.'

Kelly shrugged. 'Obviously you do things differently from us.'

She caught the contempt in his voice and her manner became cool. 'When Adolf Hitler comes to power,' she said, 'Germany will rise as England sinks.' She paused. 'Your government will destroy your navy, you know,' she ended. 'There's been a meeting in Portsmouth. I think there's trouble in store for you, Kelly Georgeivitch.'

The switch of subjects caught him unawares.

'How do you know?'

'You forget that, in addition to being German, I'm also Russian and I have some strange friends. I hear them talking.' She smiled. 'You once did me a favour, Kelly Georgeivitch. But for you, I'd probably have ended up selling myself to Red soldiers in an Odessa brothel and I promised I wouldn't forget.'

Kelly frowned. 'When was this meeting?' he asked.

'I don't know. But I understood that men from your ships, *Norfolk* and *Dorsetshire*, were present.'

'*Norfolk*'s a Devonport ship. What were they doing in Pompey?'

'What's more to the point, Kelly Georgeivitch, is what were they doing when those ships visited Kiel? I was there when they arrived and I saw the men going ashore. I imagine the first thing they saw was the war memorial painted red, like every other

243

memorial in the town. The Communists have been active there since the mutiny in the High Seas Fleet and they doubtless found a few listeners among your men. I went to a dance the C.-in-C. gave at his official residence, but it had to be held in the rooms at the back in case the lights attracted a mob and led to rioting, and two of your British midshipmen were stoned while riding. I also heard that some of your sailors visited the International Seamen's Club, and we know – and Adolf Hitler knows, too! – that that club's a headquarters of subversive influences.'

Kelly had sat up now, hardly aware of her as a woman, his interest only in what she was saying.

'Why are you telling me all this?'

She beamed at him. 'Because Germany needs the British Navy,' she said. 'We shall never be able to equal it, however hard we build, and soon we shall expect it to stand alongside us to defeat Communism in the east.'

Kelly returned to Portsmouth in a thoughtful mood. As he stepped off the train at the harbour station, he stared about him at the interminable terraces of narrow houses and undistinguished brick buildings stretching from the neighbourhood of the dockyard to the north of the city. The streets seemed to be full of bicycles, all carrying dockyard mateys in threadbare coats, dominating the trafffic as they did four times a day. Among them were a few women with shopping bags and pushing shabby prams. There was little beauty in the place but, in the brown-faced men swaggering in their best blue, their caps at a jaunty angle on their heads, arrogant despite their worries, there was a strange sense of self-assurance. The strength of a fleet was not in its ships but in its men and he hoped to God they'd never be called on to help Hitler's thugs.

As he picked up his bag, he saw Fanshawe watching him from further down the platform. He hadn't seen him since they'd met in Shanghai. He was in *Rodney* now and due to catch a train to Plymouth, and he was as uncertain of the future as Kelly was.

'I think we should repair to the Keppel's Head to celebrate,' he said. 'Sailing's likely to be postponed.'

244

'Why?' Kelly asked at once, thinking of what Vera von Schwerin had told him. 'Trouble?'

Fanshawe laughed. 'My God,' he said. 'Everybody's obsessed by this mythical trouble that's supposed to be coming! We're not expecting trouble in *Rodney*. No, Admiral Hodges has returned from leave seriously ill and they've whipped him into Haslar Hospital. They'll have to postpone sailing until they can get a replacement.'

Back on board *Rebuke*, Kelly was called to the captain's cabin where he enlightened Harrison as to what was happening. 'I made enquiries, sir,' he said, 'and I understand Rear Admiral Tomkinson, of the Second Cruiser Squadron, will be taking over.'

'Tomkinson!' Harrison sniffed. 'It'll be his first independent command – in effect, his *first* command. He was always Keyes' deputy.'

He listened to what Kelly had heard from Vera von Schwerin but he was obviously not impressed.

'Who is this woman?' he demanded.

'German attaché's wife, sir. I met her in Russia in 1919.'

'Well, nobody else has heard of any meeting. I think you're making too much of it.'

Confirmation of the change in command came later that night, and the new admiral hoisted his flag in *Hood*. The old flagship, *Nelson*, was to remain in Portsmouth to await Hodges' recovery. When Harrison returned from Tomkinson's conference, he was inclined to be critical.

'Too hurried,' he insisted. 'Taking over a ship's a long and complex business. Taking over a fleet has unlimited possibilities for going wrong. The Admiralty should have postponed sailing, and the admiral obviously thinks so, too, because he's had no guidance about these damned cuts. Surely to God they'll never permit men to lose twenty-five per cent of their pay.'

Kelly wasn't too sure. Nobody on the May Committee had ever been connected with the sea.

The lower deck was also obviously fully occupied with thoughts of the cuts, and there was a heavy resentment about the ship, so that tasks were performed sullenly and with none of the normal cheerfulness. But the ship left port spick and span with the ship's company lining the deck and the white ensign floating at the stern. The band of the Marines was bashing away for all it was worth at *A Life On The Ocean Wave*, and the bridge was packed with officers. *Hood* was already out in the channel and as *Rebuke* followed her she almost filled the narrow entrance to the harbour. There were crowds on the front at Southsea and Old Portsmouth as she cleared the Landport. The tower of St. Thomas à Becket slid clear of the ramparts, then she moved majestically down the channel past the forts to deep water. There was a light westerly wind blowing and an east-running tide, and a sullen wash spread across the sky with violet clouds massed astern, so that the gulls stood out with striking clarity. Beyond them, Kelly could see the houses and pier of Ryde to starboard and to port the power station of Portsmouth, and somehow, it seemed as if he were looking on them all for the first time.

With *Nelson* remaining in Portsmouth with the aircraft carrier, *Courageous*, the squadron had a truncated look about it as it headed east. Beyond the Isle of Wight, the Devonport Division joined the flag and they moved up-Channel past Beachy Head, Dungeness and the Forelands to the Outer Gabbard in the entrance to the Thames, where vessels of the Nore Command also joined, and they altered course towards the north.

As they drove through the iron water beyond the Thames, the dark sky became covered with a pearly overcast which threw a strange light on the angles and curves of the ships. The battle fleet – *Rodney, Warspite, Malaya, Rebuke, Hood* and *Repulse* – were accompanied by four cruisers, *Dorsetshire, Norfolk, York* and *Centaur*; the minelayers, *Adventure* and *Advance*; the old battleship, *Iron Duke*; the submarine depot ships, *Lucia* and *Adamant*; and the Fifth and Sixth Destroyer Flotillas. Butting into the wind, they reminded Kelly of Beatty's ships heading out past May Island for Jutland, all of fifteen years before.

Staring from the bridge, his eyes dwelt nostalgically on the sleek shapes of the light forces as they combed the grey seas with their washes. The big ships, he thought bitterly, were *too* big! And too damned old! The First Lord in the new government had already protested about the general ageing condition of the fleet and the money being wasted in refitting the great grey mastodons instead of building destroyers. It hadn't been

Jutland that had destroyed Germany, but the blockade; and it hadn't been the High Seas Fleet which had brought Britain to her knees in 1917, but the submarines. Light forces were what was needed, but to attack the big ships against the entrenched attitudes of the Admiralty had become like challenging the Scriptures.

At least, the old stately sarabands which had been called exercises before the war had fallen into disfavour and the run north was performed in a tight two-day convoy drill. The heavy atmosphere of resentment was still in evidence, however, and Kelly was conscious all the time of dissension below decks. Remembering Vera von Schwerin's warning, as they headed north past Flamborough Head he called the signals officer to his cabin. 'Any communications between ships?' he asked.

'Only the usual, sir.'

'I mean signals that have nothing to do with the exercises or the handling of the ship.'

'What sort of signals, sir?'

In his attempts to be non-committal, the signals officer seemed stupid and Kelly exploded. 'Dammit, man,' he snapped. 'You're as aware as I am of the feeling in the fleet about the pay cuts! Are they organising some sort of concerted action? Are signals being tagged on to normal traffic?'

The signals officer flushed. 'I've seen no sign of it, sir,' he answered stiffly. 'It's possible, of course, but surely it would be picked up by the petty officers.'

'The petty officers,' Kelly retorted, 'seem to be adopting a position of neutrality in this business. They're not for the cuts, and they're certainly in sympathy with the lower deck. No possibility of visual signals being passed?'

'Not a chance, sir.'

'Have you noticed anything?'

'Sullenness sir.'

'So have I,' Kelly growled. 'It's been quiet today but it seems to be intensifying. Perhaps they're waiting for the Admiralty signal explaining what's going on. I know damn well they're discussing what to do if pay's reduced enough to affect their way of living. Dammit, wouldn't you?'

'Yes, sir.' The signals officer clearly took the view that Kelly was chasing shadows.

Kelly glared at him. 'Well, keep your eyes open,' he said. 'I think most of 'em don't know much about it, but I don't think we should be deluded that they aren't talking about it. Do they listen to the B.B.C.?'

'It's relayed through the ship, sir, as you know. Up to now, though, as far as I can see, all the B.B.C.'s doing is speculate on the possibilities in the emergency budget. It's a pretty fragile situation ashore.'

'I think it's a pretty fragile situation at sea,' Kelly snapped.

As they drew nearer the Scottish coast, Kelly's suspicions multiplied. He'd been in the Navy too long not to be aware of subtle differences. There was a feeling in *Rebuke* that worried him, and the night before they were due to anchor he decided to make the rounds himself in an effort to gauge the temper of the ship's company. Following the Royal Marine bugler blowing G, he stalked along the passageways and through the mess-decks, alert for any subtle change in a tone of voice or the expression on a messdeck sweeper's face as he made his report, any change in the stiff faces of the sailors standing at attention or the shifting of the shrouded shapes in the hammocks in the background.

As he passed through the ship with Rumbelo and the rest of his party, he was aware of a silence of resentment. With the men divided into watches, the sailors had only limited contact with each other and they were still tired from the extra duties of the run north, but it was obvious the cuts were pressing heavily on their minds. Everything seemed to be subdued, however, and on an even keel until they came to the band room. From outside, there was quite clearly a meeting in progress and they could hear loud and angry voices.

'What's going on in here?' he asked Rumbelo.

'Meeting of the Buffalo Lodge, sir. They have that privilege. Normal Friendly Society.'

Kelly was just about to move on, wondering what the Royal Antediluvian Order of Buffaloes could be debating so fiercely, when he caught the words, 'Admiralty indifference.' He stopped dead at once and, pushing open the door, he saw the band room was crowded with men with Leading Seaman Doncaster mounted on a stool, apparently in the middle of an

248

inflammatory speech which came to an abrupt halt as the stool was whipped from beneath his feet by Rumbelo.

'This is a meeting of the Buffaloes, sir,' he said indignantly as he picked himself up.

'I don't believe you,' Kelly snapped. 'And, even if it is, it's terminated as of now. Out you go! Be thankful you're not on report.'

There was no trouble. The men filed out and headed for their messdecks in silence, and Kelly slammed the door shut behind them. It probably meant very little, but it was the first sign of trouble and he suggested to Harrison that something should be done quickly before things got out of hand.

Harrison pooh-poohed the idea. 'I think you're making too much of it,' he said. 'And there's bound to be a letter from the Admiralty when we arrive, explaining the situation.'

'Unless they're sunk in their usual elegant torpor, sir,' Kelly growled. 'I suspect they feel that while we're at sea, we're out of mischief and can be forgotten.'

Despite Harrison's decision to do nothing, Kelly called the divisional officers to his cabin. Some of them looked incredibly young and had entered the Navy in the smug days after the war when Britain was still resting on the laurels of victory. Since then a block in promotions had existed and they all knew that elevation to commander was by arbitrary selection and that a single black mark could affect their whole career. In many cases, he knew, they were only watching their own yardarms, even at the expense of others. It wasn't their fault, it was the fault of the system, but he'd come to the conclusion, nevertheless, that they all needed a good kick up the backside.

'I've heard,' he said, 'that there's talk aboard ship of strike action against the proposed pay cuts.' There was a restless movement as if they preferred not to hear it discussed and he went on grimly. 'Well, let's get it clear straight away that in the service *there's no such thing*! In the Navy "strike action" would be regarded as mutiny, pure and simple, and it's up to you people to make that as clear as you can. Point out what happened with *Lucia. Those* chaps thought they were only making a protest; the Navy still called it mutiny.'

'They feel they've as much right to strike as anybody else, sir,' the first lieutenant pointed out. 'And this time, I, for one, am entirely in agreement with them.'

Kelly frowned. 'Come to that, Number One, so am I. Unfortunately, however, according to the Act, they *haven't* that right. But they're mostly intelligent men and it's up to you to drum into them good and hard what the consequences could be.'

He also made a point of getting the chiefs and petty officers together in their mess and making the point again.

'At least try to stop them turning their resentment into public meetings,' he said. 'And watch for the big talkers. Every ship has its share of moaners and loudmouths, but I believe they're motivated less by politics than by despair. Try to stop them doing anything silly.'

He wasn't sure he'd put his point across and even suspected that concerted action *was* the only way to overcome the smug torpor at the Admiralty and in Parliament. Even the thriftiest of men on the lower deck were left with no margin for emergencies and lived permanently on the borderline of poverty.

Sitting at his desk, he was consumed with rage at the memory of the charity parties he'd been to with Christina where there'd been a great deal of champagne but not very much charity. Doubtless at that moment, Christina was in Cannes enjoying herself with the same privileged people. None of the daily papers, he'd noticed, appeared to have felt the need to drop their society gossip columns and there were still plenty of shiny periodicals about to cover the doings of the wealthy.

By God, he thought furiously, what this country needs *is* a revolution!

That night they received news of the Budget. There were increases in income tax and the cost of beer, tobacco and other things which were staggering.

'For God's sake,' the first lieutenant said. 'Don't those stupid idiots in Parliament have any idea? If they impose cuts on top of this the poor devils haven't *anything* to live for!'

'There'll be *something* for 'em,' the gunnery officer said doggedly. 'They'd never dare impose cuts of the magnitude they say they're going to impose without something to make 'em bearable.'

They entered Cromarty Firth with the sea dead calm, so that

the presence of the vast grey ships seemed like a violation of the stillness. They dropped anchor one after the other, first *Hood*, occupying the berth of fleet flagship just off the pier of Invergordon, then *Rebuke* nearer to Nigg. Next was *Rodney*, with *Warspite* opposite Nairn, *Valiant* and *Malaya* north of Lossiemouth, and *Repulse* down the Firth off Cromarty. To the south was the line of cruisers, headed by *Dorsetshire*, the flagship, with *Norfolk*, *York*, *Adventure* and *Advance* lined up on her.

Kelly had to admit that *Rebuke* looked good. Her band on the quarterdeck were going at it hammer and tongs, and the Royal Marines, their white helmets and bayonets shining, made a picture with the steady ranks of her sailors. On the forecastle men were just securing after mooring and the cluster of officers on the bridge had not yet dispersed. He knew they were being watched from the town, people staring out at the long grey hulls and the mounting lines of guns, noting how the booms for the boats swung out from the sides as if by clockwork, how the scrubbed gangways descended and the launches touched the water. Immediately boats were sent ashore for mail and newspapers, and Captain Harrison's pinnace was piped for.

As the stand-easy was signalled, the radios were turned on in the recreation spaces and at once the ship was filled with the calm voices of the B.B.C. announcers, interrupted only by morse as a ship nearby started to send. Now that the exercises were over and they had arrived, the awareness of resentment in the ship grew. Everybody seemed in a state of great uncertainty; and now that the cuts appeared to have been finalised, family budgets were being redrafted and there was a great deal of talk about hire purchase and rent that Kelly couldn't help but hear as he moved about the ship.

I hope to God the boats bring something back, he thought.

The captain returned very quickly from his business ashore. He seemed to have something on his mind but he gave no inkling of what it was. When the ship's boats returned with the mail, the excitement in the faces of their crews was obvious and their demeanour spelt trouble. The papers contained nothing but further details of the Budget, but the mail consisted largely of letters from wives who were understandably worried, and an immediate stream of men demanded from the harassed master-at-arms the opportunity to see Kelly.

251

While he was interviewing them, a message came for him to see the captain. As he entered Harrison's day cabin, a signal was tossed down.

'My father's ill,' Harrison announced shortly. 'He had a stroke and it seems it was more serious than was thought. I've been granted permission to repair ashore to visit his bedside and attend to his affairs. Captain Masterson will take my place from Portsmouth until I return, which will probably be in two or three weeks' time. With the week-end intervening, he should be here on Tuesday.'

With the captain departed on his way south by train, a make and men was piped the following day and men began to appear on deck in their tiddly suits for the half holiday, the fronts of their blouses cut illegally low, their trousers wider than regulations permitted in an attempt to dispense that curious mystique which drew the girls like magnets. There were highland games ashore and the usual Saturday afternoon cinemas and football. As Kelly watched them gathering for the liberty boats, he noticed that the chatter didn't appear to be the usual cheerful excitement, and there seemed a lot of anger.

'Go ashore, Number One,' he said to the first lieutenant. 'And keep your eyes open. If there's going to be trouble, I want to be ready for it.'

As he took a drink in the wardroom that evening, the wireless was on and the B.B.C. was reporting that service pay was definitely to be cut. He stared at it angrily. The bloody B.B.C., he decided, seemed to be on the side of anarchy, rather than law and order. Speculation without fact seemed valueless and could only cause trouble when the men reappeared on board full of beer.

There was also a reference to an Admiralty Fleet Order published the day before; he frowned, remembering no such order, and called for Boyle.

'Have you seen an Admiralty Fleet Order, Seamus?' he demanded.

'No, sir,' Boyle said. 'Nothing's appeared from *Hood*. Perhaps it contained just the usual orders about stores, modifications and appointments and wasn't issued to the fleet.'

Kelly's frown grew deeper. 'The B.B.C. seems to think it

252

contains information about the pay cuts. They also mentioned a letter from the Admiralty. Any sign of that?'

'No, sir. None.'

Kelly was on the quarterdeck waiting for the liberty boats long before they were due to return. The breeze off the shore brought with it the scent of bruised grasses and herbs, and about him was that curious tang that haunted all big ships, a compound of metal polish, drying wood, new paint, caustic soda and soap, with occasionally the hot brassy taste of funnel fumes. Then the salt sea smell came again, clearer and cleaner, with the odour of new bread from the bakery just forward of the second battery. The ship was not silent, because there was never silence in a living ship. All the time there was the draughty murmur from the mouths of the fan trunkings, and beneath his feet the steady purr of some piece of auxiliary machinery, and the slop and scurry of the sea against the ship's armoured walls. Even as she swung at her buoy, men were studying pumps and gauges, minding fans and dynamos, checking oil and water pressures, even watching by the gangway to see how she swung with the tide.

When the drifters returned, he saw at once that there were noisy arguments going on aboard them and, as he watched the liberty men vanishing below, he heard catcalls and caught the words, 'Down tools!' Turning abruptly, he called the midshipmen to his cabin and asked them what the behaviour of the men had been like.

'Excited, sir,' one of the youngsters reported.

'What sort of excitement?'

'Saturday night boisterousness chiefly, sir.'

'It was rowdiness,' another midshipman interrupted firmly. 'There was singing on the pier and in the boats. *The Red Flag* was one of the songs.'

The officer of the watch had seen nothing very different from the usual Saturday night behaviour on returning aboard. 'But I doubt if they'd heard the B.B.C. news, sir,' he added.

'They'll have heard it by now,' Kelly said. 'How did they appear to you?'

'Normal, sir. Though I did notice there was a lot of talking in undertones and that they kept well away from me. They had a strange manner.'

253

'What sort of strange?'

'Shifty, sir.'

The first lieutenant returned on board alone. He was looking grim. 'I think they held a meeting,' he reported. 'They went to the canteen and I thought they were pretty angry. I gather the meeting wasn't planned, but it took place all the same. It must have been spontaneous combustion, because it seems to have attracted no attention. The shore patrol reported nothing unusual.'

'What's your view, Number One?'

The first lieutenant gestured. 'There's something there, sir,' he admitted. 'You can't put your finger on it, but it seems stronger than it was. I think there's been some canvassing and the word's been spread.'

'What word, Number One?'

The first lieutenant frowned. 'To me, sir,' he said, 'it seems like strike action.'

5

Kelly was eating his breakfast the following morning, when the mail boat brought the Sunday papers aboard.

As the steward laid *The Sunday Times* alongside him, he idly began to turn the pages. As he browsed, the first lieutenant sat down beside him. He was obviously upset. 'Seen this, sir?' he asked, laying *The News of The World* between them. 'It's got the lot. Able seamen to get a twenty-five per cent cut. With nothing to make up for it either.'

'What!'

'It's there, sir! The unbelievable's happened!'

Snatching up the newspapers, Kelly swallowed his coffee and headed for his office, followed by the first lieutenant. '"Able seamen twenty-five per cent,"' he read out loud in a fury. '"Admirals and those receiving two thousand a year only ten. Junior officers eleven." Have they gone off their bloody heads, Number One?'

The first lieutenant looked worried. 'It's rubbish, of course, sir,' he said. 'Because it doesn't allow for extras and allowances.'

'It's still dangerous, Number One,' Kelly snapped. 'Unless they get more detailed explanations, they're not going to be aware that it's rubbish and I don't want 'em going off at half-cock. It says here the Army Council's issued explanations. Where are the explanations from the Board of Admiralty?'

The first lieutenant shrugged. 'They also appear to be quoting the Admiralty Fleet Order issued yesterday, sir – the one we don't appear to have received.'

Kelly frowned. 'Two thousand a year'll seem a princely salary to a chap getting four bob a day. Any reaction yet?'

'I wouldn't exactly say that the news has been welcomed,

255

sir.'

'I think I'd better say something at divine service. You'd better tell the chaplain to keep his sermon short and, while he's at it, he'd better put in a good word with God for us. We might need it.'

The chaplain was inclined to be lazy and seemed to spend most of his time dozing in one of the wardroom armchairs. When he'd galloped indifferently through his football-cricket-and-jolly-hockey-sticks brand of religion, Kelly held the men together and tried to speak to them. Without Harrison on board, he felt it was his duty to do so. But it was a tricky subject and he picked his way carefully through the maze of complications. He could see Rumbelo near the back, his eyes on him, but the one impression he got was of the total lack of expression on the hundreds of faces staring at him. They were regarding him politely and without a sound and he had a feeling that what he was saying simply wasn't sinking in. The hostility was there even if it didn't show.

As the men streamed away from the afterdeck, the first lieutenant drew Kelly to one side.

'I've heard from the master-at-arms, sir, that there's to be a mass meeting in the naval canteen ashore this evening, but I also understand that civilian agitators ashore haven't been given any sort of hearing at all. The complaints seem to be not against the officers, thank God, but against the government. They just appear to have lost faith in the Board of Admiralty.'

There was a distinct hardening of attitudes from the lower deck and even a feeling of derision. As Kelly had expected, a cut of ten per cent in a salary of two thousand a year was regarded with contempt.

'They must hate that bloody May Committee,' he growled to the first lieutenant. 'I shall be going ashore myself this evening, Number One, to see what's going on.'

That evening, *Nelson* arrived, without her sick admiral. She steamed into the Firth, majestic and grey against the Bay of Nigg. There was an overcast sky and, with her dark upperworks and turrets, she looked a splendid picture of grim readiness.

'With the fleet staff still aboard her,' the first lieutenant observed from behind Kelly as they watched her moved to her berth. 'I expect that's where all the explanations we were expecting are. They'd be addressed personally to Admiral Hodges and, because he's sick, the clots have filed 'em away to await his recovery.'

Kelly frowned. The first lieutenant's guess was more than likely right. The Navy had its fair share of shortsighted people.

As he stepped ashore, there were a great many men standing in groups about the pier and a lot of shouting that was not the usual good-natured catcalling. 'Good old *Rodney*,' he heard. 'We won't let 'em down!'

The officer of the shore patrol, provided by *Warspite*, greeted him warily. A meeting had been held in the canteen and there had been some disorder, the troublemakers chiefly from *Warspite*. There was still a lot of discordant singing about the town, some impromptu speeches on the pier and a few disconcerted glances from startled civilians who were clearly alarmed at the ill-feeling that existed. Kelly was aboard as the men returned. While there was singing in the boats – and he could see Leading Seaman Doncaster prominent among the singers – they came alongside quietly. But, watching through narrowed eyes, he noticed groups of men gathering on the forecastle and could hear an endless murmur of voices.

He called the officers together in the wardroom again, but the junior officers seemed not to have noticed anything at all and many of the senior officers seemed indifferent; and he realised that, since they were all in the same boat, they were probably feeling 'If they want to get drunk, let 'em.'

Sensing that a lot of them had lost touch with their men, he headed for his cabin and flung himself into his chair to sit glowering at his desk until he recovered his temper. The Mediterranean, Keyes' polo and the *Royal Oak* scandal had long since made him realise that the old attitudes were keeping the Navy the same in a changing world. Here at Invergordon, it was very definitely a *different* Navy, even a different world.

Frowning, his mind elsewhere, he got Boyle to bring in the reports, letters, signals and returns that would normally have been dealt with by Captain Harrison. He was the ship's captain until Harrison's replacement arrived after the weekend and it was something that couldn't be ducked.

'Leading Seaman Doncaster,' he growled, tossing his pen

257

down. 'Know him, Seamus?'

Boyle frowned. 'I've seen his file, sir. He's got a clean sheet, but he's got a temper and he *is* a bit of a loudmouth.'

Kelly nodded. 'I was warned about him in Novorossiisk and I notice that of all the people in this ship, he's the one I keep bumping into with his mouth open.'

He sat brooding on the problem long after Boyle had gone and was still scowling at his desk in the early hours when there was a tap at the door. It was Rumbelo. He was clearly on the side of the lower deck yet unable, in his loyalty to Kelly, to overlook what was happening.

'I think there's going to be trouble, sir,' he reported warily. 'There was a bit of mug throwing and singing in the canteen, and sometimes two or three trying to make speeches at the same time. But it wasn't a canteen brawl, sir. It was more than that.'

Kelly's smile died. 'I know that,' he admitted. 'A canteen brawl's an ancient and honoured method of letting off steam. This is different. What about you? What do you think of the rights and wrongs of it?'

Rumbelo shuffled uncomfortably. 'I think they've got a point, sir.'

'I'm sure they have. Where do you stand?'

'Where I always stood, sir. I owe you a lot, including me life, and Biddy and me family, and I'll not let you down. But I think it's wrong, sir. You can't take away a man's livelihood, not specially when he's worked hard and served his country well. And these pre-1925 men have.' Rumbelo's face was stubborn. The old warmth that had existed between them had disappeared with Kelly's marriage to what Rumbelo firmly considered was the wrong woman. 'They think that only concerted action can save their families from ruin, sir.'

Kelly frowned. 'They may be right at that, Rumbelo,' he admitted. 'But we can't look after the whole fleet. So, for God's sake, let's try to keep *our* chaps' noses clean if we can.'

The following morning, *The Times* gave the first full and genuine details of the cuts, and the parliamentary correspondent reported coldly that, however things might seem to the Members and despite allowances, an admiral's pay was being cut by only seven per cent while that of an able seaman of the 1919 class was being cut by twenty-five.

It was quite clear the lower deck had also been well informed and there was the usual stream of men waiting outside Kelly's office to see him when he arrived. During the morning, the first lieutenant brought back from *Hood* the Admiralty Fleet Order that had been missing for so long.

'Nothing about the cuts, sir,' he said. 'Just the usual rubbish about stores and appointments.'

The mail brought a telegram from Captain Masterson, Harrison's relief, saying he hoped to catch the first train the following morning and, after stopping off in Edinburgh to attend to personal business, to be aboard *Rebuke* on Wednesday morning.

'Pity he can't get a move on and report before,' Kelly growled.

As the morning progressed, *Warspite*, flagship of the Second Battle Squadron, led out *Malaya* for sub-calibre exercises in the Firth. As the remaining ships carried out their general drill against the clock, Kelly was aware of a sense of deep foreboding. Some of the jobs were being done lackadaisically, but he'd warned the first lieutenant that officers were not to chase the men. Knowing how they felt about the cuts, he gave them the benefit of the doubt and assumed they were preoccupied rather than defiant. He'd heard there'd been men from *Warspite* among the noisy crowd in the canteen the previous night, yet *Warspite* and *Malaya* appeared to have got away without trouble.

The explanation they'd all been expecting came at last in a letter from the Admiralty, forwarded from the flagship. It was out of date already and seemed to be an attempt to prove that the cuts weren't what they appeared to be.

'Written no doubt between a gossip about the weather and a pink gin at the club,' Kelly snorted. 'Doesn't it occur to those fatheads that this bloody business is dynamite and a letter explaining it is as important as a diplomatic mission? This isn't even in diplomatic language.'

'And the men will still not fail to note, sir,' Boyle said dryly, 'that the difference between four shillings and the three shillings they're going to get is still twenty-five per cent.'

'For God's sake —' Kelly tossed the letter down '— it even has the brass-bound gall to suggest that senior officers aren't paid too much, middle rank officers' pay isn't excessive, the pay of junior officers is more than necessary and the pay of the men is too high. It's enough to set a bomb off in the ships. Where have they been all this time?'

The first lieutenant was as worried as Kelly. Nothing amiss had been reported aboard but he'd heard rumours that all was not well in *Rodney*. 'What worries me most,' he said, 'is that nothing's been brought up by the petty officers.'

Something was brewing, Kelly knew. Despite the normal good relationship between the wardroom and the lower deck, he suspected that in the big ships of the Atlantic Fleet there couldn't be very many officers who knew anything of the home life of the men they commanded. Perhaps the men's very conservatism was against it.

'There's an abyss between us,' he said. 'And it's not because we come from bigger houses and better streets. Clear lower deck, Number One. I think it's about time I talked to them again.'

He had never considered himself much of a public speaker but once more he tried to tell the assembled men that it would always be better if they made any representations they had through him.

'I've organised a special office,' he said, 'with an officer and a chief petty officer, so that you can bring your problems forward.'

'And a fuckin' lot of good it'll do.' The voice from the back sounded like Doncaster's. 'They'll just get stuffed in a drawer at the Admiralty and forgotten like all the rest.'

Once upon a time, Kelly reflected bitterly, they'd shouted 'Good old Ginger' and whistled 'Anybody Here Seen Kelly?' Now he was not getting through to them and it had been going on all week-end.

Shore leave had not been stopped and he watched with the first lieutenant as the liberty men headed for the drifters. For a long time he stood frowning. He was still uneasy and he made up his mind abruptly.

'I think I'll go ashore again, Number One,' he said.

There was no sign of trouble as he stepped on to the Centre

Pier. A crowd of blue-clad men was streaming to the dockyard canteen from a football match, and the officer in command of the shore patrol, a lieutenant called Elkins, was in the officers' club. 'I've got men at the Centre Pier, the Dockyard Pier and at the canteen, sir,' he told Kelly. 'They have instructions to call me if there's any sign of trouble.'

Almost as he finished speaking he was called to the telephone. Curious, Kelly trailed behind him and arrived just as he was replacing the receiver.

'Just heard there's a meeting in progress, sir,' he announced. 'And that the canteen doors have been locked. I'm going down there. If it's trouble, I've instructions to contact *Hood*. There's a strong patrol there to reinforce me.'

Waiting near the canteen, Kelly saw him try to peer through the windows before finally persuading someone inside to unlock the doors. As he vanished inside, there were immediate shouts of 'Get out!' and 'That finishes it!' and the sound of breaking glass. Very soon afterwards, the door opened and Elkins reappeared backwards.

He gave Kelly a sheepish grin. 'Well, that seems to be that, sir,' he announced. 'They shoved me out.'

'Handle you?'

Elkins looked puzzled. 'No, sir. They just sort of linked arms and made it impossible to stay. I think it's time to call *Hood*'s patrol.'

'I'll do that for you.'

When Kelly returned, Elkins was waiting outside the canteen. 'I got in again,' he said. 'They apologised and one of 'em even said that what they were doing they were doing for the officers as well as for themselves.'

Kelly frowned. 'What the hell *are* they doing?'

Elkins shrugged. 'They're beginning to leave now,' he went on. 'I think they're heading for the football field.'

Hood's patrol, shaved to the bone and complete with sidearms, clanked up as the meeting on the football field finished and the men streamed back to the canteen. Kelly watched with admiration as Elkins managed to get inside yet again, this time with the lieutenant-commander in charge of *Hood*'s party.

There was a crowd on the Centre Pier as the men began to board the drifters for their ships. They were orderly, but strains

261

of *The Red Flag* came from *Rodney*'s boat as it swung away from the jetty. As *Valiant*'s drifter left, Kelly heard the words yelled across the water – 'Six o'clock tomorrow!'

'Six o'clock tomorrow *what?*' he growled.

As he returned aboard *Rebuke*, he saw meetings being held on *Rodney*'s forecastle and on the forecastles of other ships, and heard cheering that reminded him bitterly of the spontaneous shouts of joy he'd heard at Scapa at the end of the war.

There was no sign of trouble in *Rebuke* but there was a message from the flagship to say that a telegram had been received from Captain Masterson, whose wife appeared to have been taken ill so that he would be a day or two late reporting.

'There seems to be a bloody lot of unexpected illness floating about suddenly,' Kelly said bitterly.

Going on deck, he saw groups of men talking on the forecastle. Guessing they weren't discussing the beer they'd drunk or the quality of the football they'd seen, he wished to God Gorgeous George was still aboard or that Captain Masterson had arrived. Trouble in a ship the size of *Rebuke* didn't seem to be within the scope of a mere commander. In his cabin, he ran a hand through his hair, then he poured himself a drink and sat staring at the glass. He was just feeling desperately alone when Rumbelo appeared.

He looked uncomfortable. Honest, disciplined and clear-headed, the trouble in the fleet left him puzzled. 'I think that trouble I warned you about, sir, is due tomorrow when we sail,' he said.

'That's what I guessed. What form will it take?'

'I've heard a commmttee was formed of six ratings from each ship. They're going to run the boats and essential services and that's all. They call it strike action.'

'Then they're bloody fools, Rumbelo!' Kelly sat up with a jerk. 'Because no matter how *they* look at it, the Admiralty will decide it's mutiny. Who're the troublemakers?'

Rumbelo hesitated and Kelly gestured. 'For God's sake, man, I've got a few names myself! Let's compare them and, if they're worth it, perhaps we can stop them making asses of themselves. Anybody been at them?'

'No, sir. They're just –' Rumbelo's blunt potato face went

262

pink with embarrassment '– well, sir, they're just bloody desperate, sir. They're mostly decent men with families and I don't think in the end they'll do anything. There's only one I'm worried about.'

'Big chap? Red hair?'

'Yes, sir.' Rumbelo gave a wry grin. 'Leading Seaman Doncaster. He was in Russia with us.'

'Think he's an agitator?'

'A makee-learn I'd say, sir.'

'Can we do anything about him?'

Rumbelo rubbed his nose. 'Not at the moment, sir,' he said. 'I've got a few ideas, mind, but I'd rather keep 'em till the right moment.'

Kelly nodded and sloshed whisky into a glass. 'Better swallow that. And thanks for coming along. I'll leave it to you. What about the others?'

Rumbelo put the glass down. 'They'll not move without Doncaster and I think I can attend to him.'

As Rumbelo vanished, the loneliness came back. Command was the loneliest of all pinnacles and somehow Kelly wasn't reassured by the absence of a family. He hadn't seen his father for ages, his mother was preoccupied with her own affairs, and he had no wife and no children. His cabin was empty of family souvenirs and, for the first time in his life, he was terribly aware of the gap left in it by the fact that there was no longer Charley.

He sent for the first lieutenant and went over the situation. 'If there's trouble, Number One,' he said, 'it'll come tomorrow when the capital ships will be preparing to sail.' He frowned. 'I wish we were at sea with *Warspite* and *Malaya*.'

As they talked, they heard a burst of cheering across the water.

'*Rodney*, sir,' the first lieutenant said. 'I think it's some sort of code. It's being answered by *Valiant*.'

'Probably keeping each other's spirits up,' Kelly decided. A lunatic idea entered his head and he made his mind up abruptly. 'Number One, I'm going to shift berth.'

The first lieutenant's eyebrows shot up. 'At this time of night, sir?'

'I'm going to claim *Malaya*'s position. It's right on the end of the line and since *Rodney* seems to be the activating ship it might

263

be useful to be a long way away from her.'

The first lieutenant looked worried, but Kelly's mind was made up. 'Everybody's aboard,' he pointed out. 'Inform the engineer commander we shall need steam for twelve knots.'

'He's not going to like it, sir.'

'He's not being asked!' Kelly snapped. 'Let's have a signal off to the flagship. Inform them we have a foul berth and will have to move if we're to leave with the fleet tomorrow. Tell them we'll drop a buoy and suggest divers go down to investigate. If they don't grant permission, then we'll do a bit of Nelson's blind eye work and misread their signal.'

'Sir, this could end your career.'

Kelly frowned. 'If there's trouble tomorrow,' he said, 'and we've done nothing about it, it could end my career, anyway.'

6

The following morning dawned fine, clear and windless with a warming sun. Corporal O'Hara appeared with hot water for Kelly to shave.

'The hands have been having a bit of trouble forrard, sir,' he announced calmly as if he were giving the result of the St. Leger. 'They didn't want to turn to, but it seems they have in the end.'

Kelly's heart started to thump. He'd taken a colossal risk the previous night. With Gorgeous George attending to the affairs of his sick father – and probably thankful for it – and Captain Masterson studying the newspapers and doubtless being crafty enough to watch how the wind blew before he arrived, the whole responsibility for the ship had been on his shoulders. But *Rebuke*'s crew had been caught unawares. They had not been prepared to start work after being ashore, particularly in the mood of the moment, but, because their plans, whatever they were, had not included an unexpected move from one berth to another at short notice, they had been at a loss.

Before moving, he had carefully weighed up everything he knew about ships like *Rebuke*, and tried to behave as if moving such huge vessels was something he did every day of his life. She was underpowered, he knew, and took a lot of stopping, and his stomach had been knotted with anxiety as she had advanced down the Firth, apparently lazily but in a manner which to him seemed to indicate she was about to gallop into the harbour of Lossiemouth.

Now, as he went on deck to take a look round, the great vessels of the Atlantic Fleet stood out sharp and grim against the paler tones of the land. He had managed to get little sleep, and the night had been filled chiefly with wondering what would

265

happen when divers went down at the berth he'd left and found nothing there. Reasons in writing, even concocted with the aid of Boyle and the first lieutenant, would hardly produce anything satisfactory and he began to wish he hadn't been such a damn fool.

His bath was ready when he returned to his cabin. Outwardly there appeared to be no signs of unrest in the ship, and so far everybody had behaved with respect. In the wardroom, however, there was an air of people waiting for something to happen and he was surprised to get a cup of coffee. Everybody seemed gloomy, but the first lieutenant reported that so far everything was normal. When he went on deck again, the work of hoisting in boats ready for sea was under way. The first lieutenant's face was grave.

'There seems a lot of unwillingness,' he warned quietly. 'They keep disappearing to the messdecks on the flimsiest of excuses and it's remarkable how many men have reported sick this morning.'

'I wish to God we could get the signal,' Kelly said. 'The longer we hang about the worse it'll get.'

Accommodation ladders were hoisted inboard and booms unshipped. Here and there officers and petty officers were giving a hand on Kelly's instructions, to make sure the work went ahead, but whenever there was a pause, groups of men gathered on the forecastle, their eyes everywhere, wary, suspicious and doubtful. Staring at the sky, Kelly found himself wishing for sleeting rain. There'd have been no gatherings on deck but for the warm sunshine.

'Keep the R.N.R. men busy,' he advised the first lieutenant. 'They're doing well, and they set a good example.'

As they worked, they caught the distant sound of cheering from the direction of *Rodney*. Heads came up and everybody aboard *Rebuke* stared down the line of great ships.

'That's a damn bad sign, Number One,' Kelly said.

The first lieutenant had pulled his telescope from under his arm and clapped it to his eye. '*Repulse* sails first,' he pointed out. 'Then *Valiant*. Then *Nelson*, *Hood* and *Rodney*, followed by us.' He stared silently, a figure of tense expectancy. 'Nothing seems to be happening in *Rodney*,' he announced. '*Hood* appears to be behaving normally. Nothing much happening in *Valiant*

266

or *Repulse* either.'

'What about the cruisers, Number One?'

'Not much in *Adventure*. In *Advance* they look like a lot of ants but they don't seem to be working. Nothing in *York* except a crowd on the forecastle. *Norfolk* – they appear to be waiting to see what happens elsewhere. *Dorsetshire* – it's hard to say.'

The first lieutenant shifted his stance and Kelly saw him stiffen. 'Hello, *Repulse*'s under way, sir.'

'No sign of movement from *Valiant* or *Rodney*?'

'Not a sign. The foredecks are full of men but nobody seems to be doing any work.'

'We'll give 'em ten minutes, Number One. No more. Thank God we're a long way away.'

As he returned to his cabin, Rumbelo was waiting for him.

'I think, sir,' he announced, 'that if we don't waste too much time, it'll be all right. They're looking for Leading Seaman Doncaster to tell them what to do.'

'And Leading Seaman Doncaster?'

'He's in the storeroom aft, sir.'

'What's he doing there?'

'Sleeping. He'll be all right when he wakes up except for a bruise on his jaw.'

Then Kelly noticed that Rumbelo's right hand was wrapped in a handkerchief.

'Surely to God, Rumbelo – ?'

Rumbelo gave a sheepish grin. 'I'm afraid so, sir. Perhaps I could be excused duty so I can keep an eye on him.'

Kelly frowned. 'Well, it's a bit bloody unorthodox,' he agreed, 'but it might work. If it doesn't, then we're both sunk.'

It was Rumbelo's turn to frown. 'If this business doesn't sort itself out, sir, there'll be no navy and in that case I'm damned if I care.'

Unable to sit still, Kelly went back on deck.

'Nothing happening, sir,' the first lieutenant reported. '*Repulse* about to pass out of the Firth.'

Kelly made up his mind. 'We'll follow her,' he said. 'We won't wait for the others. Prepare to weigh. And let's have it carried out fast, Number One. Make a signal to the flagship but don't wait for an answer. So far, we still have 'em with us and with a bit of luck we'll keep 'em with us long enough to get to

267

sea.'

He turned. The bridge appeared to be properly manned and voice pipes were being answered. The forecastle party was in place.

'Weigh!'

This was the crucial moment. If something went wrong now the ship would not go to sea and that would probably mean the end of George Kelly Maguire, R.N. There'd be no medals for this affair and precious little credit. Nobody who failed to move his ship was going to get a good report. When the news got around of what was happening there'd be the biggest uproar since Jutland and at the subsequent enquiry there'd be a lot of people who'd be found wanting.

'Up and down, sir. Anchor aweigh.'

Kelly's breath came out in a loud gasp. 'Thank God, Number One,' he said. He turned to the officer of the watch. 'Half ahead both. We'll take station behind *Repulse*.'

It seemed strange to be carrying out sub-calibre firing with only *Repulse* for company, and at midday the recall came.

They returned warily, picking up *Warspite* and *Malaya* on their way in. Since their night's berth was now occupied, they moved down the line to a berth beyond the flagship and nearer the pier. The tide was on the turn and the ships had swung with their bows towards the south, so that *Rebuke* had to pass in front of their forecastles. *Nelson* was a mass of cheering men chanting slogans as she slipped past. There was some jeering, too, and it was possible to pick up the words 'Scabs' and 'Blacklegs', and the faces of the men on *Rebuke*'s forecastle grew bleak. As they dropped anchor and the cable party was dismissed, Kelly became aware of Leading Seaman Doncaster on the forecastle. He seemed to be trying to make a speech, but the men about him seemed to be unwilling listeners, and finally someone threw a wet cloth. As it hit Doncaster in the face, there was a burst of laughter. It was short and sharp but it had a relieved sound, like the mob at Kiukiang and for roughly the same reason.

Kelly's expression slipped. 'I think we're going to be all right, Number One,' he said.

Boyle appeared. 'Signal from the flagship, sir. Captain to

repair on board as soon as possible.'

'Here we go, Number One. Tell O'Hara to lay out my best uniform, Seamus, and let's have the captain's barge tarted up, Number One. If there's going to be trouble, we'll not have it for appearances.'

The normal movement of boats seemed to be unimpeded, and as they put out booms and gangways they began to arrive from other ships. The first lieutenant appeared in Kelly's cabin as he was changing.

'Only seventy-five men appeared in *Rodney* when "Special Sea Duty Men" was piped,' he announced, not without an air of triumph. '*Hood* fell in and carried on. Only P.O.s and a few men in *Valiant*. *Adventure* – they thought they were going to pull it off, but they didn't quite. *Dorsetshire, York* and *Norfolk* all seemed to have been watching each other and nothing was done at all. The men were addressed by captains and other officers but it seems without avail. *Valiant* nearly made it. They got the Marines to hoist in boats but then they just walked away from the falls. Thanks to junior officers they were still able to report "Ready for sea", but then the Chief reported that he couldn't keep the stokers below, and they had to suspend all preparations and pipe hands to breakfast. *Rodney*, nothing. In some ships, they're keeping the ship clean and working normal safety routines. In others, not even that. I gather the admiral's signalled London that they'd better do something quick-sharp or they'll have no navy left. Oh, and in *Advance* an officer was pushed overboard!'

There was a strange brooding silence about the flagship when Kelly stepped on the deck. The admiral greeted him with a grim face.

'Ah, Commander Maguire. I hope you have your reasons for shifting berth last night.'

Kelly handed them over and the admiral glanced at them.

'I'd hardly call them satisfactory,' he observed tartly. 'Needless to say, I've made no response to your suggestion that divers should investigate. Why didn't you report yourself ready for sea before disappearing?'

'I felt it wiser not to, sir. I ordered the anchor to be weighed

269

before anybody could argue. It worked, sir.'

The admiral regarded him coldly. 'Indeed it did. I'm not sure whether you should be punished or congratulated for your cool cheek. On the other hand, so that you don't take on yourself the running of the whole fleet, I'm sending Captain Corbett from my staff to take over. I trust you'll give him your full support and – ah! – the benefit of your experience.'

Captain Corbett appeared on board after lunch and immediately called for Kelly. He was a very different type from Harrison, with a grave demeanour but lively eyes.

'I think you must be a very good guesser, Maguire,' he said. 'Or else some new kind of prophet.'

It was a day of silence. The men gathered in groups on the forecastle, with the officers on the quarterdeck.

'How are they now?' Corbett asked.

'I notice a few black eyes, sir. I'm not sure whether they belong to men who favoured defiance or loyalty, but either way it seems opinion wasn't unanimous.'

Corbett picked up a signal he'd received and began to read. 'The Lords Commissioners view with the greatest concern the injury which the prestige of the British navy has suffered. . . .'

'I don't think grown men will enjoy being scolded like little boys, sir,' Kelly growled.

Corbett gave a cold smile. 'I shall not be reading it to them,' he pointed out. 'There's also a second signal saying that the exercises must take place, and one helpful piece of advice – from the Third Sea Lord's Department, of all people! It suggests a postponement.'

Verschoyle for a quid, Kelly thought. On the ball, shrewd and sharp as ever, and making sure he's squaring his own yardarm.

Night came over an uneasy fleet. Shore leave had been cancelled but by dusk the whole length of the coast was seen to be lined with cars.

'Interested spectators,' Corbett observed as they watched from the quarterdeck. 'Together, doubtless, with more than their share of newspapermen. However, the Admiralty's finally had the good sense to come out of its somnolence and cancel the exercises, and I understand the admiral's signalled them that

270

nothing will be solved unless a definite decision about pay's taken.

The first lieutenant, who had been to *Advance* to return a loan of rope, reappeared on board with a gloomy look.

'They'd had a lot of trouble,' he said. 'Things got smashed and one officer had to lock himself in his cabin. Revolver racks were stripped and ready-use lockers emptied, and they finally shoved one of the heads of departments overboard. Chap called Kimister.'

Somehow it went with Kimister, Kelly thought sadly, and he found his heart bleeding for Charley.

The wardroom was gloomy that night. There had been an unsubstantiated rumour that one of the Highland regiments had been called out to arrest the mutinous crews but had mutinied themselves in sympathy, and more than one man was weighing up his chances of succeeding as a civilian if the armed forces fell apart at the seams. The evening papers were full of accusations and wild statements. The shock of a mutiny in that most hallowed of services, the Royal Navy, seemed to have sent reverberations round the empire.

'Been a run on gold,' the first lieutenant announced from behind his paper. 'You wouldn't think a few bloody-minded seamen could knock the underpinnings from the national economy, would you?'

'The national economy,' Kelly said, 'depends a lot on people having faith in the stability of England and, with the fleet in revolt, doubtless a few of 'em are having second thoughts.'

Nobody was looking forward to the next day and Kelly greeted it almost with a groan. Nobody in authority seemed capable of making decisions and, with everybody who might help on holiday, he could only see the situation growing worse.

When 'Clear Lower Deck' was piped, everybody appeared, but they were slow. A crowd had already appeared on *Valiant*'s forecastle and a great deal of interest was being shown in the preparations for painting aboard *Warspite, Malaya* and *Repulse*. As the stages were swung out and men began to climb on to them, there was such a roar of fury they were hastily called back inboard. It was clear that if somebody didn't do something soon, the situation was in danger of getting out of control, but during the afternoon, the signals officer appeared. He looked relieved. 'Admiralty's signalled that ships are to return to their home ports,' he announced.

It was like a weight being lifted off their shoulders. Corbett sighed and Kelly knew exactly what he was thinking. The man on the white horse with the reprieve in his gauntlet had galloped up just as the noose was being put round the condemned man's neck.

7

Sailing was still by no means a certainty. In *Rebuke* the temper had deteriorated considerably and the departure for the south was far from a foregone conclusion.

When the pipe to clear lower deck went, the men moved forward unwillingly, dressed in various rigs, some even unshaven. When the first lieutenant addressed them, there were ironic cheers, but by the time Kelly went forward they seemed to have changed their mind. They avoided looking at him but there was no defiance, and they came instinctively to attention as he appeared.

'The ship's going to Portsmouth,' he said. 'You'll be seeing your wives and families again.'

'Fat lot of good that'll be without money,' someone growled.

'Better to be with 'em without money than *up here* without it,' Kelly retorted. 'Or worse still, in Scapa.' There were a few unwilling grins at that because nobody liked Scapa and he went on quickly while he had them listening to him. 'I have to tell you, too, that, although the Admiralty's promised to look into your case, they've stated also that any further trouble will have to be dealt with under the Naval Discipline Act; and I, for one, don't want that.'

There was a defiant cheer from the back, but it soon died.

'I'm therefore going to dismiss you for a quarter of an hour for you to consider your action before having the bugles sounded for both watches to fall in to prepare for sea. it's up to you now.'

As the sailors streamed aft, a cheer broke out from *Rodney*, but he noticed it was not as full-blooded as it had been and he suspected that the defiance was beginning to break as the ringleaders began to fear they were acting alone.

In dismissing the men, he realised he'd taken a great risk, but when the bugles sounded, they fell in again, though far from willingly. He appealed to one or two of them by name. Leading Seaman Doncaster was at the front, still angry from his forced incarceration in the after storeroom and looking for trouble.

'How about you, Doncaster?' Kelly said, taking a chance he'd get a mouthful of abuse in return. 'You've got five children waiting for you. Don't you want to see them?'

Doncaster scowled and opened his mouth. Then a voice from the back interrupted him.

' 'E's got one or two more in a few other places, too,' it jeered. 'Perhaps he don't want to go 'ome because 'e's got a couple in Invergordon as well.'

Doncaster scowled again and blushed, not knowing whether to be insulted or proud of his virility. Then the scowl changed to an embarrassed grin, and the tense moment passed so that Kelly tried speaking to one or two more men. They looked uncomfortable and unwilling to acknowledge him but there was no abuse and slowly they began to fall in.

Numb with shame, he remembered the German officer he'd met in *Grosser Kurfürst* when the High Seas Fleet had surrendered. Jesus Christ, he thought, this is a fine bloody way to run the King's Navee!

As they headed south past the Farne Islands off Northumbria, there was a marked sense of anti-climax and none of the sense of triumph they'd all expected. The men felt they'd achieved their ends and the officers that they'd averted disaster, but none of them denied the relief at being sent home.

Their arrival in Portsmouth was far from joyful. In the blackness which preceded the dawn they crept into Spithead, their arrival timed so that there could be no crowds along the forehore to see them appear. There were motor car headlights along the front at Southsea, however, and they all knew they belonged to newspapermen waiting to see what would happen. To Kelly their arrival seemed shifty and smacked of the war years when they'd come and gone only in darkness.

As the ships began to move along the deep water channel, there was only a subdued hum from the engines to break the silence, and the dim grey bulks slid silently out of the murk and crept past the Round Tower towards the narrow entrance to the harbour. *Hood* vanished from sight like a ghost, the stillness broken only by the querulous trillings of the bosuns' pipes. Fifteen minutes later, *Nelson* followed, heading for the flagship berth at the South Railway Jetty, another huge grey shadow moving between the buoys. By the time it was *Rebuke*'s turn it was daylight and there were people watching from Old Portsmouth and the Sally Port. There was no cheering, however. It was clearly a welcome of disapproval.

'I think there are going to be a few men listening to the sharp tongues of their wives tonight,' Corbett observed grimly. '*They* have to live with their neighbours and their neighbours have noticed that the country's lost thirty million in gold as a result of what's happened.'

The bosuns' pipes trilled, and the call, 'Hands fall in for entering harbour,' was passed along the deck. The men appeared at the double, as though they were anxious to show the people ashore that there had been no disloyalty on their part, and as the ship reached the harbour entrance, they fell in amidships, only a lone officer in the bows with the leadsmen at their stations.

There had been no more fist fights, but the mutineers were subdued by the chilly welcome. Startled at the hostility, they were chastened and unproud of themselves, and they all knew that though the First Lord of the Admiralty had promised in the House there would be no punishments for what had happened, the Admiralty was going to have to climb down over pay and would be looking for scapegoats.

'We have to hold an enquiry,' Corbett told Kelly. 'And names have been asked for. Have you any?'

Kelly thought of Doncaster and the surly stupidity on his face as he was chaffed about his children. Perhaps *Rebuke* had been lucky that her troubles had been in the hands of nobody cleverer.

'Just one sir,' he said.

Corbett gave him a sideways glance. 'You sure that's all?'

'Quite sure, sir. We were lucky. I think we should pass a little of it along.'

Corbett nodded. 'I'm inclined to agree. Officers?'

'Perhaps they deserve a little luck, too, sir.'

275

Shore leave was granted and the first watches headed as usual for the pubs. The Home Office had laid on detectives in the hope of picking up information about professional agitators, but all they got for their money were a lot of red herrings. Men who not long before had been grim and defiant were beginning to recover their sense of humour, and their murmurings about 'Ginger's going to wreck the engines,' set the detectives searching Portsmouth for red-headed stokers.

There was less success with the attempts to impress everybody that what had happened at Invergordon was not disloyalty and that they'd been forced into it by the intransigeance of the Admiralty. The city's aloofness was unbearable. The men were guilty of defiance. The officers were guilty of indifference. In pubs and hotels, people simply turned their backs on them.

To his surprise, Kelly found Charley waiting in the Keppel's Head for Kimister. She greeted him with a doubtful smile.

'I thought I ought to be here when he came ashore,' she said.

Kelly nodded. What would he have given for such loyalty? All that had greeted him on arrival was a batch of solicitors' letters, one peremptorily demanding that he clear the London house of his belongings forthwith, but not a sign of life from Christina beyond a short, sad note from Hugh from the Hotel Majestic in Cannes. . . . 'I don't like France, I can't speak the lingo. I don't suppose you could come and fetch me back to England, could you?'

'What happened, Kelly?' Charley asked.

'The lower deck lost faith in their officers,' Kelly said.

'The papers said it was Communist agitators.'

Kelly shrugged. 'If there were any Communist agitators, Charley, I never saw 'em. And the trouble didn't start among the king's hard bargains but among the men with families you'd normally expect to be reliable.'

'Is the Navy all right, Kelly?'

'I doubt if it'll be the same again for a long time.' He shifted uneasily. 'How's Albert?'

'I've spoken to him on the telephone. He says he was humiliated. What'll happen now, Kelly?'

Kelly shrugged. 'There's to be an enquiry. The gold braid will be blinding. Anybody involved in incidents will have to make reports and name names. A few heads will roll.'

'Will you be involved, Kelly?'

'They're doubtless measuring me for the drop at this moment. After this, Charley, a lot of people who thought a great deal of the Navy are going to have to find something else to give their love to. It's been a shattering experience, and those who're lucky enough to be left in will have to turn the thing upside down to make it work because it can never be the old Navy again. That's finished and done with, and I can't say I'm sorry.'

She nodded unhappily. 'How's Christina, Kelly?'

He shrugged. 'I haven't the foggiest, Charley,' he admitted. 'I don't know where she is or what she's doing. She walked out on me.'

'What shall you do?'

He shrugged. 'When the enquiries are over, I shall request leave to go to London. I've been told I have to get all my possessions out of the house there because it's to be sold.'

'You could stay with us for a while.'

Kelly smiled. 'I don't think that would be a good idea, Charley dear. And I think Albert will need all your attention after this lot.'

Gorgeous George reappeared, all smiles. It seemed his father had recovered unexpectedly, though Kelly suspected that he and Captain Masterson, despite the fact that they'd avoided an unpleasant duty with the oldest dodge in the world – attending a funeral, the excuse of every office boy who ever wanted to watch a football match – had not in the end done themselves a lot of good.

The enquiry was held in the office of the Commander-in-Chief, Portsmouth, and the weather, which had been good during the whole of the mutiny, changed to intermittent rain from a leaden sky. As Kelly had predicted, the gold lace was dazzling. In addition to the Commander-in-Chief, the Fourth Sea Lord, the Deputy Secretary of the Admiralty and all the principal port officers were present.

They sat for two days and, by the end of it, all the anger was dissipated. Both men and officers were still nervous. The shock had been great and though nothing was said about it, the condemnation of the Admiralty by everyone was clear. News had

277

finally come that the Government had climbed down. All cuts had been limited to ten per cent, which was bad enough in all conscience to men who were badly paid to start off with, but at least it seemed fairer.

At the end of the week, Admiral Sir John Kelly was appointed to command the Atlantic Fleet for one year with the clear object of curing its troubles. He was a full admiral with the prestige to make his decisions stick, and his personal investigations started at once.

London seemed as uncertain as the Navy. Winter was coming on and an election was in the offing because the country was being run by a body of men who hadn't been elected to govern. After the abysmal efforts of the Labour government, everybody expected a landslide to the right.

Most of the furnishings from the house in Carlton Terrace had already been removed and most of Kelly's belongings had been crammed into a single wardrobe. He stuffed them into a trunk with the aid of Bridget who'd accompanied him to help.

'Where will you be living now, Master Kelly?' she asked.

'Thakeham, Biddy. Or in the ship.' He paused. 'If I still have a ship.'

'Oh, Master Kelly, it won't come to that, will it?'

'It might, Biddy. It just might.'

'What about Petty Officer Rumbelo?'

'Your husband has nothing to fear, Biddy. I gave him the finest report it was possible to give any man.'

He drove her to the station and saw her off, then he went to the club for a meal. Verschoyle came in while he was standing at the bar, his usual chatty, cynical self.

'I told you the Board would make a balls of it,' he observed cheerfully as Kelly ordered him a pink gin. 'I was on duty when Tompkinson's signal arrived. It stood out a mile that the poor devil was crying out for help. But all the sea lords, the A.C.N.S., the Parliamentary Secretary, the Permanent Secretary, the Naval Secretary, the Director of Naval Intelligence, and Old Uncle Tom Cobley and all were all unavailable. Every manjack of 'em. I had to contact the Third Sea Lord myself and fill him in on a few facts he ought to have known already. In the end I got him to agree to a reply I'd sent on his behalf. I seem to have been the only bloody man in London who remembered there

278

was such a thing as a telephone.'

'I thought I recognised your touch,' Kelly said. 'How do the public regard it?'

Verschoyle frowned. 'A bit too close to Jutland for comfort,' he said. 'Faith in the Navy's been shaken again and the Admiralty's at the same game now they were at then – trying to cover its mistakes by issuing statements full of half-truths that nobody's stupid enough to believe. How bad was it?'

Kelly shrugged. 'It was bloody bad.'

'I think the public thinks the same.' Verschoyle finished his drink. 'They're pretty incoherent except in times of crisis, but then their usually half-baked arbitrary opinions have a habit of crystallising suddenly into something near to sense. The trouble, of course, is that governments have a habit in peacetime of forgetting the fighting services that save them in war, and there's been so much talk over the past few years about the last war being the war to end war they've become rather an anachronism. How're you going to come out of it?'

Kelly pushed his glass aside. 'God knows,' he said. 'You?'

'I shall be all right. I might even have picked up a little credit.'

It seemed very normal. Verschoyle could always be relied on to pick up credit from any situation. Clear-minded, cynical and coldly clinical, he could always see to the heart of a crisis and decide his best route out of it.

They said their farewells in the hall of the club. There was luggage by the door, labelled and strapped.

'I was going on leave if you remember,' Verschoyle said. 'But I decided I'd better cancel. I suppose it's safe to go now.'

As the taxi drew up, the bags were pushed aboard and Verschoyle climbed in after them. As the taxi drew away, Kelly stared after it, frowning. Then suddenly his face changed and he gave a bark of laughter that helped to relieve his grim feelings. Suddenly he could see a joke to brighten the day. Not a big joke and a joke against himself, but, if Verschoyle was up to what he believed he was up to, then it was surely against Verschoyle, too.

'And bloody good luck to you with her,' he murmured as he turned away.

Verschoyle's labels had all been marked 'Hotel Majestic,

Cannes.'

The fleet returned to Scotland to resume its interrupted cruise. Rosyth was chosen as the base this time – to save fuel, it was said, but everybody guessed it was really to save face. The winter wore on. It was a sad winter with everyone disillusioned, and in some places people so long unemployed they'd become unemployable. Joe Kelly didn't pull his punches. He decided that the men were right and the Admiralty abysmal. A few seamen were discharged as no longer required in the service, but the three port admirals concurred entirely: the cuts, like the cuts in the dole, had been cold-blooded and inhuman.

The Admiralty's reaction was vicious. The captain of *Hood* was relieved almost at once and the captains of *Rodney, Adventure* and *Advance* were informed they would not be given another command. It was clear that, like everybody else, the Admiralty was clearing its own yardarm.

To his surprise, instead of a reprimand and the information that he was to be passed over for future command, Kelly found he'd been commended for his foresight, the efforts he'd made to find out what was happening, and above all for his disobedience. 'This officer not only foresaw what was about to happen,' the report said, 'but he also had the courage to risk his career by going against instructions for the safety of his ship and the men in it.' It seemed that his career was not only not brought to a full stop but, like Verschoyle's might even have been helped a little, though there were plenty – including Kimister – who knew their careers were virtually at an end.

After a gloomy winter, the news came as a pleasant surprise, but there had been no word from Christina of commiseration or congratulation. It didn't surprise Kelly to hear that Verschoyle had wangled a staff job at Gibraltar and had left London in a hurry. He had no doubt now that he'd been involved in Christina's disappearance but he was strangely unmoved by the knowledge and unable to feel any dislike for him. Over the years, their relationship had changed from enmity to a curious sort of wary friendship, and he had a feeling Verschoyle had landed himself with a great deal of trouble if he were contemplating marriage to Christina.

A few days later, he received a letter from Christina's solicitors to inform him that the divorce would not be contested. Proof of adultery – with an Italian prince, he noted – was provided,

Even Vera von Schwerin dropped him. The elections in Germany in which Adolf Hitler had so nearly achieved power brought their affair to an abrupt end. With contingents of brown-clad thugs lining the Berlin streets, she had come out into the open in support of Hitler and his gangsters, and that, Kelly decided, was something he couldn't stomach.

When his time in *Rebuke* came to an end, he left her without even looking back at her. But leave was lonely and he spent most of his time at Thakeham making improvements and wondering, as he made them, who he was making them for. Indirectly he heard through the usual channels of information that Verschoyle, his career safely taken care of in the divorce proceedings, was contemplating marriage at last – as Kelly had expected, to Christina.

Well, he's welcome to her, he thought.

The naval assistant to the Second Sea Lord eyed him askance when he appeared to ask what his next job would be. 'You seem to have picked up a pretty good report from Captain Corbett,' he said. 'And since you're due for a spell of staff work we'll have to try to match it. How about Assistant to the Director of Naval Air Warfare?'

Kelly smiled. 'Sounds modern enough. Shall I have to learn to fly?'

'It wouldn't be a bad idea under the circumstances.'

Installed at the Admiralty and going to the R.A.F. station at Lee-on-Solent to learn to handle an aeroplane on Saturday afternoons, life became humdrum but at least reliable, and Kelly had just put down an elderly Fairey Flycatcher after soloing when a message came that he was wanted on the telephone.

It was the Director of Naval Air Warfare. 'Now's your chance to test your knowledge,' he said. 'They got a feeling in the Med – something Chatfield, the C.-in-C., said – that attacks on ships at sea by aircraft will be unremunerative in a few years' time. I think – and I think *he* thinks now, in fact – that he was too optimistic and the view was based on the unproven effectiveness of the new multi-barrelled close range anti-aircraft weapons that

281

are coming out. There's been a long interchange of opinions between him and the Admiralty on the functions of catapult aircraft and there's to be a conference at Gibraltar. I want you to go out and hold their hands. You've read everything and you know what the thought is here.'

It was a chance to get away from England that Kelly jumped at. 'I'll do that, sir,' he said. 'I'll be in London this evening and arrange my passage.'

The Director sounded pleased at his enthusiasm. 'That's all fixed,' he said. 'There's a flying boat leaving tomorrow It'll get you there faster and show we have confidence in aeroplanes. You might even get a few flying hours in, if you can persuade the pilot to let you handle the controls.'

Putting down the telephone, Kelly went to the mess to collect his belongings and celebrate his solo with a drink with his instructor. He had just emptied his glass when the evening papers arrived and there was an immediate grab for them.

'I see Invergordon's still taking its toll,' one of the younger pilots said as he backed away, the local rag in his hands.

The words caught Kelly's attention and he turned. The pilot looked like a schoolboy as he held out the paper to him. 'Inquest,' he said. 'Some poor devil shot himself. Wife said his career had been ruined by what happened. Know him, sir? Name of Kimister.'

8

The air conference took three weeks and the results were so disappointing, it was decided to hold another one in Simonstown.

Kelly flew south to Freetown where he picked up a destroyer heading for Cape Town, where, unexpectedly, the South African station seemed to have different views. Not only did they feel that airborne torpedoes might be of use at slowing down enemy ships when escaping, but they also felt they could be of value in attacks on enemy bases where crowded shipping would make missing virtually impossible.

The warm air of the Cape held Kelly for a few days more than he should have stayed, and when he reached home his report so pleased the Director he had to go through it all again and they set off on what amounted to a world tour of the naval air stations of the Empire.

His appointment came to an end with his return and they were into another new year with Invergordon a long way away. His leave coincided with his mother's death and he spent most of it helping his father put her affairs in order. As he returned from his final visit to the solicitor's he discovered a telegram waiting for him from the Admiralty. He'd been given the destroyer *Actaeon*, and was to take her to Alex as senior officer of a group of two destroyers and the minesweeper, *Glendower*. *Actaeon* was new, so they'd forgiven him the impertinence he'd shown in shifting *Rebuke* without so much as a by-your-leave, and she was waiting for him in Portsmouth, ready in every way, stored, ammunitioned, and fully manned; and the first lieutenant turned out to be Smart, whom he'd last met up the Yangtze. Things were beginning to look up.

It was quite clear the Navy was beginning to recover from Invergordon and, not only recover, but to make immense and

283

genuine efforts to repair the damage. Port committees were at work finding out things which should have been discovered long since, and departments were examining their methods and – what mattered more – their consciences. And with good reason because, suddenly, aggressive political groups led by Winston Churchill were demanding rearmament. In a rapidly deteriorating political situation in Germany, the government had fallen, the Nazis had doubled their strength in the Reichstag, and Adolf Hitler was at the head of the biggest single party. With the aid of propaganda and trickery, he'd been appointed Chancellor and it was obvious he was now set on dictatorship and even conflict, and in the House of Commons all the talk of pacifism had suddenly come to a stop as they realised at last that the war to end war that they'd fought between 1914 and 1918 had not been that at all, and that the peace they'd put together had had in it, in fact, the makings of a new struggle. Those hypnotic qualities which hid the fact that what Hitler had to say was far from new also unfortunately had the ability to reduce his audiences to delirium; and, despite those British newspapers which kept reiterating their owners' belief in peace, for the first time people were listening to the man who'd been crying 'wolf' for years. Suddenly there was the same sort of uneasy air about Europe that there'd been before 1914, with Hitler talking of rearmament and the Italian dictator, Mussolini, making bombastic claims for the Mediterranean. As *Actaeon* and her consorts were ordered to make ready, Kelly started to think about Charley again.

Smart owned a narrow three-storeyed Georgian house with bow windows in Old Portsmouth, with pillars at the door and potted geraniums on the front step. It had been a wine merchant's home when Nelson had left for Trafalgar, and it was when they asked him for dinner that he began to wonder if he dare seek her out once more.

She'd never really been out of his mind and he was also conscious that they were now both free agents again. Smart's house, full of the warmth of a woman's touches, made him long for something for himself. For all Biddy's earnest efforts, Thakeham remained cold and empty, with no one there to whom it meant home. As he left, he decided it was time to go and see her.

He was taking no chances this time and in his pocket was the

284

ruby the Grand Duchess Evgenia had given him in Malta after *Mordant* had lifted her out of Russia. Because he'd always intended it for Charley, he'd never offered it to Christina.

He found the house without difficulty. It was small and in need of paint and, in the fading light, had a lost look about it. Studying it from the shadows at the other side of the road for a moment to pluck up his courage, he was caught by a dreadful panic. Suppose she told him she wasn't interested any longer? Suppose some other man were there? Suppose she blamed him for Kimister?

Drawing a deep breath, he walked across the road and knocked on the door. A light came on in the hall and as the door opened a woman appeared. With the light behind her he thought at first it was Charley, then he saw it was Mabel. She didn't recognise him at first, then her face lit up. 'Kelly Maguire!' she said. 'By all that's wonderful!'

She looked harder, sharper, much more painted than he remembered her, with heavy lipstick and rouge on her cheeks, and he was startled to see there was grey in her hair. Good God, he thought, *we're not young any more!*

She seemed glad to see him and, ushering him inside, offered him a drink.

'I came to see Charley,' he said.

She gave him an odd look. 'I suppose you did,' she agreed. 'And you were surprised to see me open the door, eh? Well, I occasionally stayed with her and that's why I'm here. I'm not badly off again now, you see, because the fashion trade's picked up a lot in the last year or so.' She shrugged. 'All the same, I'm damned if I want to spend all my life in it and it seems to me time I got out. I'm getting married and I'm here to collect a few things.'

He grinned, delighted for her. Their relationship had never been one of enmity 'I thought you'd land someone as long ago as 1914,' he said.

'So did I. I ought to have done.' She smiled at him, tough-minded, self-reliant and cheerful, a new Mabel who seemed to have lost her chances but found her senses. 'I had all the attributes. Damn it, I was even willing – a damn sight more willing than most girls! – but it didn't work. The men I chose seemed to have a depressing habit of getting themselves killed. First, that chap in the dragoons – I've even forgotten his name now – then the R.F.C. man. There were a few others as well, but they all seemed to disappear to France and vanish. When the war ended I found I was twenty-seven, and still not fixed up.'

'Who is it, Mabel?'

Mabel smiled. 'Met him in Shanghai,' she said. 'I thought at the time it might be James Verschoyle, but he was too cagey and always slipped through my fingers. Then I met George. He was a captain in the Devons. When I went down to Hong Kong, he followed me. We made a good foursome, me and George, and Charley and Albert Kimister.' She paused and frowned. '*That* was a disaster, Kelly, you know.'

Kelly pulled a face. 'It wasn't the only disaster that came out of China,' he said. He glanced round for some sign of Charley but could see nothing of hers that he remembered. 'Go on about George,' he urged, chiefly because he needed something to say and was afraid of mentioning Charley. 'Which George?'

'George Dunbar. He's retiring as a lieutenant-colonel. He's a bit of a boozer but he's a good-hearted soul and he needs some-one.'

'To keep him sober?'

'Good God, no!' She gave a hoot of laughter. 'If George wants to get drunk, he can get drunk. I don't mind. He doesn't became maudlin and he doesn't sing or fight. He just grows a little more dignified, that's all. He's perfectly house-trained and he has money. For years he had to dance attendance on Mummy and perhaps that's why he got drunk. Now she's dead and he won't have to any more. We're doing it at Aldershot in May.'

She lit a cigarette and Kelly waited. She offered him another drink and he found she was looking curiously at him.

'I bet you didn't come here to hear about George,' she said suddenly.

'No, I didn't,' he admitted, and he was just about to ask where Charley was when she spoke again.

'How's Christina?'

He shrugged. 'I've heard she and James Verschoyle are con-templating getting hitched.'

She nodded thoughtfully. 'It fits.'

'I think it does,' he agreed. 'Perhaps he did me a good turn

286

even, because the marriage never worked.'

'Neither did Charley's'

Her voice was unexpectedly sharp and accusing, but it was something he'd known all the time.

'Albert Kimister was wet,' Mabel said firmly. 'Wet as a winter Sunday afternoon. And after spending all her life expecting to marry you, being married to him came as an awful shock to her.'

He could find nothing to say and Mabel reached for her drink. 'It was your fault entirely,' she went on. 'All you had to do during those years when she was waiting for you was stick an engagement ring on her finger and she'd have waited until the Last Trump. Did you know that?'

'I ought to have done.'

'She went on waiting. Like me. But in my case it was because I couldn't make up my mind. And look what I got – George Dunbar. He's not at all what I expected, bless him, but I'm too old now to quibble and I intend to make a good job of it if I can.' She finished her drink and stared him squarely in the face. 'But you're no George, Kelly, and Charley's no Mabel. That sister of mine has the most faithful of hearts.'

'I'm sure you're right.' Kelly was growing puzzled, wondering where Charley was and why Mabel was so anxious to talk.

'I often thought you were a dirty dog, Kelly,' she went on. 'Especially when I came to stay with her in this ghastly little house which was all her precious Albert could manage to leave her. I expect you're wondering where she is.'

At last they seemed to have reached the point he'd been waiting for.

'I've even got a ring in my pocket, Mabel' he admitted uncertainly. 'A Russian grand duchess gave it to me and I always intended it for Charley. I heard about Kimister just before I left for the Mediterranean. It turned out to be rather a long trip and I've only just got back.' He found he was talking because he was uncomfortable in front of her.

She gazed at him. 'She got over Albert Kimister,' she said unexpectedly. 'There wasn't much to get over.' It was an illuminating comment and he shifted restlessly.

'I think I was a bit of a fool some years ago.'

'I think you both were.'

'I've come to try to make up for it. I'm not much of a hand at making speeches, Mabel, but five years isn't a lifetime and it ought not to have left an indelible mark on either of us. I want to do what I ought to have done years ago. I want to ask Charley to marry me. As soon as possible.'

There was a long silence as she stared at him and, with a curious sense of foreboding, he felt his heart sink. When she spoke, however, her voice was sympathetic. 'You know why I'm collecting my things, Kelly?' she said gently. 'It's because the house is up for sale.'

Kelly's heart dropped to his stomach.

'She's gone, Kelly, my love. You're too late. She left for New York in the *Mauretania* on Monday. She got a job there – a good one, with some British export firm – and it was so sudden she asked me to look after everything for her.'

Kelly drew a deep breath. It seemed painful in his chest. Charley was heading one way and, as usual, he was heading in the other. 'Perhaps I can write to her?' he offered. 'I meant what I said, Mabel.'

She shook her head. 'Oh, no, Kelly,' she smiled. 'Not again! She's had enough. Besides, there's someone interested in her. An American. That's why she took the job. She met him while he was here on business. I'm sorry for you, Kelly, because you seem to have found your senses at last, but I'm damned if *I'm* going to give you her address when she's got a chance of pulling something out of the fire. She's still young and, unlike yours truly, she doesn't look jaded. What's more, he's no Willie Kimister. He's a hell of a nice man and I hope she marries him and has lots of good American kids covered all over with stars and stripes.' She looked at him sadly. 'You may be hell on wheels as a sailor, Kelly, but as a hearts and flowers type you're an absolute dead loss.'

Two weeks later, *Actaeon* led *Adroit* and *Glendower* out of Portsmouth harbour en route for Gibraltar. A large crowd of relatives and friends had been given special permission to enter the yard and wave their farewells from the jetty and, as the last wire fell away and *Actaeon*'s stern came out for her turn for the harbourmouth, Kelly saw the handkerchieves appear at once in a fluttering rash of white.

288

He was beginning to get over Mabel's news a little by this time. The sense of loss had staggered him. He hadn't been able to accept it at first and had gone to a Southsea hotel and quietly got drunk. He was feeling better now, however, occupied as he had been over the last two weeks with the thousand and one things of his command that needed his attention. Perhaps in the end, he had decided, it was as well. For naval wives, marriage was only an endless routine of pack and follow, something they did for the rest of their husband's career, living a nomadic life, dragging the trunks from the garage on their own, and emptying their lives into them without turning a hair, ready always, like a desert Arab, for instant departure.

The women's eyes were on *Actaeon* and her consorts as they passed, the grey ships that were their rivals for the affections of their men, the ships that would always come first and break their hearts every time they vanished over the horizon. They had looked on in silence as the kitbags and suitcases and tin trunks went off, the place where they lived already wearing a stripped look; and now they were watching the slow diminishing of their lives as their husbands vanished from sight. Their eyes were fixed on the sailors lined up on deck, printing their faces in their minds in a way they hoped would last throughout the empty months ahead, and there was a little quiet weeping going on, he knew, behind the brave waves, and more than one hard lump in the throat. Some of the men wouldn't see their wives for three years and it was always hard to keep a home together at a distance of a thousand miles, especially where a shortage of money made a lodger necessary to make ends meet.

He picked out Smart's wife. In her breast would be the quickening fear that every woman felt as she watched her husband's ship leave, and he saw her lift her head a little higher as the wind tugged at her hair. Thank God I didn't inflict this on Charley, he thought.

But in the next breath, he knew he was lying to himself. Knowing you left someone behind waiting for you, longing for your return, always made departure easier, and he suddenly realised how over the years, when he'd seen other men receiving letters from their wives, how empty his life had been.

'God bless this ship and all who sail in her,' he murmured to himself. 'And God bless the wives who wait at home.'

Slowly, with the ship at the Still, they passed *Vernon* to port and Fort Blockhouse to starboard. He heard the bosuns' pipes as he stood at the salute then quietly they slipped past Southsea Pier and into the chop of the Channel where a fresh blustery breeze was blowing. The gulls mewed round the mast as he smelled the chill salt tang of the sea and caught the faint hint of spray on his face. Beyond the Isle of Wight, the water was grey and hazy and the horizon was blurred by rain squalls.

Smart appeared alongside. 'Forecastle secured for sea, sir,' he announced.

'Thank you, Number one.'

Kelly nodded and tugged the gold-laced peak of his cap down over his eyes. The ache in his heart was growing easier now, the sense of disappointment and loss fading slowly. Life wasn't always as kind as you expected it to be but it *was* possible – it had to be – to get over the fact that the woman you loved preferred someone else. Fortunately the Navy had to come first. If it didn't, it couldn't exist. And that, in a way, was a sort of consolation prize, because not far round the corner was war, which would make parting even harder. Of that he was as certain as he had been in 1914. Indeed, it would really be the same war they'd fought then with only an interval for half-time and a suck at a lemon.

It might take a year to arrive, he decided. Or five, or ten. But it was coming, because already in Germany there were ambitious men rattling their sabres in their scabbards, while in the rest of Europe there were only the unimaginative politicians who had failed again and again yet always seemed to be in office, bewildered, tired men, devoid of both guts and ideas. When it came, he thought, men would die and women would go through agonies, so if they were all heading for self-immolation what in God's name did love and tenderness matter in the end?

He drew a deep breath that was almost a sigh and decided he was becoming as cynical as Verschoyle, because love and tenderness *always* mattered.

The familiar outline of Portsmouth drew into a thin blue-grey line. No one spoke very much. Nobody could fail to be touched by the poignancy of parting and the knowledge that they wouldn't be seeing their homes and families for another two or three years. They all had a hard knot in their chests as the Horse Sand Fort came up, and the navigator began to exchange information on course, speed and weather with the officer of the watch in a way that seemed to indicate that his thoughts hadn't yet quite parted from the girl he'd left behind.

The navigator turned to Kelly. 'Horse Sand Fort abeam, sir,' he reported.

'Thank you, Pilot.' The interruption broke into Kelly's thoughts so that the parting from the land became complete.

The wind was from the south-west and the ship began to feel the first of the open sea as they left the shelter of the Isle of Wight, digging her nose into the waves and lifting water over the bow to be blown by the salty gust into glittering fans of rainbow hues. The deck canted and Kelly's heart suddenly and unexpectedly began to sing as he felt the fresh clean air dance in his lungs.

He turned, cut off at last from the land as if by a surgical operation, his problems cast aside, a deep-sea sailor in his own element again, his eyes far ahead and concerned only with the King's business and the affairs of the Navy. Occupied for the thousandth time with the mundane but always exciting procedure of taking his ship to sea, he felt whole once more, his own man, caught as he never failed to be by the mystique and mystery of the ocean. New ships, he thought, new cap tallies. It was all part of the picture.

'Know who *Actaeon* was, Number One?' he said.

'No, sir. Who?'

'Bit of a huntsman. Bit of a voyeur, too, as I remember. Came on Artemis bathing with her nymphs and rather liked what he saw.'

'Made rather a cock of it, I'm told, sir,' the officer of the watch said. 'Changed himself into a stag to get a better view and got eaten by his own hounds.'

Kelly laughed. 'Hope *we* don't,' he said. '*Adroit*'s a bit close on our stern. Signal her to watch her station.'

It was going to be all right, he told himself. The Mediterranean command had changed hands since he'd been there. There were men there now who saw the Navy not in terms of privilege or social events, and the hard facts of the European political situation were being faced, because they knew that Mussolini,

291

the Italian dictator, with his bombastic claims that the Med was an Italian lake, was going to be the first to start the dance.

There was going to be work, he thought, plenty of it, and it would keep him from thinking. Yes, he felt, it was going to be all right.

MAX HENNESSY is a pseudonym for John Harris, author of *The Sea Shall Not Have Them*. Ex-sailor, ex-airman, ex-newspaper-man, ex-travel courier, he went to sea before the war from his job as a newspaperman, going into the Merchant Navy and doing his first trip in the Windjammer, *Lawhill*. During the war he served with two air forces and two navies, was twice reported lost at sea, and had to swim for his life on more than one occasion. He returned to newspapers after the war but is now a full-time writer. He lives by the sea and for many years kept up his interest in flying with a private pilot's licence.